The First in line

SLEEPER CHRONICLES

Ray Zdan

D0293643

Copyright © 2021 Ray Zdan

All rights reserved.

ISBN: 9781999737795
ISBN-13: 978-1-9997377-9-5

It was painful even to think. His entire body balanced between the dull numbness and the scorching ache of an open wound. He had been beaten – he vaguely remembered that – beaten mercilessly and with methodical accuracy, leaving not a square inch untouched. Some spots were less painful, but others were almost unbearable. He had probably fainted a few times. Still, they kept him alive.

He was naked. Cool air touched his skin, and waves of shiver passed down his body – one after another. It was a trouble to open his eyes – he wasted a few attempts trying, though not much was visible when he finally succeeded in getting his eyes to focus. The room – not large, as far as he could judge – was dark, dimly lit by a single candle, flickering at his feet.

He growled, trying to lift his head – failed. His forehead was fixed firmly to the table, strapped down by a wide belt. The table's surface was metal, chilling and numbing his skin, and he tried to move again, this time his right arm. Failed again. It was strapped to the table, as was the rest of his body, but his fingers, still numb and stiff, discovered a plastic tube passing along his right arm. He couldn't guess its origin with the pain wrapping him like a burning blanket, but he was sure its tip was inserted into his body somewhere. Was he in a hospital? That hope faded as soon as it appeared. He couldn't remember how he had got here, but the place didn't look like a hospital. Why was he here?

He tried to growl again, but his chest refused to comply, causing him to fall into the most terrible bout of coughing. Then he heard footsteps, and the door squeaked, opening somewhere to his left.

"He's awake," a harsh male voice cracked through the gloom.

He heard more footsteps, unhurriedly approaching through the door. He squinted at the dark silhouettes but couldn't see much. It was too dark and all too painful.

"Give him a mug of water," someone ordered. The voice was deep, almost hypnotic. "He needs more fluids to make more juice!"

He flinched when the mug appeared in front of his face, and a cold metal touched his lips. He felt thirsty and grateful when the liquid ran into his dry mouth. Still, it felt like a trap. They almost had to force another mug down him. Then they waited.

They did something with the tube. His heart pounded insanely when a wave of weakness passed down his limbs. And it got colder, much colder.

He tried to speak, but his tongue felt stiff and too tired and nor did anything he could say seem important anymore.

"He's getting too weak. I think this round should be the last before we go to another phase," said the deep voice. "Your turn, Paul."

Paul, a shaggy young man with a dark beard, came closer to the candle, his face tense, dark eyes glistening fearfully in the flickering light.

The man on the table moaned as shadows stirred and moved around him. It was cold. Damn, it was so cold! His body shivered uncontrollably. He squirmed, trying to get a better look at Paul, but his sight failed him each time he tried. One of the shadows passed a goblet to

Paul – the red goblet.

"Don't waste a single drop if you want to live until tomorrow," the deep voice warned Paul. The guy silently nodded and began to drink. His lips were red when he lowered the goblet a few minutes later.

The man on the table growled weakly, his voice fading.

"Don't you dare slip to the other side!" the deep voice hissed angrily at his ear. "You must die here!"

The warning came too late – the man fainted, and his troubled mind was already seeing a dream. The same dream he had seen for a very long time.

The night was cloudy and seemed chilly, and he was shivering despite the several deerskins wrapped tightly around his body. The fireplace was still hot, its embers blazing in the soft breeze, but its heat seemed insufficient to warm him. He turned his head to the right, where several grass houses stood in a semi-circle by the quietly splashing creek. A drum beat there, softly, like a wounded heart, and a husky voice chanted the Mortal Way. He listened to the chant, but the meaning of the words slipped his mind as water seeps through a sieve. There was not much time left, and he knew this.

A dark silhouette stirred to his left.

"Is it near?" a voice asked – firm but caring.

He nodded. He was too weak to speak.

"Here," the silhouette extended a ceremonial pipe, no doubt filled with acha and carefully placed the mouthpiece between his cracked lips.

"May the journey be peaceful, brother."

He slowly inhaled, the acrid smoke filling his lungs and lifted his eyes to the sky. The clouds were dark, covering the silvery face of Wyrna and the Road of Gods.

"Hardly peaceful," he breathed out between the puffs, feeling his body becoming light and numb. "I expect a bumpy ride."

The silhouette next to him was silent, waiting.

He took a few more puffs, listening to the drum and chant. Then he screamed as unbearable pain ripped his chest and spread down to his navel. The pipe fell to the ground, scattering red-glowing ashes of acha. Suddenly it was unbearably hot under the deerskins as the sticky remains of blood oozed from the open wound.

The silhouette barely moved, but the strike of the yatagan was lightning-fast and precise.

"Goodbye, brother," the shadow whispered, covering the body with a deerskin and picking up the pipe. "Will see you on the Road of Gods."

The chanting stopped.

The morning was chilly. The moss and ferns were damp, and large dewdrops hung from the pink blossoms of morning glories. It was deadly quiet as well. The silence was disturbed only by the peaceful snoring nearby.

Will looked around. Half of his face was damp with several pine needles sticking to his skin, and he wiped them off before allowing his gaze to wander any further.

It seemed just moments ago that he had boarded the night train to London and walked down the aisle searching for a quiet corner, passing through a few coaches until he found one. He had then placed his head on his rucksack, trying to find some comfort for his big muscular body, squeezed into the narrow seat. He closed his eyes just to give them a little rest without any desire to take a nap. In no time, though, Will was in the land of nod. The transfer was so quick and seamless that he spent a few seconds wondering where he was and how he had got there. Then came the terrifying realisation that it was *the same dream* that he was fated to see until the end of his days. Or so he had been told.

Will leant against the rough trunk of a tree. The sound of snoozing came from a large black shaggy shape lying on the moss a few paces away under the shade of some ferns. Will watched how it barely moved with each breath and grinned guiltily for thinking wrongly about Qu Sith – the sphinx hadn't run away as Will had thought yesterday. He was sleeping next to him.

That didn't make any difference, though. They weren't friends. They just used to sit in neighbouring cages, and it was time for them to separate. Will had to find the lost blue orchid, and this was his most important mission. He didn't care too much about what was on the sphinx's mind.

It was early in the morning, and he decided to stretch out those few minutes of quiet still left him. Will closed his eyes, trying to remember all the precious features of the woman he loved. Hel's Black Castle seemed miles away, and her heart was behind the wall of ice unreachable. *It was his fault!* He had built that wall with his own ignorance. *Damn!* Now he was forced to bang at that ice, hoping that her heart was there still waiting for him, hoping that he still had the chance of another try. If only he could somehow succeed in finding that lost orchid.

He must go where the river of lava had been blazing a week ago – it should have hardened by now – and find the blue orchid he had placed on the dead body of that stupid girl Gudula before pushing it into flames. It was a silly moment of weakness, an impromptu decision that Will hated even to remember. *Why hadn't Hel told him how special that flower was to her?* He would never have let it out of his hands. The blossom had been carried away by the flow of molten rock, and although the search might seem like a hopeless and stupid idea, it was the only hope he had. Will had been told – more often than once – that Hel's flower wouldn't burn in flames. He must find the orchid and take it back to the Black Castle. Maybe, Hel would forgive him then?

The rising sun painted oblique streaks of light, breaking through the intertwined branches, leaves and pine needles of the treetops. Everything seemed quiet and peaceful. The faint smell of burnt flesh was the only indication of that cruel massacre last night of the Rybbaths' village just a few hundred paces away when he and the sphinx had only just escaped inevitable death. Will frowned, thinking about the villagers who had been burnt alive but could not force any compassion into his thoughts for the savages who had been eager to sacrifice him or Qu Sith – depending on who would win the mortal combat – to their imaginary Gods. The death of the Rybbaths had been horrible, and Will flinched, reliving the flaming serpent's attack on the village. He had almost died too. *But almost doesn't count, does it?*

The only thing that had saved him and the sphinx from death in the flames was distance – they would have been roasted alive if the cages had been any closer to the village. Will tried to remember the frightening moment when the flaming monster had towered above their cages. The next moment the creature had been shattered to pieces by the timely eruption of the geyser. Will's lips shaped into a smile – he was alive, and that was all that mattered.

That was yesterday... Will stretched his muscles, yawning; his legs moved and shuffled the dead leaves. Qu Sith instantly raised his head, darting a few worried glances around. Then his black eyes in that human-like face, framed by a shiny black mane, focused on Will.

"Oh, you're awake already," the sphinx observed, then rose and stretched like an overgrown cat. "I thought you'd be ravenous after all those mashed parsnips the Rybbaths fed you, so I brought you some real breakfast."

"That's very kind of you," Will acknowledged. "What is it?"

The sphinx pointed at the charred chunk resting on the leaves between him and Will. It was as black as charcoal with uneven streaks of red raw meat bursting through gaps at either end.

"It's much bigger than a rabbit. What is it?" Will repeated his question as he moved closer.

"It used to be a piece of venison," Qu Sith told him. "You humans have a strange habit of burning your food before you eat it. I don't know if I burned it enough or too little – I'm not good at this. I think it's a waste of good meat if you ask me. And don't blame me if you find it doesn't suit your taste."

"Thanks anyway. You only had the best of intentions in mind," Will poked at the charred hard surface. If there was any edible meat inside, he had to break through the tough outer layer of burnt crust.

"You still have that knife, don't you?" Qu Sith demanded. "Your teeth look too small to tear into it."

"I hope I haven't lost it. Last night was quite adventurous, though," Will told him as he began to search his pockets – the knife must be somewhere. He finally found it in the breast pocket of his jacket.

The knife wasn't designed for cutting meat – its curved blade was more suitable for pumpkin carving, but Will gave it a try.

"You are indeed a bad cook," he announced, inspecting the cut. The meat was raw inside, and just a finger-thick layer between that bloody red flesh and the outer charcoal seemed suitable for consumption.

Qu Sith flashed an angry glance, and Will instantly began to regret his remark. "There are plenty of edible pieces," he quickly added, cutting deeper through the charcoal, "which are well-done but still with some blood. I'll eat those. Thank you for breakfast."

"I'm glad you found something to suit your palate," the sphinx spat out at him flashing his black eyes. "At least, you won't starve.

I hate moaning humans."

"I'm not moaning," Will chuckled. He placed the bloody piece in his mouth and began to chew. The taste was weird but not entirely terrible. Venison probably is supposed to taste weird, especially when prepared by a sphinx. Will winked enthusiastically at Qu Sith before cutting off another piece and placing it into his mouth. Blood squeezed through his teeth as the chunk was too large and had some raw meat attached, but Will bravely gulped it down, keeping his face straight.

"You're not starving yet. You'd be moaning later if left hungry," Qu Sith observed flatly.

The beast took a dozen paces to the left and casually wiggled his butt between the two thick shrubs. Will looked away, but the unmistakable sounds gave away the fact that those mashed parsnips were still battling for a place in sphinx's guts.

"Do you know what that flaming creature was that attacked the Rybbath village?" Will swallowed another piece and asked the sphinx a few minutes later. "Are they common in this part of the world?"

"I'm not sure, but I think that viper was one of those ancients they call Night Crawlers," Qu Sith whispered as if afraid that some imaginary dark creatures lurking in the bush might overhear him.

"Why Night Crawlers?" Will asked.

"Because they crawl at night, obviously!" The sphinx cast a few glances around and added. "Legend has it that the Gods didn't clear this world properly before they gave it to us. They just dumped us here behind the mountains and left, abandoning us completely."

"Bullshit!" Will sneered.

"Where?" the sphinx sprang to his feet and sniffed the air. "If there is bull's shit somewhere, there must be a bull too! We need more meat!"

"It's just a saying," Will calmed him down. "And we have enough meat for both of us here."

"It is a strange thing to say when there's no bull and no shit. Humans have such a vivid imagination," Qu Sith spat with disappointment in his voice, then sat down, looking away. "Thanks for offering, but I don't like that terrible taste of burnt flesh. I'll go hunting later."

Will shrugged. "Do you believe that nonsense about the Gods?"

"I believe everything about the Gods, but they've never answered my prayers, no matter how hard I've tried. It must be all about belief. Maybe mine isn't strong enough," the sphinx sighed. "But yes, I think they abandoned us."

Will's relationship with religion was simply non-existent. He lived the life of a simpleton. Faith didn't fit into his everyday routine, nor did he ever give it a serious thought while running between his gym and his bed. He had never given a damn about that imaginary someone's eye in the sky that was supposed to see everything. That eye was only a concern to those grumpy old ladies usually keen to worry about things that nobody else would. Will had never met a celestial being and didn't know anybody who had. Those cranky ladies were well known for inventing things, and all that heavenly nonsense had been dreamed up by them too – Will was certain. Anyway, he had more important things to worry about than that. The fact that he was speaking with a sphinx in his dream didn't trouble him at all.

He looked at the beast with a poorly concealed pity in his eyes, like one would look at a grown-up man who still believed in elves and fairies.

"I had in mind that other crazy thing – about clearing the world?" he mumbled. "Never heard nonsense dumber than that."

"I don't know much about the Creation," Qu Sith closed his eyes and gathered his thoughts before continuing. "But the world we have feels like a cage. Our lands are framed by the mountains – you can't deny this if you've seen enough of it, and no one knows what's behind those mountains. The peaks are far higher than the clouds could traverse. No living creature can breathe in those high passes. No one has ever seen what's on the other side, though many have tried. No one has ever returned to tell. Only those terrible monsters seep through the holes in the ground; you've seen one with your own eyes. Yes, it seems like this is the true state of affairs in our relationship with the Gods. This world is their unfinished and abandoned creation."

"Have you seen those flaming monsters before?"

"No. I've seen many strange creatures in my life, but none as terrifying as that," Qu Sith admitted without a moment of hesitation. "It scared the shit out of me. That flaming snake wasn't hunting for food, that's for certain. Did you see its eyes? It sought pure extermination. I was sure we were about to die like those bloody Rybbaths."

"Yes, for a few moments, it was very scary, indeed," Will admitted, chewing.

"A few moments?" Qu Sith chuckled nervously. "I nearly screamed my soul out!"

"Well... Your soul is still in place, is it not? We were just lucky," Will shrugged. "That flaming snake is dead! Done and dusted!" He put another piece of meat into his mouth. "But it did indeed seem deadly when it was alive."

"Can't argue with your observation," the sphinx said blankly. "But if the rumours are true, that viper didn't seem big enough to be a true Night Crawler. It must have been just a baby Night Crawler."

"That monster was taller than any tree!" Will stopped chewing.

"If it was just a baby, how big is its mummy then? Mummies usually keep their babies close."

"Bigger, I suppose," Qu Sith assured him, and Will could swear he heard a note of terror in the sphinx's voice. "Much bigger."

Will glanced around at the grim-looking dusk in the underwood. He wasn't afraid of its shadows. The woods seemed creepy, but he was fine with them as long as no flaming snakes crawled out anywhere from behind those crooked tree trunks. If the baby could leave the village in smoking ruins with no survivors, Will preferred to stay away from its mum.

"You can relax now. They are *Night* Crawlers," Qu Sith traced Will's gaze with a hint of impatience. "We won't see much of them in the daytime."

"Are you sure?" Will paused before cutting another piece of meat. He felt almost full. "Where are they hiding then? I can't imagine anything that big capable of hiding somewhere. Still, you can't see them in the daytime."

"I'm not sure about their hiding places," Qu Sith shrugged. "I know nothing more than the rumours say. Night Crawlers can wipe out entire kingdoms. No wall or castle would keep anyone safe. No army can defend against them."

"Still, that indestructible monster was killed by a mere splash of water," Will observed.

"Honestly, never before have I heard of a Night Crawler being killed," Qu Sith left the words trailing.

"You've seen it with your own eyes," Will mumbled, chewing. "That viper shattered to pieces when a splash of water landed down upon its head."

"It was a giant splash of water, by the way." Qu Sith shrugged. "That might be a worthwhile observation for you."

"Why?"

"Swamps might save your life, human," the sphinx said, looking away. "The only problem is, it's hard to find any in this part of the world."

"Things here are getting more and more dangerous with every passing day," Will observed, refraining from further comments about things he didn't know. "It seemed so peaceful at the beginning, not counting the volcano."

"Oh, yes, these lands are perilous," Qu Sith nodded. "I've always wanted to live on the other side of the Great River, away from all those flames, eruptions and lava flows, but I can't cross the river, especially one as wide as Braaid. I'm not a creature who can swim or fly."

"Don't people have any boats here?" Will asked.

"A boat for a sphinx? You must be joking! No human would agree to take me on board," Qu Sith chuckled.

"Have you asked?"

"I don't talk with my food," the sphinx said proudly.

"Then don't moan about still being on this side of the river," Will stopped chewing. "You gave an oath not to taste human flesh again, remember?" His grasp tightened around the knife – it was his only weapon, no matter how pitiful, and he put the piece of meat he had just cut aside.

"I'm not crackbrained," Qu Sith barked sharply. "Your back is safe from my teeth, don't worry."

Will squeezed a tight smile. "Now, since we humans are safe from your teeth, you might try to ask a ferryman for a lift," he shrugged. "You might be surprised."

"I can't go to the river," the beast mumbled. "Not yet."

"Why?" Will asked as he casually cut another piece of meat.

Qu Sith squirmed uneasily but chose to remain silent. Will glanced at the black eyes of the sphinx and decided against pressing the matter. It was none of his business anyway – he knew that curiosity killed the cat, so he turned his full attention to cutting a few more pieces of meat.

"I still have some unfinished business in Patna," the sphinx said at last. "Life on the other side of the river might become irrelevant if I succeed in my affair, but I might consider the journey if I fail."

Will didn't respond as his mouth was full of meat. The sphinx was babbling in riddles – but all of this was none of his business.

He had his own quest.

Qu Sith patiently waited until satiety filled Will's stomach, and he had wiped away the blood dripping from his lips.

"So... What are you going to do next?" asked the sphinx as his unblinking gaze fixed on Will. "We're free at last. Where are you going?"

Will shrugged before answering.

"I'll go on searching for the lost blossom. I must find that blue orchid Hel gave me. Then I'll be able to return to the Black Castle and beg Hel for forgiveness," he mumbled, scratching his head. "I've been told the blossom won't burn in lava. I know this sounds crazy, but I must try. It's my only option."

"Death gave you a flower, and you tossed it into the lava?" the black eyes of Qu Sith widened. "You must be insane."

"Well, it wasn't exactly that I tossed it into the flames," Will was reluctant to reveal the whole truth – the circumstances didn't seem relevant. "There was an accident, and it ended up in the lava and got carried away. By the way, Hel is a nice pretty woman. Why are you calling her Death?"

Will could almost hear the eyes of the sphinx popping. "Are all humans this dumb? Or just you?" the beast asked at last. "Or have you been locked somewhere in a dungeon until now and only just broken free? She is the master of the Tower, and whoever rules in the Tower of Whispers is called Death. You must have fallen out of the sky if you don't know this. And yes, the flowers of Death are indestructible."

Will squeezed a silly smile – he had no idea what the sphinx was talking about. The beast was sure about the flower, and that was the only thing that mattered. Everything else seemed like utter nonsense. Yes, he had seen the Tower and heard ghosts whispering there. The place was eerie, and it was strange that such a beautiful woman as Hel chose to live in such an eerie place, but her lifestyle choices didn't make her Death. *Death?* He simply couldn't believe that.

"Are you sure that the orchid will have survived the flames?" Will still felt the need for further confirmation.

"Yes, but you might be in trouble if the blossom has been carried across to the other shore," observed the sphinx. "You'll never get across the flow."

"You've spent too much time in that cage, my friend," Will grinned widely. "The volcano exploded shortly before I got into the cage next to you, and the lava found a new path on the northern slope. I saw it with my own eyes. The old flow must have cooled down and become hard enough to step on while we were sitting in the cages of those bloody Rybbaths. I'd be able to find that blossom even if it was carried to the other shore. I must find it."

"You might just be one lucky bastard," Qu Sith gave him a

wide grin revealing his sharp pointed teeth.

Will shrugged but chose to drop the issue. "Thanks for breakfast. I'd probably better hurry then. And you – where are you heading? You never mentioned what brought you to these lands while we were sitting in those cages."

The sphinx yawned before answering. "We never talked much, and you never asked. I'm heading to the ancient sacred city of Per Hathor, if you must know," he said in a plain voice.

"What is so ancient and sacred about that city?" Will chuckled.

"It's not a city anymore," Qu Sith didn't seem willing to go into any lengthy explanations. "Did I mention the word *ancient*? Not much is left of that great city by now. Mostly ruins. Still sacred, though."

"Why do you need to go to those ruins then?" Will asked seriously. "Are they hiding treasure? Then I'll go with you after I've found that orchid. I'd love to do some treasure hunting."

The sphinx squirmed at the question and this just added sparks of curiosity to Will's eyes.

"It's not about any treasure," Qu Sith was quick to assure him. "It simply might be too dangerous for you to go there. You might be killed if she spots you wandering around."

"She?"

The sphinx growled and lowered his head.

"*She?*" Will repeated his question, grinning.

Qu Sith flashed an angry glance at him, but Will carried on grinning widely and even winked.

"Yes," the beast admitted at last. "I've heard some rumours that a female sphinx lives in those ruins. I must check that out. There's not too many of us left in the world. It's my duty to couple up and produce some offspring."

"There's no shame in still being a virgin," Will dropped his grin. "You can tell me afterwards how wonderful it was."

"I don't suppose that you'll ever understand this," Qu Sith lifted his black eyes and looked at Will. "I must find her. She's only ready to lay eggs just once a century. It might be a long wait till the next time if I miss this chance."

"Were you hatched from an egg then?" now it was Will's turn to find his mouth gaping open. It was hard to believe that large and fearsome sphinxes were hatched from eggs like some trivial chicken. "I see nothing even remotely resembling a bird in you. How is that possible?"

"Crocodiles, lizards and turtles don't even remotely resemble a bird either, but you don't run around shouting about them hatching from eggs! And it's not entirely true that I've nothing that birds have – I've got a few black feathers on my paws," Qu Sith seemed embarrassed to discuss the matter. "You may think that it's not much, but this doesn't make me a lesser sphinx than those who have full talons. My brother Qu Barn even has wings, for example, but he is no greater sphinx than me!"

"You have a brother?"

"Yes, I do. A few of them," Qu Sith admitted. "I haven't seen much of Qu Barn since we hatched as he was the first to leave the nest."

"So, you hatched from an egg, not like humans are born," Will grinned. "That makes you a bird in fur!"

Qu Sith growled. "I'm a sphinx! I'm not a bird! And I'm not a bloody human!"

"What's wrong with being a human?" Will shrugged.

"You, humans begin your life as parasites," Qu Sith spat out with rage. "And I've heard some of you carry on living like parasites! It's in your blood! We, sphinxes, are different!"

Will stopped himself from slipping out another joke about birds. He had no objections when the beast called humans parasites. In fact, he could agree with this, but the avian issue seemed too sensitive for the sphinx.

"You're right," Will decided that a simple agreement would put out the sparks. "You seem to be entirely independent since the very moment of hatching, not like me depending on my mum for so many years."

"Yes," the sphinx told him proudly. "We sphinxes are not like bloody humans. We face our fate with pride from the very beginning. As I said – there's not too many of us left alive, and it would be great to have a few small sphinxes of the Qu clan running around if she's ready for it."

"Glad that you've decided to become a father," Will winked. "It's good to watch your offspring grow."

Qu Sith glanced at Will with apparent disdain in his gaze. Will shrugged with a silly expression on his face.

"You don't understand, human," said the sphinx at last. "Your mind is clouded by that perverted strange friction you call sex. We're made differently. Mating for a sphinx is an act of unconditional love and sacrifice. I must give some part of myself to my mate to produce eggs, and I don't know if I'll continue to live without that part. I'm almost sure I'll die in the process, but my life will be passed to my offspring, and they'll grow to explore the world, learn its wisdom and pass it to their offspring if they're lucky enough to find a female sphinx ready to mate. I don't expect you to understand this, human. You're too different."

"That's sad," Will's smile faded.

"No, it isn't," Qu Sith said in a calmer voice. "It's a purpose in life that you humans don't have."

"I'm not talking about your mating, sphinx," Will stood up and stretched his muscles. "It's always sad to lose a friend. But you probably wouldn't understand that. You, sphinxes, don't have friends."

Qu Sith flashed an angry glance at him but kept his unease to himself. "Nobody is perfect," he admitted a few seconds later.

It was pointless to argue.

"Well, it was nice to have your company, but I must go now. Thank you again for my breakfast," Will mumbled under his breath, suppressing another yawn. "We've both already wasted too much time in those cages. I wish you the very best of luck in your mating quest, but I must find that flower before someone else does."

Qu Sith rose to his feet as well, stretching his spine like an outsized cat. "There's no need for us to separate yet," he observed calmly. "The sacred city of Per Hathor is downstream of the lava flow. I don't think your orchid will have been carried that far, but we must check everywhere."

"We?"

"I'll help you to find your lost blossom," Qu Sith stood up and, without waiting for Will, began to move down the barely visible path between large ferns and flowering vines. "If you don't mind my company, of course."

"Let's go," Will shrugged and began following the sphinx.

The woods grew darker and creepier as they carried on but were as silent as before. Qu Sith strolled confidently down the path that winded between the tangled roots, fallen trees, large black boulders and arched cliffs protruding from the grey and green moss. Will followed, trying hard to keep up with him.

Half an hour later, they were still wandering among the centennial trunks and struggling to get out. The arches, cliffs and boulders looked exactly like those they had passed before, and an uneasy suspicion crept into Will's soul.

"Are you sure you know the way?" he asked the sphinx.

"Oh, yes, I know the way," Qu Sith responded without slowing down. "We just have to skirt around the village of the Rybbaths, and the lava fields will begin shortly after that."

"The village has been destroyed with no survivors," Will observed. "Why can't we go straight through it if that's a shortcut?"

"I didn't think you'd want to see those cages again," the sphinx mumbled but kept on going forward. "We're nearly out."

"I'm not that sensitive," Will shrugged. "There's no need to protect me. But if we're nearly out…"

The path was still the same – dark and creepy with tangled roots and branches. They passed another few arches covered with grey mould, and Will could swear he had seen them twenty minutes ago. He got the knife out of his pocket and quickly scratched a big cross on the face of one of them as they walked by. Qu Sith carried on ahead without slowing down, and Will had to dash forward to keep up.

They passed another field with ferns and a small clearing where Will caught a glimpse of the gloomy, cloudy sky. Then the woods grew dark again, with countless paths tangling and intersecting on their way. Yet, the sphinx carried on without a hint of hesitation, and Will wondered how the beast was so sure of his tracks since each path he took was no different from any other.

"Let's rest for a bit," Will said, breathing heavily fifteen minutes later and stopped next to the arch, which was covered in a grey mould with a crooked cross scratched on its uneven surface.

"I guess we can take a short break," Qu Sith agreed and sat down.

Will placed his palm on the arch. "Could you explain this while we rest?" he asked the beast, pointing at the cross.

"What is this?" Qu Sith, a frown on his brow. "The symbol is unfamiliar to me. I can't explain it."

"I scratched this a while ago. That means we've been here before," Will said calmly, looking into the black eyes of the sphinx. "Why are we going round in circles?"

"I must have taken a wrong turn," Qu Sith's voice trailed off as he gazed away. "Sometimes, it's difficult, especially when I can't rely very much on my sense of smell."

"What happened to your sense of smell?"

"It's the burnt village," the sphinx complained. "I can't smell the track properly with all that stench."

"And so, we've been going round in circles instead," Will

shook his head in disbelief. "Why keep it secret?"

"I wasn't entirely certain," Qu Sith squeezed a small guilty smile. "I was sure I'd be able to pick the correct path, given time."

"Are we lost?" Will demanded. "Can you find the shortest way out of these woods?"

"I'm trying," Qu Sith said flatly. "It's very confusing."

Will punched the arch angrily.

"Then we're lost, I guess," he observed, shaking the palm.

Qu Sith shrugged, but his face remained expressionless. Will cursed. They were stuck in the woods, and this stupid animal hadn't even bothered to mew this to him, dragging them in deeper and deeper into the woods until they were utterly lost.

Will growled in frustration. He circled the arch several times but didn't risk punching it again. Qu Sith's eyes followed him silently, his mouth remained shut, offering no apologies.

Then Will stopped, struck by a sudden idea. "Do you still sense the smell of the burnt village?" he asked.

"I'd be out of the woods by now if for not that stench," Qu Sith said sadly. "Of course, I sense it! That smell just make things worse! How can that help?"

"Very well. Let's go where that stench is the strongest – to the village of the Rybbaths then," Will nodded, grinning. "It will be much easier to find a way to the lava fields from there."

"Are you sure?" the sphinx asked. "The village is completely devastated with charred bodies everywhere. Are you sure you want to see that? Won't those cages and the Lifeless Pond stir up some unpleasant memories in your head?"

"I'm not that sensitive. I've told you that already," Will said firmly. "Let's go."

Qu Sith stood up reluctantly. "Are you sure you want to go there?" he asked again, carefully sniffing the air. "I hate moaning humans."

"Yes," Will urged him. "I'm sure. I won't moan, don't worry."

The sphinx hesitantly took a few steps down one of the barely visible paths tangled in front of him, then stopped and leapt to another.

"This is so confusing!" Qu Sith complained but kept on going. Will followed him closely.

The path wound between fallen trees and arched cliffs again, but this time the sphinx wasn't so sure in his tracks – he stopped now and then, shaking his head and sniffing the air again, then resumed strolling just to stop again a few paces later.

"Why do you want to see that village, human?" he asked during one of those stops. "There's nothing there. Everything's burnt."

"Great," Will shrugged. "Then we'll not need to hide. Dead people don't attack, do they? Let's go back to the Lifeless Pond, sphinx. As you said, the lava fields are straight to the South from there, left from our cages. We'll be able to find the way even with our eyes closed."

"Very well..." Qu Sith uttered under his breath. "As you wish, human."

The sphinx turned sharply right and carried on straight through a thicket of ferns without any path, breaking a few branches of vines on his way. Will almost had to break into a run trying to keep up. The woods were still creepy and dark, but the way didn't look familiar anymore. Most of the time, Qu Sith walked in a straight line ignoring the vegetation. They had to find their way around massive boulders a few times, but the sphinx didn't stop even then.

The scenery hadn't changed fifteen minutes later, and Will began to wonder if they were lost again, but then a gust of wind brought the distinct stench of decaying flesh to his nostrils, and he knew they were getting close.

They had to find their way around a fallen tree, and then Qu Sith led them to the same place where they had begun their journey that morning – with the flattened moss and broken ferns where Will had spent the night. Even the charred venison leftovers were still resting on dead leaves with traces of knife cuts deep into the red meat as Will had left it.

Will cursed silently. All that strenuous jogging around the woods for the last few hours had been a complete waste of time. "I think I can find my way from here without any trouble," he observed, halting his run.

Qu Sith stopped a few paces later but didn't say a word. The sphinx looked away with his gaze wandering aimlessly towards the woods, clearly avoiding any eye contact with Will. Then the beast lowered his butt on the moss.

"I guess you want to rest a little before we go on," Qu Sith grunted, still looking away. "I don't understand why you want to go back to that horrible place. We could find our way around through the woods."

"After wandering in circles for a whole week?" Will chuckled ironically.

The sphinx shrugged. "It wasn't supposed to be like this," he said a few moments later. "Maybe, I've been sitting in a cage for too long."

That sounded like an apology, but Will didn't need one. A few hours had been wasted, and he felt angry. They could have been searching for the orchid by now but had gone back to where they had started instead. At least the village of Rybbaths, or what was left of it, was near – it would certainly be easier to find their way in the open space rather than wander around the dark woods.

"Let's go," Will urged the sphinx. "We've wasted too much time already!"

"As you wish," Qu Sith moved aside, making way for Will to

pass.

Will stepped slowly, parting lush shrubs with his hands. Qu Sith had said that everybody in the village was dead, but how could he know that? Everything had happened so quickly yesterday, and it had seemed like the end of the world. Still, there could be survivors. They might be angry about what had happened and willing to sacrifice the escaped contestants on the spot. Will wanted no surprises. He had had enough of sitting in the cage and waiting for his turn to die. He had no time for this shit.

Will stood quietly for a few minutes and listened.

"Well?" Qu Sith asked impatiently. "Are you still willing to go there?"

"I can't hear anything," Will admitted. "Maybe they still obey that silent fasting thing, though?"

"They're all dead!" the sphinx spat with disdain and then unexpectedly roared with all his might. Will flinched, but nothing else moved as the echoes died in the woods. "See? There's no one waiting to be saved!" Qu Sith shrugged. "Can we go around it? Now you know the spot where the village was."

"I want to have a closer look," Will said firmly. Qu Sith just sighed and shook his mane.

Will went with the sphinx close at his heels. The sickening stench of death hung in the air when he finally left the woods behind and entered the Rybbath's cemetery.

The Rybbaths had a strange way of burying their dead, as weird as all their other customs. Will knew the place – those cages where the Rybbaths had kept him, and Qu Sith had been placed on a narrow strip of sandy land between the cemetery and the Lifeless Pond. But still, he flinched and squirmed with a wave of chill when he found himself face to face with one of the graves. It was a vertical wooden pole in the long grass with the body of a large man loosely wrapped in a cloth that had once been white. The corpse stood tall, tied to that pole and faced the woods. Will glanced at the empty eye sockets and flinched again. The man's head was resting on his left shoulder with his slack jaw, giving the impression of a silent scream. Thick vines crawled up his legs and wrapped around his waist, and their small red flowers looked like splatters of blood barely moving in the wind.

The stench was worse than he remembered. Will glanced briefly at the long line of graves on the left, stretching at even spaces in front of the dark wall of the forest. All the cadavers faced the woods, the same as the other rows of graves behind them.

"Savages..." Qu Sith mumbled with disdain apparent in his voice as they moved forward, where two piles of rubble marked the spot where their former cages had stood.

Will's heart trembled as he got closer. The image of the flaming viper attacking the village was still fresh in his mind. It seemed like a bad dream now, like a nightmare that he remembered only vague bits of – images of distant fires consuming the straw roofs of the village looked like an old silent movie as the Rybbaths met their death without a sound or a scream. Their strange belief kept their mouths shut even during the extreme pain of being burnt alive.

Will clearly recalled the chilling horror that had frozen his joints when the fiery creature spotted the cages and began its approach along the shore of the Lifeless Pond. *Was it really a Night Crawler?* He almost screamed as the recollection flooded his mind like the live horror, and he had to force the image away to the farthest corner of his mind. Will was sure that the same painful death had been waiting for him and the sphinx too, if it had not been for that timely eruption of the geyser. But he wouldn't have died silently. He would have screamed his lungs out in the process. He wasn't a bloody Rybbath.

Piles of sharp black volcanic glass lay at the spot where the wall of water had struck the flaming viper. Will carefully stepped around the rubble, keeping the distance as great as he could, afraid that those rocks would somehow meld together, rise, ignite into flames again and bite him. Nothing happened. He noticed that Qu Sith kept close to him as well, almost touching his heels.

They went along the shore of the Lifeless Pond down the

narrow path to the village.

"Maybe, we could just turn left and go south to search for your orchid?" Qu Sith suggested as they left the Lifeless Pond behind. "It's getting late."

"I didn't think you scared that easily," Will grumbled without looking at the sphinx. His eyes were fixed on the smoke that slowly rose above the village. "I want to have a quick look at that before we go."

He moved forward.

"Why?" Qu Sith stopped but then had to take a few leaps to keep up. "There's nothing left there!"

"How do you know?" Will asked without slowing down.

The sphinx didn't answer.

The village was deadly quiet, with thin strands of smoke slowly rising above the piles of ashes where houses had stood just a day before. Here and there, shy flames still licked the remnants of wood, but most of the conflagration had already died down.

Will stopped in the middle of what had been the hard-dirt street with houses lining each side. It resembled a narrow sandy path between smoking rubble. It was quiet – no screams, no sobs, no motion. Just then did he begin to notice the charred bodies of the villagers. There was a blackened arm sticking out of the rubbish with two missing fingers. A little further down the road was the charred corpse of a woman clutching the corpse of an infant. The whole tribe of Rybbaths was gone.

Will's eyes wandered around the devastation. He wasn't sorry for the tribe – they had intended to kill him, either through mortal combat with the sphinx or by sacrificing him to the Gods. He didn't feel sorry for them, but their fate still seemed horrible. Then his eyes stumbled upon the charred corpse of a large young man a little further down the road. Will slowly approached.

The body was naked with its arms spread wide, and the empty eye sockets in the charred face gazed at the sky. His left leg was gone. In fact, not the entire leg was missing – the bloodied calf with its charred foot was just a few paces away. Will looked at the piece of bone sticking out of the wound, and a sudden realisation turned his stomach into knots.

"It wasn't venison, was it?" Will whispered, turning to face Qu Sith. The beast jumped a few paces away, his fur raised.

"Why waste a piece of good meat?" the sphinx asked guiltily. "And it was already burnt to your taste!"

Will felt weak, engulfed by a wave of nausea. *It's only some protein*, flashed the thought, but that didn't feel comforting.

"You've broken your oath!" Will hissed and dropped to his knees, but the spasms in his stomach were empty – the meat was too far down the road already. "You promised never to eat human flesh!"

"I didn't," Qu Sith stated plainly from a safe distance. "You did. I just trimmed the ends!"

The world went black for Will as he slumped down on the dust.

❧ ❀ ❧

The transfer from the dream was abrupt, and he was back in the brutal real world. Will lifted his head slowly, realising that the train wasn't moving anymore. A grey-haired woman was gently shaking his shoulder but stepped back as soon as he opened his eyes.

"What happened?" he asked, frowning.

"We've arrived," she told him. "We're in London. You have to get off here."

She went on minding her own business and barely cast a second glance back at Will.

What am I doing here? The thought buzzed in his head with the persistence of a thirsty mosquito. Yes, Will could understand his mother chucking him out. He had angered her by running away from the hospital. He had his reasons but would never be able to explain those to her. She was mad at him. Righteously furious. *But why had she called the police?*

Unless...

The thought was so unsettling that Will gasped. *Had she met Jill?* That was possible – Jill *was* in the hospital spreading madness at the same time as his mother was looking for him. *No, that couldn't be true!* Will shook his head vigorously, but the thought returned with the persistence of a fly. Would Jill dare to talk to his mother? *Yes!* Will gasped again with his heart sinking. *That crazy blob of fat could do anything!* Did Jill tell her about him? Did she tell her about *that* sex? About *that money*?

That could certainly drive his mother over the edge, Will was sure. It was Jill's fault that he had to run away from the hospital. And it was Jill's fault that his mother had chucked him out. *Damn that fat monster!*

The police had scared him away from home, and Will had done a stupid thing, but why had he run this far? *What am I doing in London?* The thought kept buzzing in his head as he collected his rucksack and headed out of the carriage. He could sleep around the town for a few days, wait until his mother had calmed down then everything would go back to normal.

Why had he come to London? Will still had no answer to that question.

He stepped out of the carriage onto empty platform number 13. It was brightly lit and looked alien and frightening. All the other passengers had already left the train, rushing out as per their usual morning routines. Will was the only one dawdling towards the exit without any haste.

It took a few minutes of searching through his pockets and rucksack before he succeeded in finding the ticket needed at the exit. Only then did Will notice the price printed out on the yellow-orange sheet of paper, and his heart began to sink as he stepped through the gate. Of course, nobody was waiting for him here.

Will looked around. It was an early hour, but the vast waiting hall was full of people casually bustling about on their own tracks, buying their morning coffee and sandwiches from the abundance of coffee shops, reading the morning papers or staring at the orange-lit timetables on the wall.

The young lad in a casual suit in front of Will suddenly stuffed almost a whole cheese and ham croissant into his mouth and dashed to catch his train as he sipped coffee from a paper cup on the go. A wave of pleasant food aromas followed the guy, tempting Will to visit the nearest eatery as he gulped back a mouthful of saliva, but he marched off to find an ATM first, ignoring the loud wailing in his gut – he must check his savings first before indulging in any treats. *Maybe just one croissant?* He stuffed the card into the machine and frowned as his heart skipped a beat when he saw the numbers on the screen. *Too little... Too little... Too little! Damn!* He wouldn't be able to take a train back!

Will cursed loudly and retrieved his card. *Shit!* What was he doing here? He carefully replaced the card in his wallet and quickly left the station. He was too poor for even a glance at a croissant.

Outside it was chilly. Will looked around with a bit of surprise. He had expected a wide, busy street framed by grand buildings, but London met him with a surprisingly narrow square framed by still closed cafes and gift shops. The towering building on the left was even less impressive – not even remotely grandiose, just another grey box of glass and steel! Will glanced at it once and turned right along the black walls of Euston Station, sinking into an even deeper depression with each step. He stopped a few paces later, unsure where to go. He had reached London. It was his own silly idea, the bravado of an impulse, and now, probably for the first time in his life, he was scared to face the consequences.

He was in this enormous city, entirely alien to him, and his scarce financial resources couldn't even buy him a ticket for the train journey home. Will cursed. This was a stupid decision. *Why did I buy that ticket to London? Damn! Why?*

He slowly stepped alongside the station building. A bronze cat was sitting on the ground and watching him with its sad eyes. The man crouched behind the cat was made of bronze too. He was measuring Western Australia with a large divider and paid no attention to Will. Nobody paid him any attention. *What am I doing here?* The thought bounced around in his head like a frightened bat as he carefully touched the cat as if trying to find a way out of this nightmare – the metal surface was cold and dusty. The miracle didn't happen. Will brushed his palm on his trousers and looked around. Nobody even glanced at him.

Another train arrived at the station, and a small crowd burst from it, carrying Will to the end of the yard, then he turned left, squeezing between the two tall buildings.

The place felt alien and strange, and Will lowered the hood over his face as far as it would go trying to shield himself from everything. But, in fact, this wasn't necessary as he seemed to be almost invisible to everyone. People rushed to and from the station past his muscular shape as if he was just another statue, not worthy of a second glance from the hurrying commuters. *What am I doing here?* The thought kept returning as Will crept towards the street.

He needed a plan for how to get his life back.

Two red double-decker buses rushed past him when he turned left and crossed a roundabout with an obelisk at its centre. A shady square lay ahead, and Will slowly ambled towards it, hoping to find a place where he could sit on a bench, calm his racing heart and organise his thoughts. His life had got messier with every step, and indeed he needed a plan on how to get his grip back. And he needed a quiet place to come up with that plan.

Will had spent the night on a train, and that train had taken him too far beyond the point of no return. He deeply regretted that daring impulse of frivolity. Why hadn't he just ignored the ticket seller and left the train station after eating that baguette yesterday? Why had he thought of buying a ticket? *Why London?*

His mother was still mad at him, Will was sure. It was the first time in his entire life that he had dared to tell her a firm no, and that direct contradiction had seen him dumped from his home. It was Jill's fault, of course, but he had been on the receiving end when all that shit she had created hit the fan. Now he must wait for those raging flames to burn out. Would his mother change her mind? Will hoped she would – she just needed a few more days to calm down. He must wait for those few days to pass, and then she would call him. He was her only son, after all. He couldn't ask her for any help until then. *Did he need help?*

Will went left along the black-painted metal fence until he found the entrance to the square. A flock of pigeons pecked something on the paved path that wound across the square, and Will scared the birds away, creeping along that path like a ghost searching for an empty space. It was early morning, but people were already sitting on the benches. A few had their luggage with them, nervously glancing at their watches, clearly waiting for a train or a bus. Others were staring ahead of themselves with the same empty gazes as Will's – some clutching their meagre belongings, some sorting their newspapers or eating something. A few were sleeping, covered by sheets from newspapers or ripped cardboard boxes. Nobody spoke.

The place felt alien, and Will was painfully aware of the chill biting at his bare hands. Those people must have spent the night here, and he might be forced to join them unless he could find another solution. He desperately needed a plan.

The empty bench he spotted was a bit further away from the others, and Will sat down, placing his rucksack next to him. He felt like a white crow in a flock of black birds with his bulging muscles, the same but different, and he didn't like the feeling. It was an entirely different experience from being in his gym, where he enjoyed being in the spotlight and at the centre of everybody's attention and gossip. Here he just wanted to blend in with the bench. The change was frightening.

More people rushed towards the train station as the day slowly broke. Will noticed they were trying to avoid the square and preferred to take the longer routes around rather than go straight down the winding path among the benches. Why? They were strange people with their peculiar habits, and Will just shrugged, hunching on his bench.

He still had no idea what to do next or where to go. He had become almost used to the nightmares he had each night – sometimes they were scary, sometimes boring. But now, his real life was turning into a nightmare too, and he just hoped to wake up and regain at least a part of his sanity. How had he ended up here? Yes, he had got what he wanted so desperately – a tattoo with Hel's face was on his chest, but the price he paid was too high. He hadn't expected his life to crumble.

Still, Will couldn't believe his mother had been able to find out that Jill was the source of the money for his tattoo and especially what nastiness he had to do to get it. It was the most embarrassing business, and he would rather forget it entirely, but that crazy blob of fat named Jill reminded him of the fact with his every step. Even now, his phone was quietly vibrating every ten or fifteen minutes notifying him of incoming emails. Jill's emails. It was utter madness. *Damn her!*

Will was alone in a strange city where he knew no one. He had no idea where to go, and each passing minute seeded dismay in his mind. *I'm big enough. I can handle everything,* he decided firmly. Half an hour later, his determination had evaporated like camphor, giving way to fears and panic, and he had to begin the self-persuasion again.

It was nearly noon when Will finally dared to leave the bench, still having no plan of where to go and how to resolve his issues. The waves of panic hadn't helped with the planning either. His phone was silent, except for the steady stream of Jill's emails – his mother had neither texted nor called him. Will would gladly answer her call but still didn't feel brave enough to take the first step and dial her number. She might reject him entirely. He must wait.

Will crossed the street and turned right – the direction was random, as good as any when there was nowhere to go. The crowd that crossed the road along with him rushed the other way, and he felt a slight relief as he unhurriedly strolled down the almost empty pavement. The few people he met never glanced at him twice, and he indeed felt like no one, like a shadow sneaking down the street.

"Any spare change, please?" a barely audible whisper slashed him like a whip.

Will stopped. A sheet of cardboard was placed on the pavement, and a dark man dressed in rags sat on it, leaning on the building wall behind him. Will had never seen any human that skinny. His bones stuck out everywhere with no meat attached to them. His joints seemed enormously swollen and almost pierced the skin. His hair was long and messy, black with just a few stray strands of silver, and his eyes were hidden behind his palms that were raised in front of his face as if in prayer.

"Please..."

He glanced at the man's rags and his bare feet on the pavement as the cardboard was shorter than his length. Will's stomach growled in compassion, and his left hand slipped into his pocket without consulting his brain. There was a banknote there that Ali had given him as a change when he'd ordered the Manly Meal yesterday. Will pressed the tenner into the man's hand and dashed forward.

"Thank you, sir!" an exclamation caught him from behind. "God bless you, sir!"

Will rushed forward, lowering his hood. *I could have bought a few sandwiches with that money...* But the man was so skinny! He probably hadn't eaten for several days! These thoughts were unsettling and were followed by loud moans from his own stomach. Will sighed, still feeling sure about his impulsive act. *Let the skinny man eat,* he decided without regret, but the decision failed to whisk away his own hunger.

Will had no idea where he was going. He still felt the man's eyes on his back and heard a flow of pompous gratitude addressed to him. He hunched over, feeling uneasy and rushed left at the first crossroad. *Don't look at anybody! Don't give away your last remaining money!* He knew he might need to survive a few days until his mother's anger had faded enough for a call. Will hoped she would call him. *If not today, then maybe tomorrow...*

The street was busy with young people rushing back and forth – some talking and laughing, some worried and concerned clutching books and papers. Will realised that he was crossing the college campus, and he hunched over even more, feeling alien at this temple of knowledge. *Go away. What are you doing here?* And he went on, allowing his feet to choose the random way.

A few blocks later, he turned right, leaving all that topsy-turviness behind. It was quieter here, and he slowed down, aimlessly dawdling forward and trying to avoid eye contact with whoever faced him on the pavement. Will had to ignore the quiet whisper for "any spare change" from a tired woman there – he had given all his cash to the skinny man. *I can't feed everybody. I can't. I'm hungry too. I need to eat something.* The thoughts were disturbing as he painfully felt the begging eyes upon him.

I can't give away everything I've got. I must eat something too.

The thought had a driving force, and Will began to move faster. He still had a few quid left on his card, but he must use this wisely – save it just for food and avoid paying cash. *I must avoid cash. I won't ever have any spare change then.* He cast another glance at that woman, but she was already begging somebody else. Will sighed with relief and carefully stepped around the orange tent on the street corner. Somebody was sleeping inside it with trashed boots sticking out from behind the loosely hanging flap, and Will rushed forward, hoping that whoever was in that tent wouldn't have enough time to wake up and ask for money.

He turned left, heading south along another busy street, still unsure where the flow of traffic and people rushing around would wash him ashore. He went slowly, hiding under his hood, painfully aware of smiling faces sitting at cafés and having lunch or people snacking on the go. The street seemed designed to offer food, and everybody gladly accepted this – everybody except him.

A few crossroads later, Will finally dared to sneak into a corner shop and looked at the snacks and sandwiches neatly lined up on the shelves waiting to be selected and eaten. He knew how little money was on his card, and any spending felt like a luxury that brought him a step closer to being completely busted. He carefully read the labels and checked the prices, searching for the best investment of his scarce money until security began glancing at him. It was time to make up his mind, and Will meekly picked up the cheapest sandwich he could find among the discounted stuff and a small bottle of still water. He paid with his card.

Will's stomach was playing loud grateful marches when he got back onto the street, stepped aside from the constant flow of pedestrians and bit into the sandwich. Will forced himself to chew it slowly and thoroughly to make it last longer, but the sandwich was small, and he finished it without reaching any feeling of satiety. He gulped a few mouthfuls of water and put the bottle into his rucksack.

Then Will checked his phone again. It was silent – no missed calls or new texts if you didn't count that steady influx of emails from Jill. That was strange. He knew how bad his mother's temper could get, but the rage never lasted for very long. It was about time for some rift to appear in those dark clouds above him. Still, the much anticipated sunshine failed to show up. Will sighed, replaced the phone into his pocket and went on down the street, dashing past the pleasant aromas leaking from every café and teasing his sense of smell.

Will turned left at the first crossroads. The side street was a quieter version of the one he had just left and slightly resembled the High Street in his humble hometown at peak hour. He lowered his hood and went on, trying to avoid any eye contact. That wasn't difficult. Nobody paid any attention or looked at him more than once. Sometimes he even doubted his own existence, feeling like a spectre among the living. He went through the strange maze of streets and squares heading south until the river stopped him.

What am I doing here? The thought pounded through his brain in panic as he looked at the muddy waters of the Thames rising at high tide. The river had halted his aimless wandering, but now Will stood hesitating where to go next. He didn't want to go too far away from the train station – it might be quite hard finding it again later. He looked across the water at the crowds slowly moving along the south bank with an old-fashioned carousel playing its tunes across the Thames on the right. He could cross the bridge, but the north bank was less crowded, so Will turned left without a second thought and went down the pavement between the busy street and the rising river.

The city around him beamed with life, but Will went hunched and hiding under his hood and absentmindedly counting his steps. There was no need to count them, but this kept his mind busy and the waves of panic at bay.

Will slowly crawled forward, keeping his eyes on the river, and almost bumped into someone. He jumped back instantly, mumbling apologies and eyeing the unexpected obstacle. The oriental man in front of him looked like a Buddhist monk dressed in light brown robes. His body faced the river, and his right hand extended out a small picture of his deity glistening in gold. It seemed to be a strange meditation or prayer since nobody was standing in front of him, and the deity's eyes on that picture observed the murky waters while the monk observed Will. A wide smile was frozen on his face, but the man's eyes weren't smiling – they looked empty and soulless. It was weird, and Will stopped, unsure of what to do.

"I'm sorry if I scared you," he apologised again, but the monk remained silent with that silly expression still on his face.

Will shrugged and backed away a few more steps closer to the river. The man didn't move. His body remained frozen like a statue, still extending out the picture, but the monk's face seemed to live a life of its own, separate from the rest of his body and followed Will with the same wide smile. *The man was crazy* – Will decided and rushed forward. He didn't like dealing with crazy people. Still, he felt those weird eyes fixed on his back. Several paces later, he glanced over his shoulder. The monk's body was still set in the same strange pose with his right hand clutching the golden picture, but his eyes, sharp like a pair of daggers, followed Will with that same silly smile still attached below them. *Damn!* Will dashed across the road, almost causing an accident, and slipped into the first side street, heading away from the Thames, away from that crazy man. The monk didn't follow – Will glanced back several times just to be sure.

The strange city hummed around him like a beehive – strange with its sounds, smells, people and customs. That monk had been the weirdest so far, but Will was sure he'd come across more.

Will hurried down the street, leaving the river behind. "Crazy people," he kept mumbling under his breath until the northern bank of the Thames was completely hidden behind several rows of buildings.

He met no more monks on his way. It was less crowded here, and he paid attention to nobody and did his best to avoid eye contact. Will stopped briefly by the metal fence that framed a small park just to check his phone. There were no missed calls and no texts, but the flashing red light made his heart sink – the battery was almost empty!

Will leaned against the fence as a sudden wave of weakness

passed through his body. Obviously, he couldn't wait any longer for the call – he had no way of charging the phone! He wasn't ready for the conversation and wasn't sure if his mother would be willing to forgive him yet. Still, the circumstances were pressing.

Will took a few deep breaths and crept along the park fence until he found the entrance. He must gather all his courage and call her. He must call his mother and beg for forgiveness. He must do that right now!

Will circled the park three times until he found an empty bench far enough away from other people. He expected this conversation to be difficult and didn't want anybody to eavesdrop. The bench was in the shade of a giant willow, and he sat there staring at the flashing red light on his phone for nearly an hour, still unable to gather enough courage. *What if she refuses to listen? What if she turns him down? Would his mother be able to forgive him?*

He must call her! He couldn't wait any longer!

Will took another deep breath and scrolled through the contacts list until he found the required number. His heart skipped a few beats as he pressed the call button.

"Hello," she answered almost instantly as if she was waiting for the call, but there was a hesitation in her voice. She had recognised his number, Will was sure.

"Hello, mum," his throat suddenly became dry. "It's me..."

"Who..." the line went dead unexpectedly, leaving the question unfinished.

Damn! Large drops of sweat rolled down Will's back as he sat clutching the phone. He had no time for any lengthy explanations. The battery was almost exhausted, and it was probably his last chance to call for help. He had no idea where he could charge the phone for another attempt if this call should fail.

Will pressed the call button again and patiently waited until she answered.

"Mum, it's me, your son Willy. Please, don't talk and just listen. The battery has almost run out, and I don't know how long it will last," he took another deep breath, trying to speak as quickly as he could. "I'm in trouble, mum. I was silly enough to end up in London, and now I don't have enough money to get back home. I know you're angry but, please, forgive me. I'd like to ask you to lend me a few hundred for the train ticket. I'll find a job as soon as I get back. I'll pay everything back to you, don't worry. I'll be a different person – I've learned my lesson, and I'll always do as you tell me. Just help me now, please. You'll never have a reason to get angry again, mum. I'll change my ways. I'll be the best son to you. Help me to get home, please. Mum... mum?"

The phone was silent. Will looked at the black screen with hot tears suddenly pooling in his eyes. The battery was flat. Had his mother had the chance to hear him before the phone went dead?

Could he hope for her forgiveness? Would she be willing to help him to get back home? Would she accept him back after all he had done?

He sat on the bench for another hour, clutching the phone. The day was dying, and the sunset cast long shadows in the park. Freezing waves of fear crept into Will's heart. Where could he find a place to sleep? He couldn't afford a hostel.

"Any spare change?" a quiet voice asked to his left. Will glanced at the tired-looking girl and shook his head sadly.

"It seems like we're in the same boat," he sighed, replacing the phone in his pocket. "I've no change."

The girl took a seat next to him. "I hope you don't mind if I sit down for a bit," she said. "I'm Sheila."

Will eyed her with suspicion. The girl was small with her greasy auburn hair tied in a knot. She wore a shabby grey tracksuit and dusty pink trainers. She tossed her plastic bag on the ground next to the bench as if there was a tangle of venomous snakes in it.

"I'm Will," he uttered with some hesitation.

"Nice to meet you, Will," Sheila flashed a quick smile, and Will noticed a few teeth were missing. "Are you a newcomer on the streets?"

Will shrugged.

"It's difficult to admit it at first, isn't it?" she asked quietly.

"You keep on clutching that silly little thing called hope even when it's completely gone. Welcome to the real world, beauty."

"I'm not homeless," Will cut her short.

"Oh, silly me," Sheila sighed with a wry smile. "You're just enjoying the evening view in the park, and a lush bed is waiting for you just around the corner."

"I'm waiting for some money to be transferred," Will explained proudly. "Then I'll buy a train ticket home."

"And I'm waiting for my invitation to Buckingham Palace," Sheila chuckled. "It's got lost in the post, I guess."

"I'm serious."

"Me too," the girl stopped smiling. "Haven't you ever heard of Princess Sheila?"

It was a silly remark, and Will smiled, for a moment forgetting his troubles. Then he remembered.

"I must find a cash machine," he grunted and stood up. "It was nice to meet you, Sheila."

"I'll show you," Sheila took her plastic bag and rose to her feet. "There's one nearby."

"I can find it myself, don't you think?" Will mumbled and strolled down the path. He didn't wait for her.

"I just want to observe your moment of glory," she told him, trying to keep up. "I hope you'll be generous enough to give a fiver to the princess. I'm not asking for much."

Dusk was spreading its shivering tentacles across the park. Most of the busy people had left, rushing to the pub to meet their friends or heading back to the quiet harbours of their homes. Now new ghostly shadows crept across the park carrying all their lives with them in plastic bags. Will tried to look away as they sat on the benches spreading out cardboard or newspapers. Some were rich enough to have a blanket.

Will stopped at the rusty gate, hesitating.

"It's on the left," Sheila whispered. "A few hundred yards up the street."

Will turned left. He didn't look to see if Sheila followed. His steps were firm, but his confidence was just skin deep. *Had his mother been able to hear his plea for help?* She was still mad at him, Will was sure, but would she be willing to help? It was a clear case of an emergency! He was her only son, anyway! She couldn't just abandon him. *Could she?*

Every step up the street brought him closer to the ATM, but his heart sank deeper into uncertainty. Will was almost in a panic when he finally stopped in front of the machine and took the card out of his wallet.

The monitor only confirmed his worst fears. His scant savings had grown even lighter after that sandwich, and there had been no transfer from his mother.

Will retrieved the card and carefully replaced it in his wallet without withdrawing a penny.

"I guess that means there's no fiver for the princess," Sheila sighed behind him. "And it means you have no place to go."

Will shrugged and turned his face away. Moisture pooled in his eyes against his will, and he shook his head, trying to hide it.

"I understand," Sheila pulled at his sleeve and turned right. "Let's go."

"Where?"

"We need to find a place to spend the night safely," she told him firmly. "It's London, beauty."

Will stepped after her hesitantly. He had no plan B. *Maybe his mother would do the transfer tomorrow?* Yes, he needed a place to spend the night! *Everything will be fine tomorrow. She just needs some time. She'll understand him.* Although these thoughts were comforting, they didn't instil any confidence, and Will followed Sheila, barely paying attention to where he was going. The city pulsed around them, sparkling with lights and colours, celebrating with music and laughter, but they moved between the happy crowds like two shadows.

Sheila tried several side streets but always returned, shaking her head disdainfully.

"We waited for your miracle for too long," she sighed. "All the best places are already occupied."

They hurried across the tangle of streets. Sheila took the lead, making seemingly random turns at crossroads, sometimes sneaking into dark inner yards each time returning to the street and dashing forward, and soon Will lost all track of time and direction. He was deadly tired and was nearly asleep as they went. Each cul-de-sac seemed as good as another to him, and Will couldn't understand what this strange girl was looking for. He was too tired even to wonder.

"Here," finally, she stopped with a satisfied smile in front of a large plastic bin in the dark, quiet corner of one of the cul-de-sacs.

"What's this?" Will asked.

"Our bed. Get in," Sheila opened the lid.

"Are you crazy?" Will's sleepiness evaporated in an instant. "It's a bin!"

Sheila glanced at him and shrugged.

"It's not exactly the Ritz," she told him, sounding like an expert. "But far better than the pavement, believe me. Get in."

Will glanced in. The inside of the bin was as black as a bottomless smelly pit, and he shrugged, hesitantly shaking his head. Sheila chuckled.

"Help me in," she tossed her plastic bag inside. "And don't be silly. It might rain tonight. Unless you have a million pounds on your card and can afford one of those extravagant hotels."

Will glanced at the sky. The city lights dimly reflected in the low clouds, and he realised that she might be right. It seemed like rain was coming.

"Will, give me a hand!" Sheila hissed angrily. "Good places don't stay empty for long."

Will lifted her like a bunch of rags and tossed her into the bin without thinking about it too much.

"Lovely," she announced a minute later. "Don't go too far to the left; there's broken glass there. But still, there's plenty of space for the two of us. And someone's dumped a blanket. You'll be sleeping like a king. Get in!"

Will frowned, but a gust of cold wind brought some soft drizzle and brought an end to his hesitation. He wouldn't be able to sleep on a bench, that was certain, and this was the only roof he could afford.

"Get in and close the lid," Sheila said from the seemingly bottomless smelly abyss.

Will looked around. The cul-de-sac was empty, and nobody could see him. *This is for one night only. Nobody will know.* He took a firm grip on the plastic and hoisted up his muscular body. Sheila moved aside as he landed on the garbage. The smell inside wasn't as bad as he expected; all the refuse was carefully packed into plastic bags. He just had to be careful not to pierce them.

Will placed his rucksack under his head and closed his eyes. Then two hands embraced him as Sheila spooned him from behind.

"I've never slept with such a muscular guy," she crooned, feeling his pecs.

"I've never slept in a garbage bin," Will said as he slipped his left hand into his pocket, firmly clutching his wallet. Just in case...

"We should get you some sort of superhero outfit, and you could pose for photos in Covent Garden," Sheila's hand wandered down onto his manhood. "People would pay good money for those."

"I'm too tired for all that nonsense," Will pushed her palm away angrily.

"Pity," Sheila sighed, withdrawing her hand. "Big, handsome, muscular and a bloody faggot..."

"Let's sleep," Will said firmly. He felt no obligation to prove anything to her or anybody else. Sheila said nothing.

Sleep didn't come easy. Angry and desperate thoughts swarmed in Will's brain, keeping him awake. His life was going down the drain faster than he could handle. A few days ago, he had had a roof over his head, his own room and his own bed and enough food to fill his stomach. Now he was hungry and sleeping in a bin with some crazy girl! *Damn Jill!* She'd stolen his life.

He listened to the raindrops softly drumming against the lid. Finally, Sheila's breathing grew quiet and deep, and only then did Will permit his mind to wander away.

It was the stench of smouldering flesh that pulled Will's mind out of the darkness. The sun smiled in the east, peeking over the forest, and he jumped to his feet and glanced around. The place was devastated but familiar. It used to be the middle of the village of the Rybbaths, but now, just piles of ashes marked the spots where people used to have their homes. Qu Sith sat in the morning sunshine absentmindedly licking his paws. The beast smiled at Will, stirred and stood up, stretching his body.

"Good morning," the sphinx parted his lips in a smile exposing two rows of sharp teeth. "I'd never have thought you'd be *that* sensitive. You fainted like a girl and were out for the whole night! I thought you might even be dying!"

Will acknowledged the greeting but chose not to comment. He was still too confused.

"I've carried all the bodies I could find to the burial grounds. You mustn't worry," Qu Sith told him proudly. "And I've got a boar roasting for you. A *real* boar. Get up and have some breakfast."

Will's throat felt as dry as the smouldering ashes of the burnt village. "Good morning to you too," he mumbled at last with his tongue barely moving. "I need a drink first."

"There's a spring a few paces down the street," Qu Sith suppressed a yawn as he spoke. "It is surprisingly clean, bearing in mind what happened here."

"Good..." Will stretched his aching muscles and looked around. There wasn't much he could see – just a smouldering wasteland surrounded by the distant dark green walls of the woods as he went down the street to where the sphinx had pointed. The spring was indeed just a few paces away, neatly framed with black rocks, and Will rushed to quench his thirst.

The rocks framing the spring were intact despite the turmoil and tragedy just a few days ago. Even a dried, carved pumpkin had been placed next to the stones as if inviting one to take a drink. But the surface of the quietly bubbling water was covered with floating ashes. Will cursed, turning the pumpkin in his fingers and circling the spring. A narrow creek leaked from it at the other side, where the water found its way through the rocks and gravel, leaving the sooty sediment behind. The stream was shallow, rippling downhill on a rocky bed, but the water there seemed cleaner. Bloody red stains marked the black rocks a few paces downstream where the sphinx had drunk his full after his hunt. Will stopped a few paces upstream to these, knelt down and first washed out the pumpkin.

The water was warm and tasted odd. Will frowned but drank his fill without risking a closer look at the spring. His stomach started to rumble when he finally stood up.

"Where's that boar you mentioned?" he asked the sphinx. "I hope you've no more surprises with this one."

"If you don't mind that I've eaten my half of it raw," Qu Sith mumbled, indicating the smoking pile of ashes where a large family house had stood just a few nights ago. "I'm a bad cook, but I've already warned you about that."

Indeed, there was a boar – just the head and shoulders of it, to be precise, resting on the hot ashes, half burnt, half raw – you shouldn't hope for more when the sphinx is a chef. Will didn't dare to complain – Qu Sith was sticking to the rules, even if the rules were against his nature.

Will had to find a stick to poke the boar out of the hot ashes. He turned its burnt side up and grinned as the pleasant aroma of the roasted meat leaked through the deep cracks in the charred skin. Perhaps the embers had not been as hot as yesterday, or maybe the sphinx had gained a little experience.

Will took his knife and made a few deep cuts through the burnt flesh. This time he found a thick layer of well-done meat between the bloody red and the charred outside, more than enough for breakfast, and began to eat. Qu Sith patiently waited a couple of paces away.

"What's next?" the sphinx asked as Will ate his fill and washed his hands in the stream.

"Let's go," Will said. He closed his eyes, trying to remember the view he had seen from the Tower of Hel's Black Castle. It wasn't quite the same thing as a map, but they had nothing else. "We need to go Southeast, I guess," he said firmly and stood up. "So now our path lies towards the sun."

Qu Sith shrugged. "You know best," he mumbled but followed.

They entered the dark wall of woods, leaving the Lifeless Pond on their left. Will led the way with the sphinx following closely at his heels. The woods were as creepy as they had been yesterday, blocking the sun halfway to the ground before it could have any chance of reaching the damp kingdom of fungi and moss. This time they had a guide – a quiet stream that left the Lifeless Pond and slipped into the woods, weaving around cliffs, rocks and arches on its way. Will wasn't sure if it was the right thing to do to follow the stream, but it showed the way downhill, and it was too wide to cross safely anyway.

They went silently, listening to any rattle of a falling branch or shuffle of wind in the brown dead leaves on the ground.

Everything else was silent in the dusk of the woods, although Will had the disturbing feeling of being watched a few times. He stopped and looked carefully around but couldn't see any human or animal eyes peeking at him. *It must be his imagination…*

"Tell me more, please. How do you humans deal with human females?" Qu Sith asked hesitantly half a mile later. "What do you do when you want to mate?"

"Why do you need to know that?" Will grinned without looking back.

"We may be in Per Hathor sooner than I thought," whispered the beast, although the woods were silent, and it seemed there was no one to eavesdrop. "I still have no idea how to present my case to the lady sphinx. I need a bit of advice. It's unlikely I'd ever ask any other sphinx for theirs, therefore, any sensible advice will do. Have you mated before?"

"Yes, lots of times!" Will exclaimed without stopping. He suddenly blushed – the only real experience he had had was the pitiful performance in Jill's boudoir, but he was ashamed to admit that. Luckily, the woods were too dark for the sphinx to see the bright colour blooming on his face.

"Great! I'd appreciate the advice of an expert. I understand that it's much easier for you humans because you've got a lot of females running around, and, I assume, you might get picky. I must be careful about your words, but you're the only source of information I have," Qu Sith mumbled. "Tell me everything, please. What do you do if you see a female and she's suitable for you to mate with? How do you let her know your intentions?"

"It's quite a complicated thing," Will shrugged hesitantly. "I don't know if I could advise you properly. You're not human."

"Please, tell me the truth," Qu Sith almost begged. "It's a question of life and death for me, and don't worry, I'll make my own assumptions. So how do you begin?"

"Mating, mating, mating…" Will mumbled. *Damn! It would be hard to explain to the sphinx the trick of placing an advert on the internet!*

"Well?" the beast demanded expectantly.

"Everything starts with a look," Will said, trying hard to remember what he had ever heard or fantasised about on the subject. "You look at her and wait until she looks back. You try to hold eye contact if you can. You repeat this several times until you're sure that she's looking at you and not at somebody else."

"We could easily cut that part short," Qu Sith observed. "It's not likely that there will be another sphinx for her to look at. So what do you do next?"

"Then you try to smile," Will shrugged. "If she smiles back, then you know she might be interested."

"A smile?" Qu Sith stopped abruptly. "Is a smile her only hint of potential mating? I thought there's much more involved. I've seen humans doing that, but it was difficult to understand. I think she might need other hints too. If you present her with a couple of sexual organs from a plant, would that serve as enough of a hint for her to get excited about mating? Or do you need an even bigger hint?"

"Sexual – what?" Will stopped as well.

"Flowers! Flowers!" the eyes of the sphinx shone with excitement. "I've got it! They're the key to mating! Now I understand the logic – it's so obvious! She needs flowers to understand your intentions! Have you ever tried animal sexual organs? She could eat them afterwards. Meat is very good for the laying of eggs."

"You've got it all wrong," Will told him and resumed his journey alongside the creek. "You give her flowers to make her happy. She'd admire them, smell them and understand that you cared about her."

"Smell them? Admire?" the sphinx sat down on his butt on the moss. His eyes had almost popped out in disbelief. "That's disgusting! Humans are so perverted! That makes no sense at all!"

"Then you need another gift if you don't like flowers," Will shrugged. "I guess a gift is a key, the way to show that you care. I don't know what gifts are valued by a sphinx, but you'll need to give her something if you want access to her private parts at any time later."

"Oh! Now I understand!" Qu Sith dashed forward with a broad smile, trying to keep up with Will. "It's a kind of trade. I'd never have guessed that something so complex as mating could be reduced down to the level of mere merchandise."

"It's not always the case," Will was glad the woods were dark enough to hide his blushes. "But you want the quickest way? If you offer her something that is of value for a sphinx, she might want to see you more often, and then things might move on to sex quite quickly. Still, I don't think you should expect to get intimate on the first date."

"Date? What's a date?"

"A date is when you meet up with a girl. You try to impress her while she's making her mind up about you," Will explained without stopping. "It may take a few dates if she's slow to decide. It's not a quick process, I told you," he glanced at Qu Sith over his shoulder, "but you may get on a bit quicker with presents."

"You're the expert," the sphinx frowned. "What do you do on these dates?"

"It depends on the girl you're trying to impress. Some girls like just to walk around with you. Others prefer fancy food. Some want you to tell them stories or sing," the explanation sounded awkward, and Will added after a few moments of hesitation. "Usually, jokes work well if she's got a sense of humour."

"I see..." Qu Sith mumbled with disappointment. "It sounds

very complicated indeed."

"I told you," Will shrugged. "It's a lengthy process, but don't be disappointed if it takes too long or if the girl doesn't like you after all – there's always another one waiting. You can always have another shot."

"Sphinxes are different," Qu Sith said sadly. "I doubt if I could find another female if I fail in Per Hathor. There's too few of us left in the world. She might even be the last female sphinx alive unless another female hatch from her eggs. I won't have another shot if I fail this time."

"That's an enormous responsibility then," Will observed. "You might need a very big present to impress her."

"Any suggestions?"

"I don't know what it might be," Will glanced back and shook his head. "You're the first sphinx I've ever met. I can't advise. I'm not familiar with your ways of living. Think about something that would please you – probably it would please her as well."

"Why is it all so complicated?" Qu Sith moaned and carried on mumbling something indistinct under his breath.

They went downhill between the ancient trees with their proud crowns obscuring the light. The moss was damp as barely visible strands of fog rose from the stream and followed their footsteps before merging with billions of droplets of dew on the dark green ferns, emerald vines and red and brown mushrooms.

It was very quiet. Too quiet. Not a sound pierced the woods except for the barely audible rippling of water in the creek. Will felt uneasy with that silence. Was another flaming viper lurking somewhere? He decided to keep as close as possible to the stream – water had saved them once, and he wanted to have an escape route in case of danger. Qu Sith was still indistinctly arguing with himself under his breath and barely paid any attention to the surroundings.

They went on like two goblins following the stream, weaving around occasional crags and arched cliffs on their way, and Will cringed each time he stepped on a dry branch and a loud crack echoed downhill between the ancient trunks. "Is Per Hathor far from here?" he asked, trying to find a way through the thick shrubs.

"Probably, two or three days downhill," the sphinx stated in a flat voice. "Why do you ask?"

"I'm just trying to figure out how long we'll stick to travelling together," Will shrugged without looking back.

"Am I too boring?" the sphinx stopped. "Are you counting the days till I die?"

"No," Will cut him short firmly. "I'm making plans how to survive without you. I'm a bad hunter."

"But you survived somehow without me until the Rybbaths got you," Qu Sith observed, resuming their stroll. "You didn't seem that worried when you were put into the cage."

"I'm worried now," Will shrugged.

A bird's cry pierced the silence, and they stopped.

"Do you hear that?" Qu Sith whispered.

"What? A bird?" Will chuckled.

"No," Qu Sith still was whispering. "The *other* sound."

Obviously, the sphinx had better hearing. Will listened carefully, but there was just the sound of leaves shivering in the light breeze – he shrugged uncertainly and shook his head. Qu Sith quietly sneaked past Will then disappeared into the shrubs ahead. Will dashed after him, but the creature was faster and moved among the shadows like a ghost.

After a while, Will stopped, breathing heavily. Finally, he could catch the low rumbling and slurping sound ahead but still couldn't understand what it was. The sphinx was out of sight somewhere behind the shrubs ahead, and Will stepped at a slower pace, casting cautious glances around.

The sound became louder with each step, muting all other sounds of the creepy woods. Will parted the low branches of the fir trees barring his way and found Qu Sith there. The sphinx faced the rumbling waters where the creek ended abruptly and disappeared underground in an insanely circling whirlpool, making those slurping sounds like a hungry mouth.

"This is where it ends," Qu Sith had to shout over the loud

noise. "Death is certain if you fell in there! It looks like a bone breaker!"

A few ribs, a shoulder blade and a bloodied skull rested grimly on the other bank of the whirlpool among a few pieces of the torn white cloth – that was probably all that was left after the sacrifice they had witnessed a few days ago. And it wasn't the first sacrifice. Will noticed that other bones, blackened with time, were scattered along the shores on both sides. Some were apparently human; some were not. And some lost appendages weren't even bones.

"We might have ended up here as well!" the sphinx told him. "Dreadful place and dreadful Rybbaths!"

"But we're out of all that, luckily," Will responded, patting the shaggy back of Qu Sith. "Let's go!"

"Let's go," the sphinx began moving.

They curved around the whirlpool, keeping as far away from the shore as possible. The slurping and rumbling subsided as they went. Half a mile later, it was gone.

Will stopped uncertainly. With the creek and that slurping sound gone, he wasn't sure which way to go anymore. The slope here was barely visible, and the sky was obscured by thick vegetation. It would be very easy to get lost and begin going round in circles again with no apparent sense of direction. A row of black arches stood on the left, and thick dark fir trees barred their way on the right. Ahead were black waves of basalt covered with moss with barely visible paths intertwined between them. Which way to go?

"Do you need any help?" crooned Qu Sith behind him.

"Are you sure you know the way?" Will asked. He didn't trust the beast and remembered perfectly well the last time they had run around in circles.

"Of course, I know!" the sphinx hissed disdainfully. "I can find the way with my eyes blindfolded and my ears plugged with wax."

"Let's go then. You lead!"

The sphinx marched proudly left, straight into the thick ferns where there was no visible path. He glanced back a few times, his eyes shining with determination. Will could do nothing else but follow. They strolled along silently, skirting around only the largest obstacles. The beast regarded all the shrubs and low-hanging fir branches as non-existent, and Will silently cursed him, doing his best to keep up.

They almost broke into a run for a while, but the scenery didn't change much, with the dark and creepy woods around them looking just the same. Qu Sith only stopped a few times, once when he had to leap over a fallen tree and twice when they ran into towering crags that barred their way. Will felt entirely lost. His sense of direction had failed, so he could do nothing else but follow that shaggy black butt ahead.

The woods around them were as silent as before. Too quiet. No birds sang, no insects buzzed. Even the wind didn't rustle the leaves that sat on the treetops as still as mushrooms sat down on their roots.

The forest grew taller as they went, with the trees becoming thicker and wider apart. The black basalt boulders were now more frequent, getting taller and bigger, sometimes arching above the dense undergrowth.

"How do you know the way?" Will demanded. It seemed they were going deeper into the woods rather than running in circles.

"You're sense-deprived if you don't feel this," Qu Sith said wryly without slowing down.

"Probably," Will agreed. "I don't feel anything. What is it?"

"Heat! It's faint, but we're hitting waves of heat as we get closer," the sphinx said on the go. "The lava fields must be very near."

"Then we're heading the wrong way," Will stopped with frustration.

"Why?"

"That lava flow we're seeking is supposed to be frozen by now. If you feel any heat, it must be from the new flow," Will tried to explain, but the sphinx wasn't listening. "We're looking for the old flow, not the new one."

"Silly human," Qu Sith mumbled angrily. "A lot of things may happen to a volcano when you're not looking, and they don't happen the way you're expecting. They have their own way happening."

"Damn," Will cursed. "Then the flow must still be too hot. I won't be able to pick that orchid up even if I do find it!"

"I hate moaning humans," the sphinx spat and leapt forward. "Wait until you see it!"

Several hundred yards later, their advance was stopped when a weird high wall barred the way. It stretched both ways beyond their visibility and was much taller than the tops of the nearby ancient trees.

"I could swear this wasn't here before," Qu Sith grunted, gazing at the rough brown surface streaked with red and white. "Things are ever-changing on a volcano, I've told you. We sat in those cages for far too long. Still, I can feel those waves of heat rolling. We just need to get over to the other side somehow."

Will didn't feel any heat but chose not to comment. The senses of a sphinx must be much sharper.

"I'd hate to climb this, especially if you feel any heat coming from the other side. We need to find a way around it," Will shrugged. "If there is one."

"I won't climb it either – I'm a sphinx, not a monkey," Qu Sith said seriously. "Downhill or uphill?"

"Let's go uphill," Will had no hesitation. "I might miss the orchid if that wall carries on down for too long."

"That will take us away from Per Hathor, but you're the one who seeks that blossom. We'll do as you say," the sphinx turned left. "Let's follow the wall and see what happens."

They went alongside the wall with not too many changes in the scenery. Will noticed the charring of the tree trunks that stood close to the wall. Still, he couldn't feel any heatwaves like Qu Sith could. The forest was silent around them with no life stirring – no birds could be heard in the trees, nor did they soar in the sky. They didn't startle any deer or rabbit or even a mouse. It was an uncomfortable feeling, and soon Will was almost running without even realising this. The sphinx stopped a few times and carefully sniffed the wall, then shook his head in disappointment and leapt forward, trying to keep up.

"What is it?" Will asked the sphinx after one of those stops.

"It's a bizarre thing," Qu Sith shrugged before leaping forward. "That wall is huge – nothing that big appears overnight. It must have been here for a while, but it has no odour, no traces of anything on it, no moss or dampness. This is a forest, and animals are supposed to be here in abundance, but not a single predator has marked its territory! No bird droppings! Can you explain why that huge thing is still pristine clean in the middle of the woods?"

"Maybe it was only recently built?" Will suggested.

"Built? Do you see any signs of a recent build? Any tracks?" Qu Sith whispered. "Any signs at all?"

"It doesn't look like frozen lava either," Will observed. "What do you think?"

Qu Sith stopped and carefully sniffed the air.

"Anything?" demanded Will getting closer to the wall. Now he too felt a faint warmth leaking from it. He extended his hand. It felt even warmer.

"I'd advise against touching it," the sphinx whispered while slowly retreating. "It doesn't feel right. I don't know yet, but that thing feels menacing."

Will passed his palm a few inches away from the rough brown surface. "It's still too hot to touch," he announced as he carefully probed it with the tips of his fingers. He had to jerk his hand back at once – the surface was hot enough to fry eggs on. "Another flow of lava? We might be stuck here while it cools down."

"Don't touch it," Qu Sith whispered with a note of terror in his voice. "I think I know what it is."

"Well," Will retrieved his hand. "What's your best guess?"

"A Night Crawler... the mother of the viper that killed the Rybbaths!"

"I see no flames," Will shrugged. "The one who killed the Rybbaths flamed, as I clearly remember."

"It's daytime," Qu Sith seemed tense like a coiled spring, ready to leap away into the shrubs. "That creature is sleeping! Don't disturb it. Let's get away while we can!"

Will shrugged, but the note of terror in the voice of the sphinx ignited an uncomfortable flame in his own mind that urged him to flee as fast as he could, although he tried to suppress this before it reached the level of panic. The memories of the flaming village of the Rybbaths were still alive, and he realised that the beast might be right. They'd seen the viper in action at night, but it may look different while it was asleep. *And if this was the mummy of the baby who had destroyed the village?* Will didn't like the thought but didn't dare test it either. "Let's go," he whispered. "We need to walk around it anyway."

"Can we keep a greater distance from that thing?" Qu Sith was visibly disturbed. "I don't feel comfortable *this* close."

"As you wish," Will attempted to sound brave but was glad to follow the sphinx who had already leapt away.

They sneaked back into the shadows of the creepy woods until the strange thing was barely visible among the crooked trees.

"We must move quickly," Will said, glancing over his shoulder. "If you're right, there might be a lot of forest fires here this evening."

"Yes! Yes!" Qu Sith whispered. "But let's keep quiet. We don't want the creature to wake up early!"

They hurried uphill – Qu Sith sneaked a few paces ahead like a black shadow, and Will tried to keep up with the sphinx, glancing at the mysterious wall to his right from time to time. He could also feel the waves of warmth rolling through the forest but still wasn't sure if those were real or simply his mind playing tricks with his imagination.

The trees grew shorter and more distorted as they went. It was difficult for things to grow on these slopes, but pines and firs somehow still managed to raise their twisted limbs and scarce green needles into the sky. The black boulders were scattered everywhere Will could lay his eyes on, thickly covered with green moss at first, but then they grew bald as they made their way further up the slope.

The woods ended a mile later. That strange thing they had been following had pierced the forest line and gone a few more hundred paces up the slope and then abruptly slipped underground under an enormous pile of rocks. It was still and lifeless and, at a glance, looked like a massive weird-shaped stone formation. *Was it?*

Qu Sith was as scared as Will. They sneaked forward, trying to hide behind the crags and boulders, dashing through the open gaps between them. The way uphill was slow, with not too many places to hide. Will sighed with relief when they finally got around that wall and began descending on the other side. They tried to keep the strange thing as far as possible at the edge of visibility as before.

The way was strenuous, and Will announced a halt. "Let's rest a little," he said, gasping for air. His heart trembled, either due to the arduous long trek or the invisible menace emanating from that thing with the apocalyptic images of the burning village still alive in his mind. "I guess we've nearly got away."

Qu Sith stopped and glanced back at the brownish wall that looked like an ugly brown scar on the volcano's slope in the distance. "It won't move until dusk if I'm right," he said dryly. "We might have some time to rest."

Will sat down on a flat rock. The ground trembled slightly, and he could hear a few muffled explosions high up the slope where the volcanic caldera was. He had almost forgotten that feeling during that captivity by the Rybbaths.

Qu Sith took a few paces further and climbed a large crag.

"You're a lucky bastard," he told Will. "That lava flow is indeed black now, as you told me it would be. Let's hope it's cool enough to walk on."

Will sighed. "What about that Night Crawler?"

"It hasn't moved," Qu Sith announced moments later. "But don't rely on that. You've seen what that other creature did to the village. We must get as far away as possible. I don't know how far away it can smell a human."

"But you're still not sure if that flaming creature and the thing on the slope are of the same kind, are you?" Will rubbed his calves which were aching after the brisk climb.

"No, I'm not," admitted the sphinx. "But I wouldn't like to take a risk, would you?"

The question trailed unanswered while Will frowned, tracing that worm-like thing with his eyes – down the slope from the giant pile of rocks until it dived into the woods and hid behind the charred crowns of crooked trees. It could be just another lava stream that had escaped from the volcano's depths and had frozen to stone on its way down the slope. Was Qu Sith just being paranoid with his suspicions? That thing looked entirely different from the flaming viper that had obliterated the village of their captors. *Didn't it?*

"Let's go," Will said firmly and stood up. "That lava field can't be too far away."

"It isn't," Qu Sith responded from the top of the cliff. "I can see it. It's no more than half a mile down the slope to the left. So, where do you want to begin your search?"

"Any place will do," Will said and shaded his eyes, looking down the mountain. He couldn't see anything the sphinx described without getting on top of that cliff. The flow was beyond the piles of rocks and trenches that barred the view as well, not just the way.

"Wouldn't it be wiser to begin at the place where you dropped the blossom? It's a small thing and could easily have got stuck between the rocks quite quickly," Qu Sith said as he carefully went down the cliff.

"It got carried away down the slope quite far, a few miles, at least," Will shrugged. "I saw that." He didn't want to go all the way up to the black castle and meet Hel there without finding her orchid first.

"I would never have thought your eyes would be that good," the sphinx observed before jumping down onto the crag next to Will. "The blossom is a small thing, not so easy to see, especially among those flames... A few miles, you say? That's very impressive."

Will wasn't ready to reveal all the circumstances but, before he was even able to think about opening his mouth, a white light, brighter than a thousand suns, flashed above in the sky, followed immediately by a deafening thunderclap. A shockwave threw them onto the ground, and the earth trembled and shivered the nearby cliffs. Seconds later, all had reverted to a standstill, apart from the usual tremors of the volcano.

"What was that?" Will asked as he tried to stand up.

"Stay low," Qu Sith whispered and placed his heavy paw on Will's shoulder.

Will followed his gaze. A giant warrior in shiny silver armour stood with a lance in his hand next to the pile of rocks where *that* thing was emerging from the ground. His eyes glared like a white flame through the narrow slit in his helmet as he looked around, scanning the slope. Will held his breath as the warrior's gaze passed over them without stopping.

"Who's that?" Will dared to whisper when the warrior looked the other way.

"He is a god," a few heartbeats later, Qu Sith answered, keeping his voice as low as he could. "I don't know the name, but he's a god, I'm sure."

"There are no gods," Will began to protest, but the sphinx pressed him firmly against the rocks.

"He is a god, not one of the Sacred Trinity but still a god," the sphinx repeated in the same barely audible voice. "Stay low whatever happens. It's our only chance. Look!"

A sudden strike of the lance shuddered the ground, ejecting pieces of rock high into the sky. Will raised his arms to shield his head as waves of small gravel began to fall on them. He didn't see the next few strikes but felt the ground shuddering at the mighty blows.

"Let's back off," Qu Sith hissed between the two strikes, his voice hushed by falling gravel. "We're too exposed!"

Will nodded and moved on all fours like a crayfish. They slipped behind the arched crag that provided some shelter from the falling gravel but risked collapsing from the tremors on the ground. Then a wave of intense heat passed over them.

Will dared to peek out from behind the crag.

The warrior-god had already passed a few hundred yards down the slope. His lance flamed blue and sang out high-pitched notes as it flashed in his hands like a thunderbolt hitting the brownstone wall. The thing had been entirely destroyed where the warrior-god had made his way with just small brown fragments scattered widely in the fields of black basalt.

Qu Sith stood next to Will with his black eyes nearly popping out of his head with curiosity. The waves of gravel stopped showering on them as the warrior-god moved further down the slope, reaching the first crooked trees. These didn't slow him down, though, and his lance flashed with increasing frequency, and the gravel showers were now accompanied by the broken branches and even the trunks of trees.

"I've heard the Night Crawlers are invincible," Qu Sith observed.

"It isn't even fighting back," Will said and stood up, shading his eyes to get a better view. "But you need to be a god to destroy it."

"Indeed," the sphinx sighed.

Then everything changed.

A long line of flames flashed through the crowns of the trees, stretching a few miles towards the horizon as if a flaming sword had instantly pierced the dark forest. The warrior-god still struck out with his lance, but now flames and molten rock splatters showered everywhere, not just gravel. The progress slowed as the trees got bigger and the flames grew higher. Then, finally, the head of the flaming viper rose above the woods in the distance. It looked around for a few moments as if wondering who had dared to tweak its tail and then attacked.

"Now we're doomed," Qu Sith whispered.

"That thing looks pissed off," Will muttered under his breath. "I'm glad we left the woods."

"But we have nowhere to hide," Qu Sith kept his voice low as if either of the creatures clashing a mile away could hear him over those mighty blows and earth tremors. "There's nothing but rocks here!"

The warrior-god continued to strike the flaming creature with his lance. The viper circled him several times but didn't dare to get any closer. Its tail moved, and the warrior-god had to jump around after it, casting occasional thunderbolts. The head of the flaming reptile kept its distance as if teasing or playing, avoiding the blows of the lance. The thunderbolts seemingly did not affect the viper even if they made a direct hit.

The clash was of titanic proportions. Centennial trees flew around aflame like bunches of grass. Will flinched every time the ground shuddered under the mighty blows of the warrior-god. The viper attacked silently, but its strikes were just as powerful and deadly. The fierce battle continued for nearly an hour. Most of the forest was now aflame or already burnt, but neither side was winning.

The viper screamed as the warrior-god dug his lance deep into its body, and then it split into two smaller versions of itself. The two of them attacked from different sides, striking and burning everything to the bare ground. Then the vipers split one more time. Then again, and again. And again...

The forest had no trees anymore – it had turned into a fiery lake, rippling with heat and slowly circling like a giant whirlpool, threatening to suck the warrior-god into its depths. He fought with all his might, but his lance could do no damage to the flames. The power wasn't equal, and the warrior-god was losing.

His shiny silver armour now glowed red, and small flaming vipers crawled upon his legs and chest like leeches. The warrior-god stopped fighting. He raised his head to the sky and screamed. It was a strange voice – undulating, sharp and loud like a siren, and Will had to shield his ears as it painfully reverberated in his eardrums.

"Shit!" Qu Sith cursed.

That scream pierced the heavens, and the sky answered with a low rumble. Six thunderbolts flashed, and six more warriors descended. The earth trembled as they set their feet on the flaming ground and raised their weapons – swords, axes and maces. The vipers hissed, and flames rose high, painting the sky in red, and the weapons sang their song of war, hitting the enemy with mighty blows.

The vipers continued to split and grew smaller, but their army became larger in numbers as they fought. The flaming creatures were now countless, covering the ground like blazing caterpillars. The mighty blows simply splattered them around without doing much harm, but the vipers – as they grew smaller – couldn't cause any damage to the warriors either. The battle was exhausting, but neither side was winning or losing.

From a distance, where Will peeked from behind a crag, it seemed like seven warriors were splashing about in a lake of flames. Then the lake began to thin and retreat. The vipers slipped into trenches and crevices and disappeared underground – getting away, out of sight but hardly defeated.

Half an hour later, the flames had gone, and the seven warriors lowered their weapons. Then thunderbolts flashed, and they were gone too, leaving the devastated land behind. What had been a lush and tall forest hours ago was now burnt down to bare rocks with trees, moss, all the undergrowth and whatever lived there gone. The abrupt silence was deafening.

"I thought we'd die," Qu Sith whispered and sat down, looking utterly exhausted. "That flower of yours would have been quite handy. Luckily, it's over."

"Why are you saying that?" Will asked.

"Don't you see, it's over?" Qu Sith snarled. "The flames went back underground where they belong."

"No, it's not about the flames," Will sat down in front of the sphinx. "Why are you saying that the flower would be handy? I see no advantage of having that flower if any of those had chosen to attack us."

"Don't you know?" Qu Sith made a surprised face. "Don't tell me, you don't know. I can't believe this – you were given a gift by Death herself. Don't you know the meaning of that gift?"

"She didn't tell me," Will shrugged. "What is it?"

"The gifts from Death are special," the sphinx said mysteriously. "They give you protection. You can't die while you hold that flower."

"I see…" Will let his voice trail off as the horrific recollection took on an entirely different meaning. That damned girl Gudula had been dead when he pushed her body off the cliff. It had been the decision of a moment to place that orchid on her corpse. He felt that she had earned a small farewell. Then she screamed, carried away by the lava flow. *Damn! She was burning alive!*

The realisation hit with a mighty blow like a hammer, and Will gasped, trying to swallow his guilt. *That stupid girl was being burnt alive...* That's why he had heard her screaming. It wasn't his imagination!

Qu Sith waited patiently, sitting in front of him. "You had no idea what was in your hands," he stated at last. "I can't believe how ignorant you are."

Will only nodded. Gudula had been a stupid girl with all those notions about loving him. It had been her crazy idea, not his, but he hadn't wished anything horrible to happen to her. He hadn't seen how or when she died. It was her own fault that she had wandered where she wasn't supposed to. All he wanted was to burn her corpse, not to resurrect her. Will closed his eyes, and the horrible screams of Gudula filled his mind as he tried to force out the memories of her flaming body being carried away by lava.

"Let's go," Qu Sith woke him from his reverie. "We still have some daylight left for a little search. That old flow must be hard and cool enough to stand on by now."

Will sighed and stood up. That entire incident hadn't been his fault, but the sense of guilt was crushing. He silently followed the sphinx down the slope where the black frozen river of basalt wound between the crags and cliffs in the distance.

The wind blew from the smouldering remnants of the forest, bringing smoke and soot that was painful for the lungs and eyes. They went silently, saving their breath. The sphinx led the way, stepping among the frozen waves. Will walked with his head down, keeping close to the sphinx's heels. It was supposed to be a joyous moment – they were alive, free and had reached the spot where they could begin their search for the blue orchid, but, for some reason, Will felt sad. He flinched whenever the scream of Gudula flashed through his memory.

"We could start here if you're certain that the blossom has been carried this far," Qu Sith mumbled, stepping on the bank of the frozen flow. "That thing is still warm," he observed moments later, "but not too hot. Let's go! You said it was blue?"

"Yes," Will stopped and looked at the top of the volcano – Hel's castle was barely visible from there. He was sure the screaming corpse of Gudula had been carried away by the lava further than that. "It was a blue orchid."

"I don't think it will be hard to spot if you look carefully," the sphinx marched across the lava field. "I'll take the other side, and you look down here."

It was far more complicated than Qu Sith had anticipated. The surface was uneven as if someone had poured hot dark chocolate down the slope, and it had frozen in waves and jagged chunks with countless trenches, holes and even small caves. Such a small thing like the blossom of an orchid could easily end up in any of these, resting in the shade and entirely missed by any glance. So, every crevice, every shaded spot had to be checked!

Progress was slow. It was like searching for a peculiar single bentgrass stem in a heap of hay. It could be anywhere.

Half a mile later, they still had no result.

"I need a rest," Qu Sith announced when they met in the middle of the lava field. "I feel exhausted."

Will shrugged and carefully lowered his butt down onto a flat piece of basalt. His muscles ached as they used to after the most strenuous routine in the gym when he squeezed his chest, back and legs days into one crazy workout. "It's getting dark," he said in a flat voice. "We need a place to sleep. I'd hate to sleep too close to the place where those flaming snakes went underground."

"I don't think they'll show up any time soon," the sphinx observed. "Or those gods wouldn't have left so quickly."

It was a crazy statement. Will didn't believe in gods, and those warriors they'd seen fighting with the Night Crawlers must have some different explanation other than being divine. *Gods wouldn't clash with those flaming vipers – they would simply flood them.* Those warriors were *fighting*. They weren't gods. Will cursed silently. Not only was this world weird, but it was also getting weirder with every passing day.

"Let's go to the other side," Will said a few minutes later and stood up. "I'd hate to sleep here, and it's getting too dark to search for that orchid. We might unknowingly miss it within a foot in the dusk like this."

"I've seen a few crags on the other shore that could give us some shelter," the sphinx offered a wry smile. "We could go there if you prefer the cliffs and not the remnants of the forest. It might mean an uncomfortable sleep and no breakfast, though."

"I'll survive, don't worry," Will mumbled as they went across the lava field. "Anyway, you won't be able to hunt in those ashes."

The crags Qu Sith was speaking about were almost a hundred paces uphill. It was a formless pile of large flat rocks with a dark hole beneath, looking like the luxury palace of a single caveman. Will crawled in on all fours without too much hesitation. He felt exhausted, and dusk was already slowly thickening around them. Qu Sith followed him.

As the sphinx predicted, there were just bare rocks inside, and it took some time for Will to find a comfortable position. He had to pick up a few stones and toss them outside since the cave was so tiny and two of them were sharing it.

Qu Sith settled into the darkest corner leaving Will to enjoy the view through the entrance hole. There wasn't much to look at – the lava field and the smouldering embers of the former forest on the other side – and Will placed his head on a rock, listening to the distant hooting of a lost owl.

The sphinx squirmed in the darkness, trying to fit between the pebbles and still unable to find a position that would be comfortable enough to snooze. This hole was worse than the refuse bin back in London – the thought strolled lazily across Will's mind, which began to cloud, preparing to slip away. Then another thought flashed like lightning.

"I know!" he exclaimed, smiling.

"What?" the sphinx's question hung in the darkness for a while until Will was able to collect his spinning thoughts.

"There is a way for you to watch your offspring grow up," he said at last.

"Don't give me that shit about the Road of Gods and some happy afterlife. I won't buy it."

"Shut up!" Will cut the sphinx's moaning short. "Are you certain about the properties of that blue orchid?"

"It's a well-known thing, human," Qu Sith chuckled. "You're strange, indeed."

"Then we must find that damned orchid," Will was smiling widely in the darkness. "I'll pin it to you before you make love to that female sphinx, and you'll be able to come out alive. Then, you'll be able to tell me how it was and watch your offspring hatch from her eggs!"

There was a nearly full minute of silence. Qu Sith was slow to digest the thought. "It makes sense," he said at last. "I might succeed if she doesn't tear me into pieces."

"You're a sexual partner for her, not food," Will shrugged the concerns of Qu Sith away. "She needs you so she can lay eggs.

And you'll have the blossom."

"She might be hungry or angry or not in the mood," Qu Sith sighed in the darkness. "You can't ever guess what's going on in the mind of a female sphinx. And the blossom will make me immortal but not invulnerable. It would be no use if only pieces of me were left crawling around."

Will chuckled.

"What's so funny?" Qu Sith asked angrily.

"Nothing," Will still secretly smiled in the dark. "Do you think it's worth trying?"

"I know for sure that my death is imminent if I choose to make love," the sphinx said after a little while. "But I don't know if my death is essential for her to lay eggs."

"You'll only have one chance to find out," Will said seriously. "Would you prefer to go to meet her prepared and protected, or would you rather leave everything to chance?"

Qu Sith sighed.

"Thank you for your kindness, human," he said at last. "I'll do as you say. I want to see my children grow."

"Great," Will said. "But I'll lend you the blossom only for a one-time action. I'll take it back as soon as you've finished with your lovemaking. I need to bring it back to Hel."

"Agreed," Qu Sith assured him. "I'll use the blossom just once. Let's sleep. I feel deadly tired."

"Let's sleep," Will agreed.

But sleep didn't come easy. The surface was hard, and one pebble or another pressed into his skin as Will squirmed, trying to get into a comfortable position. The sphinx had no trouble snoozing – soon, his deep breathing filled the cave, but Will still was listening to the hooting of an owl in the distance. He didn't notice the moment when he drifted off.

It was the nasty stench of rotten fish that hit him first. Will opened his eyes. It was dark all around him, and he didn't realise at first that he was still sitting in the refuse bin.

"Sheila!" he called softly. Nobody answered.

Will stretched up his arm and lifted the lid. Grey morning light hit his eyes painfully, and they began to water. He shook the tears away and opened the lid even higher. Princess Sheila was nowhere in sight.

Will's right hand still clutched the wallet in his pocket, and it took a few minutes for him to realise that his phone had gone. *Damn!* That girl had sneaked in with him just to rob him. Will cursed aloud. *Damn Sheila! Let her burn in hell!*

He frowned, trying to remember his mother's phone number – he'd seen it hundreds of times, but it was conveniently stored on the phone and had never managed to stick in his memory. *Damn!* He was in real trouble. He couldn't remember his sister's phone number either!

Will climbed out of the trash, cursing everything – his bad luck, the damp weather, the smelly bin, London around him, Sheila and Jill. Jill, most of all. His rucksack was open, and Will quickly inspected the contents – his old trainers and smelly sweatpants were still there. Sheila probably hadn't found anything in there worth stealing.

The cul-de-sac was empty, and nobody had seen him leave the stinky den. Will quickly lowered the lid and dusted off his garments, trying to brush away as much of the smell as he could.

He cursed again. The feeling was dreadful, and he hated Sheila for that too. Just a few days ago, he could never have imagined that he would be sleeping in a bin, with almost no money, nothing to eat and no place to go. He felt like an octopus in a desert with its fish tank suddenly cracking as it helplessly watched the leaking water, knowing that the end was near. Now with his phone gone, he had no way to contact home. *Damn Sheila! And damn Jill!* They had turned his life into a mess.

Will wasn't sure if his plea for help had got through to his mother yesterday. He was ready to swallow his pride and call her again. He could have somehow charged the battery, but Sheila had stolen even this last chance from him. *Damn her! Let her choke on that damned phone!* He'd find a way to contact his mother, Will was sure. He just had to remember her phone number somehow.

Will looked at the red double-decker bus that passed the crossroads at the far end of the cul-de-sac and forced his feet forward. He had no reason to hurry.

The large city around him softly hummed as the day broke through the heavy clouds above the rooftops. It wasn't raining, but the pavement was still damp from the late-night downpour. Will turned left at the crossroads and headed south, carefully avoiding the occasional puddles.

The street was busy with cars dashing both ways like angry beasts, and the growing crowds rushed in and out of the tube, waiting at bus stops, grabbing their morning coffees and snacks in shops and cafés along the way. Will's rumbling stomach reminded him that he needed some food as well. He touched his wallet and decided to delay any spending until the very last moment. It wasn't easy – he was painfully aware of all those pleasant aromas and saliva pooled in his mouth each time he laid eyes on someone biting into a croissant, sandwich or sausage roll or sipping coffee. Will lowered his eyes and went forward, hunched over. That helped a little – he could escape the sights, but those aromas still haunted his nostrils.

He negotiated a few more crossroads on his way and went slowly, placing one foot in front of the other without looking too much at the surroundings. He felt like an alien. He didn't belong there. Still, London gripped him firmly like a fly on sticky paper, offering no means of escape.

He decided to check his bank account again at the nearest ATM. Will had a tiny hope – maybe, his mother had changed her mind? A hundred quid would make a huge difference.

That thought gave purpose to his movement, and Will crossed another street in search of a machine. When he found one, his happy demeanour faded to grim disappointment, squeezing his heart with icy pliers. There were no incoming transfers.

He stared helplessly at the indifferent screen before retrieving his card and stepping away from the machine. Life bubbled and flowed around him – close, within reach but at the same time still bending around him as a rippling creek would curve around a rock. It was a new and frightening feeling that made him hunch over even more. But before Will began to crawl away with his soul drenched in self-pity, his eyes stumbled upon the red and white sign of a nearby building on the corner. It said "Post Office" and caused a manic smile to break out on Will's face – he couldn't talk to his mother, but he could send her a letter! That wouldn't cost a fortune.

He sneaked inside. The place was small, and Will had to walk along shelves stacked with snacks and drinks before he reached the glass partition on the counter at the far end where a sleepy Asian woman in her fifties sipped her morning latte.

He stopped with that silly manic smile still beaming across his face.

The woman placed her coffee aside. "How can I help you, young man?" she asked seriously.

"I need to send a letter," Will told her.

"You've come to the right place," she nodded as a slight smile passed her lips. "Where's the letter?"

"I haven't written it yet," Will shrugged. "But I need everything to write it."

"Paper, envelopes and pens are on that shelf," she pointed. "Choose what you want and come back for stamps."

Will went back along the aisle. *Damn Sheila!* He was sure he could have talked that nice Asian lady into charging his phone, and then his mother and his salvation would be just a call away. Now he had to use a system that would deliver his message at the speed of a drunken turtle. He had never written a letter before. It was confusing. More than a dozen types of envelopes were there – all in packs, none single. The plain paper was in packs of five hundred sheets as well – he had no intention of writing five hundred letters! He only needed one sheet.

Will cursed silently, almost ready to abandon the stupid idea, but he had no alternatives. He took the cheapest bag of envelopes but buying the whole pack of plain paper still seemed too silly. Bunches of coloured paper were much smaller but cost even more, and Will hated the thought of writing on green or blue. He considered buying a card for a few moments – it had an image of a sad puppy with the huge word "Sorry" on top, but it was way too expensive – he could buy a decent sandwich for that money!

A few paces down the aisle, Will found a stack of notebooks on the top shelf. He could tear a page or two out, and they would fit nicely into his envelope. He took the cheapest.

It was easy with a pen. He returned to the counter.

"Would you like a first class or second class stamp?" the Asian woman asked, scanning his possessions.

"What's the difference?" Will shrugged.

"Second class is a little cheaper but takes longer to deliver," the woman explained. "There's not a huge difference anyway – just a few days, I guess; it depends on the address."

Will frowned – a few days of rough sleeping seemed like an eternity. "First class, please," he mumbled unhappily.

"Half a dozen or a dozen?" the woman asked and opened her drawer.

"I only need one," Will said firmly.

The woman stopped messing about in the drawer.

"Then come back with your letter," she said and closed the drawer. "You'll pay the price of one stamp, and I'll send it."

Will nodded quickly. That sounded like a solution to his complex problem. He paid for the stuff he had selected and left, clutching the envelopes and the notebook in his hands. He needed a quiet corner to sit down, gather his thoughts and pen a massive apology to his mother.

Will looked around. The street was busy, with the only tranquil islands being around the cafés, but, of course, they wouldn't allow him to sit at their tables without buying anything. Will squinted at their prices. Even the least expensive tea was out of the question.

Will turned right and went down the street looking for inspiration. He had to cross a few more crossroads before stopping in front of another cul-de-sac. It was away from busy crowds and seemed suitable for a bit of meditation in the shade of a leafy lime tree.

He sneaked forward, looking for a dry place to sit down.

Just behind the overflowing bin, Will spotted a familiar plastic bag. Princess Sheila was lying on the bare ground next to it, facing the brick wall. It wasn't the most comfortable place to sleep with her legs soaking in a puddle.

Will felt a wave of anger building up in his stomach. He jumped closer and pushed the bin aside.

"Do you know anything about my phone?" Will squeezed through his teeth angrily. "Give it back to me!"

There was no response – still sleeping, probably.

"Sheila?" Will took a few steps closer and then froze. Something didn't seem right. Sheila's eyes were wide open, with their empty gaze still on the brick wall. A shadow ran across her face, but Will could clearly see the grey-blue colour of her skin and the bloody foam covering her mouth despite the shadow. A plastic syringe was next to her in a pool of vomit. Princess Sheila wasn't moving. She wasn't breathing either.

Will dashed into the street without wasting another second.

"Somebody help! Please, help!" he cried out. "Something's wrong with a woman down there!"

His cry halted the steady flow of life in the street for only a moment. A few men stepped out of their tracks and rushed into the cul-de-sac where Will was pointing, followed by a group of curious youngsters. They looked at Sheila and stepped back. No one touched her. One of the men took out his phone and called the police. He talked for a while, answering some questions and checking the name of the cul-de-sac on the wall. The youngsters stared shamelessly and took pictures – some of them even dared to take selfies.

"Did you know her?" the man with the phone asked Will. He was still on the line.

Will shook his head vigorously. He felt embarrassed to admit that he'd slept in a bin with her. He wasn't a vagrant. Not yet, at least. She was. And he didn't know Princess Sheila well.

The youngsters left as soon as the police arrived. They closed off the cul-de-sac and sent everybody away. Sheila's body was behind the bin, not visible from the street, and the onlookers quickly dispersed, hurrying back to their own routes. Will went with the flow. There was nothing else he could do, and his phone was now lost forever. Nobody stopped him.

He felt strange about Sheila. The short outburst of anger fell aside, leaving his heart empty. She was a thief, she had robbed him of hope, but his urge for vengeance slipped away and faded. The phone wasn't worth her life. *It was all her fault*; this thought flashed at the back of his mind but could no longer spark any anger. Instead, he felt just pity and sorrow – for her, at first, and then for his own fate.

Half a mile later, Will realised that he was still clutching his notebook and envelopes. He must write that letter, write it now. That was the most important thing to do – even more important than finding some food or shelter. It was his way out of this mess. He must return home or end up like Sheila, dumped somewhere next to a bin. This realisation seriously shook him, and Will cursed aloud. An elderly lady limping down the street suddenly jumped away at his outburst and gave him an angry look from a safe distance.

Will apologised, but the lady limped on, mumbling something angrily under her breath. He needed a quiet corner to collect his thoughts. He must get away from these hurrying crowds, away from Sheila's body and away from that sense of self-pity. He must grab the chance while he had it and write that damned letter.

He went down an unfamiliar street, wondering if there were any quiet corners in this giant ever-rushing anthill. Sheila *was* dead, but it wasn't easy to get rid of her. She kept sneaking back into his mind, blaming him for her fate. She would have been alive if he had guarded his phone with greater caution. *It was her own fault* – he tried to remind himself again – *she sold the phone and bought some shit that was stronger than she could handle. Her fault!* Still, the thought was unsettling, and that sense of guilt melted away his confidence like an acid.

The shops, cafés and offices seemed endless, as did the faceless crowds streaming in and out of them. Will strolled down the street, keeping his gaze down on the pavement but still painfully aware of the occasional begging glances and quiet whispers for "any spare change". He wasn't homeless – he firmly decided. He was just away from home. That *was* a big difference, but that would grow less distinct after a few more nights in a bin, he guessed. He must get out of here somehow, get back to his former life where everything was clear, consistent and orderly – food on a plate and a roof over his head, a nice soft bed to sleep in. All that luxury now seemed light-years away.

A shy smile sneaked across his face when he caught a glimpse of the rounded square at last – one of the many scattered in the tangled labyrinth of streets of London. It appeared on the left when Will emerged from around the corner and seemed suitable for the purpose. The square was small but shaded by the mighty crowns of tall trees, and several scarce shrubs offered defence from the noise of the swiftly moving traffic beyond.

Will had to cross the street and follow the long, brick-laid border until he found the entrance to get inside. It was too early for lunch, so most of the benches, scattered in abundance around the gate, were empty. Will turned right and went along the perimeter, seeking more privacy. Vagrants occupied a few benches further down the path, and Will hurried on towards the empty one next to the tall glassed cabin of the lift to an underground car park.

It was a quiet spot. Will sat down and got the notebook out. He then spent almost fifteen minutes staring straight ahead with unfocused eyes, trying to collect his thoughts. It was a difficult and unfamiliar task, very different from his usual choice-making between training routines. He sighed and grabbed the pen as if it was the fuse of a grenade. He *must* get this job done.

"Dear mom," Will scribbled on the first page and stopped. Sheila's bluish face with the bloody foam on her mouth persistently haunted his mind, and he couldn't concentrate properly. Will had never thought he was the sensitive type, but that death had shaken him deeply. It didn't matter that he barely knew her. Shivers ran through his body as he imagined her ghostly arms embracing him and touching him in all the inappropriate places. She laughed as he shook his head, trying to concentrate on the letter. "I beg you to forgive me," carefully he wrote the first line.

Will had to stop again and brush a few shy tears away. Princess Sheila was laughing in his ears and mumbling something indistinct that he couldn't understand. Will shook away her toothless smile and forced his eyes closed. *Am I going insane?* The thought flashed and vanished. It was terrifying. *No! I won't let that happen!* Will felt his heart tremble and took a deep breath, trying to calm it down. Sheila resisted but not for long. She sighed, and the cold ghostly hand squeezing Will's manhood vanished. Her hushed chuckles were still nearby but now didn't feel so disturbing. *I need to concentrate on the letter. I won't get a second chance.*

"I'm guilty of several things that I'm not proud of," Will wrote. "But I'm still your son. I'll do my best to change, and you'll never have a single reason to get angry with me again."

The image of Sheila faded as he carefully wrote down the words, strictly adhering to the blue lines on the paper. Suddenly, it felt like a floodgate had broken down – the words came out effortlessly, and he had a hard time trying to hastily put them down on paper while keeping the scribbles legible at the same time. It had been a while since he had spoken with his mother about anything more serious than a chicken breast or his so-called searches for a job. Having a conversation with his mother was always difficult, but it was easier to pour the words out into the notebook. The sheets of paper accepted everything without any judgement or objection.

Princess Sheila faded away, no longer haunting his imagination, and Will could pour his heart out with no one troubling him or interrupting his thoughts. London softly hummed around like a giant hive. The sensation would be otherwise numbing as if swarms of real bees were buzzing around, but Will forced the great city out of his mind too, seeing nothing else but the blue lines on the paper that guided his pen.

Will filled three sheets without even realising the effort. Then he stopped. Would his mother understand him? He didn't want to anger her even more. Would she be able to forgive him after reading this scrawl?

Will frowned and read the text he had just laid down on paper. *Shit!* He sighed. It was supposed to be a letter begging for mercy and maybe offering a few explanations for his occasional odd behaviour, not a tell-it-all memoir. How could those stupid confessions of the occasional trying of steroids or smoking of a few cigarettes help him to regain the lost trust? And that affair with Jill sounded entirely outrageous! He cursed and tore out the sheets.

An ambulance wailed down the road, flashing blue. Will

glanced a few times after it, then stuffed the torn sheets back into his rucksack and closed his eyes, trying to collect the erratic thoughts that swarmed around his mind in some weird Brownian motion. He must try harder.

"Dear mom," he began on a new sheet.

Progress was slower this time. Each word fiercely resisted being pinned to the blue line, and Will had to fight his way each time he attempted to organise them into something meaningful. The blue face of Sheila watched him from a distance but didn't dare to interfere. The text was clumsy with multiple strike-throughs and corrections, less emotional and without any embarrassing and unnecessary revelations.

Will wasn't sure if the job was done correctly but was reluctant to make a third attempt. It was a very tiresome activity, and his brain felt betrayed from being food-deprived and forced into something more complicated than tending to the chiselled body. But would this letter be enough to convince his mother? *Would she be willing to help him to return?*

Will read the text several times. Then, still hesitating, he transcribed it onto a clean sheet, correcting a few mistakes as he went. His heart trembled as he carefully tore the page out of the notebook, folded it and placed it in the envelope. Then he wrote down his home address.

He sighed and glanced around. The job was done, but it hadn't brought any relief. He still had to survive those few days on the streets while the letter made its way to his mother. *If she is willing to help, I might be sitting on a train in three days. If she is willing…* Will sighed. He had to find that post office again.

And here was another problem. Will had no idea where he was or how to retrace his way back to that nice Asian lady who had promised to send his letter. He was reluctant to go anywhere else where he might be forced to buy six stamps instead of one. He cursed aloud, scaring the pigeons.

Carefully, Will placed his notebook, all the discarded sheets with his scribbles, the remaining envelopes and the pen into his rucksack and stood up, stretching his already numbed muscles. It was well past noon, and his stomach annoyingly demanded its rights, but Will had decided to address that issue later. Sending the letter felt far more important.

Will's gaze followed a red double-decker that unhurriedly moved down the street when his eyes stumbled upon a suited guy who was standing probably ten paces away, clutching a luxurious bitten baguette with lush pieces of smoked salmon in his right hand. Will froze. The guy was staring directly at him with his dark brown eyes darting strangely in the expressionless face. The guy's mouth was open with a bite of the baguette still visible behind the chiselled white teeth and a drip of saliva slowly rolling down his chin. *Another weird Londoner*, Will thought disdainfully and was about to move, but the guy was barring the way. He was tall and big, not as muscular as Will, but was still an obstacle standing in the middle of the path with his right hand outstretched. Meanwhile, the guy's left hand was hidden in his pocket.

Will wasn't in the mood but dared to accept the challenge. "What do you want?" he asked, getting closer, face to face with the man.

The guy didn't answer. Tiny beads of sweat glistened on his forehead, but his face and his body didn't move, frozen in that unnatural pose in the middle of a walk.

"Stop staring at me!" Will barked angrily, pointing his finger at the man's chest. "I'm not your girlfriend!"

The insult faded unanswered. The guy didn't even blink, nor did he step out of the way. His face remained expressionless.

The lack of interaction was weird, and Will waved his hand in front of the guy's eyes but failed to achieve even a blink – the dark brown eyes were focusing on Will, but the rest of his body remained frozen.

"Is this a prank? A game? Playing at being a tree? Fine!" Will felt like a fool. For a few seconds, he stared at the bitten baguette in the man's hand – the lush pieces of salmon, salad and cheese stared back at him, and he was unable to resist the temptation as his stomach growled. Will grabbed the baguette before even realising what he was doing. "You're too fat anyway," he said in a harsh voice. "Don't even think about following me!"

The man didn't respond.

Will quickly left the square, taking the first street to the left, as it didn't matter which way to go in search of another post office when he was feeling so utterly lost. He only knew that he must find one and mail that letter.

The baguette was soft and tasted like the food of the gods. Will savoured every single crumb until it was gone. He glanced back over his shoulder several times – the strange man hadn't followed him, but he hurried away anyway. He was ashamed and embarrassed about stealing the baguette, but his stomach felt full and grateful. That man was a bully anyway – Will had had to teach him a lesson.

The post office emerged no more than two crossroads later, occupying the entire corner of the building. It was a bit crowded, and he had to wait in a long line before he finally got to the front and faced the tired-looking blonde woman behind the counter.

"I'd like to send a letter," he said and extended the sealed envelope out to her.

"Put it on the scales," the lady barked without even blinking.

Will did as was told. "I need it to get there fast, first-class," he attempted a smile. "But I don't need six stamps."

"Standard, signed or guaranteed?" the woman barked in the

same commanding voice.

That sounded like a foreign language, and Will felt lost. "I want it to get there fast," he muttered. "What's the difference?"

"What's inside? Any valuables?" the blonde woman frowned, turning the envelope in her hands with two-inch-long purple claws. "There's no return address."

"It's a letter," Will blushed. "And I don't have a return address here."

A few seconds of awkward silence followed.

"Do you need to know if it was delivered? You can track it on the internet," the woman asked, still inspecting the envelope.

Will blushed even more, painfully aware of his situation – he had no phone, no way to track that letter on the internet either. "No," he said at last.

"That will be sixty-seven pence then," the woman announced.

Will nodded quickly and got out his wallet. The woman placed the stamp on the envelope, and he paid with his card.

"When will she get that letter?"

"In a day or two," the woman said indifferently and tossed his precious letter into a large sack that was hanging on a stand next to her.

"Thank you," Will muttered and rushed away. He had to survive that day or two somehow.

Will turned left. He had no idea of his whereabouts but headed south along the busy street, trying to keep the sunshine on his face. The baguette he had snatched from that weird guy still warmed Will's stomach, and he hurried past occasional cafés as soon as their pleasant aromas began tickling his nostrils. However, the feeling wasn't as painful as before. He'd have to buy some more food but not until later in the evening.

The ghostly shape of Sheila still haunted his imagination. Will saw her from time to time – a transparent apparition following him down the street, sometimes weirdly laughing and indecently gesturing, sometimes just chuckling with her eyes fixed on him.

"Go away," he told her at the next crossroad.

Sheila chuckled and faded away, only to reappear a few steps later. Will chose to ignore her entirely. This was crazy. Was he going insane? Was Sheila's death shocking enough to affect his imagination? He barely knew her!

He squinted at the apparition, then lowered his hood as far down as it went over his eyes and hurried along without saying a word to Sheila. He turned right at the next crossroad and slipped in amongst the crowds, slowly moving both ways. A few paces later, he stopped and glanced around. The spectre had gone.

This street was even more crowded than any before. Will hunched over, seeing all those happy faces and hearing the music, he rushed across the road in the gap between the moving red double-deckers. All that happiness and entertainment around him drove him mad. He must somehow survive these next few days until the letter had been delivered. Then everything would depend on his mother. He knew her temper. She might regret her decision to evict him, but she would never admit that. Still, there was a chance that his mother might change her mind if she thought he had already learned his lesson. The odds were small, indeed, but it was all he had.

Will squeezed through the crowds oozing from the underground station and turned left behind the red brick building. The street was wider here but less busy. Will strolled downhill until he found an ATM to check his account – still no income. That desperate phone call had been utterly useless. He only hoped that his letter contained sufficient explanations and assurances to be more successful. Will sighed and replaced the card in his wallet.

He strolled down the street without paying much attention to the surroundings. His biggest problem remained the same – how to get some money, enough to return home. He wasn't entirely sure if he still had a place he could call home – everything depended on his mother and her decision. Will cursed, squeezing his fists in his pockets. *Why had he gone to London in the first place?* What kind of mind eclipse had he had when he bought that silly ticket? He had no answers. Time was his enemy, but he couldn't do anything about it except to unhurriedly place one foot in front of the other while keeping his eyes low and his gaze fixed on the pavement. And wait. Other pairs of feet rushed around him in both directions as he quietly navigated forward, trying to avoid collisions. Will had to lift his eyes from the pavement as he crossed a few streets on his way. Smiling faces moved in front of him. Quick glances slipped over his body as if it was made from glass, but then those faces moved on, never giving a second glance.

The street ended abruptly at a tall Tuscan column and a broad flight of steps descending towards another road paved in red. Some people were sitting on the steps, so Will decided to take a break as well. His wandering had no purpose, and any place to rest his legs was as good as another. He lowered his body next to the wall on the right without even bothering to have a look at who was sitting on top of that Tuscan column. It was irrelevant.

The street in front of the stairs wasn't busy, with just the occasional car slowly passing by. Still, the pavements were flooded with wide-eyed tourists, mainly moving right with their cameras out and phones on selfie sticks in anticipation of some wonder. Will eyed them absentmindedly and then lowered his head. The sun was smiling cheerily upon the stairs and at the people climbing up and down them, sitting in the bright light and chatting, drinking soft drinks or eating ice cream. Only he chose to sit in the shade, merely observing life rather than living it. He *must* get out of this mess somehow. He must get out before it became too late.

A pair of feet slowly climbed the stairs in the shadow and stopped in front of him. Will cursed. The feet were transparent. He raised his head wearily and glanced at the ghostly figure.

"Waiting for the Queen?" Sheila asked with a wide smile. Her teeth weren't missing this time, and her face wasn't blue anymore.

"Have you ascended to the throne already?" he asked bitterly.

"No. Of course, not!" Sheila chuckled, then gasped and half faded out of existence. "Do you see me?"

"Yes," Will shrugged. "You're my vivid hallucination. I must have eaten something laced with drugs."

"But I'm not a hallucination!"

"Then shut up and go away! I'm having a bad enough day without your silly questions," Will snarled.

Sheila backed a few steps away, looking at Will intensely, then stopped, leaning against the wall. "Aren't you going to cage me?"

"Cage? You're crazier than I am!"

"But... You *see* me," Sheila said hesitantly.

"So what?" Will spat. "I've no obligation to look after you. Your problems are not my problems."

"Sorry for the phone," Sheila whispered. The ghostly figure came closer and sat down next to him. "I didn't mean to cause you pain."

Will didn't answer. Several black cars rushed down the street to the left, stirring the crowds of onlookers into motion.

"That was the Queen," Sheila observed, but Will didn't even raise his head, studying the streaks of pink instead in the rock under his feet. He didn't say a word either.

"You seem more troubled today," she told him. "What happened?"

"I've seen your dead body," Will replied wryly.

"So, what?" Sheila shrugged. "I've seen it too. It wasn't that horrible, no need to make a face. It was just a body."

"It's not that it troubles me very much," he shrugged. "But that image is still somehow stuck in my imagination because I can't get rid of you. I'm probably going insane if I can see ghosts."

"It's nothing to do with your imagination. You must be blessed by Death if you can see me," she said. "I'm dead, and you won't see much of me quite soon. I'll be returning to the Tower as soon as I bump into some more determined *nesyn*. You were nice to me, but I messed everything up. I could repay you a little, though. I'll show you a few places where you could spend the night safely."

"Tower?" the word jolted Will's brain.

"I wasn't supposed to say that, yes? Is it a secret? I'm sorry," Sheila gasped. "The rules are very complicated. But, please, don't punish me."

"Punish?"

Sheila put a finger to her lips and shook her head. Her transparent face remained calm, but her eyes seemed frightened. She didn't seem to be joking. Will shrugged but wasn't keen to drop the subject. *How did she know about Hel's Tower in his dream world? Did she know Hel as well?*

"You're not giving up any secrets. I know about it already," Will told her seriously. "I've been to the Tower, and I met the woman who lives there. I'd like you to tell her a few things if you do meet her. Could you do that for me?"

"And you're living in the flesh but still remember the Tower?" Sheila whispered. "How is that possible? Haven't they blocked your memories?"

"They?"

Sheila shrugged but still refrained from answering. Will noticed that she didn't fade away either.

"What else do you remember?" she asked cautiously.

"There's not much to remember," Will said in a quiet voice. "I was only there once, a couple of weeks ago. The Tower was empty. I went to see the woman who lives there, but she was away."

"The Tower is never empty!" Sheila let her voice trail off.

"Yes, I met a few ghosts like you on my way out," Will admitted. "But I thought it was empty when I got there."

"Did you go to the Tower in your own flesh? No human can

enter the Tower – it's only for soulings!" Sheila gasped. "Then you're a *nesyn*! I'm doomed to slither the life of a snake in my next incarnation for dealing with you! Damn! A couple of centuries are wasted! I hate hatching from an egg and eating frogs!"

"What?" it was Will's turn to gasp. "What is that, *nesyn*?"

"Forget it," Sheila said firmly. "I won't say another word! I don't want any more problems!"

"Problems?" Will chuckled. "You're dead! They'll dispose of your body properly, don't worry! What other problems might you have?"

The question triggered a few stares at him, and Will realised that he was talking to an empty space as far as any outsiders were concerned since nobody else could see Sheila.

"Let's go," he whispered. "People are staring."

"Since when are you afraid of people?" Sheila mocked him loudly. "You were fine to sleep in a bin, and now you're afraid? Anyway, we can go now. The Queen's entourage had already passed."

She sprang to her feet and rushed down the stairs without waiting for Will to keep up. He dashed after her, trying not to crash into oncoming people – surprisingly, a crowd, probably a few groups of tourists, who had slowly crawled left down the red street before, abruptly went upstairs towards the column with their cameras ready.

Will hunched over and lowered his hood murmuring apologies on his way. The ghostly silhouette moved down the stairs several feet ahead without stopping and without looking back. He did his best to keep up.

They crossed the red street and went left, leaving the park on their right. It was less crowded there, and Will found himself walking next to Sheila.

"Where are we going?" he whispered when no eavesdroppers were around.

"South Bank," Sheila said firmly.

"What's there?" he asked.

"I'll show you a few places where you can spend the night," she said. "I don't have much time."

"What's making you rush?" Will began protesting. "What's wrong?"

"It's probably wrong to help you," Sheila shrugged as they turned left at the next crossroad. "I feel the strong pull of the Tower already. Damn! I'll be punished. I knew it wouldn't end well. No good deed goes unpunished!"

Although Will decided not to press this any further, the issue continued to nag at the back of his head. He had no idea what she was babbling about, but she was going to travel to the Tower and would probably meet Hel. "Would you be able to pass a word to the woman named Hel if you meet her there?" he asked with a humble smile. "Just tell her that I'll bring her flower back. She doesn't need to worry."

"Is she a souling? A ghost?"

"No, she's a person," Will shrugged. "She lives there."

"That's hardly possible," Sheila squinted at him. "Masters of the Tower never talk to any lost humble souling like me. And the Master of the Tower is a man named Mantus, I do remember now. But he is rarely in the Tower. He loves to travel the world. You must have been visiting another Tower."

"Another? I'm quite confused," the statement didn't make any sense, and Will frowned, staring at the ghostly eyes. "How many Towers are out there?"

"Just one per world," Sheila said flatly. "It means you were in another world when you visited that Tower, but I still don't understand how is this is possible? Unless..."

"Another world?" Will gasped. "Yes, it seemed like another world, indeed. How do you know this? How did I get there?"

"It's weird you don't know this," Sheila looked at him with a serious expression. "A *nesyn* is supposed to know everything. My humble knowledge is very limited, and even those bits are released only by death. I can't see the big picture. And even those few little things I do remember will be taken away by my next birth. You're supposed to know this too. Unless you're not a true *nesyn*."

"I'm not a *nesyn*, whatever that means," Will mumbled. "But you're right. It was a different world. I don't know how I got there. The moon in that world was much larger and entirely different."

"Unless you're not a *nesyn*," Sheila repeated slowly for the third time, her gaze wandering somewhere ahead. Abruptly she stopped. "Have you seen that other world in your dreams?" she asked, facing Will.

"Well... yes," Will admitted and stopped as well. "What does that mean?"

"That means that you must run and hide, dear big boy," Sheila lowered her voice. "You're a Sleeper, and that is far more dangerous than any slip of my tongue. Much more dangerous. Damn! I'm so unlucky to have met a Sleeper on my dying day!"

"I don't understand a word you're saying," Will complained. "Why must I hide?"

"They'll hunt you, dear," Sheila smiled sadly. "Once in another life, I had a Sleeper friend who was stupid enough to ramble on high and low about the wonders of her dream. Nobody ever saw the poor bastard after they got her."

"Who?"

"There are too many predators around for a Sleeper," Sheila's voice trailed off into a whisper. "You must find the Sanctuary to stay alive."

"I must get home," Will sighed.

"You must find the Sanctuary, you idiot!" Sheila cut him abruptly. "It's too dangerous for Sleepers to be anywhere else."

"Where is that Sanctuary?" Will asked.

"Sorry, bunny, I've no idea," Sheila frowned. "It's not here, that's for sure."

"Why do you think I'm a Sleeper?" Will demanded.

Sheila shrugged and resumed their stroll. "It was you who saw the other world in your sleep, not me," she told him without looking back. "I'm just a humble deceased soul. I don't want to be involved in your business."

"I don't have any business," Will mumbled. "You told me that you're going to the Tower and I asked you to pass a message to a friend. That's all!"

"And I told you exactly why I couldn't do that," Sheila snapped, keeping her voice low. "Your friend is out of this world."

"They're your words, not mine," Will said. "She is real, and I even have her portrait to prove it."

"Portrait? Have you met Picasso?" Sheila chuckled.

Will blushed but firmly lifted his T-shirt and let her inspect his tattoo. "See?"

"I don't know her," Sheila shook her head with a note of disappointment in her voice. "Is this the place where you've seen the Tower?"

"Yes," Will nodded, pointing at the tattoo. "It's slightly higher up the slope of that volcano."

"Then that Tower is different too," Sheila whispered. She didn't seem very surprised by the revelation. "Every world has its Tower, and every Tower has its Master. Our Master is Mantus. You have seen another Master, so I can't deliver your message," she smiled sadly and shook her head. "I'm just a mere grain of sand in this vast ocean, Will. I wasn't good enough to ascend to any higher world, so I'll probably stick with this Tower waiting for one more lifetime here if they don't banish me to the underworld."

"Where is your Tower?"

"I don't know," she sighed. "The place is freezing and covered with ice, and the Tower is deep beneath it. That is all I remember."

"Not much, but that's not important," Will told her. "I won't be trying to get there anyway. I need to speak with a woman named Hel, and she lives on a volcano, not under thick ice."

"I wonder which Tower will take you when you die," Sheila shrugged with a wry smile.

"I don't believe in all that nonsense," Will cut her.

"It doesn't matter if you believe it or not," Sheila stopped. "Have you seen some strange places too?"

"Yes, I've seen a few strange things," Will admitted.

A police car stood in the middle of the road, flashing blue and red and blocking the way. A shapeless angry crowd was right behind it, cheering at the speaker, waving flags and threatening somebody with fists. Will had no interest in any protests and went on, but Sheila stopped abruptly and pointed with her transparent hand at the police car where a man in a uniform was leaning against it with his right hand lazily resting in his pocket. Then, suddenly, he lifted his left hand and waved to Sheila.

"Shit," Sheila said with terror in her voice. "He's seen me! Shit!"

The man's gaze lazily swept over Will without stopping, but his eyes were fixed on the transparent shape of the deceased princess.

"How can he see you?" Will shrugged. "You're a ghost!"

"And he is a *nesyn*! He can see me as well as you can!" Sheila took a few steps back. "I'll be doomed for helping you! They'll punish me, I'm sure! Bye-bye, my dreams for a better life! I'm so stupid!"

"I'm sorry," Will mumbled.

The crowd began screaming and chanting frantically. The police officer didn't move, but his eyes still followed Sheila.

"I'll find you on the South Bank!" Sheila whispered. "Just cross the river! Go! Don't wait for me!"

"Is there any way around that crowd?" Will asked. He wasn't

keen even to try to get through that rabble.

"Go left and find any bridge," she vanished before finishing the sentence.

Will looked around. Sheila must be paranoid. That police officer was just doing his job trying to keep order. He didn't say a word and then turned his back on Will, watching the agitated crowd. Why had his stare seemed so frightening for a ghost? Will placed a guilty smile on his face and turned around, retracing his steps back to the park. He glanced a few times over his shoulder. The police officer was looking the other way.

Will shrugged before turning right at the crossroad. Nobody followed him.

He went between the park on the left and the grand houses lining the right-hand side of the street. He only met a few other people, and they hardly paid a second glance at the figure hiding beneath the hood. Indeed, Sheila was too paranoid. But who would judge a ghost? *Being dead was a big enough reason to be paranoid*, he guessed. That explained something but still not much about those things Sheila had babbled about. *Who is that damned nesyn?* Will had no idea.

Luckily, that police officer had given him no reason to worry. Will wouldn't have noticed him, he was sure, if not for that stupid ghost. She raised hysterics, and he had to crawl around and find another bridge across the River Thames. Still, Will couldn't understand why sleeping on the South Bank was better than on the North Bank. He must be crazy to believe what the ghost had said, and he must be crazy to believe in ghosts in the first place. Sheila's babbling had all indeed sounded like one grand nonsense. Will sighed – he must get a tighter grip on his imagination. His tricky situation and Sheila's death must have driven it over the edge. But, there was no reason to worry. He just had to wait a few more days, and he'd be back home, sleeping in his room, eating his chicken breasts, going to the gym. He just had to find a nine-to-five job to make his mother happy, and his life would be back on track in no time!

Will smiled, sneaking along the edge of the wide sanded square to his right. The sky was clearing again, and the sun warmed his heart and lifted his mood. *Everything would be fine!*

He reached the same red street at the next crossroad and turned right. The sun was shaded here by mighty trees, but he went on not minding the slight shadows. Sheila had told him to cross the river – but he had to find a bridge first. It was nowhere in sight, as far as he could see. He couldn't see the river either.

The street ended abruptly – a tall four-storey building blocked the way with a strange inscription on top of it. The letters were familiar, but the words they formed were strange, if not weird, difficult to understand. Will gave up trying. It didn't seem important.

Large arches ran through the building, letting cars pass through to the other side. Two smaller arches were for pedestrians on either side of the road. The way wasn't barred, and Will rushed forward.

The other side was disappointing. There were no angry mobs, but he couldn't see any bridges or the river either. A few paces later, he hit an almost steady line of traffic around a small roundabout in front of another square with another Tuscan column scratching the sky. Will stopped, unsure where to go. The tangled knot of the streets did not indicate which way the river was. *Where is Sheila when she is needed?* Will cursed and took the first street to the right, hoping that it would lead somewhere.

There was no traffic, but the thick crowds moved slowly on both sides of the pavement. Will went with the flow, trying to keep closer to the buildings. A few crossroads later, the way was blocked again by two police cars, and several officers were directing pedestrians. The same angry mob was shouting and waving flags behind him, and Will realised that he needed to find another way.

Where was Sheila? He crossed the empty street and took the first side street he could find. After all those crowds, it seemed nearly empty, and Will hurried forward, hoping that it wouldn't end in a cul-de-sac. It didn't.

The street ended by the river, and there was a bridge to Will's left. He widely grinned as he crossed the street and climbed the few flights of stairs to the bridge. He had made it! It was a late afternoon already and about time to search for a suitable place to spend the night. *Where was Sheila?* Will crossed the bridge looking at the disturbed waters of the Thames rising to a high tide. The wind blew in chilly gusts as he went on hunched over with his hood pulled low over his eyes.

It seemed warmer on the South Bank. Will stopped unsurely and looked at the old-fashioned merry-go-round playing tunes next to the London Eye. People were selling grilled meat and sausages, ice cream and waffles, and those aromas hit his nostrils painfully. Will clutched his thinning wallet and went the other way as far from the celebrations and music as he could. *Why did Sheila want to meet here?*

He went on, grim like a rainy cloud until he had left everything behind. Will couldn't escape the happy crowds wandering back and forth, but he found a place where the smell of food wasn't as strong.

Will sat down on a bench under the branches of trees richly wrapped in the warm light from electric garlands. The light breeze barely swayed the lamps and weaved the darkening shadows on the pavement into an intricate moving carpet. Hundreds of feet stomped along that carpet. None of those feet was transparent. People walked unhurriedly in both directions –

smiling, laughing, mostly in pairs or small groups. Will frowned, looking at all that happiness and feeling – not for the first time – alienated and lonely.

The dusk thickened, and some of those gusts of wind sweeping from the Thames brought an evening chill. *Damn! Where was that damned ghost when you needed her?* Will cursed and looked around. He had managed to reach the South Bank, as agreed. *Where was Sheila?*

He waited for another hour. Once he saw a homeless man in the distance carrying a large cardboard box and dragging a supermarket trolley containing all his possessions. Will hadn't got too many possessions, but that cardboard box seemed like a treasure. He looked after the man until he had slipped away behind the moving crowds.

Darkness fell, and it became clear that a quiet place to spend the night was entirely his own rather big problem. Neither Sheila, with her extensive knowledge of good places to sleep, nor any other solution appeared. He had to move or risk spending the night sitting on a bench.

Will decided to find a cardboard box first, but that wasn't as easy as he anticipated. He couldn't see any large ones anywhere in the vicinity. His best shot was around the food wagons. It was torture in itself as the food aromas made his stomach knot in convulsions, begging for a little bit of any tasty bite. Will couldn't permit such a luxury and tried to concentrate on the waste. A few times, he spotted a large box in the distance, but it had a bad habit of vanishing as soon as he got closer as another shadowy figure snatched it from under his nose. He needed a different approach. Would a few smaller boxes do the trick?

Will suppressed the loud rumbling of his empty stomach and began circling a park behind the busy pizzeria. He was rewarded with five pizza boxes half an hour later. One of the boxes even had a few remnants of pizza – someone wasn't keen on eating the stuffed crust, leaving half-eaten chunks in a box. Will gulped them down without thinking too much. His stomach fell silent, but it wouldn't be for long – he knew that.

Will picked one more pizza box from a bin and sneaked deeper into the park. The place seemed crowded, and he carried on looking for any quieter corner. The benches were all occupied, mostly by talking and laughing couples; some of them were kissing, and Will realised that it would be deep into the night before the park would be empty.

He crossed the street that pierced the park in half and went down the paved path between the dark shrubs. A few paces later, the path ended, and he sneaked into those shrubs with just a moment of hesitation. The place was empty and had probably been used before as he found another cardboard box stuck between the branches. The ground wasn't bare either – it was richly mulched with wood chips and peat and smelled of damp earth and fungi.

Will carefully checked the pizza boxes before spreading them out on the ground. He found just a few slices of pepperoni and a small piece of cheese. He must buy something to eat. He was reluctant to spend any of his remaining money, but it seemed inevitable. *Tomorrow*, he decided as he spread his muscular body on the ground. It wasn't as comfortable as it had been in the bin, but it wasn't as smelly either.

Will placed his rucksack under his head and stuffed his wallet into his underwear, deep under his manhood. He must protect that money at all costs.

He glanced at the sky just before he closed his eyes. The stars glanced back indifferently, and Will sighed, wishing for a clear night. Some merry tunes played in the pizzeria, and lazy gusts of breeze brought the aroma of fried food. He ignored them. He ignored everything as his mind was slowly carried away into the land of dreams.

Will was alone in the cave when he opened his eyes as he stifled a yawn. The sphinx was gone. This wasn't a big surprise. The beast was mischievous and was now probably darting across the frozen lava field, searching for that orchid. Sex must be a thing to him, and the orchid offered an opportunity to try it as many times as humans do, not the way sphinxes normally would. If he could have sex more than once in a lifetime, would he grab that chance?

Will cursed loudly and crawled out of the cave. *Why had he been so stupid to tell that beast everything?*

"Shut up!" a sudden hiss stopped him.

The broad shaggy back of Qu Sith barred the view, and Will squeezed a small smile, instantly regretting his moans. The sphinx was sitting at the cave mouth and observing the basalt field in front of him. At first glance, there was nothing unusual, but Will noticed the beast's fur raised on his back.

"What is it?" he whispered, trying to follow the sphinx's gaze.

"That lava field was full of those flaming snakes overnight," Qu Sith whispered without moving a muscle. "They're still there."

Will shaded his eyes. "I see none of them," he admitted after a while.

"They aren't flaming anymore," the sphinx glanced at him just briefly. "Remember that thing in the woods?"

Will frowned, scanning the basalt field. It looked the same as yesterday – splashes of rock frozen in strange, bizarre formations and cracked waves. Not a hint of sparkle was there.

"I still can't see anything," Will gave up trying.

"One of them is less than a dozen paces away," Qu Sith whispered and pointed with his paw. "Look at that stone."

Will crawled out of the cave and sneaked a little closer. Indeed, that elongated brownish boulder had the familiar strange texture. The boulder was small, far from the size of the wall of stone that had barred their way the day before, but they had seen how easily the giant monster dispersed into little flaming vipers equally as deadly despite their size.

"How did that happen?" Will asked.

"They came in the night," Qu Sith said quietly. "I thought it was the lava returning at first. I got up to have a look, but it wasn't lava. It was Night Crawlers. Many thousands of them. They came from the top of the volcano."

"Have they seen you?" Will asked. He began to notice similar boulders scattered across the lava field as far as he could see.

Qu Sith barely shook his head. "I don't think so. I didn't move. Sphinxes can sit for a very long time without moving – it's in our blood."

"We must proceed with greater caution then," Will observed. "It's dangerous, but it must be done."

The sphinx sniffed with disdain. "Are you going to tiptoe around this wreckage?"

"I need to find that blossom," Will said firmly. "You can stay away from it if you're too afraid to move." He stood up and patted the sphinx's shoulder.

Qu Sith squirmed with his fur still raised. "I don't know if this is a good idea," he mumbled with less certainty. "You've seen how dreadful it can be. Even gods can't handle them."

"Dreadful?" Will slowly went ahead. "Maybe this will inspire your courage?" He got out his manhood and emptied his bladder right onto that strange brown stone.

Qu Sith gasped as clouds of steam hissed, escaping the surface, but it didn't turn into a flaming viper. The rock didn't shift or move, and seconds later, it was as dry as before.

"See?" Will flashed a content smile and adjusted his pants. "It's daytime. You can piss on them!" He went on, laughing. "They're sleeping!"

"I don't know if that was a wise thing to do," Qu Sith began protesting.

"Do you want to survive that lovemaking?" Will threw the question over his shoulder. "Let's go! Just try not to step on them as they seem to be hot, and you'll be fine!"

The sphinx didn't answer.

Will went forward carefully, avoiding the brown stones. His heart trembled behind all that bravado. It had been a stupid idea to soak that creature, but he had to encourage Qu Sith somehow, or they would be stuck forever by that cave. He silently cursed, trying to calm down. He *must* find that blue orchid. He had wasted too much time already!

Will carefully chose his path between the crevices and solidified splashes, trying not to touch the brown rocks. He could feel waves of heat emitting from the Night Crawlers, but not a single spark escaped the surface.

He stopped in the middle of the lava field and looked back. Qu Sith was still sitting next to the cave mouth and cautiously sniffing the air.

"Let's move!" Will waved to the sphinx. "We both need that blossom! Time is ticking, and I guess we don't have a full day. We must get away from here well before dusk!"

"Very well…" Qu Sith sighed and lifted his butt. "I'll check this side of the flow."

They went on searching – slowly and carefully, watching their steps as they leapt from one black basalt rock to another, trying to stay away from the ones that had even the slightest shades of brown. Qu Sith moaned continually and mumbled something incoherent but slowly proceeded while doing his best to keep close to the shoreline. Will paid him little attention. He went along the path he had followed yesterday, looking into each dark crevasse and ravine, trying hard to spot any hint of blue. He felt silly. He still couldn't believe that something as fragile as the flower blossom could survive the heat of the molten rock despite everybody telling him that Hel's gifts were indestructible. That statement simply refused to connect with his sane mind.

Will sniffed loudly. *Sane mind?* This dream world kept pushing his sanity beyond its limits. Everything was strange here. He chuckled at the thought – he was hopping around a basalt field like a bunny, doing his best not to step on the sleeping rocks that might turn into flaming vipers if disturbed too much, and he was using the help of a complaining sphinx in this quest. Still, it felt more comfortable than sleeping rough in London.

He was firmly determined to find the lost blossom. A few weeks had already been wasted, but he must achieve the impossible, and then an even more onerous task was awaiting him – to go back and try to persuade Hel to forgive him. *Did he still have a chance?*

Will stopped. It was painful to doubt this. He sighed and resumed the search. *There must be a way out of this mess.*

"Anything?" Will looked back at Qu Sith, who was leaping between the brown boulders like a crazy monkey.

"Nay," the beast sighed. "Was it big?"

"A little smaller than my palm," Will scratched his vertex, trying to recall.

"And it was blue, you said," the sphinx sat down on a black boulder and looked around. "Then it can't be very difficult to spot. Or maybe somebody has already found it? Anybody could do that with a little luck."

The remark caused Will's back to stiffen in an instant. He growled as an abrupt realisation of the amount of time wasted struck his brain like a razor. *Yes, anybody could pick Hel's gift up with a bit of luck!* That was why she was angry. He must try harder! And faster! Will cursed before resuming the search. Hel would never forgive him if her precious blossom had ended up in somebody else's hands. *Damn!* Will's heart skipped a few beats as he looked around with his eyes open widely. The basalt field was enormous. It would be easier to spot a needle in a haystack than finding that small blue flower here, even without all those Night Crawlers. *Damn! Damn!* Why had he lost his luck when he needed it most?

Qu Sith went forward between the rocks, raising his paws high in the air like an overgrown cat on a hot tin roof. The beast was paying more attention to putting his paws down rather than searching for the orchid. The entire effort seemed next to useless. They would never be able to find the flower – not with so many obstacles.

Shit! Hel would never forgive him. She would never speak to him again!

He must try harder!

They had barely moved a hundred paces downstream so far. Will checked their progress using the line of twisted woods on the right bank. Still, not a hint of blue was visible anywhere between the black rocks, but he couldn't be sure with a surface as rugged as this. Any deep crevice could hide the blossom, and he wouldn't be able to spot it before almost stepping on it. The task was almost impossible, and Will went on cursing loudly. Would Hel accept his apologies if he failed to find the flower? She probably wouldn't... *Damn! This was entirely the fault of that stupid girl Gudula. She had spoiled everything that had seemed so promising in the beginning!*

The curses didn't bring any help but simply vented the anger he felt, and Will sighed, slowly looping down the slope on the lava field. The day promised to be long and strenuous.

The petrified vipers leaked some heat, and soon Will felt like he was walking in an oven. The occasional breeze, which came in waves, brought some transient ephemerous relief, but then the heat baked him again. Thick clouds slowly gathered around the volcano with their dark grey bellies painted pink. Will hoped for some rain – he felt thirsty and hungry, but the clouds only shaded the sun.

"Anything?" Qu Sith asked as he leapt on a high crag overlooking a crevice.

"Nope," Will said, firmly keeping his gaze on the ground.

"Could we take a little break?" the sphinx asked and licked his lips. "I'd like to go hunting. We need something to eat."

"I've no time for that," Will mumbled under his breath.

"You must eat something," the beast was persistent. "Or you'll become weak and start to moan."

"I must find that flower!" Will cut him short fiercely.

Qu Sith just shrugged and carefully got down from the crag, then sighed and fixed his sad gaze on the crevice. A sharp gust of cold wind swept over the field as Will leapt over the nearest Night Crawler and glanced around. Then something white flashed over his head – as white as a thunderbolt, but no rumbling followed. He froze and lifted his gaze to the sky. Something big was moving within the clouds.

"Run!" Will screamed, casting a quick glance at Qu Sith.

He wasn't sure what or who was moving above them. The thing was a monstrous shadow obscured by the low clouds and blocking the daylight. A strange chill froze Will's joints, but he forced himself into motion. Whatever it was, a sense of danger emanated from it that felt almost physical. His heart fluttered like a frightened rabbit as Will sprinted towards the crooked trees without choosing his way. The sphinx flashed past him like black lightning.

Will looked back only when he had reached the woods. The dark shadow took a few hundred paces up the volcano's slope and then descended onto the ground, covering the entire width of the basalt field.

"What is it?" Will asked, trying to keep his voice as low as possible.

That monstrous thing was as black as the deepest pit. Just occasional red and yellow sparks appeared here and there then instantly faded, consumed by the shapeless blackness. Will frowned, gazing at that thing. His brain hurt like hell, refusing to comply with the black absence of any existence on the slope of the volcano. It looked like a hole in the fabric of the world with utterly nothing shining through.

"I've no idea," Qu Sith responded a few seconds later. "Let's get away from here."

"I won't abandon that orchid. I can't," Will whispered. "I must find it. And may I remind you that your life depends on it too."

"I can still postpone my mating for another century or two,"

THE FIRST IN LINE | SLEEPER CHRONICLES

the sphinx muttered hesitantly. "I'm in no rush."

"I can't postpone my meeting with Hel for a century or two. I don't have that much time," Will cut him dead firmly. "And I need that damned flower!"

"Don't shout, please," Qu Sith whispered. "Let it be as you say. Let's just get a bit away from that… that black thing before it's too late. It won't hurt to keep low until it goes away."

"If it goes away…" Will retreated a few more paces. An undulating sound appeared at the edge of perception – a high pitched ringing that drilled into his eardrums like fine needles.

Qu Sith shook his head with a sour expression. "Do you hear that?" he asked.

Will quickly nodded. "Better hide until that thing calms down. Look at that!" he almost screamed.

Quivering black tentacles extended from that absolute darkness. They looked like strands of black fog slowly descending onto the ground. Then a white spark was born in the depths of that utter blackness that pulsed at first and then began to shine like a distant sun. The ringing increased in pitch, as did the pain it caused, locking Will's head in a hot metal band.

"Let's get away. *Now!*" he squeezed through gritted teeth. "This can't end well, whatever it is."

They sneaked among the thorny shrubs getting away from that shapeless black monstrosity as fast as they could, and the sound with its unexplained sense of danger forced them to move even quicker. Will uttered a loud curse – even the flaming vipers didn't look that scary anymore.

They were almost fifty paces into the forest when Will finally dared to stop and look back. The same instant, he began regretting doing so. The thing was as big as a mountain with tentacles shading half of the sky – it seemed there was no way to outrun it. *Was this the end?*

The white spark turned orange and began pulsing in the depths of the blackness and every rock and crag touched by the tentacles exploded, pulverised to dust.

"Run!" Qu Sith roared from the top of his lungs.

They dashed across the woods without thinking twice. The trees behind them shattered to splinters with the sound of thunder as the black tentacle unhurriedly passed the edge of the forest where they had been standing just seconds before. It seemed like chaos itself had descended on the mountainside and moved down the slope devouring everything in its way.

Will ran as fast as he could down the almost invisible path winding between the crooked trees and boulders. Qu Sith kept at his heels. Half a mile later, they stopped, panting heavily.

"Are we far enough away?" the sphinx asked as he looked back over his shoulder.

A few thunderbolts flashed through the tumultuous clouds,

with the sound of thunder barely discernible through the cacophony of explosions on the mountain slope. They couldn't see the dark monster but could hear it perfectly well. The ringing was less intense here, but the sounds of the explosions still were deafening.

Will shrugged and shook his head with a desperate expression. He couldn't run anymore, even if his life depended on this. The salty taste of blood was in his mouth, and he had a hard time swallowing the dried saliva before being able to speak.

"I don't know," he said and sat down, leaning against the nearest boulder. "I hope so. Let's wait and see."

"It might be too late when we do see it," the sphinx observed, still breathless.

"I need some rest anyway," Will forced out and pointed with his trembling finger. "By the way, your side is bleeding."

"Am I going to die?" Qu Sith gasped, looked at his side and then passed out.

Will cursed over the rumbling. *Now he would have to carry the beast if there was imminent danger!* He couldn't just leave Qu Sith behind!

Thunderbolts flashed almost constantly, but the rumbling sound didn't get any nearer. In fact, it was slowly diminishing. Was that a good sign?

Still breathing heavily, Will crawled closer to the sphinx to look at the beast's injuries. The black fur on the sphinx's right side was soaked with blood, and he had to part it with his fingers to get a better look. It wasn't as terrible as he expected – just a few scratches, and Will had to remove several thorns that stuck out of the beast's skin. The sphinx must have caught himself on something as they ran through those shrubs.

A few more thunderbolts flashed through the sky, but a cacophony of explosions drowned the sounds of thunder as the dark monster consumed the mountainside. Gusts of wind combed through the woods bringing a numbing smell of burnt iron. *What was going on out there?*

Will sat cross-legged next to the sphinx and absentmindedly watched the bright red streaks on the beast's side slowly turning brown. A few times, he flinched when something hissed just a few hundred paces away, but he couldn't see anything – the trees and rocks obscured the view.

The rumbling and explosions weren't getting any closer, but it still didn't feel safe. Will would have preferred to sneak another half a mile deeper into the woods, away from the darkness, but he was too tired to carry the sphinx.

The ground shuddered a few more times then the painful ringing in his ears eased a little. Will wiped beads of sweat from his face as he listened to the sounds of chaos from the other side of the woods. He had no clue what was going on there, and his imagination ran wild swirling scary apocalyptic visions in his mind. *Is this the end?* If the darkness headed their way, there was no way he could survive that.

"Am I dead?" Qu Sith asked weakly.

Will's smile was crooked with fear. "No, you're not!" he tried to sound encouraging. "But let's get away from that thing. Can you move? Those wounds are just scratches, but it would still be helpful to find some water and wash them."

"That might be a good idea. The smell of blood could attract a predator. I know this. I'm a predator myself! The wind can carry the smell of blood for miles," the sphinx moaned as Will helped him to his feet. "What is that thing? Did you get a better look?"

"I thought you would know that," Will shrugged. "You know almost everything here."

A series of explosions ran down the mountain, and the winds swept back, bringing the acerbic smell of soot and burning sulphur.

"Did you get a good look?" the sphinx repeated his question.

"All I saw was darkness with just a spark inside," Will said. "Let's go." And he went down the barely visible path. Despite the noise and explosions, they didn't run this time, and the ringing diminished as they went deeper into the woods.

The sphinx crawled after him, moaning and mumbling. It was irritating, and Will did his best to ignore him. The beast wasn't dying – those few scratches would heal without a trace. He even had fur to cover them. They might have been a little painful at the beginning, but why moan now?

"What?" he stopped a couple of paces later.

"I still can't believe how close to death we've been," Qu Sith sighed.

"Now we're out," Will cut in. "Stop worrying. That thing went down the slope – or at least it sounds that way. We're not in any danger!"

"We're safe, yes, if that thing doesn't turn in our way," the sphinx agreed sadly. "But it may destroy Per Hathor. I'll never find another female in my lifetime!"

"Shut up," Will said harshly. "Let's worry about one thing at a time. We must get away from that monster first and find some water to wash your wounds. You'll have your chance to worry about your sex life later."

"You don't understand, human," the voice of the beast was sad. "But I'm not blaming you. There's nothing you can do about it."

"Then stop moaning, or some predators might hear you," Will told him. "You're slowing us down."

Qu Sith didn't say another word. They went carefully selecting the way, still flinching when loud explosions rolled over the volcano. The woods seemed darker and creepier than before, but they went on, urged by fear. Will's legs hurt, and he had completely lost track of time. They had probably been going along the tangled paths for just a few hours, but it seemed like the better part of the day. Will stepped between the twisted trunks and crooked branches, occasionally glancing back to check if the sphinx was keeping up. The beast had stopped moaning but still muttered something quietly under his breath. Will went on paying no attention.

All his thoughts circled the blue orchid – what had happened in that lava field? Would that fragile flower have been able to survive all those explosions if it had survived the flames? Could it end buried under the gravel? Or had it been destroyed by that monstrous blackness? Was there any hope left there?

Will didn't think twice about choosing the way. He just tried to keep the rumbling at his back, and this took them away from that dreadful monster. *Was it far enough? Was it safe here?* He realised that it might take them another half a day to get back to the lava field and resume their search.

Qu Sith was mumbling something incoherently but did his best to keep up. "Let's go faster! Faster!" he urged from time to time. "It's still not safe here!"

"It's not safe anywhere," Will observed but continued to push forward.

The woods ended abruptly. Will stopped, surprised, and the

sphinx almost bumped into him. There was a vast field ahead with just rocks and scarce occasional shrubs – some still green but most of them losing the browned leaves they had – with a new lava stream blazing brightly almost a mile ahead. The way was barred, but there was no need to go any further.

Will looked back at the rumbling thing far behind. The sky was black there, and he could see the ghastly tentacles moving among the boiling clouds and flashing thunderbolts. It was slowly moving south, down the slope.

"There's some water down there," Qu Sith observed as Will eyed the sky.

"Great! I need a drink," Will looked where the sphinx was pointing with his paw. A steaming stream emerged from the depths of the mountain a few hundred paces away and cascaded down the slope in a series of rocky pools and small waterfalls. A few crags rose high into the sky at the last pool, where the water spilt over the edge and rushed down the slope in a rippling creek. Its troubled waters boiled white among the black boulders framing the bed before calming down and disappearing into the dark woods almost a mile below.

"This is what we need!" Will rushed forward, smiling happily.

"Be careful…" Qu Sith's warning was left to trail off.

Will joyously hopped between the rocks like a spring rabbit, suddenly feeling thirsty and filthy. The sphinx crawled at a distance behind him, cautiously sniffing the air and hesitating with every step he took. That dark, shapeless monster was still creating chaos on the other side of the forest. The sounds of explosions rolled over the woods but muffled before spilling over the line of trees that stood like a dark wall a mile below. The new blazing lava stream slowly moved down the slope on the right. Some dead trees still smouldered where the fervid flow had found its way across the woods. Those pools of water on the rocky slope looked like an island of tranquillity.

Will paused at the shore of the nearest rocky basin and patiently waited while the sphinx stopped moaning and reached him. The water was crystal clear, sweating thin strands of steam, and Will frowned, barely touching the surface with his finger. It was hot – not scalding but still too hot to risk dipping a hand in.

"The water is always freshest at the source," Qu Sith said in a humble voice. "Could you wash my side here?"

Will straightened his back and cast a few glances at the black grains of sand rippling in the depths of the basin. "Let's go further on," he said firmly without answering the question. He carefully stepped along the rugged rocky shore of the pond, where a small waterfall cascaded down a few feet and splashed into the next pool. The water was steaming here as well, so Will didn't even bother to check it. He followed the winding stream, went round a high black cliff towering above the creek, and stopped in front of the next basin.

A few more loud explosions ripped through the rumbling on the other side of the forest and shook the ground. Will flinched and squatted down, waiting for the shockwave to pass, but it was more than just a shockwave. A series of blinding white thunderbolts escaped from the tumultuous clouds, and the shapeless blackness on the other side of the forest began to rise. A giant murky tentacle slashed across the woods, shattering the stately trees to sawdust and shaking the ground again. A wave of cold air rolled after the shockwave, and that high pitched sound drilled into Will's eardrums again. The shifting shapeless blackness, high as a mountain, rose even higher, obscuring the larger half of the Southern sky. Will tried to suppress the rising panic but failed. Qu Sith seemed scared to death as well. His shaggy body shook as the beast pressed himself hard at Will's side casting glances at the blackness spreading high above them.

"Watch out!" Will roared. "That thing may descend on us!"

"We're going to die!" the sphinx moaned. "It's the end! We're going to die!"

"Shut up!" Will cut him short abruptly, barely keeping his teeth from chattering. "You're making too much noise!"

"Let's hide!" the sphinx leapt into the nearest crevasse. "I don't know where its eyes are! It could spot us here!"

Will followed the beast. The hot water in the rocky basin

rippled and splashed. It seemed the whole volcano had gone into convulsions, shaking and trembling, as if something huge had turned within it, ready to break free.

The cliff towering over the creek collapsed, and Will closed his eyes, silently saying his prayers.

Then the rumbling, tremors, and that high pitched sound ceased. A few thunderbolts flashed through the sky and the shapeless darkness lifted from the ground, hovering over the forest. The monster seemed to be resting on its tentacles as if making its mind up or gathering strength. Then it jumped.

Will closed his eyes instinctively as a giant tentacle passed high over their heads, hitting nothing. Qu Sith let out just the tiniest of gasps, barely audible over the tremors of the ground.

"I'll be damned," whispered the sphinx a few moments later as the black monster hid behind the clouds. The sudden silence felt deafening at first, but then the splashing of the water soothed the eardrums. "We can come out, I guess. It's over."

The dark mass in the clouds spat out a few more thunderbolts and then glided to the East with increasing velocity until it hid behind the horizon. Will sighed with relief.

"Are we safe now?" he asked. "Do you know what that thing was?"

"I've no idea," the sphinx admitted without any hesitation. "It seems that the gods decided to use different weapons to fight the

Night Crawlers this time. I hope it dealt with them."

"Then we can go and deal with that blood on your side," Will said flatly. "That pool might be still too hot for the purpose, though. Let's try those further down the slope."

Qu Sith didn't answer, and Will didn't wait for the beast to keep up. He left the crevice and cast a few cautious glances around. Will's heart still raced despite the fact the dark menace had already gone. He had to steady himself and lean on the nearest boulder as he scanned the vicinity. The rocky slopes hadn't changed much – just a few of the largest crags had collapsed due to the tremors. The stream still escaped the depths of the volcano, filling the pools and running down the slope to meet the forest, which had changed beyond recognition. Large clearings ran across the woods where the tentacles of the monster had hit the ground. And it was not only the trees that were missing. Not a single shrub, crag or even boulder was left behind, and the clearings seemed as smooth as freshly laid tarmac. The remaining trees seemed almost intact except for missing branches or sometimes even half of their crowns that had been in the path of the black monster.

"I'll be damned if I understand a bit of this," the sphinx said as he got out of the crevice. "But I'm glad we left the woods. I hope Per Hathor is still standing. That thing didn't seem to get very far down the slope."

"Everything will be fine," Will observed. "Nobody died, and you'll be able to tend your hatching offspring in no time. We just need to find the orchid."

"Yeah..." Qu Sith sighed. "If only that monster hasn't destroyed it."

Will carefully walked down the slope along the rocky bed of the rippling creek. The ground still trembled slightly, and he had to watch his steps for any loose stones. The sphinx crawled behind him, gasping at each stronger tremor of the ground.

"Do you think it's over?" the beast asked as they approached the next pool. "That thing might have gone, but is it safe for us to return to our search?"

Will stopped in front of the pool and carefully touched the rippling surface before answering. "I don't know. We'll see." He straightened up with a sour expression.

"Still too hot?" Qu Sith asked.

Will only nodded and went on. The monstrous thing had moved away, leaving an aftershock of silence behind, and the sky remained covered with thick grey clouds blocking the sun. They wouldn't be able to see if that murky thing returned unless its tentacles began to protrude through the cloud cover. It might be too late by then, but there was no place left to hide and nowhere to flee. The Northern slope of the volcano had been barred to them by the flaming flow of lava.

They must move away and fast. Will realised that they might not get a second chance when the monster returned. If it returned... and they needed to find the orchid on their way. *Damn, that was so difficult!* He had thought it would be as simple as picking a pebble. It might be, but he had to locate the correct pebble. Will sighed and stopped in front of the next pool. It was shallow but much larger than the previous ones. The waterfall on the left still leaked some steam while the waters dropped from a height of almost ten feet. The surface rippled around the three large boulders resting in the middle of the pool like a herd of river-horses with their backs slightly raised above the surface. A crystal stream leaked excess water on the right, finding its way through the jagged surface to the smallest last pool no less than a hundred paces away. Will looked at the black arched crags towering over the last pool in the distance, then sighed before bending down and touching the water.

"Is it still too hot?" the sphinx asked with a note of impatience in his voice.

Will shook his head absentmindedly as he submerged his palm and tasted the water. "It's warm and a bit salty," he announced at last. "It's fine to wash in, but it might hurt if it's poured on a wound, but I see no alternative if we're going to get rid of that blood on your side. The water is the same in all those pools."

"It's safe, but it will hurt," Qu Sith sat down on the shore with a wry expression. "I got that…"

Will dipped his hand into the pool again, then cupped up some water and splashed it on his face. It was too warm for his liking. Still, it washed the sweat away.

"You said that you didn't want to attract any predators," Will reminded the sphinx. "You said that the smell of blood could be sensed miles away. So now you decide if you want to take that risk or not."

"I'm not sure," the beast said, looking at the rippling surface. "If it hurts…"

"We're wasting too much time," Will stated the obvious, then stood up and stretched his muscles. "We need to snatch that blossom quickly in case that monster returns. Just take a splash when you're ready, or let's just go if you're in the mood to attract a predator. Have you seen a predator bigger than you in these lands?"

"No," the sphinx admitted. "But a bunch of small carnivores could kill you just as easily."

"Very well," Will suppressed a yawn. "Make your decision then."

"Don't bully me," the beast hesitantly trampled his paws without taking any step closer to the water.

Will rolled his eyes and looked down the slope at what was left of the woods – they must get down to one of those clearings and get back to their search. Time was pressing, and he had no intention of wasting even more of it. Then his breath froze in the middle of a yawn.

"What's that?" Will gasped, and his heart skipped a few beats in slow realisation.

"Where?" Qu Sith sprang to his feet and looked down the slope as well.

The remaining tufts of woods seemed to be in motion, with billions of sparks flickering in the underwood like dancing fireflies. It was pretty at first glance only. Even from here, Will could see tiny strands of smoke rising among the crooked branches and dispersing in a light breeze just above the tree crowns.

"Night Crawlers!" Qu Sith gasped. "We're doomed unless we find a good place to hide."

"There's no such place," Will lowered his voice to whisper without even realising this. "They can get into any crevice or hole."

"We're doomed! We're doomed!" the sphinx pressed his mighty body to the ground like a frightened kitten. "We'll die tonight. We can't run any further!"

"Stop moaning!" Will cut him short harshly. "We have a solution!"

"What solution?"

"The water! We'll get on those rocks in the middle and wait," Will pointed to the pool. "The vipers won't follow us there while they're flaming!"

"They could reach us across that puddle with no trouble at all if they're as big as the one that attacked the Rybbath village," Qu Sith whined. "We'll die, that's certain! We'll die!"

"Shut up! None of them is that big," Will told him and shaded his eyes. "I can see flickering in the undergrowth only – there's none taller than a foot! We have no other options anyway!"

"They'll merge into bigger ones if they see us," the sphinx couldn't stop trembling. "We've seen them splitting. I'm sure they could merge as well."

Will watched how the flaming army of caterpillars slowly emerged from the woods and began advancing up the slope of the volcano. It looked enormous, like a wildfire spreading through a dry prairie. There was no way they could outrun them, nor was there any safe path.

"We'll submerge ourselves as much as we can and wait until they pass or petrify," he said firmly. "That's our only chance."

"Submerge?" Qu Sith nearly fainted. "Sphinxes can't swim."

"You won't have to," Will assured the beast and began unbuttoning his shirt. "The pool is shallow, and we'll walk to those stones in the middle and wait there."

"We'll die! We'll die!" then the moaning of the beast stopped suddenly. "What are you doing?"

"Undressing," Will shrugged. He took off his shirt and began to untangle the knot of a rope holding his pants. "I don't want to get my clothes wet."

Qu Sith watched while Will slipped off his pants and, stark naked, began to fold up his garments.

"I hate naked humans," the sphinx spat with disgust. "You look like a monkey with some terrible mange. That fur is disgusting. It neither covers nor protects."

"I'm not asking you to admire me," Will looked down at his torso with obvious disappointment remembering that his marvellous chiselled body was sleeping rough in London. And this body was just... average! "Get into the water! Now! Or would you prefer to die in flames?"

Qu Sith sat down and passed his front paw over the rippling surface, still hesitant to get wet. "You said it would hurt," he groaned at last.

Will lost his temper. "Get in!" he jumped closer and began pushing the beast with all his might. "I won't watch you die on the shore! Move! We won't get a second chance! The Night Crawlers are coming!"

Qu Sith stopped resisting and went in with a splash, jumping up as soon as his paws touched the bottom. Still, he stayed in the pool with his eyes wide with terror. Will jumped in after him.

"It isn't as bad as I thought," the beast observed after a few seconds. "Why isn't it hurting yet?"

Will collected his garments from the rocky shore and placed them on a boulder in the middle. "I don't know," he shrugged. "Maybe you haven't soaked your wounds properly, or it may not hurt at all. I might be mistaken. Let's get to the middle and wait." He sat down, leaning on a rock and placed his head on the folded clothes, submerging his body up to his chin. The warm water soothed Will's muscles, but his brain remained on high alert as he peeked down the slope at the approaching flames.

The Night Crawlers hadn't covered a third of the way yet. Will's heart fluttered as he watched the sea of flames slowly approaching. Remaining calm was difficult. He had to suppress the rising panic more than twice and stop senselessly fleeing away from the death that was closing in. The left flank of the vipers had reached the creek, which was escaping the series of pools and carrying the moisture to the woods. There were no hesitations nor any attempts to cross the stream. The Night Crawlers turned right and began moving uphill along the rocky shore, bending around the occasional crags. That felt encouraging.

"Are they close?" Qu Sith whispered.

"Not yet," Will told him, keeping his eyes on the flames and his voice low. "They couldn't cross the creek, so now they're trying to find a way around it. They won't go into the water, so we might be safe if we sit quietly."

"Unless..."

"What?" a wave of chill carried on down Will's spine despite the warmth of the water.

"Unless the gods send that black monster back," the sphinx's teeth snapped with a sound of a closing trap. "We won't be able to escape if that comes down on us. The end would be ghastly but quick."

Will sensed the truth in the sphinx's words. He glanced at the sky, where low clouds gathered around the volcano. He realised that they wouldn't see that black thing descending until it was too late, and that was the most disturbing feeling. "It isn't coming," he whispered. "Not yet, at least. We might still have a chance."

"We're sitting ducks down here in this pond," Qu Sith kept on whining. "I have the sense of a predator. We're cornered and doomed!"

"We're still alive! Shut up!" Will cut in harshly. "We're going to make it unless you jump out of the water and begin running around like a mad cow. Be quiet!"

The beast stopped moaning, and Will turned his eyes back to the approaching nemesis.

"We could outrun them," the sphinx whispered. "If they can't cross the creek, we could run safely down the other side and wave them goodbye when we reach the woods!"

"Be quiet!" the terrified sphinx was irritating Will, and, shading his eyes, he scanned the field between them and the woods, which was slowly filling with flames. He could barely suppress his panic, watching the countless vipers no bigger than a foot finding their way around the scattered boulders. They looked like floodwaters rising but were much deadlier than that. Almost half of the field was filled with them, but endless hordes of the flaming monsters still emerged from the smouldering woods.

"We could outrun them if we started to move now!" the sphinx repeated his crazy suggestion. "They're slow!"

"There's no place to hide down there even if we make it to the woods," Will whispered. "The forest is already smouldering. We won't be able to hide in flames, and I see no more pools down there. The creek might be too shallow to dip into if they got to us. Be quiet! We're not moving anywhere!"

"We're doomed! We're doomed..." Qu Sith kept mumbling. "We're doomed..."

"Shut up!" Will snapped and gasped as another wave of Night Crawlers emerged from the woods on the other side of the creek and began their ascent up the slope, heading to the fiery flow of lava. "We'd be dead and fried by now if I'd listened to your advice. Those woods are jammed full with them!"

"Oh!" Qu Sith just growled as he gazed at the approaching creatures. It seemed as if the whole world had gone on fire, and their tiny puddle was like the last drop of tranquillity in a sea of flames.

The clouds were moving low, and a few thunderbolts flashed in the distance. Will quickly scanned the sky, but that dreadful black monster was nowhere in sight. Yet, the thunderbolts kept on flashing, and a few gusts of wind brought some chill air from the west.

"We're as good as dead if that black thing comes back," Qu Sith whispered.

"Relax," Will told him, trying hard to keep his teeth from chattering. "We're not dead yet."

The sea of flames slowly moved up the rocky slope of the volcano. The first Night Crawlers on the left were just a few hundred paces away from them, but the end of the moving fiery carpet was still somewhere in the woods, out of sight. The vipers on the creek's right bank were moving slowly yet steadily like a colony of gruesome fire ants seeing nothing but their target. Will only hoped that the flaming creatures would not target them.

"Get down," Will whispered with his eyes fixed on the nearest Night Crawler. "Submerge as deep as you can. They're keeping away from the water."

"I can't go any deeper," Qu Sith complained as he squirmed in the shallow water.

Will cast a glance – the beast's mane had risen a foot high

above the rock and looked like a messy crane's nest with his black eyes tearfully blinking at him from beneath it.

"Turn around and lie on your back," Will hissed. "It might attract their attention if you stay like that. Your mane is too big."

"I can't," the sphinx moaned. "My back isn't as flat as yours. I won't be able to keep still."

"Lie on your side then," Will snapped at him angrily. "At least part of your mane will be under the surface, and I'll splash some water on the rest."

"Water. I hate water," the beast mumbled but obeyed.

"Be quiet!" Will got the sphinx's mane soaked, but when he turned back, the army of Night Crawlers was already less than a hundred paces away. "They're getting close!"

The Night Crawlers on the creek's right bank had changed direction abruptly and turned towards the flowing lava, but the vast field on the left was blazing bright with countless twisting snakes slithering up the slope in an attempt to get around the flowing water. The biggest swarm was marching along the bank.

Qu Sith only sighed, not daring to move a muscle. Will stretched his body in the warm pool as well, resting the top of his head on a rock and gazing at the clouds. His heart raced insanely – he just hoped it wasn't visible through the rippling surface, disturbed by the falling waterfall on their right.

Will watched the heavy clouds slowly moving north over his

head and prayed for rain for the first time in his life. *Please, let it rain! Pour some water down, please...* He looked at the grey bellies floating above in god-like indifference and hoped for a few thunderbolts and a torrential downpour. *Let it rain, please!* He needed a miracle. Water had saved his life once and shattered the flaming viper to pieces. *Please, let it happen again.* Even a short sprinkle would be better than nothing. *Please!*

The passing minutes seemed endless. Qu Sith sighed a few more times but didn't dare say anything. And not a drop fell from the sky. The grey clouds were heavy with water but carried it towards the majestic peaks far in the north. The moisture wasn't meant for the volcano.

"We're going to die," Qu Sith whispered.

"Shut up!" Will answered in his lowest voice.

Let it rain, please! Please...

Will just blinked his eyes helplessly when a wave of heat rolled over the pond announcing that the flaming vipers had finally reached its shores. He silently squeezed the sphinx's paw and squinted to his left. The flames crawled over the rocks no more than five paces away. The pond was too small and its protection ephemeral, but it was all they had.

Will slowly turned his face to the left to get a better view of the shoreline. It looked like an entrance to hell. Billions of vipers slithered over the rough surface among flames and sparks. The black boulders grew dark ruby upon their touch, and waves of heat rolled over the pool. *This is certain death*, the thought stated the simple fact, but it froze Will's heart with primordial fear as the realisation struck his mind. They were nowhere near any sort of safety.

The water was still comfortably warm, and Will could feel the tiny grains of sand rippling against his bare legs. Still, his heart beat loudly like a pneumatic hammer in a forge, and he was afraid that those slithering snakes might hear it.

Qu Sith was breathing quietly next to him. At least, he wasn't moaning or whining. Will was sure the sphinx was as paralysed with fear as he was. He just hoped that the beast would be able to hold back any hysteria or nerve breakdown. Any screaming, shouting or running would mean certain death in their situation. There was no safe place around.

Time seemed to be almost frozen as the flaming hordes of vipers crawled uphill, keeping just a few paces away from the shore. They didn't like water, that was obvious, but Will wouldn't even think of testing the boundaries. His body grew numb and wrinkled, soaked in the warm stream. Still, he didn't move a muscle, even under the rippling surface.

A thunderbolt slashed the clouds, followed by a loud rumbling. *Let it rain, please, let it rain!* The sky grew darker.

"Oh, shit!" a sudden exclamation from the sphinx made Will

flinch.

Then he flinched again when misty tentacles protruded through the clouds. The field went into instant turmoil as the flaming vipers dashed around, creating utter chaos. It resembled a piece of rotten meat with the worms within suddenly stirring and fleeing at the sight of an approaching bird. Some Night Crawlers tried to jump over the creek, landing in the water but never coming up above the surface again. The majority rushed uphill, desperately trying to crawl around the site where the spring and the steam escaped from the depths of the mountain and gave birth to the creek.

"Watch out!" Will sprang to his feet as one of the flaming snakes jumped into the warm waters next to him. It went black in an instant and then cracked into several pieces before hitting the bottom of the pool.

"We're doomed!" Qu Sith jumped to his feet as well and shook his mane, splashing water all around him.

Will lifted his eyes to the sky. The tentacles hadn't descended. They were slowly hovering several hundred paces above the ground and seeding chaos among the Night Crawlers.

"The gods have gone mad!" Qu Sith wailed. "We'll die, that's certain!"

"Shut up! Don't attract their attention!" Will snapped at him sharply and pushed the sphinx back under the water. "We're not dead yet!"

The utter blackness was above them, still hiding in the clouds and blocking out the daylight. The tentacles moved slowly, hovering no more than a hundred paces above the ground. And that dreadful high pitched sound was missing.

Hell was still being unleashed on the flaming slope. The vipers were frantically dashing around; some were splitting into smaller versions. It seemed chaotic at a glance, but the flames slowly moved uphill, then curved around the jagged cliffs where water was escaping from underground and rushing towards the lava.

Qu Sith stopped moaning, and they both patiently waited, immersed in the warm water with only their eyes and noses sticking out. The air was hot to breathe, and Will had to soak his dried nostrils a couple of times. He lost track of time entirely as the flames ranged across the rocky field, and the giant black misty tentacles stirred the clouds. Probably it was several hours that had been filled with heat and panic. Twice he had to wrestle Qu Sith and submerge him again. Luckily, the beast didn't shout too much.

The heat remained even when the flames had faded. The hordes of vipers skirted around the stream on their way to the lava flow, but they left behind red-hot rocks and boulders scattered across the field. Will didn't notice the moment when the ghostly tentacles disappeared from the sky – one moment, they were still hovering over the ground and then the next moment, they had just faded away.

The sky brightened a little but remained covered with dark grey clouds, slowly moving North without releasing a single drop of moisture.

"It seems we've survived," Will muttered before raising his head and glancing around.

Qu Sith only sighed. He wearily put his front paws on the spine of the rock he was leaning against and shook his mane. "I'm not meant to sit in water," he said at last. "But I'm grateful that you made me do it."

"You're welcome," Will sat down on the rock. Waves of heat rolled over his naked skin as he scanned the blazing field in front of him. Nothing and nobody moved there, and the stream looked like a black crack in a dark ruby.

"That was the worst day of my entire life," Qu Sith stated sadly. "A very long life."

"It's not over yet," Will observed.

"I won't survive another hour of soaking in that water," the sphinx hissed angrily. "Don't tell me more of those creatures are coming!"

"No," Will said calmly. "Not yet."

"Do you see any of them? Do you?"

"No, but the ground is still too hot to step on," Will shrugged.

"We could walk down the middle of the stream, but I don't know what's waiting for us in the woods."

"It's late, and I'm not going anywhere," Qu Sith got out of the water, crawled up on the flat spine of one of those three rocks and sat down. "We have a sanctuary right there in the middle of the pool. Let's sleep here."

"We might be in trouble if that black thing returns," Will said flatly. "I think the ground was too hot for it to do whatever it was doing. Those tentacles might return when it cools down."

"We'll get out of here in the morning, as early as possible," the sphinx was almost begging. "I can't go now. And you don't know what's waiting ahead. Wouldn't it be wiser to wait and see?"

Will shrugged uncertainly. "We're wasting too much time," he said.

"But we're alive!" Qu Sith growled impatiently. "You won't find that damned flower if you get roasted somewhere in the woods by those snakes! It's getting late anyway."

"It's getting late..." Will echoed. "Very well. Let's sleep here!" He crawled on a flat spine of the rock in the middle of the pool and gathered his clothes into one bundle. His body looked pale in the fading light, and those perfectly honed muscles he used to chisel for long hours in the gym were gone. The body in this dream was far from perfect – was this the reason why Hel had turned him away? The thought chilled his spine, and Will carried

173

on a closer inspection of his image. The sphinx was right – that scarce ginger hair on his chest, legs and around his manhood looked disgusting and needed shaving. *Damn!* It seemed like a lot more work was waiting for him. Finding that orchid was just a part of the problem. He had to put on some decent meat before expecting Hel to take a closer look at him.

"Have you lost something there?" Qu Sith asked before lying down on the nearby rock. "Your fur isn't thick enough to hide anything."

"No!" Will flinched at the question. "Everything is fine…"

He placed the bundle under his head and closed his eyes. The sphinx muttered something indistinct, but Will paid no attention. His mind was busy building routines for his necessary workouts and making plans to survive another day in London. He didn't notice the moment when his consciousness was carried away by the   darkness.

Something soft brushed his right hand as Will's mind still hovered at the edge of dark oblivion. It was a vague feeling as if a feather had barely touched his skin and was withdrawn the same instant. Then there was the sound of the tearing of cardboard.

Will opened his eyes. His gaze was bravely met by a pair of brown unblinking eyes that belonged to a cheeky red fox. The animal froze just for an instant. Then it ripped a piece of the grease-soaked cardboard from under Will's leg and dashed away. An instant later, the fox was gone.

The morning was early and damp. Strands of thin fog leaked through the intertwined branches of the shrubs around Will, covering his garments with tiny droplets of dew. The chill brought shivers to his body, and he stretched his muscles before getting up.

Will peeked his head over the shrubs that surrounded him and glanced around. It was early morning, and the park was still almost empty with just a few dark figures moving among the strands of fog. It took some time for him to realise that these were fellow rough sleepers unhurriedly gathering their possessions and creeping away. He waited until they had gone. Will just couldn't walk with them. He wasn't homeless, just out of his home. And out of money, in fact. *Temporary!* He made an angry face and gathered the pizza cardboards he had collected yesterday into a neat pile under the thick shrub – he might need them that evening if his mother hadn't given his bank account a boost.

Maybe she had already? Will brushed the shy, hopeful smile away and sighed. He had to find an ATM and check that. He wouldn't stay here for another day if he had any means to leave.

He squeezed the remaining few drops of water out of the plastic bottle he had bought two days ago and dumped the garbage into the bin. Then he placed his rucksack over his right shoulder and went in search of a cash machine.

Will crossed the park following the deserted path on the right. The River Thames met him with a low tide that exposed its naked muddy banks and a faint stink of rotting fish. He stopped hesitantly, unsure where to go. Several lonely joggers pierced the thin strands of fog in both directions on the South Bank, and this didn't help him to decide. He glanced both ways and then turned left.

It would be wise to stick closer to the train station if his mother had decided to help him. Will had to cross the river first, but then he had no idea which street to follow. Everything here was so unfamiliar.

He forced himself into a hopeful mood, and his gait as he climbed the steps to the bridge seemed almost gleeful, but then his pace slowed down. The city still looked drowsy under the dissipating blanket of fog and was slowly stirring into motion. Will imagined millions of hands grabbing the usual mug of morning coffee with invisible clouds of pleasant aroma rising over London. He could almost smell the delightful dark brew.

A wave of loneliness stabbed his heart unexpectedly, and Will had to stop in the middle of the bridge. He gazed at a flock of seagulls hovering over the muddy waters, and shameful tears began to pool in his eyes. Will hastily brushed them away and lowered his hood as far as it would go, but the feeling still crushed his chest like a massive globe of flint. He gasped and steadied himself, grasping at the railing. *Please, mom, take me back home... Why have you abandoned me?* No one answered, of course.

He was alone on the bridge. Will took his time to shed a few more tears and then shook them down into the muddy Thames.

"Everything will be fine," he whispered. Still, he didn't believe that. His previous gleefulness had evaporated like camphor.

A few joggers passed behind him on the bridge, and he finally managed to get his senses under control. Will dried his eyes and went on, heading towards the television tower that flashed neon lights into the morning sky high above the rooftops.

He dived into the tangle of streets on the North Bank, trying to walk faster, keeping up with the image of an average Londoner and pretending to make his way to the gym. Will dropped the pretence fifteen minutes later. It was useless – nobody knew him here. Nobody cared or paid attention to him. No one cast a second glance at him as he passed down the street.

It took nearly half an hour to locate a cash machine. Will's heart trembled as he put the card into the slot and entered his code. Then the ruthless machine crushed his hopes to dust. He sighed before retrieving the card and replacing it in his wallet.

And he went on, paying no attention to where his feet were taking him. Each street he passed looked the same as the one he had just left behind – beaming with life, luring and inviting, but his empty wallet firmly built an invisible wall between him and all those sweet temptations that he passed with a blank gaze. He went slowly among the rushing people, absentmindedly probing the unknown waters, towering over the crowd with his large frame, like Titanic, but still unsure where to find his iceberg.

Will made a face when two pizzerias – one painted in black and the other in green – appeared in front of him with all those inviting smells, and then he hunched under his hood, sneaking right at the corner. The side street was short, ending a few paces later in front of a leafy square. Will's stomach churned in knots, still sensing the sticky smells of that fresh pizza following him. He sighed, clutching the wallet in his pocket. Those pizzas were a luxury he couldn't afford.

Will crossed the street and went through the gate, searching for an empty bench. His legs needed some rest after a few hours of aimless wandering. He stopped and looked around uncertainly.

Several paved paths crossed the square, meeting in the middle where a strange small timbered house rested in the shade of magnificent plane trees. It looked tiny and alien, surrounded by the grandiosity of central London, and Will wondered who might live there. He didn't have much time to guess since people with lunch boxes and paper bags began filling the square, trying to catch a little sunshine during their lunch break.

Will spotted an empty bench in the right-hand corner of the square and rushed there to claim the space before anybody else could reach it. He sat down and placed his rucksack next to him, selfishly taking up the larger part of the bench. His legs numbed gratefully, and Will closed his eyes, trying to push his problems away, at least for a few moments.

When he opened his eyes a few minutes later, three girls were sitting on the grass in front of him, just a few paces away. They were chatting agitatedly and laughing before opening their lunch boxes containing carrots, celery and hummus.

It was bizarre food but still – food. For a few minutes, he absentmindedly followed the travels of the carrots and celery sticks from the lunch box into the hummus dip and then into the constantly chatting mouths, then gulped down his own saliva, cursed silently and closed his eyes. *Damn!* He must survive this somehow. He promised himself he would buy a sandwich in the afternoon, or maybe even later. Then he would go to sleep somewhere with a full stomach.

Then a light breeze delivered the divine smell of fresh coffee.

Will kept his eyes closed, doing his best to ignore whoever was feasting nearby, but the smell of coffee just grew more assertive. He could even distinguish the faint notes of vanilla and caramel in that odour. He spent a few more minutes in torture with his stomach loudly requesting its share of food and then opened his eyes with a growl.

A large paper cup was only a couple of inches away from his nose, and it took him a few seconds to focus. The girls giggled and continued to devour their celery, but they were not responsible for the prank.

A guy in a tracksuit with large sunglasses peeking from under the hood was holding out the cup. He didn't move it even when Will growled at him with a hushed curse.

"Take it," the guy said calmly.

"Why?" Will asked but took the cup before this strange guy

could change his mind.

"I think you need it," the guy said with the same calm. He wasn't eating or drinking, and not a trace of a smile crossed his lips as he spoke.

Will tried the coffee – his nose hadn't lied; it was a vanilla cappuccino. The taste seemed as divine as the smell had been, and he gulped a mouthful feeling the pleasant warmth spreading down his throat.

"Here..." the guy extended him a paper bag.

"What is it?" Will asked before taking another sip.

The guy shrugged. Will took the bag that the strange guy was offering – inside was a generous baguette with chunks of roasted chicken and cheese and two muffins with blueberries.

"I've no money to pay for this," Will said, returning the bag. His stomach began to protest.

"Did I ask for money?" the guy sat down on the narrow free part of the bench. "Eat that. You need it."

The chats and giggles had been silenced, and celery sticks froze mid-air as Will fished out the muffin. He winced at the girls before taking a generous bite with a vengeful smile. The guy was silent, staring away through his sunglasses as Will devoured the treat. The baguette seemed endless as he gulped it down in large chunks without waiting for the guy to change his mind. He took a deep breath after the last bite and then got out the second muffin.

The girls quickly packed their celeries and went away silently. Will didn't mind them, but now his own throat felt dry, and he blinked, forcing the food down. He regretted not saving any coffee.

"Here," the guy produced a water bottle and handed it to Will. "I bought still water – I wasn't sure. Maybe you'd prefer sparkling?"

Will gratefully gulped the liquid and then finished the muffin. "Thank you," he told that strange guy. "I really appreciate this. I've warned you, though – I've no money to pay for this feast. So what do you want in return?"

"I want you to come with me…" the man was still looking away.

"I'm not gay!" Will cut him dead harshly. The idea of selling his meat for a sandwich seemed repulsive, even in great need.

"That innuendo might sound tempting, but it's not what's on my mind," the man glanced to Will's side just briefly, then fixed his gaze on the bark of a nearby tree. "I need to talk to you."

"Do I know you?" Will demanded.

The guy glanced around before taking off his dark sunglasses, then closed his eyes and turned to face him. Will gasped with instant recognition, and the guy quickly slipped the sunglasses on, turning his gaze away.

"How is this possible?" Will asked, still failing to believe his eyes. "I've seen the pictures."

"Have you ever heard of image editing?" Ben sighed. "What are you doing in London?"

"I really don't know," Will shrugged. "It was an impulsive decision."

"Strange decision, but okay," Ben stood up. "Let's go. We need a safer place to talk. Where are you staying?"

Will sighed before shaking his head wearily. "I ran out of money on arrival."

Ben didn't comment. He turned left and led the way without saying another word. They quickly passed the paved path and slipped through the gate, leaving the chatting crowd behind. Ben glanced back a few times, but nobody was following them – or, at least, Will thought so.

They turned right on the first street. Ben still didn't drop a word, just lowered his hood. Will kept close as they made their way through the crowd of wanderers. Ben silently extended an Oyster card to Will a few hundred yards later and turned right into the underground station. Will was barely able to keep up. He couldn't understand why they had to hide or who was after them. Ben must have his reasons – probably, those horrible fake pictures were enough reason to go into hiding and stay low.

They boarded the train. Ben was silent, with only his dark sunglasses visible from under his hood. The coach was crowded, and Will clutched his rucksack and squeezed between two sweaty gentlemen trying to keep up with Ben. They didn't travel for long. At the next station, the crowd oozed out, carrying them along.

"Faster!" Ben said quietly through gritted teeth as they sped down the corridor towards the Piccadilly Line. Will glanced back a few times but didn't see anything suspicious. People rushed in both directions, nobody paid any attention to them, and Will shrugged but moved faster. They hurried onto the westbound platform where the train was waiting already and slipped inside just before the doors closed. Ben lowered his chin, scanning the platform over the top of his sunglasses as the train accelerated and passed into a tunnel.

Again, the journey was brief. They sped down the platform at the next station, heading hastily to the Bakerloo Line. Ben wasn't offering any explanations, so Will had no other choice but to follow him. Anyway, Ben, the young doctor, was the only person he knew in this grand city. They got off the train at Baker Street, but this wasn't the end of the road either. Will's legs had gone numb, but he was afraid to complain, so he squeezed his teeth and did his best to keep up.

The journey was endless and dizzying, and Will couldn't understand why they were running or who was after them. He kept his eyes wide open but couldn't spot any prying glances – everybody seemed to be minding their own business.

They almost ran across the enormous hall at the end of the Jubilee Line and took the escalator to the second floor. Then Ben stopped abruptly.

"Stay behind me whatever happens," he squeezed quietly. "Don't let my eyes see you."

That was a strange request. Will was about to voice a question when Ben's body froze with his hand almost touching the handrail, his head began moving in slightly jerky motions, and his eyes scanned the crowd in the hall below like a floodlight.

It was an eerie sight, but nobody else seemed to notice. Will did as was told, trying to stay away from Ben's gaze. He carefully peered down at the hall below and gasped. A strange girl stood there looking around with the same absentminded expression and the same jerky motions. Her body froze in mid-step; a large brown leather bag slipped down from her right shoulder, but she didn't make any attempt to stop it. A crowd of commuters parted around her, barely noticing any strangeness.

Will jumped back a few steps, waiting, as the eerie pantomime continued. Minutes later, Ben's hand landed on the handrail, and his head stopped moving; his body, though, remained frozen. Will couldn't see the girl from where he was standing and simply waited. That didn't last long. Abruptly, Ben turned around and dashed past Will, hissing on his way, "Quick! Let's get out of here!"

Will glanced back before rushing after Ben. No one was following them. *What had all that bizarre pantomime been about? Who was after them? And why they were running round in circles?* He had no chance to voice his questions aloud as Ben had crossed the spacious platform and was already slipping onto the red coach of a train.

"Where are we going?" Will asked, rushing after him.

"To a safe place," Ben whispered. "Trust me, please."

"I won't go anywhere unless you give some explanation," Will watched the door close behind him as the train set into motion. "Why are those people after you?"

A small smile crossed Ben's lips. "They're after you," he kept his voice low. "And we're going to my place. Keep low. I don't want them to connect you with me. Not yet."

That sounded like another damned nonsense, but Will bit his tongue – the guy had fed him, maybe he'd help him to get back home? Still, Will couldn't understand who might be after him. *He had no enemies! He knew no one here!* He grimly watched the moving scenery outside the train window. His life had indeed become strange lately, but who was the enemy behind all these misfortunes?

They got off the train a few stations later. *All Saints* was the station, and Will squirmed, glancing around. Several guys and a girl boarded the train, then it carried on, leaving the platform empty.

"Now, what?" Will asked.

Ben silently moved on, and Will was forced to shut up and follow. They emerged onto a busy street. Ben glanced around through his sunglasses a few times before tugging his hood even further down and turning right. Will lowered his hood as well and stepped after the young doctor silently. All this dizzying rush around London had burned out his already depleted resources, and he felt hungry again.

They turned right at the first crossroad. The street was quiet, but Ben rushed forward without slowing down. Will tried to keep his head low, but it was difficult to hide in the empty street with his mighty physique. No one followed them. He checked a few times.

Several two-storey buildings painted light green lined the street on the left, and Ben briefly stopped in front of the first of them, glanced back a few times and unlocked the front door. They took the stairs to the second floor and stopped. Ben sighed before opening the door, labelled D.

"Come in, quickly," he let Will inside and locked the door. Only then did Ben remove his hood and smile briefly. "I hope nobody saw you."

Will shrugged. "Nobody knows me in London."

"Don't be so sure," Ben squeezed past Will. "Come in. Are you hungry?"

Will blushed. It was the question his mother used to ask. He didn't expect the same thing from a guy he barely knew. But those few days on a starvation diet had mercilessly killed his pride and butchered it to mincemeat. He quickly nodded, walking behind Ben.

The flat was small – the sitting room served as a kitchen, and a messy bed was visible through the open bedroom door.

"You might want to wash your hands," Ben told him, opening the fridge. "I don't have anything special – I hope you like lasagne."

Saliva pooled in Will's mouth as he dutifully went to the bathroom. He still had no idea why Ben had been searching for him, why he had brought him home and what was the meaning of all that secrecy. *Food!* The thought brought a broad smile to his face as he scrubbed his palms with liquid soap and washed his face. He even rinsed his mouth out before drying everything with a towel.

A big slab of meaty lasagne sat on the kitchen table waiting for him. Ben stood next to the window facing the yard outside with his back turned to Will. He didn't turn around, and Will stopped hesitantly at the door. The strange silence extended into minutes, and when Will was at last about to announce his presence, he noticed a few jerky motions of Ben's head. The guy was probably having one of those fits again.

Will patiently waited, tortured by the divine smell of food waiting for him on the table. Suddenly, Ben collapsed without emitting a sound. Will dashed forward to try to catch him, but he was too far away. Before he could get close enough, the young doctor banged his head on the cupboard and slumped to the floor like a bunch of rags. His face was chalk-white, and Will had a frightening thought that the guy might be dead. He pressed his ear to Ben's chest and listened carefully. The young doctor's heart was beating, and Will sighed with relief but didn't know what to do next.

He must be uncomfortable on the floor, the thought flashed, and Will carefully lifted Ben's limp body in his arms. The guy wasn't heavy. Will was used to greater weights in the gym, but the body wasn't a barbell and uncomfortably kept on slipping away from his grip.

He dashed to the bedroom and tossed the blanket away before lowering Ben onto the bed. Only then did he notice blood leaking from the young doctor's head. The wound wasn't deep, but the red stain on the pillow continued to grow, and Will realised that he had to do something about that. He looked around, but nothing suitable caught his eye, and he cursed, remembering the towel hanging in the bathroom.

He soaked the towel with some cold water and rushed back.

Ben's eyes were still closed, but his chest moved with deep inspirations.

Will placed the towel over the wound and pressed it lightly. There was nothing else to do but wait.

The bleeding stopped a few minutes later, but Ben's eyes remained closed. Will sat down on the floor next to the bed and closed his eyes too.

The situation was strange. He had no idea what was going on. Was Ben ill? It was a peculiar and frightening illness if it was an illness. *Was it contagious?* He must ask. Ben was a doctor. Perhaps he had an explanation.

Will sighed. *What if the guy died?* He would be in a tricky situation then. He would have to call the police and explain how he got here. His story might sound like utter nonsense, and he might end up in jail. The thought was only frightening at first. *Was prison a better place than sleeping rough on the street?* But he wouldn't be sleeping on the street for much longer. His mother might be reading his letter at this very moment. Will wasn't sure if she would be willing to help him after all those things he had done. But he was her only son!

Will opened one eye and glanced at Ben. The guy seemed to be sleeping. His chest moved smoothly with every breath, and some colour had returned to his face. Still, his eyes were shut and his face expressionless.

Will shrugged and shut his own eyes again. Strangely, he didn't feel any panic – not about the police, not about jail. And not about Ben. *The guy would be alright*. He was almost sure. He only waited.

A few more minutes passed in silence.

"How did I get into bed?" Ben murmured.

Will smiled before answering. "I brought you here," he said and got up to his feet. "You collapsed in the kitchen and banged your head. You'll probably need a new pillow."

"I'd forgotten how strong you are," Ben smiled weakly. "Have you eaten your lasagne?"

Will shook his head. "No, I couldn't leave you bleeding."

"It's not my first injury," Ben sighed. "And certainly won't be the last."

Will helped him to get up. "Are you okay?" he asked. "Maybe you should go to a hospital and see a doctor?"

"I'm still a little dizzy, but I'll be fine, don't worry," Ben brushed away Will's concerns. "I'm a doctor, remember? I'll go to the bathroom and have a look in the mirror. I know that I'm in a situation where no medicine can help me. No one can, in fact, so let's not worry about things we can't change. Better still, let's reheat your lasagne."

"You know best," Will shrugged.

Ben went back to the kitchen, limping slightly. Will dutifully followed.

"Have a seat," Ben invited him with a gesture and stuffed the lasagne into the microwave.

The machine buzzed for a few minutes, and they both waited silently.

Will's stomach victoriously growled when Ben placed the meaty dish on the table and handed him a spoon. He carefully probed. The taste seemed divine, and Will sank the spoon into the fleshy treat again.

"I must wash my hair," Ben said and left to go to the bathroom, leaving Will to enjoy his food alone.

Will hadn't noticed how fast the lasagne disappeared from the plate. He heard the water running in the bathroom and was busy stuffing his stomach before Ben changed his mind. He enjoyed that warm and heavenly numbness in his belly – the feeling he had almost forgotten while wandering around London.

Later, Ben appeared carefully, rubbing his wet hair with a towel. There was a small sticky plaster on the spot where his left temple had met the kitchen cupboard.

"Are you all right?" Will asked.

"I'll be fine," Ben frowned. "It's not the worst wound I've had."

That didn't sound convincing, but Will felt in no position to press the matter. Ben *was* a doctor. He probably knew how to handle this.

Will watched Ben take his plate away and wash his cutlery. Only seconds later, a realisation struck him, and he said in a guilty voice. "I should have washed my plate, sorry," he gave a guilty smile. "Thank you for feeding me."

"It's the least I could do," Ben mumbled, still busy with the plate. "Don't be offended, but your clothes are a bit smelly – they need washing since you've spent a few days on the street."

Will sighed and carefully sniffed his armpit while Ben was looking away. It *was* indeed stinky. No wonder – he had spent a few nights sleeping rough and even a night in the garbage bin. He hunched over, afraid of Ben deciding to point him towards the door. He didn't want to lose the safety he had found here.

"You can take a shower if you want," Ben said and placed the plate on the rack. "I could put your clothes in the washing machine. They'll be dry in a few hours."

"That's a good idea," Will quickly nodded. "I hope you won't mind me using your towel."

"I'll get you a fresh one, don't worry," Ben went to the bedroom. For some time, Will heard him shuffling through cupboards. A minute later, he returned with a green towel and a folded bedsheet in his hands. "I'd forgotten how big you are. I have nothing suitable for you to change," he said, handing everything to Will. "Wrap this around you while your clothes are washed and dried."

Will accepted the bundle and stood up. "Thank you," he said. Ben just nodded.

Will locked himself in the bathroom and slowly stripped. Ben was right. It was a good idea to get those smelly clothes cleaned. He might need a more respectable appearance when he bought a ticket and boarded a train. *Soon,* he sighed. *Now, really soon. Maybe even tomorrow.* He hoped that his mother was no longer angry. A few quid in his account would make a big difference. A few quid would help to get home.

He turned the tap on, and streams of lukewarm water hit his skin. It felt soothing on the surface, but a little later hit his deep strings as well. He felt so close to normal life again that hot tears pooled in his eyes and rolled down his cheeks, mixing with the streams of water. *Men don't cry,* he told himself firmly and wiped them away. *It must be soap...* But his heart calmed down a few moments later and felt lighter.

Will turned the tap off and thoroughly rubbed the soap into his skin. He smiled at the fresh scent of citrus and turned the water back on, washing everything crispy clean. He felt human again.

For a few minutes, Will just stood and watched how the clear stream of water carried the foam away. Then his heart sank with realisation – he was still stuck in London, homeless, hungry and penniless. Ben had been kind enough to feed him and offered to wash his dirty stuff, but he must get back to the streets when his clothes were dry. He had no right to abuse Ben's kindness and had not a single reason to stay.

He sighed before turning the water off and stepping out of the shower.

His skin was shiny pink when he rubbed it dry with the towel, but this time somehow this didn't embarrass him. Will looked in the mirror. The tattoo on his left pec was as he remembered. He carefully touched the lovely features of Hel on his chest and brushed a few droplets of water away from her hair. He smiled, hoping that she would forgive his carelessness if he succeeded in finding her blue orchid. Then he sighed again – there were too many uncertainties in his life, too many ifs and buts.

Will wrapped the bedsheet around his waist and collected up his clothes. They were indeed stinky, and he frowned as he touched them with his clean hands.

Ben was waiting for him in the kitchen. He took his rags and stuffed them into the washing machine without saying a word. Will took a seat at the table.

"Would you like a cup of tea?" Ben asked, still busy with the washing machine.

"That would be great," Will smiled gratefully. He watched as the other guy fiddled about with the teapot and cups.

"Do you want sugar and milk?" Ben asked as he poured the brew.

"Yes, please," Will nodded. He still felt hungry and watched with some impatience as Ben placed the cups on the table and arranged biscuits on a plate.

They drank their tea and ate their biscuits. Will blushed when he caught Ben secretly glancing at the tattoo on his bare chest.

"It's nice artwork," Will said, tracing the flow of lava with his finger.

"I know," Ben sighed with some sadness in his voice. "Sorry for staring. It's been a while since I saw the picture. It stirred up some memories."

"I only got it recently, you probably remember that from the hospital, and the man said he could only ink it once," Will began to explain, but Ben waved his words away. "It's unique."

Then Will's heart sank – was Ben one of those other guys who had failed to find the money for that tattoo? He bit his lip, waiting to hear what the young doctor would say.

"I'd seen the sketch," he told Will. "Then I saw you in the hospital."

"Oh," Will made a silly smile. "You wanted to have her inked on your chest?"

"No," Ben said quietly. "I saw Eric drawing it."

"Eric? Who is Eric?"

Ben turned the cup of tea in his hands and placed it on the table without taking a sip. "Eric is my boyfriend," he said, at last.

"He is a Sleeper, like you."

"A Sleeper?" Will tasted the word. That crazy ghost of Princess Sheila had been mumbling something incoherent about Sleepers, but he hadn't paid much attention – he'd had more pressing matters at the time.

"He's travelled a lot in that dream world," Ben shrugged. "That's where he met Hel. That's why he sketched her in front of her volcano."

"Still, what's a Sleeper?" Will demanded. He needed a proper explanation this time.

"You don't know?" there was a pure surprise on Ben's face.

"One crazy girl tried to explain it to me," Will admitted but was too embarrassed to call Sheila a ghost. "She failed."

"Why didn't you ask her again?"

"She died."

Ben sighed. "Well, that explains something," he said. "Let's start from the beginning then. When did you begin to see the black castle and the volcano in your dreams?"

"A couple of weeks ago," Will mumbled. "Or a little longer, maybe."

"Do you remember the first time?" Ben suddenly growled. "Was it related to that tattoo?"

"It had never happened before this tattoo," Will said firmly. "It began *after* I had it inked."

"That just means the tattoo is genuine," Ben whispered. "And you have Eric's spark in your blood."

"Stop these riddles, please," Will said softly. "What is that spark? Will I die too?"

"We all die – sooner or later," Ben sighed. "But you might be hunted for that spark if you're not careful."

"Hunted? Like a rabbit?" Will's eyes widened. It sounded like utter nonsense.

"Sadly, yes," Ben slowly nodded. "And it's much easier for the hunters when their prey doesn't know the rules and wanders naively around their traps."

"And who are those hunters?" Will asked, his heart beating faster.

Ben sadly shook his head. "I don't know. Eric didn't tell me. He tried to keep me out of trouble."

"Then how do you know the danger is real?"

"Eric is missing," Ben stated that as a fact.

Will shrugged. That sounded serious enough.

"Then I must be doomed too," Will's voice was steady, but his heart fluttered. "I can't escape if I don't know what that trap is or who those hunters are. I don't want to sound ungrateful, but how can I be sure you're not tricking me into something too?"

Ben blushed, and Will instantly began to regret the words that had slipped from his mouth. He half expected Ben to start to scream at him and shove him out of his flat. Will blushed too, but for a different reason – he was *naked*. It was frustrating enough to wander around London fully clothed, but it was unthinkable to do that naked!

"Sorry," Will mumbled, still as red as a boiled lobster. "I didn't mean to insult you."

Ben waved his shy apology away. "You're right," he said calmly. "I can be dangerous for you too, but still, I can help you if we act wisely. Maybe this will help me to find out what happened to Eric and where he is. I must try to save him if he's in trouble."

Will felt as if he had moved an inch away from an abyss. He must be more careful with his tongue. "Why are you dangerous?" he asked carefully.

"I'm an Eye," he paused, studying Will's reaction. "You've probably noticed that already."

The statement didn't ring any bells. Will had no idea what the guy was talking about.

"Cool! I don't know what that is but if you know a lot about that world, maybe you could help me find something? It's getting too complicated there, and I'd appreciate a bit of advice," Will cheerfully nodded, but Ben didn't share his enthusiasm.

"It doesn't work that way," he sighed. "Eyes are not Sleepers. Our relation to that world is different. I've never been there, never will. All I know is what Eric told me."

"I'm lost," Will growled. "Eyes? Sleepers? I don't know what you're talking about."

"I've broken too many rules already," Ben mumbled, staring into his cup. "Unlike you being a Sleeper, I gain nothing by being an Eye. I can't explore the other world, and my dreams are ordinary. It's someone somewhere in the other world who explores our world through my eyes. That someone sees what's in front of me but can't move my body."

Will put his cup down on the table, suddenly feeling uncomfortably naked. "Hello," he squeezed a silly smile and waved his hand in front of Ben's eyes.

Ben chuckled. "No, not like that, not constantly," he shook his head and added with a sad note. "My mind blanks out when they access me. You won't be able to miss that. So, please, stay out of my sight when I'm having one of those vacant fits. I don't want them to know you're here. Not yet, at least. I still need to find out how they're related to those dangerous people who are hunting Sleepers."

"Okay," Will nodded seriously. "But how do you know it's the same other world peeking at your life through your eyes?"

Ben shrugged. "I don't know. Some *borwil* Eyes have dual way communications with the other world, and they rule over other Eyes. I'm not that lucky," he admitted. "My mind cries in the corner when they force me out of the driver's seat. I'm lucky they don't have much access to my motor functions. You'll know that I'm on a long-distance call when my body freezes."

"I know what you mean," Will smiled. "I've seen a few weirdos..." he suddenly choked on the word and guiltily added. "Sorry. I didn't mean to offend you."

"I'm not easily offended, but apology accepted," Ben said. "Have you seen them in London?"

Will nodded.

"Damn," Ben squeezed his fist. "They might know you're here. I must be more careful."

The silence that followed was uncomfortable. Will hesitantly took the biscuit then put it back. Did this mean that he must leave? *But he was naked!* His clothes were tumbling around the washing machine. He blushed, trying to imagine himself running down the street naked and crowds of silent weirdos staring at him as they transmitted the images somewhere out of this world! *That was utter nonsense!*

Ben sighed and sipped his tea.

"Why did you try to find me if you knew it would be dangerous?" Will asked.

Ben shrugged before answering. "Probably, on impulse," he said slowly. "I love Eric and felt utterly lost when he disappeared. He was desperate to find the Sanctuary because there was no other safe place for Sleepers. When he vanished, *borwil* allowed me to go to London and search for him. Maybe he just needed a new Eye here. I don't know the ways of the high, and they usually don't offer any explanation. I'm a small guy, just trying to pick up the pieces of my life. With Eric missing, I've not got too many pieces left."

"You still haven't me told the reason why you brought me here," Will was persistent.

"This is the reason," Ben pointed to Hel's face on Will's chest. "Eric knew her, and I hoped to find out what happened to him. Maybe she knows, and maybe you could ask her."

"That might be much more complicated than you think," Will sighed.

"Why?"

He had to tell him. Maybe Eric was one of those guys whose bodies he had pushed into the lava. He had no way of knowing. He didn't know them. It was that crazy girl Gudula who had taken them to their death. He had just burned the bodies.

It was a long talk, and Ben listened without interrupting. A few times, he made more tea and placed some biscuits on the table and once he heated up what was left of the lasagne. Will skipped a few small things, but most of his story was as accurate as he could remember.

"I'm away from the castle, away from Hel. And I'm not sure if she'll speak to me if I can't find that damned blue orchid," Will said after he had finished his tale. "The situation is as complicated as it could ever get. I must find the flower first."

Ben sighed with disappointment. Will shrugged. He had been honest with the guy and had told him everything.

"I didn't think it would be easy," Ben mumbled. "I understand. You need more time."

"And a lot of effort," Will reminded him.

Ben nodded. "Oh, shit!" he suddenly cursed. "We forgot about your clothes!"

He jumped to his feet and opened the washing machine. The clothes were clean but wet. He glanced guiltily at Will wrapped in a bedsheet and rushed to hang the clothes on an airer. Then he prepared one more cup of tea.

"It's getting dark," Ben observed, sipping his tea. "You must get back to your quest. You must find the flower."

"Yes," Will agreed. "But I can't go back onto the street naked."

"You don't need to," Ben told him. "You don't need to sleep on the street. You can sleep here. The only problem is that the flat is small and I just have one bed."

"I don't sleep with other guys," Will cut him but then blushed. "Sorry, I didn't want to offend you."

"I know," Ben nodded quietly. "You don't need to worry about that. I'll give you a separate blanket."

"I don't have any other options, really," Will sighed. Ben didn't comment.

When the lights went off, Will secretly brushed a shy tear from his eye. It had been a while since he had slept in a normal bed. It felt like home – well, almost like home if you didn't count the young doctor quietly breathing next to him.

"Thank you..." Will whispered. Ben didn't answer.

Minutes later, Will drifted into darkness as well.

The morning was damp and not only because of the water surrounding the rocks where Will and the sphinx had spent the night. A soft drizzle fell from the sky. The forest remnants down the slope had vanished completely in the milky fog. It looked like a white lake from a distance with only occasional treetops piercing the surface like black islands.

Will sat up. He was naked on the rock but didn't feel cold. The water around was warm, and the stone he was sitting on felt the same. He grabbed his bundle of clothes and looked around. Qu Sith was sleeping on a nearby rock and twitching his legs as if he was running. Will smiled. The beast was still dreaming, but it was time to wake up. They had wasted too much time already.

"Wake up, you lazy bum," Will said quietly. "Your lady is waiting for you!"

Qu Sith stopped moving. He lazily opened one eye and glanced at Will.

"You're not my lady, human," the beast yawned. "And you look disgusting naked. You better put your rags back on."

"Your lady sphinx will find another lover if you sleep for too long," Will chuckled.

"That's unlikely," Qu Sith grunted but got up and stretched his body like an outsized cat. "There are no other sphinxes in the vicinity. In fact, I hadn't seen another sphinx since those ancient times when I left the nest. Have those flaming serpents gone?"

"As far as I can see – yes," Will lowered his legs into the pool. "Let's go. We're probably still too close to them. We need to cross that damned forest – or what's left of it – and get back to the old lava fields. I don't know what happened there, but if the orchid is indestructible, I need to find it."

"Are you saying that I'll have to swim across that lake?" Qu Sith asked, still sitting on a stone.

"It's not a lake. It's a puddle," Will placed his bundle of clothes on top of his head and lowered himself down, waist deep, into the warm water. "I'm not going to carry you," he observed. "You're too heavy."

Will took a few steps forward.

"Let's go!" he said without looking back.

"I'll starve to death on this rock!" Qu Sith's voice begged. "I can't swim! Don't abandon me here! Please!"

Will stopped and looked at the beast. "You didn't complain too much yesterday," he said. "I thought we were already over this. The water hasn't changed overnight. It feels exactly the same. Just do it!"

"It was a matter of life and death yesterday," Qu Sith mumbled. "Today, everything is different."

Will cursed. They were wasting time again.

"Let's face it," he said, looking at the beast. "You're at least twice as big as me. How can I carry you? Yesterday you were fine to get wet."

"You pushed me in," the sphinx reminded him.

"I could push you in again," Will told him dryly. "If that's what you want."

Sphinx's eyes flashed red as he roared angrily.

"I'd advise against making that noise again," Will didn't move a muscle. "Unless you want to attract all those ghastly creatures to this lovely pool where you're sitting on that rock."

"I'm not a fish!" Qu Sith hissed angrily, but his mane shrank back down.

"You won't have to swim. It's shallow here," Will said calmly. "The banks are still too hot to walk on anyway, and you don't have wings to fly."

"It's cruel to make fun of a cripple," the beast mumbled, still sitting on the rock. "And I am not mentioning the bald ape."

"I'm not making fun," Will grunted. "If you know a way of

getting to that forest without getting wet or burnt, please, don't hold back. I'd prefer getting wet to being burnt."

Qu Sith growled and shook his head. Then suddenly, he leapt high into the air. Will flinched as the black body passed over his head and landed in the pool with a loud splash.

"Happy now?" the sphinx's eyes flashed with anger as he looked back. "There's nothing more pitiful than a wet cat. Enjoy!"

Will kept a straight face. "Let's go," he sighed without getting into further conversation. Qu Sith said nothing either.

They crossed the pool where a stream ran over the bank and escaped down the slope winding between three large boulders. Qu Sith did indeed look pitiful when he emerged from the pool and stepped into the shallow stream – water dripped from his mane, and his big, tufted ears looked like the wings of a bat. The beast went on, angrily grunting and shaking his head, and Will didn't dare to say a thing, but nor was there any need to say anything as long as they kept moving. The rocky fields on both sides of the creek still pulsed with heat, and Will was keen to get out of this hell as soon as they could.

Will put his shirt on as they went, but his pants remained tightly rolled up in his hand. The rocks were slippery, and he had to step slowly and carefully. Qu Sith moved a little faster on his four legs, still skidding from time to time.

Halfway to the forest, they dived into a wall of thick fog. The world seemed to cease to exist as Will moved on, seeing nothing. There was just the slippery rocky bed of the creek under his feet and the milky emptiness around him. Qu Sith went faster and quickly disappeared from his sight, and Will strolled on alone. The experience was frightening – he was almost sure that monsters and deadly predators lurked behind the wall of fog. He just couldn't see them, and his imagination was killing him. His bare butt made him feel even more vulnerable, and Will allowed himself to stop briefly to put his pants on.

There was no sign of the sphinx as he went, but his mind painted invisible shadows on the banks of the creek. They looked like dead Rybbaths attached to the poles, with vegetation consuming their flesh and dismembering their joints. But the very moment he tried to get a better look, they vanished without a trace just to reappear as soon as he turned his glance away.

It was slow torture of his mind. A few times, Will wanted to stop and cry out to Qu Sith. The mumbling of the sphinx was much better than the dead silence and the white wall around him.

He flinched when crooked black hands suddenly appeared above him. At first, they looked like just another monster painted by his mind, but they didn't vanish when he frowned and peeked at them. It took some time for him to recognise. Will sighed. They were the blackened bare branches of a tree. He had crossed the plains and reached the woods at last.

The fog was even thicker here, and Will went on still trying to stick to the middle of the creek. At least his feet soaking in the lukewarm water would point him in the direction. He passed a few more trees. The forest was silent, and he stopped several times to listen. It was almost dead calm. He hoped to hear the footsteps of the sphinx somewhere nearby, but there was just the faint sound of a light wind squeezing through shivering leaves. It was strange as he couldn't feel any wind, and the trees he passed had only bare branches.

More trees emerged from the fog, and the sound grew a little louder. Will looked at the branches – still no leaves.

Will had no time to scream as the ground disappeared from under his feet and he dropped down surrounded by falling streams of water into almost complete darkness. A few hundred feet later, he splashed into a deep pool. The water was cold here, and he nearly choked getting back to the surface.

"Damn!" Will cursed aloud – it was dark except for the grey hole in the ceiling, probably a couple of hundred feet away, which let in some dim light filtered by the fog and streams of water. The light was too faint to see anything, and he cursed again, swimming in circles.

"The land is this way," a calm voice said in the distance.

Will turned his head to the sound. A pair of eyes barely glowed red in the dark a few hundred feet away. Will couldn't see the beast. He had no other choice but to swim towards those eyes. He couldn't stay in such cold water for much longer.

"I've been waiting for you," Qu Sith disdainfully spat as Will crawled onto the shore. "It was your bright idea to follow the water. Here we are!"

Will shivered. The water felt as if thousands of sharp icicles were painfully poking his skin. "Shit!" he cursed again, stepping onto the bank.

"No, it's not shit. It's mud," Qu Sith observed calmly. "I *was* frightened, but not that much."

Will probed his way and sat down on a rock. "How did you get here?" he asked.

"The same way as you," the beast said disdainfully. "Isn't it obvious?"

"What happened to your sense of smell? To your intuition? To your predatory instincts?" Will spat out the water, which tasted salty.

"I was distracted," the sphinx admitted. "What happened to you?"

"I was running after you," Will told him fiercely. "We'd still be walking outside if it wasn't for your carelessness."

"It's too late for regrets now," Qu Sith sighed. "We're already here."

"Yes, we are," Will sighed. "Now – what?"

"Now we die," Qu Sith said in a low voice. "There's plenty of water, so thirst is not a threat for us, but we'll starve to death unless these caves are riddled with rats. I know it is a bit degrading to eat rats, but I doubt we'll be lucky enough to find them here anyway. Or we might be lucky if a wandering deer or moose fall through that hole by accident."

Will glanced around in the dusk. The beast looked away. He couldn't spot the red glow of his eyes anywhere. "We'll find the way out," he said, but his voice didn't sound very confident.

"It's unlikely that you'd be able to kill me with your bare hands," Qu Sith whispered. "But I could end your suffering if you would like, and your body would prolong my own humble existence."

The statement sent chills down Will's back. He wasn't sure if that was just the cold or if fear drove the shivers.

"You gave an oath, remember?" he reminded the beast.

Qu Sith sighed. His red eyes looked at Will from the dusk, but he didn't make any attempt to get closer. "Yes, I remember," he said at last. "I won't touch you unless you ask me to."

"That sounds encouraging," Will said, trying to suppress the tremor in his voice. "We'll find a way out, don't worry."

Qu Sith chuckled. "No need to search, human," he said ironically. "There's a way out – right above us, but neither of us has wings to reach it. Not to mention that we'd keep falling into the water."

"There must be another way," Will said firmly.

"What makes you think so?"

"That falling water!" Will pointed to the ceiling. "All those streams are falling in here, but the water in the pool isn't rising! There must be an underground river somewhere. We might be able to follow it and get outside."

"It's fine if you want to delay the thought of imminent death by keeping busy in a pointless search," Qu Sith didn't share Will's enthusiasm. "I don't believe there is a way out, and we don't have any light to prove you're wrong."

Will growled in frustration but had no intention of giving up easily.

"You don't know that for sure," he told the sphinx. "That water is going somewhere. We only need to find out where it goes! And we don't need any light to find the way out."

"I'm sure humans can't see in the dark," Qu Sith mumbled. "It's too dark here, even for me!"

"I don't need to see anything," Will began to lose his temper. "We'll walk along the shore at the edge of the water, and, sooner or later, we'll find the stream. Then, with a little luck, we'll get outside!"

"I don't think we have any more luck, human," Qu Sith sighed. "But I'll play along with you. I don't mind if you want a little entertainment before you die."

Will squeezed a fist but chose not to comment. He had become almost used to all the complaining from the sphinx. At least he had got the beast moving.

He went along the shore, carefully probing the way with his feet. Qu Sith stepped close to his heels. Will kept his right foot in the pool while his left skidded in the mud. It was fine at first, but the water was icy cold, and his right foot grew numb and then began to ache.

"Are you sure we're going in the right direction?" the sphinx asked.

"No, I'm not," Will mumbled.

"Then why are we going this way?"

The question remained unanswered as they stumbled upon a large rock on the shore. The stone was too big to climb over, and Will had to soak both his feet in the cold water, trying to get around the obstacle.

"A few more rocks like this, and I'll feel more like a fish than a sphinx," Qu Sith moaned but followed.

Will carried on silently. He knew that it was a hopeless venture but wasn't ready to give up. They stumbled on two more large rocks and had to get knee-deep in the water to get around. Then there was a wall – a steep cliff that went straight into the pool, and Will couldn't reach its end even by getting waist-deep in the icy water. He didn't risk going any further.

"Well, you have your answer," Qu Sith observed sadly. "There's no way out of here."

Will leaned against the wall, visibly shivering. *It can't end like this!* He punched the rock and cursed. "We'll go back and check the remaining part of the shore," he told the sphinx. The beast just sighed.

They went back – cold, hungry and unhappy. Will grew numb with cold, and the wet clothes that stuck to his skin only made things worse.

An hour later, Qu Sith stopped. "Maybe we could rest a little?" he asked.

Will didn't have the strength to object. He took a few steps away from the water and sat down on the ground. He didn't care if it was sand or mud under his butt. He just rubbed his feet, trying to get some feeling back into them.

"How big is this cave?" the sphinx asked. "That waterfall now looks far away."

Will raised his head. Indeed, the hole in the ceiling was barely visible in the darkness, and the sound of the falling stream was muffled as well. He shook his head sadly, but, of course, the sphinx was unable to see this. "I don't know," he mumbled. "But that pool now looks more like a lake."

"It was a stupid idea to go looking for a way out," the sphinx observed. "The farther we go, the darker it becomes, and I'm not sure if I like that."

"It was stupid not to look where you were stepping in the first place," Will cut short the moaning.

"I didn't expect there to be any holes in the middle of the creek," Qu Sith said quietly. "And nor did you."

It was pointless to argue. Will sighed, still shivering.

"There must be a way out of here," he muttered under his breath. "We just need to follow the shoreline. That falling water can't just disappear."

"I think it's hopeless," the sphinx said flatly. "But I'll help you to kill the time you have left."

They rested a little more, but it wasn't a rest Will could appreciate. It was strange to encounter such a drenching cold on the volcano, and that chill painfully drilled into his bones. *A little fire would be helpful or a warm blanket...* The thought drowned in waves of fear. Will began to believe that the beast was right – *they'd die here!* That stream might not save them even if they were lucky enough to find it. It might just go deeper underground where they couldn't follow.

"It isn't resting. It's a slow death," Will said at last – warmth leaking from his limbs. "Let's go!"

He couldn't see if Qu Sith rose to his feet. The beast said nothing, and Will crawled in the mud until he found the water again. "Let's go!"

"As you wish," the sphinx sighed in the darkness.

They carried on. It didn't matter how hopeless it was. Will knew that he must keep moving. He was hungry, but his moving muscles provided some of the heat he so desperately needed, depleting his energy resources as well. *I must go on until I fall* – the thought flashed through his mind. The journey was arduous, but he went on, skidding on the slippery rocks and in the mud but placing his numb feet one in front of the other. The cold in his legs combined with the pain and numbness, but he did his best to ignore this.

Will didn't look back to see if the sphinx was following. It had become his own fight. The beast must take care of himself. He wasn't his nanny.

A couple of hours or more passed as they struggled on, trying to keep to the shoreline in the dark. Will could barely feet his feet anymore when a steep rock wall barred his way again. He felt around, but the rock blocked the way completely.

"What?" Qu Sith stumbled at his heels.

Will cursed. All their efforts had been in vain. If there was a creek leaving the pool, it went underground, unreachable, useless. He growled in rage and pushed the rock with all his might. Strangely, it moved a little. Will pushed again. Then something banged high above them.

"Careful!" Qu Sith leapt away.

Will jumped aside as well. Something big splashed into the pool. Its depths suddenly lit up as if a giant eye had opened to look at the disturbance. The purple light stung like razor cuts, and Will backed away from the shore, hiding behind the pile of rocks. Qu Sith was already there.

A few moments later, everything became black again and calm.

"What was that?" Will whispered.

"I don't know," the sphinx answered. "But I'm not going near that water again. You can kill me here."

Will carefully lifted his head and glanced at the pool.

"Whatever that light was, it's gone now," he told the sphinx. "You can relax."

"It's not far away, I'm sure," Qu Sith whispered and repeated. "I'm not going near that water again."

"Let's get away from the shore then," Will suggested. "We both need some rest, and it's difficult to relax in the cold mud."

"Away!" the sphinx leapt a few paces. "Away!"

"Wait for me!" Will straightened his back and frowned, peering in the darkness. Then the pair of red-glowing eyes showed him the way.

"We can't go any further away, human," Qu Sith said sadly. "There's only steep walls there."

"Then we'll rest by those walls," Will shrugged. "We need

another plan, but I can't think when I'm so bloody tired. Are you still sitting in the mud?"

"No," the sphinx told him. "There's a solid rock here."

"Great!" Will approached the beast. "I need to dry my pants."

"Be my guest," the red-glowing eyes moved a little to the left, making room for Will to sit down.

They sat quietly for some time, looking at the distant grey hole in the ceiling where the stream of water fell. It darkened a little, but it wasn't clear if it was just a rain cloud or evening dusk that killed the light. Their hopes of breaking out of that cave had gone long before.

"I hate to point this out," Qu Sith whispered after some time, "but we could get warmer if we shared our body heat."

"What do you have in mind?" Will asked.

"We'll both get warmer if you lean against me," the sphinx explained. "You can hug me if that helps you get closer."

"We can try," Will agreed and got closer to the beast. "But don't expect a kiss."

The fur was soft but a little damp as he touched it. He pressed his back against the side of the sphinx, trying to find a comfortable position. But then he remembered the mighty fangs of the beast – just an inch away from his neck. The thought was unsettling, and Will backed away.

"What happened?" Qu Sith asked.

"Your mouth stinks," Will lied. "But this is a good idea. Would you mind if I leant against your back?"

The red eyes flashed just for a second.

"Do whatever you want, human," Qu Sith said with bare irritation. "Just stop moaning!"

Will found his way in the darkness. He placed his cheek on the sphinx's shoulder and brushed away some shy moisture in his eyes. Death was inevitable. Now he was sure of that. It was just a question of time. The slow death of starvation seemed more frightening, and the idea of being ripped to pieces by the sphinx didn't seem that crazy anymore.

Will sighed. An hour had passed in dark thoughts before he slipped   away.

Will woke up shivering and spooning Ben. The young doctor was still soundly asleep, and Will carefully backed away to his side of the bed. For some time, he observed Ben breathing quietly under his blanket and then soundlessly mouthed a curse. This place was supposed to feel safe, but his mood could not lift at all from its nadir. He was stuck! He was bloody stuck! And he didn't know what to do.

Will closed his eyes, trying to gather the last crumbs of his confidence. He failed. The fear that gripped his soul was too great. He couldn't believe the way his life was going downhill. Where was that proud boy who teased the girls at the gym? Again, Will almost cursed aloud. Just a few weeks ago, he had none of these problems. *Look at me now!* Will forced his eyes shut, trying to hold back the tears. He was homeless, useless and close to dying.

He sighed and only then realised that Ben's breathing had changed. Will opened his eyes to have a look.

Ben was looking at him, surprise in his eyes.

"Good morning," Will mumbled.

"What's worrying you so much?" Ben asked without returning the greeting.

Will shrugged. "Bad dreams," it was a half-truth.

"How bad?" the concerned expression didn't leave Ben's face.

Will sighed. He was indeed stuck, and he needed a little advice. He told the young doctor everything. Ben listened without interruption as Will poured his heart out. That cave was cold, dark and frightening. He had done his best to find the way out but had failed. He had simply run out of options.

Ben sighed when he had finished. "The situation is difficult, indeed," he agreed. "And probably fatal unless you can find some alternative solution quickly."

"What solution?" Will sat up, and the blanket slipped down, exposing his tattoo.

Ben's eyes grew moist as he reached out, but his arm froze mid-air and didn't touch the picture. "Sorry," he whispered and jumped out of bed. For some time, Will heard him busy in the bathroom.

Ben returned with Will's clothes in his hands. "You might want to get dressed while I make some breakfast," he muttered, placing the folded clothes on the bed before he left without saying another word.

Will's heart skipped a beat. Did this mean that he must get dressed and go? He felt he had still been invited to have breakfast. Had he done or said something wrong? *Could he stay for another night?*

He hastily dressed and slipped into the bathroom, still unsure how to put his plea into words. Will looked in the mirror. His face looked tired, he had a beard, and he looked a mess. *Shit!* Those few nights on the streets had engulfed him, captured him and made him look and feel just like any other vagrant begging for some spare change.

Will rubbed his face vigorously until there were no more traces of weariness. He splashed some water on his beard, trying to give it some sort of respectable appearance. His looks improved but were still far away from his liking. He didn't dare to borrow Ben's toothbrush and so just placed a few drops of toothpaste on his finger. He felt cleaner when he'd finished, but his heart still trembled like an injured sparrow. *One more night, please!*

Ben was waiting with two mugs of coffee. "I've put milk and sugar in," he shrugged with a guilty smile. "I don't know if that's how you like it. And I've just some scrambled eggs. I'm not a genius chef."

"Thank you," Will blushed and sat down at the table. He took his mug and tried the hot coffee before he was able to gather all his courage. "I'd like to apologise for all the inconvenience I'm causing you. I'm sorry if I've unknowingly said or done something inappropriate. You've been very kind to me, and I don't have anything to repay your kindness with. I wrote a letter to my mother. I'm sure she'll send me some money to get back home. It's just a matter of a day or two, I guess, no more. I was wondering... if you could... let me stay here for that day or two? If you say no, I'll leave. I don't want to be a burden."

"You're not a burden," Ben interrupted him. "Yes, you can stay."

"Thank you," Will tried to reach out to shake the young doctor's hand, but Ben's serious glance stopped him. Feeling awkward, Will attempted to hide behind his mug.

"Your situation is much more difficult than that," Ben sighed. "You may feel safe at home in this world, but you're still in great danger in that underground cave. You won't live in this world if you die there."

Will slowly nodded, fear gripping his soul again.

"You need to find another Sleeper and ask them for help if they happen to be near that damned cave. It's the only way I can think of," Ben told him seriously before sipping his coffee.

"How could they help me?"

"Well, at the very least, they could drop you a rope down through the hole where that damned creek goes underground."

"I don't know any other Sleeper," Will admitted sadly.

"That's why you need to find the Sanctuary," Ben shrugged. "There are many Sleepers there."

"Do you know where the Sanctuary is?"

"Sadly – no," Ben slowly shook his head. "Eric was searching for it, but I don't know if he succeeded. He kept secret those bits that he found, even from me."

"Then it's hopeless," Will admitted. "I've not a clue what you're talking about."

Ben was silent for a few long moments. "I was really hoping to avoid this, but there are no other options left. I'll do my best to help you," he said at last. "I know a few Eyes, and we'll start asking questions. It's dangerous and might take some time before we stumble upon a *borwil*. And there's no guarantee that we'll get any answers even then."

Will had to hold back the tears before he was able to speak. "Thank you," he whispered. "I don't know how I'll ever be able to repay you."

"You don't need to repay me," Ben told him quietly and pointed to Will's chest where the tattoo was. "It is entirely due to this. I'm being a bit selfish in helping you. I'm hoping to find Eric."

Will bit his tongue – it was all between Ben and that tattoo. His chiselled, muscular chest was simply the medium that carried the tattoo. He didn't understand the strange situation when someone was so concerned about a picture that he would go the extra mile to help him. But his life had been full of strange situations lately. At least he had the promise of a roof over his head and some food in his stomach for a few days. He sighed and thanked Ben.

They ate their scrambled eggs and drank their coffee in silence. Will washed the plates when they'd finished eating.

"We'll be trying to contact other Eyes today. It's against every rule I can think of and is very dangerous," Ben told him seriously. "Please, stay behind me, especially if you notice that I stop moving."

"Okay," Will agreed without thinking too much.

"Let's go then," Ben sighed and rose to his feet.

Will felt uneasy about Ben mentioning certain dangers, but he had no idea what those dangers were. Still, he had had enough of them and took the young doctor's advice seriously. He was stuck in a game, the rules of which he didn't know or understand, and nobody cared to explain them properly to him.

He picked up his rucksack, but Ben stopped him. "You'd better leave that here. It will be more of a nuisance than an asset," he told Will. The guy seemed fragile and frightened at the thought of being forced into foreign territory too.

They left in silence.

The weather was great. Will briefly glanced at the bright sunshine in the clear deep blue sky and went after Ben, keeping a distance of a few paces. The street was quiet. They went under the shade of the chestnut trees, meeting no one. Things changed when they reached the crossroad and turned left. Busy London was there, just around the corner, and Will had to be careful not to lose Ben in the crowd. The doctor stopped nowhere and talked to no one, hiding under his hood and dark sunglasses all the time. Will lowered his hood too. He had no idea where they were going.

They turned left into the Tube, and Ben passed the Oyster card to Will. The platform was crowded, and Will had to be extra vigilant not to lose his companion among the other hooded silhouettes waiting for the train there.

When the train arrived, they squeezed in, leaving the empty platform behind. For some reason, Will felt guilty, occupying too much space with his big muscular body. Ben was just a few steps away with his absent gaze fixed on the dark window as they moved underground. *Was he having one of those fits again?* Will wasn't sure but kept quiet.

Five stations later, Ben moved towards the door, and Will followed closely. They were on the platform when it happened. Ben stopped abruptly within the moving crowd. Someone bumped into him, someone pushed, someone stepped over, someone didn't.

Will jumped forward like a lion, pushing the crowd aside. "Watch your steps!" he roared. "Watch your steps! The man is down!"

That worked a bit as it became less crowded around him. He reached for Ben and pulled the man up. His body wasn't limp as he expected – it was hard and stiff as if cut from wood. *It's one of those fits*, the thought flashed as he looked helplessly at the receding crowd, but no one offered any help. Seconds later, they were left alone on the platform.

Ben's eyes were open wide and moved in jerky motions, scanning the space in front of him. His body was as stiff as a plank, but it couldn't keep its balance, so Will embraced Ben from behind, keeping him upright and avoiding the gaze of those strange eyes as he had been told to.

The next train arrived a few minutes later, but it seemed like hours for Will. Another crowd oozed out and rushed past the two strange guys embracing in the middle of the platform.

Will hunched under his hood, feeling a little embarrassed about hugging a guy, but that wasn't important. Nobody knew him here, and he was sure he wouldn't meet any of these passengers again. Still, the feeling was a mixture of fear and shame, but his concern for Ben was much stronger than either of those.

"Are you all right? Do you need any help?" a girl stopped in front of them – a gorgeous girl. In different circumstances, Will would be ready to stick his tongue out and clap his ears. Now he just shook his head slowly.

"No, thank you," it was Ben who answered the question. "I feel better already."

Will sighed with relief. He gazed at the curvy backside as the girl walked away and only then realised that he was still embracing Ben.

"Thank you," Ben muttered as soon as Will released his grip. "Let's go."

They left the station and turned right on the busy road in front of it. Will kept the distance shorter this time, just in case the young doctor fell into a fit again. *It must be torture to live a life like that.* But his own life didn't seem any better, hopping between the hopeless and deadly in both worlds.

"How often do you get knocked out?" Will asked carefully, still walking a pace behind Ben.

"A couple of times a day at most," Ben mumbled. "Usually, less than that. This time I was unfortunate to get caught in the crowd. I'd have fallen if I hadn't been pushed. Thanks again for saving my neck."

The guy sounded embarrassed, and Will decided to quit questioning. He didn't want Ben to feel like a cripple, but that sudden freeze of his body and the eerie gaze kept sending chills down his own spine each time he remembered the situation. Ben wasn't the first Eye Will had seen. That creepy man in the hospital who had decided to keep him in a coma must be the *borwil* – he felt like a commanding authority. Then he remembered those other weirdos, standing frozen on the streets and gazing at him. They must have been Eyes too – he realised – the same as Ben!

They went on silently. A couple of hundreds of yards later, Ben turned right towards the entrance of another station. They went down the stairs to the platform. The red-painted train was already there, and they had to run to catch it.

"Where are we going?" Will whispered.

Ben didn't answer. He kept staring through the window, and Will worried that he might be falling into another fit on the train. He got closer, ready to grab Ben if necessary.

"Are you okay?" he asked quietly, but Ben didn't respond. The doctor's eyes wandered through the window without focusing on anything much. Will didn't understand what was going on but didn't dare to interrupt.

The train moved on, stopping briefly at stations to let people on and off. Will watched Ben with suspicion. *Had they already missed their station?* Will wasn't sure. He had no idea where they were going. He stood close to Ben and waited, ready to intervene if any unexpected stampede threatened to ground him again.

A few stops later, when the train was standing still letting passengers off, Ben's eyes closed after a short series of jerky motions. He sighed. The tension was gone when he opened them a few seconds later.

"Are we still going forth or heading back already?" he asked quietly.

"Forth," Will whispered, keeping his voice just as quiet.

"Good."

The train sped on into the tunnel under the Thames. The day grew murky as it emerged on the other side, briefly stopping at Greenwich. Ben said nothing, just sighed as they passed over the muddy shores of Deptford Creek, exposed to the elements by the low tide. Will had become increasingly nervous about the situation. Who was this person they were travelling to meet? Why did Ben feel so restless? He had none of the answers as he wrestled the growing crowd away from Ben. It wasn't difficult with his massive frame, and it kept him busy until the train stopped at the final station and everybody oozed out.

"Where are we going now?" Will asked as they ambled down the platform at the tail of the receding crowd.

"Just follow me," Ben muttered, explaining nothing.

"Is it dangerous?" it was a silly question for a big guy like him to ask, but Will felt a strange restlessness emanating from the young doctor.

"You'll be fine."

They turned left outside the station. The sky greeted them with a soft drizzle, and Will raised his hood again, hunching over. Ben went a few paces ahead, slipping through the crowds of people who were waiting for a bus. The rain didn't seem to bother him, and Will had to move faster to keep up.

They crossed the street and turned left again. Ben went, glancing around, searching for somebody. Sometimes he slowed down to almost a complete halt, sometimes he dashed forward, nearly running. It seemed like an ordinary street to Will, the same as many others – with shops, banks and small eateries littered on both sides. Ben saw it differently. He dashed forward, almost bumping into people, and Will had to run, afraid to lose him in the crowd.

Even bigger turmoil lay ahead where the spacious square between the shopping centre and the street was scattered with the stalls and tents. A band played their music on an improvised stage, but it seemed that nobody was listening. People were busy trying to grab a better bargain or just strolling around, looking at what was on offer.

Ben stopped in the midst of all that cacophony, and Will rushed closer, ready to catch him. *Was he having another fit?* Ben wasn't – as he moved closer, Will saw the young doctor glancing around uncertainly like a bloodhound who had lost the scent. Will glanced at all the turmoil too, but he had no idea what they were looking for.

"Are we lost?" Will asked quietly, drawing closer.

Ben glanced at him and then dashed through the crowd like that same bloodhound, short only of howling. Will ran after him.

They squeezed among the sellers of fruit, clothes and bags, past the smelly stall selling fish. Only then did Ben slow down, looking at the young black girl who was leaning against a plane tree in front of a pawn shop. The young doctor slowly approached her as if afraid to scare her away. Will secretly glanced at her delicious curves in a tight pink blouse and lime green lycra and blushed. Her long hair was glossy, black and probably fake, but that didn't seem important. The girl's black eyes drilled into Ben, and her bored expression quickly morphed into one of distaste.

"Hello, Vanessa," Ben said, getting closer but keeping his eyes away from her. "I've been looking for you."

"Why?"

"Have you seen any *borwil* recently?" Ben stopped in front of her.

"You're crazy," the girl gave him a long stare. "We're not supposed even to mention such things."

"I know," Ben sighed. "This is a situation of life and death, though, and you owe me a favour."

Vanessa snarled and punched the tree.

"Who's dying?" she asked.

Ben silently pointed to Will.

"He doesn't look very sick," she scanned Will's bulging

muscles with a spark of interest.

"He needs some help on the other side," the young doctor whispered.

"I see..." Vanessa suddenly looked away, and her voice trailed off.

Ben grabbed Will's hand and pushed him behind the tree, away from Vanessa's eyes. Will had no idea what was going on but obeyed silently after a single glance at the frightened face of Ben. The next moment the young doctor joined him.

"What just happened?" Will asked.

"She has a long-distance call," Ben sighed, glancing at the girl from behind the tree. "I don't want us to appear on the scene too soon."

That explained nothing.

They likely looked like two idiots, peering at Vanessa from behind the tree, but Will didn't give this a second thought. Vanessa didn't move, and they waited patiently.

A few red buses passed along the street behind them. Will was conscious of the glances – curious and speculating, but Ben didn't seem bothered.

"Shit!" exclaimed Vanessa at last and sighed. "You can stop hiding."

Ben straightened his back, emerging from behind the tree. It was obvious that the ensuing conversation would be unpleasant.

"You know it's against the rules, Ben," Vanessa hissed when they had emerged from behind the tree. "It's simply unbelievable how you've managed to hook up with Sleepers and keep creating a mess. Now you need a bloody *borwil* to sort it out!"

Ben's face blushed from light pink to dark crimson.

"You owe me a favour," he reminded her seriously.

Vanessa growled, casting an angry look at the young doctor. "You don't scratch a horse for free," she hissed, punching the tree again. "Do you?"

"You're not a horse," Ben observed calmly. "And that wasn't a scratch."

The black girl's eyes flashed with rage as she struggled to contain her temper.

"Please…" the word was barely audible from Ben's mouth.

"No, I haven't seen any lately," Vanessa snarled. "There was one crazy Indian bitch around – the big boss of a big company, but I've no idea if she's still here or where to find her. You'll have no chance of getting any closer even if you do see her. It's London, and she's guarded. Look elsewhere, darling. She's not the only *borwil* around, I guess."

"Where?"

That single word made Vanessa flinch. She stared at Ben with her large unblinking eyes, and Will began to fear that she might be on another 'long-distance call' again.

"You know it's illegal," she said at last.

"It won't be the first illegal thing you've done," Ben met her gaze calmly.

Vanessa considered the accusation for a few seconds; her face remained expressionless. "The name won't mean anything to you," she said at last.

"True," Ben agreed. "Then show us the way."

"I'm busy," Vanessa grunted. "You're wasting my time."

"Haven't wasted it yet," Ben said. "We're not very busy and could spend a few days in the neighbourhood if you'd care to become the heroine of my transmissions."

"It's a matter of life and death, as I recall," Vanessa gave him a tight smile. "We could try to find out whose transmissions are more interesting."

Ben gulped, but it was at this moment that Will lost patience. He gently pushed the young doctor aside and got closer to Vanessa, placing his left hand on the tree trunk next to her right ear.

"Lady," he said. "I've no idea what you're talking about. I'm in real trouble. Please, help me if you can. I don't have much to repay your kindness, but I'm begging you. I'll go down on my knees if you want but help me, please. I can't end up in the wrong Tower with Mantus."

Her black eyes almost popped out of her head upon hearing

the name. "You can't mention his name," Vanessa gasped and then turned to Ben. "You promised not to tell anyone!"

"I haven't told anyone," the guy mumbled quietly. "I didn't tell him."

"Please, help us," Will whispered. "We're desperate."

"Don't make us shout that name from the rooftops," Ben added. "We've nothing left to lose now."

There was a struggle on Vanessa's face. Obviously, she was deliberating between breaking down in tears or slapping Ben. "I'll show you the way," she said at last. "But you pay all transportation costs; we'll need to catch a train. And I don't want to see either of you again after that."

"You won't see me again," Will was quick to promise.

"I'll pay for the tickets," said Ben.

"Both ways," Vanessa poked her finger to Ben's chest. "I'm wasting my time, but I don't want to waste my money."

"Okay," Ben nodded before she could change her mind.

"Let's go," Vanessa began moving without waiting for them. "We need to get to the train station."

Will sighed with relief behind her back. They crossed the street and turned left, where two bus stops lined the pavement.

They waited for the bus without talking too much. Vanessa rolled her eyes and sighed from time to time, but Will and Ben stood on either side of her, ready to stop her way of escape. She calmed down when they boarded the bus, and Ben paid for all the tickets.

The weather was still murky as they passed down the street. The bus stopped now and then, letting people off or on, but none of them looked at the changing crowd. Vanessa and Ben sat down as soon as they spotted empty seats. The muscular frame of Will towered above them. Nobody spoke.

The journey wasn't long. The bus turned right at the traffic lights, and they got off at the next stop.

"We need to cross over," Vanessa took the lead.

"You go first," Ben told her and then cast a glance at Will.

Something's not right, the thought flashed in Will's head, but he had no time for any more thoughts as Vanessa dashed across the street, dodging between the moving traffic.

"Shit!" Ben cursed but ran after her. "Crazy bitch!"

Will had no other option but to follow them.

The beeping of horns and stream of profanities followed them as they ran. Twice they almost collided with moving cars. Vanessa panted as she reached the safety of the pavement. Ben looked no better. Will was the last to join them, but his body had managed the effort more efficiently.

"Why did you do that?" Ben growled like a wounded wolf.

Vanessa shrugged but didn't answer. She went on, and they followed.

They crossed a bridge over railway tracks, but the black girl didn't even glance at the entrance to the train station. Instead, she hurried down the street without bothering to explain anything. Ben shrugged but followed.

The next railway station was just a few hundred yards away, on different tracks. Vanessa marched straight through a shallow puddle and stopped in front of the ticket machine.

"Who agreed to pay for the journey?" she asked, messing with the touchscreen.

Ben sighed, reaching for his wallet. Will approached the machine too, as Vanessa stepped aside. The amount of money on the screen was ridiculous – he could easily buy a ticket home for that much if he were that rich! The thought of home squeezed his heart with icy pliers, and his eyes grew moist for a moment. He turned away as Ben paid for three return tickets.

Unexpectedly, Vanessa pushed him away from Ben.

"What happened?"

"I thought we'd be lucky enough to avoid that old bitch," she hissed, rolling her eyes and making an upset face. "Now they know!"

"Who!"

Vanessa silently pointed across the street. It took several attempts for Will to spot an old woman leaning on her umbrella. She stood on the other side of the road, beyond the heavy traffic, her face expressionless, like most other faces you may see on any busy street, but her pale blue eyes stared at them, unblinking. Several red double-decker buses slowly passed along the road, obscuring the woman for a few moments but her eyes still followed them when she came back into view.

"Hurry up with your card!" Vanessa hissed at Ben and pushed Will away, rushing him up the stairs to the platform.

They dashed through the platform, away from the street. Will glanced back, but that old lady beyond the heavy traffic was already out of view. A few minutes later, Ben ran after them, clutching the tickets in his right hand.

"I knew I was in trouble the very first moment I saw you," Vanessa barked at him. "What shall we do now?"

"We stick to the plan," Ben said firmly.

"She's old. Maybe she couldn't see us clearly," offered Will but was waved away by Vanessa.

"She was in transmission," the black girl spoke through her teeth. "Her age doesn't matter."

She slapped the railing, flashing angry glances at Ben. "Why did I agree to help you?"

"We made you," Ben told her calmly. "You had no choice, and it wasn't your fault. Calm down – nobody will blame you."

"She saw us!"

"That doesn't matter now," Ben sighed. "I'll take the blame, and the punishment will be mine."

"What punishment?" Will demanded. It sounded weird, and he couldn't understand why someone needed to be punished. The train arrived, and nobody answered him.

The carriage was almost empty as they took seats around the table. Vanessa was still biting her lips, and Ben turned his gaze towards some rooftops beyond the window. It was clear that Will wouldn't get any explanation. It was some odd Eye thing that he had to accept without question, along with a few other things lately.

The journey wasn't long. Vanessa dragged them out onto Bromley South Station.

"We need to catch another train," she said before hurrying them up the footbridge to the other platform. "We've got ten minutes," she added after consulting the board.

The place was crowded, and they waited in silence. Will glanced around, but there were no more weirdoes anywhere in sight, and no one stared at them. Pleasant aromas from a nearby café irritated his nostrils, but no one mentioned any food, nor had they any time for that.

The train arrived packed, but most of the passengers got off as soon as the doors opened and rushed towards the footbridge and out onto the street where red double-decker buses proudly moved like overgrown ladybirds.

They got on, but Vanessa stopped Will before he was able to take a seat.

"We can't sit facing each other," she hissed as the doors closed, and the train began to move on. "I can still get away if they think that it was a coincidence. I'm sure they'll want to have a look."

"What do you suggest?" Ben looked uneasy but determined.

Vanessa dragged them back to the door, ignoring a few curious glances from the other passengers. She placed Ben next to the door facing the window and leant against his back, facing the wall of the loo.

"You'll guard us," she flashed a glance at Will and then quickly turned away. Her face became expressionless with just her eyes darting around.

Ben seemed nervous but still hadn't been gripped by a fit. Will backed away a few steps and waited as the train left the city and sped East among distant green hills. He caught a few curious glances from the fellow passengers, but no one was *staring* as Eyes do.

It all ended ten minutes later.

"Shit!" Vanessa exclaimed. "I've never been gripped twice in a day."

"I have," Ben sighed but kept looking at the green hills outside the window.

Will said nothing. His life was going down the drain, but his guts turned to knots as he watched the Eyes. He had no idea how Ben and Vanessa managed to cope with their 'transmissions'. *Their life must be miserable,* he sighed. And they get nothing in return. Will felt privileged with his dreams, despite the situation he had created there.

They travelled the rest of the way in silence as if waiting for a disaster.

"We're here," Vanessa told them when the train stopped at some little grey station.

Will looked around as they got off – nothing exciting met the eye except for the green palanquin of treetops and a pretty steep bank of a ravine rising away from the tracks. It was covered by a thick carpet of nettles and vines with just occasional limestone ribs protruding through the greenery.

The train sped on and disappeared around a curve in the track a mile later. They were alone on the platform.

"Well?" Ben asked, still looking away.

"Let's go," Vanessa took the lead. Will followed a few steps behind.

They crossed the footbridge over the railway tracks. The station building, as grey and dull as everything here, was closed. Vanessa led them round and crossed the car park where a few cars awaited their drivers return from London.

A neat house hid behind a tall wooden fence on the left, and

Will looked at the windows, trying to spot that mysterious "Indian bitch". He was sure that she lived here. But Vanessa didn't even glance at the gate. Instead, she went on to the street ahead and turned left.

The road was as quiet and empty as the station. They met just a few passers-by on their way, but no one gave them a second glance.

Vanessa seemed to hunch over and shrink as they carried on uphill but didn't slow down. Ben sighed a few times, walking next to her. Will went after them, suddenly deeply in doubt if they were doing the right thing. Yes, his situation in Rehen was hopeless, but these two Eyes now seemed like two lambs approaching a lion's den, and he hated to place people in danger. Will didn't know the rules they said they were breaking, but those rules seemed important, and this mysterious *borwil* seemed powerful. What if they were about to die because of him?

They reached the top of the hill, and Vanessa stopped abruptly.

"It's there," she waved her hand to the left, where a long white two-storey building hid behind the green shrubs. "I won't go there. She's the big boss in that building. Her name is Adrika. That's all I know. You're on your own now."

Ben shaded his eyes and looked at the building. "Okay," he said at last. "I know where to find you if you've been telling lies."

"It's all I know," Vanessa said firmly. "But I don't have any desire to get any closer to that *borwil*. This is all your business, not mine."

Ben shrugged but nodded.

"May I have my return ticket?" she demanded. "I must get back to London."

Ben produced several yellow-orange slips of paper from his pocket, shuffled through them and then extended one to Vanessa.

"Thank you," she said. "Good luck."

Will glanced at her curvy outline as she went back downhill back towards the train station. The girl was strange – she had brought them to the middle of nowhere and dumped them at the roadside. Still, she was a pleasure to look at.

Ben looked tense as he regarded the white buildings beyond the green shrubs and the half-empty car park. His brows furrowed and his lips were tightly pressed together as he stood gathering courage and determination. Will realised that they were about to do something dangerous and probably even illegal, although he failed to understand what dangers were lurking in the attempt to speak with the big boss. Even if she were a bitch, as Vanessa had said she was – she wouldn't bite. Not physically, at least.

Ben took a deep breath and sighed. "Let's go," he murmured. "We need to move fast."

And they went fast.

"Where are you rushing to, young men?" a security guard stopped them as soon as they slipped in through the automatic door.

"We need to see Mrs Adrika," Ben told him. "Urgently."

The guard nodded knowingly. "The second floor," he said. "Mrs Patel's office is in the middle of the corridor on the left."

"Thank you," Ben said and took the stairs before the guard could think of another question. Will hurried after him.

The corridor on the second floor was empty as they quietly sneaked forward. The doors were open, and they could see people working behind computers or sorting piles of papers. Some glanced at them, but most remained immersed in whatever they were doing.

"Here," Ben stopped in front of the only door that was closed. A yellow metal plate was on the wall next to it, "Mrs Adrika Patel, CEO", it read.

"Should we knock?" Will asked.

Ben shook his head, took a deep breath and opened the door. Will peered inside too. The room wasn't big. He noticed a window on the left and a large dark brown door on the right. Between those two was a table littered with several stacks of paper and a computer monitor on the left end. A blonde girl was behind the desk sipping coffee, eating a muffin and staring at a computer monitor with an openly bored expression. She wasn't Indian.

"We must see Mrs Patel," Ben told her. "It's urgent."

She eyed Ben first, and a faint shadow of disdain crossed her lips. "Mrs Patel is very busy," the girl said, then laid her eyes on Will's muscles. "She has a meeting in thirty minutes and will be leaving for London after that. Let me have a look, and maybe I could squeeze you both into her schedule at some time next week."

"We can't wait until next week," Ben groaned. "It's urgent."

"I'm sorry," the girl shrugged. "All the slots for this week are full."

"It's a matter of life and death!"

"There's no need to shout. I understand," the girl put her muffin down on a plate. "But there's nothing I can do. I've no free slots showing on the computer. Everything is fully booked."

"It's my life that's in question!" Will lost his temper and didn't even notice as he jumped closer and loomed over her table. "Do you want me to die?"

"Julie? What's happening? What's all that noise?" an intercom on the girl's table asked in a soft voice.

Julie blushed before answering. "Two young men want to see you, Mrs Patel. They say it's a matter of life and death, but I've no free slots for this week."

"Nonsense," said the intercom. "Let them in."

Julie silently extended her right hand and, with a fierce glance, pointed to the brown door. Then she picked up her muffin again and took a small bite.

Will followed Ben closely as they approached the door. He half expected to meet a one-eyed monster behind that door since everybody seemed to be afraid of her, even Vanessa. Ben's hand slightly shook as he turned the doorknob.

The office of the "crazy Indian bitch" was painted white, and there was a soft, light grey carpet on the floor. The furniture was black.

Mrs Patel stood by a large window as they entered and looked over the sleepy town's greyish rooftops. She turned to face them, and, for a few moments, she just silently stared, saying nothing. Neither Ben nor Will dared to break the silence of the *borwil*.

"You're not the young men I was expecting," she said, at last, her face remaining expressionless. "But come in anyway..."

"I'm..." Ben began.

"I know who you are," she cut the young doctor short, but her black eyes drilled into Will's face.

"I've got a problem," Will began hesitantly.

"I know your problem," Mrs Patel said. "You never listen. We told you to find a safe place. We told you we would force you to do that. Here you are, wandering around London. But it's not the Sanctuary. This place is even more dangerous than your hospital bed. You need to find a safe place, or you'll die."

"My problem is not here," he told the *borwil*. "It's in the other world. I'm stuck underground."

"Last time we helped you, you were stuck in a cage," said Mrs Patel. "How did you get underground?"

Will told her all that had happened. She listened without interrupting him, without any reaction on her face. She remained silent when he had finished.

"Could you contact someone who could drop a rope through that hole in the ceiling?" Will asked.

"No."

"Why?"

"We don't have any Eyes in that part of that world," she told him. "And we don't contact Sleepers."

"The man in the hospital mentioned that my proceedings are especially interesting," Will shrugged. "Aren't they interesting anymore?"

"They are even more interesting," Mrs Patel admitted. "But there's no way we can help you. You need to find a Sleeper close to your location. It would be impractical to seek help from someone on the other side of that world. You'd be long dead before they arrived at the hole where you fell underground."

"Do you know someone nearby?"

"No."

"It's useless," Will sighed and turned to Ben. "Let's go."

"You must find the Sanctuary," said Mrs Patel. "Many Sleepers are there, and maybe someone could help you out."

"Where is that Sanctuary?"

"We don't know," said the *borwil*. "We don't have any Eyes there. But you must find it. It isn't safe for you in London."

"I won't be here for long," Will assured her. "I'll be going home as soon as my mother transfers a few quid for a ticket. I can't imagine a safer place than home."

Mrs Patel silently stared at him for longer than a minute. "You don't have a home anymore, young man," she told him coldly. "You won't get that money transfer, and you won't be going back. You need to go forward and find the Sanctuary."

"That's not true," Will almost choked on his words as hot tears began pooling in his eyes. "My mother loves me in her own way. You can't take that from me. It's simply a lie!"

"You must forget them and move on – move to a place where you can be safe. At least, on this side of reality," she said in her dreadful monotonous voice.

"No! Never! I'll never forget my family!" Will's outburst made no impression on the *borwil*.

"I guess I must explain something to you," Mrs Patel crossed the room and sat down at her table. "Have a seat, young men," she gestured to the chairs in front of her.

Will shook with anger, and Ben had to guide him to the chair

Mrs Patel had indicated. Then he sat down too. The *borwil* silently stared at them with her dark eyes showing a peculiar insect-like interest.

"My mother loves me..." Will whispered as he quickly wiped away the few drops of moisture rolling down his left cheek.

"Your mother doesn't remember you anymore. Your sister doesn't remember anything about you either," her voice was chillingly calm and monotone.

"What have you done to them?" Will began to stand up, but Ben stopped him.

"They are obedient," the *borwil* explained. "They have no memories of you."

"Why did you do that? How?"

Mrs Patel took a pencil from her table and began to turn it between her fingers absentmindedly. Her face remained expressionless, and that simple motion was the only hint of nervousness she permitted to slip through.

"I think we've broken too many regulations with you already," she admitted at last. "You began your journey when you had some blood from Eric Penrose injected into your skin. That was your decision, and now you must face all the consequences of that decision. There are people out there hunting for what is in that blood. You have become prey, the same as Eric was, and the only way for you to survive is to find the Sanctuary. It's not in London.

We're sure about that."

"Who was hunting Eric?" Ben asked quietly.

Mrs Patel focused her dark eyes on him, and the young doctor seemed to shrink in his chair. "The Pyrite Man and his gang," she said without twitching a muscle in her face and turned back to Will.

"Do you know where Eric is?" Ben was persistent.

"Yes."

"Where?"

"Dead."

"Dead the same way that man in the hospital tried to convince me about Ben?" Will demanded.

"Sadly, no," Mrs Patel said indifferently. "He was eaten by the gang led by Mantus. We have a secret Eye amongst them."

Ben began to shake his head, tears in his eyes.

"What kind of bullshit is that?" Will chuckled. "No one eats people these days. Why would someone want to do that?"

"They were after that part of Eric's blood that now circulates within you as well," Mrs Patel said. "They failed."

"Did they eat him alive?" Ben gasped.

"He was alive while they drank his blood but not for long. Then they ate the rest of his body..."

Ben fainted, and Will jumped up to support him. Mrs Patel stared at the scene with indifferent eyes.

"Stay away from the man with fool's gold in his ring," she told Will. "Or you'll end up like Eric."

"Shut up!" Will cut her dead harshly.

"He wanted to know..."

"Shut up, for God's sake!"

The door quietly opened behind them.

"Is everything okay, Mrs Patel?" Julie asked.

"Yes," the *borwil* didn't even raise an eyebrow. "These guys are just about to leave."

Will cast a quick angry glance at Mrs Patel as he half carried Ben out of the room.

"Could we have a glass of water, please?" he asked Julie as she held the door open for them.

"Sure," she smiled a wry smile and closed the door to the *borwil's* kingdom.

Ben drank the water gratefully. He was still as white as a sheet of paper, and Will had to support him with his shaky legs on their way out. No one stopped them. In fact, no one even glanced at them, although they met a few worried faces as people rushed up and down the corridor. They crossed the car park, and Ben collapsed on the grass, still shaking.

"Let's rest a bit. Please..." he mumbled, and Will sat down next to him.

Ben looked like a shadow and trembled like an aspen leaf on a windy day.

"I can't believe he's dead," he whispered, keeping his eyes away from Will.

"I can't believe they ate him," Will said. "That woman is mad! She was talking bullshit!"

Ben shook his head hastily and then abruptly turned away, splashing a projectile of vomit on the grass. Will patiently waited for the convulsions of the young doctor to subside. The guy was a wreck and Will half-considered carrying him all the way to the train station – maybe he would get better before they got back to London.

"I can't believe he's dead," Ben uttered, searching his pockets for a tissue. "He meant the whole world to me. Now he's gone and in such a dreadful way. Eric had been terrified lately. I saw that, but he never complained, never mentioned anything, never answered my questions. He didn't want to worry me. Now he's dead..."

Will shrugged silently. He didn't know what to say or how to comfort the guy.

"Last time I saw him, he was planning to go to London. He rented that apartment. We kept calling each other and texting, but then he just vanished. I had a terrible feeling that he was in trouble when I went to search for him," Ben shut his eyes tight, tears rolling down his cheeks. "I didn't expect this to happen..."

Will looked at the crushed young doctor, and a certain terrible feeling sneaked into his soul too. *Was that strange lady telling the truth?* Had they indeed somehow performed intricate surgery and cut him out of his mother's mind? Was that even possible? It was crazy, and he bravely laughed it off. Then it sneaked back. His mother had been silent for too long. Could that crazy thing the *borwil* had been talking about indeed be true?

He sat stunned next to lamenting Ben for several minutes. *No!* That crazy woman had been talking utter nonsense. But if she was lying about his mother, maybe Eric was still alive too?

"Calm down," he embraced Ben's shoulders. "I'm sure she was lying."

"About what?"

"About everything," Will shrugged. "She has no reason to trust us, and we have no reason to trust her. She just made fools of us."

Ben cried for a few more minutes, shaking his head but said nothing.

"Calm down," Will tried clumsily again to comfort him. "We must return to London."

Fifteen minutes later, he succeeded in getting Ben to move.

"Let's go," Ben nodded, wiping his tears away.

Will had to support him all the way downhill to the train station. Ben's legs were shaky, but he stepped on, barely lifting his gaze from the ground. They didn't talk.

The train arrived half an hour later, nearly empty. They chose random seats, and Will stayed close to Ben. He didn't care if some crazy bitch could see him through Ben's eyes.

They got off at Bromley South and took a bus to Lewisham.

"I don't think she was lying," Ben said gravely, staring at the traffic outside the window.

"What makes you think so?"

"She's a *borwil*."

"That explains nothing," Will shrugged. "She had no obligation to tell you the truth, and she could invent things as she spoke."

"Why would she do that?"

"She's a *borwil*," this seemed a good enough explanation to Will.

"You have no proof that she was lying," Ben sighed.

"You have no proof that she was telling the truth!" Will said. "Wait until Eric comes back to you!"

"That won't happen."

Will embraced the young guy and patted his shoulder. "Wait, and you'll see. She *was* lying."

Ben only sighed as tears began to pool in his eyes again, but he squeezed his teeth and shook them away. Will didn't dare to say anything else.

They left the bus silently. Neither said a word as they boarded the red-painted DLR and later switched to the underground.

Crowds of commuters moved swiftly around them as a mighty river moved around solid boulders. They walked at their own pace like two shadows, not seeing much around them.

"I don't have the strength to mess with any food preparation," Ben said when they reached home. "Do you mind if I just order a pizza?"

Will didn't mind.

They ate when the pizza arrived. All the time, Ben was looking away, and Will didn't dare to say a word.

Later, when they were lying in bed under their separate blankets, Ben began to sob again.

"I'm sorry," he apologised. "Never in my life have I felt lonelier."

"I could hold you until you fall asleep," Will offered.

"Please..."

It was utterly dark. Will opened his eyes but couldn't see anything. And it was quiet except for the distant sound of water falling. Had Qu Sith sneaked away?

He extended his hands out, feeling around him. There was only dust, but the dust on his right-hand side was much softer than on his left. He sank his fingers deeper, seeking for the rocks beneath...

"You can stop scratching my balls, thank you," the voice growled. "I didn't know you were sexually attracted to sphinxes."

The beast was here.

"I can't see anything," Will complained, ignoring the insult.

"Maybe it's still too early for the view," Qu Sith snarled.

"Maybe..."

Will sat up, leaning against something soft. The stench of the beast's breath was to his left.

"Any bright ideas on how to get out of this hole?" Qu Sith

asked.

"No, not yet," Will sighed. "Have you thought of anything useful?"

"We wouldn't be here if I had," the sphinx spat out. "Isn't that obvious?"

Will didn't answer. They sat in the darkness, listening to the distant sound of falling water and waited. An hour later, a grey spot appeared in the ceiling where the warm creek slipped underground into the chilly grip of the grotto.

"It seems that the sun is up," Qu Sith observed in the darkness.

"I still don't see anything around," Will sighed.

"Me neither..."

"But your eyes are supposed to be better in the dark!"

"It's too dark."

"Damn!"

"We'll die here."

"No!"

"Do you have any magical solution?" Qu Sith growled. "If not, then keep calm and stop moaning. I hate moaning humans!"

"I think I've got a solution," Will said, standing up. "There's one idea we need to try."

"May I remind you that I can't fly, and I can't climb those walls – they're too steep," the beast mumbled. "You're welcome to try if you want, and I might have my last supper if you crash back down."

"Do you remember your oath?"

"I do, don't worry."

"Don't make me regret freeing you from that cage," Will said, facing the barely visible grey opening in the ceiling. "We simply need more light, and then we could find the opening and the way out."

"Have you made friends with some fairies in your sleep?"

"We don't need fairies," Will said. "A few large rocks might just do the job."

"Are you serious?" Qu Sith jumped to his feet, but Will couldn't see that – there was just the shuffling sound of disturbed pebbles in the dark. "You want to wake up whatever monster lurks under the surface? Just for fun?"

"We only need a few flashes of light, and you might see the opening," Will explained patiently. "Your eyes are more sensitive than mine."

"It's a bad plan," the sphinx growled. "You risk angering the monster, and those flashes are blinding! I won't be able to see anything!"

Will was determined to try their luck. "You must look the other way, not at the flashes. You must look at the walls! If there's any tunnel out of here, you'll see it. Then at least, we'll know where to go."

"Silly plan..." the sphinx spat out disdainfully.

"Do you have a better one?"

"No. But it's too risky. We might not have time to run for safety if you wake up whatever lurks under the surface. Silly plan..."

"I think we should try it," Will said firmly. "I just need to get a little closer to that pool."

"Bad idea. Very bad idea..."

"Are you coming? I'll throw those rocks anyway. You better look closely, or you'll miss our opportunity to get out!"

Qu Sith sighed. "What curse clouded my mind when I decided to stick with this silly and stubborn human..." he moaned, choosing his way in the dark.

"That silly and stubborn human has saved your life a few times," Will dropped as he moved on.

"I know. I remember. I'm still grateful."

"The plan is good," Will tried to sound encouraging, failed. "If we die, we die with fireworks."

"What are fireworks?"

"Never mind..."

They slowly crawled forward, stumbling upon rocks in the darkness. Will almost fell a few times, and the sound of shuffling pebbles and curses in the dark told him that the sphinx was moving too. The chill spread up his limbs as he got nearer to the underground lake, and he kept glancing at the grey spot in the ceiling to make sure they were going in the right direction.

He stopped when the water touched his feet. Then he backed away a few paces, feeling around for a suitable rock.

"What do you want me to do?" asked the beast.

"Look away from that hole in the ceiling," Will weighed a boulder in his hand, then dropped it next to his feet and kept on searching for bigger ones. "I'll tell you when I'm ready to throw the rock!"

"I'll do as you say, human," the sphinx sighed in the darkness. "Just promise you'll warn me if that fiery thing in the lake tries to bite my ass off."

"I will. Don't worry," Will found a suitable rock and stood up, resting it on his right shoulder. "Are you ready?"

"No."

"Why?"

"I've turned around but still don't think it's a good idea."

"Just don't close your eyes and don't blink!" Will's arm went up with the force of a coiled spring of steel. The rock arched in the dark and landed in a pool a few yards away with a loud splash. There was nothing at first, and Will was about to sigh with disappointment when it hit something deeper under the surface, erupting a flash of the purple light.

Qu Sith screamed.

"Did you see the hole?" Will asked.

"No. I didn't see anything. The water monster grabbed my tail, and I closed my eyes!"

Will cursed. "It wasn't a monster, silly. It was just a splash of water when I threw the rock, and it will splash you again when I throw another rock. Get your tail away from the pool and keep your eyes open!"

"Very well," Qu Sith sighed. "Give me a little break while I get higher. I like the idea that the water monster will feast on you first. I might be able to get away by then."

Will got down on his knees and felt around for another suitable boulder. It wasn't easy, and he had to move twice along the shore.

"Ready?" he asked and placed the rock on his shoulder.

"Almost..." the sphinx mumbled somewhere in the darkness. "Now!"

"Don't close your eyes!" Will threw the rock as high as he could.

A loud splash was followed by a painful flash of purple light from the depth of the pool, leaving blue and green stains swirling in front of Will's eyes.

"Did you find an exit?" he asked.

"No. There's none on the left side of the pool. I could clearly see the walls. No holes there."

"Very well," Will mumbled. "Now, let's try the other side.

Don't waste a throw!"

"Wait! This might be dangerous! I'm not ready!"

"Take your time," Will uttered, feeling the ground around him for one more suitable rock.

The water quietly rippled, splashing tiny waves upon the dark shore. This was a new sound, and it took some time until it broke through the door to his consciousness, suddenly flooding everything with bestial fear. Will stopped searching.

"I don't like this," he whispered, backing away from the wall of chill emerging from the dark pond.

"What?"

"Let's move!" Will whispered, pushing the beast away from the water.

"What happened?"

Will kept his voice low. "Move to the right!"

"Why the right?"

"You said there was no exit on the left."

"I'm not sure," Qu Sith mumbled but followed the lead. "I was hoping for a second look. Why are we suddenly running away?"

"I think we've angered something..."

"I told you! I told you! Now we're doomed!" the sphinx sounded breathless. "I'm too young to die!"

"Shut up and move!" Will snapped. "We don't have much time!"

Waves were now hitting the invisible shore more vigorously, and the chill was spreading more quickly.

They rushed uphill, stumbling into countless obstacles, invisible in the dark. It was a small wonder that no bones were broken after all those falls, and Will was sure that his body was covered in wounds and bruises and that some of those wounds were bleeding.

They were stopped by the steep wall of the grotto and began running along next to it.

"Are you sure there was something there?" Qu Sith asked, trying to keep close to Will's heels. "My predator instinct was silent. I thought you were braver."

"I won't toss another pebble in that pool..." Will's voice was cut by the sound of breaking waves accompanied by something that sounded like crinkling cellophane.

They stopped just for a second. First, there was a barely perceptible flash of dark purple light, and then, a few seconds later, an enormous pillar of purple sparks emerged from the depths of the pool, hitting the ceiling of the cavern high above. It looked like an explosion but didn't emit a sound apart from the slightly louder sound of crinkling cellophane, making everything seem like an eerie movie on a faulty TV.

The grotto was now brightly lit by an eerie purple illumination, and Will could now clearly see all the errors of his blind wanderings. The cliff he had assumed to be a wall yesterday was an arch – he could have passed through it if he had taken a few more steps to the right.

"Escape is there," he happily pointed as they ran, now stumbling and falling less, aided by the shimmering purple illumination.

"Where?"

"The blackness... behind that arch!"

Will cast a quick glance at the pool. The pillar of sparks was still there, but a thick fog rose around it and steadily spread towards the shores. The temperature dropped even further.

"We must run faster!" he said, sprinting under the arch. He didn't turn to have a look if the sphinx was following.

The dark mouth of the corridor was almost three hundred paces behind the arch. Will ran as fast as he could as the chill bit at his heels. He took just a few steps into the blackness of the corridor as it was too dark in there to run on without risking breaking his neck. Qu Sith bumped against his leg and stopped too. The corridor mouth was an opaque milky wall with purple flashes and strange shadows moving inside when he looked back.

"What was that?" Qu Sith squeezed between gasps for air.

"I don't know," Will leaned against the wall. "It seems we're safe. For a while, at least."

"I told you not to throw those stones," the beast dropped down on his hind legs. "That thing almost got us. Now we're stuck in some stinky hole. How can we get back?"

Will was still too breathless to have a good laugh out loud – he only managed a few short chuckles.

"You're crazy, human," Qu Sith spat out.

"No. You're ignorant," Will said. "Unbelievable!"

"What shit had made you so happy?" the sphinx growled. "What exactly am I failing to see? That thing raging and making it impossible for us to go back? Or the fact that we're sitting in some black hole and shitting on our heels?"

"It's not a hole," Will patted the nearest wall. "It's our way out!"

"It might just be a dead end."

"No. We have a creek here," Will pointed out the obvious. "That will guide us out."

Qu Sith looked around. "We're doomed if this is your way to salvation."

"We don't have any other."

"As you say," Qu Sith sighed. "But I need a break. I'm too tired already."

"Let's rest before we go," Will offered, suddenly afraid to leave that scarce light leaking from the mouth of the corridor although it was subsiding. He glanced at the darkness that was waiting for them down the corridor and sighed.

They sat on the ground several paces away from the entrance, ready to spring to their feet and run away if necessary. Something strange was still happening in the grotto – shadows still moved in the fog, but the purple light slowly subsided. Fifteen minutes later, it was gone. The darkness was absolute.

"Congratulations!" mumbled the sphinx. "We've saved our skins from whatever it was just to get utterly stuck. I can't see anything past the end of my nose. Maybe it's better to go back?"

"Why? Unless you grew a pair of wings while we ran."

"It's rude to make fun of a cripple. I don't have wings, but I might still have a scorpion's sting in my tail!"

"Have you?"

"No."

Will shrugged in the darkness. "I see no point in going back," he said. "Unless you hope for some sort of rescue army to lower their nets and get you out. Even then, you would need to swim to the middle of that pond over whatever lurks below the surface. Are you ready to do that?"

Qu Sith growled. "Very well, human," he spat. "There's a certain dubious logic to your statement. We'll do as you say. I just need a bit more rest."

"We can have a bit more rest," Will said as he stretched his muscles.

They sat for another fifteen minutes.

"Are you ready to go on?" Will asked.

"No," Qu Sith growled. "We sphinxes are creatures of the sun and heat. You're dragging me into some dank, dark dungeons, and I'll never be ready for that. I can't see what's in front of us or what monsters are sneaking up behind us from that cave. I wonder how you can be so sure that this passage leads to the way out."

Will sighed. He wasn't sure himself, but this corridor must lead somewhere, and that place might happen to be better than the hole they were sitting in right now. Or worse... He wasn't sure of anything.

"We can come back if we get stuck and try something different," Will said. "We can peek into the grotto before we go in to make sure that no monsters are following us if that will make you feel safer. I see no other possibilities but to go down that corridor."

"Why not wait for some help?"

"Why have you kept it so secret that some rescue army is coming for you?" Will chuckled. "No one is looking for us. No one cares. Even those bloody Rybbaths are dead. We're on our own!"

"It's frightening..."

"The unknown is always frightening," Will snapped, getting up. "You'll never have your nest and see your offspring if you're afraid to take the first step. Everything you want is on the other side of your fear. Gather your courage while I check the grotto."

Qu Sith only sighed. It was difficult to go back those few hundred paces in the dark, but Will was determined to take a glimpse at the pond. He went slowly, touching the rocky wall with the fingertips of his left hand. The mouth of the corridor was just a slightly lighter shade of black in the dark, and he kept his eyes firmly fixed on it, trying to ignore the monstrous shapes his bored brain painted. It was just flickers of light at first, but later, the images became more complex and frightening. He stepped on regardless. It was difficult, but he succeeded in convincing himself that he was not afraid of those images. *Were they just images?* Will couldn't be sure.

Do as you preach, the thought pierced his brain. *You must descend into the darkness to see the light!*

He cautiously peered into the cavern and looked around. It was cold, much colder than before, still as dark. It seemed like frost glistened in the faint light, but he couldn't be sure. The underground lake was dark. The purple lights and the pillar of sparks were gone.

Will listened intently, but all he could hear was the sound of water falling in the distance. Nobody and nothing moved around. He almost jumped when a voice next to him asked quietly: "Are you afraid?"

Will peered in the direction where the voice had come from, but there was nothing there to see – only blackness inside the blackness. "Do I know you?" he asked a dumb question, his voice trembling slightly.

Someone sighed in the gloom. "I hadn't had any real hope that you would remember me," the voice said, but nobody appeared behind it.

Will frowned. The voice wasn't threatening and sounded familiar. "Kanykei?" he asked.

Someone chuckled.

"You remembered!" the barely visible transparent form of a girl emerged from the darkness. "Did you find that flower?" she asked.

"No, not yet," Will shrugged. "But I keep on searching."

"Good luck then..." Kanykei turned to go.

"Wait!" Will stopped her.

Kanykei turned around, or so it seemed – it was difficult to tell with someone as transparent as a ghost.

"Has Hel returned home?" he asked.

"No."

"Could you tell her that I'll find that flower? When she returns, of course."

"I doubt that you'll find it. You should have done that long before."

"I had a few obstacles," Will blushed. He hoped that this wasn't obvious in the darkness.

"What obstacles?"

"You never mentioned the crazy religious fanatics who hunted people for their crazy religious rituals!"

"Oh! You met the Rybbaths!" Kanykei chuckled.

"And you never mentioned some bloody flaming snakes that are taller than trees!"

"You've met the Night Crawlers too! We suspected that something was wrong when whole villages began returning to the Tower. You have indeed been busy."

"You never told me how dangerous it might become!"

"You never asked," the ghost shrugged. "It would be bizarre to explain what is common knowledge, especially to a guy who is so much in love."

A chill thought drilled through Will's brain. "Are you jealous?" he asked cautiously.

"No," the transparent girl shrugged. "Why should I be jealous? You're not my type of a guy anyway."

Will bit his lip, but it was too late. He couldn't clearly see the expression of the transparent face, but her voice sounded disappointed.

"Will you tell her?"

"No."

"Why?"

"I don't believe you can find it," Kanykei said. "Too much time has passed already. Anyone could have picked that flower up by now. You've spent too much time getting into trouble and sitting in holes like this."

It was pointless to ask her for help.

"Could you help me to get out?" Will risked anyway.

Kanykei looked around before answering. "I can't," she sighed. "We're not allowed to touch any living beings. And we can't touch this forbidden cavern. You're on your own, I'm afraid."

Will sighed.

"Could you tell me if there is any way out of here?" he asked.

"There is," Kanykei nodded. "You're standing right at the beginning."

Will forced a weak smile and nodded. "Any dangers down there?" he asked, gesturing to the corridor behind him.

"I've no idea," the transparent girl shrugged. "I've never been there."

"How do you know it's the way outside if you've never been there?"

"Trust me. Or don't – you decide..."

"Thank you," Will sighed. "You don't believe in me, but I'll bring that flower, and you'll be able to have a look as I promised."

"Good luck! You'll need it..." Kanykei whispered before

vanishing.

The grotto seemed even colder as Will stared into the distant hole in the ceiling where the warm waters of the creek fell into the underground lake a few hundred feet below, barely visible in the dusk. With Kanykei gone, he felt lonely and abandoned. Nobody would help them – he suddenly realised – not in this world and not in the other world. It was his own struggle and his own fate. His quest was to find that damned flower, return to Hel and beg for her forgiveness. And he couldn't be of much help to the sphinx either – the beast must solve his mating problems himself. They simply must get out of these caves.

Will turned and entered the tunnel, leaving the frosty cavern behind. It was even darker than before, and he stepped carefully, touching the wall with the fingertips of his right hand. The rock was cold at first but grew a little warmer as he carried on.

"Are you still there?" he asked softly a few dozen paces later.

"Did you expect me to run away?" Qu Sith growled ahead of him in the darkness. "Or did you plan to run away yourself?"

"This is the only way out," Will mumbled, taking a few more steps.

"We'll see..." Qu Sith sighed.

"Keep on talking," Will asked the beast. "I don't want to stumble on you or step on your tail."

"My tail is safely tucked away, don't worry."

Will took a few more steps. "Shit! I didn't expect the darkness to be this absolute!" he complained, keeping hold of the wall. His next step stumbled into something soft.

"It's me," the sphinx growled. "How can we go through this tunnel when we're as blind as moles."

"You said it!" Will suddenly rejoiced. "It's a tunnel! We can't wander away in the wrong direction!"

"Still, we could break our necks if we fall into some hole in the dark," the sphinx didn't sound enthusiastic. "You can't see shit! A true hell only awaits us there – first we get hurt, then we get damaged, then we go insane, and finally we get dead! Is that what you're after? Suicide?"

Will ignored the moaning and grinned widely in the darkness. "We have a guide here," he said.

"Who?"

"It's not a person. It's this creek. We just need to follow where it flows, and we'll get outside!"

"Or into some goddamned cavern which is even deeper and creepier than the last one," the sphinx moaned. "I'm not getting my feet wet again! I've had enough of water in my life!"

"I'm going," Will said firmly. "You can stay if you want..."

"Don't leave me!" there was some shuffling in the dark as the beast had probably jumped to his feet. "Please..."

"I'm not afraid to get my feet wet," Will said. "You can stay on the shore."

"And wander away somewhere while I can't see anything? No, thank you! You won't get rid of me that easy!"

"I've no such intention."

"You're just saying that..."

"Have I ever left you behind?"

The sphinx was silent for a few minutes. "No," he admitted at last. "But that might happen any minute in the dark, and you wouldn't even notice."

Will mouthed a silent curse. It was next to impossible to stop the creature from moaning, but he must find a way to get the beast moving. They had plenty of water but would starve to death if they continued to jib at the entrance to freedom. The thought of food made Will's belly growl louder than Qu Sith. It had been a few days since they had eaten last time, and he was becoming increasingly aware of the emptiness in his gut. He could clearly imagine the same sensation in the gut of the sphinx and wondered how long the oath not to eat humans would hold.

"I'll walk in the creek, and you can walk on the shore," he sighed.

"You're saying that on purpose, aren't you?" Qu Sith spat. "You'd be pleased if I wandered away in the dark."

"I could hold you by your tail..."

Qu Sith roared in the dark, and the sound echoed from the

corridor walls, spreading through the guts of the mountain and then waning.

"Have you the slightest idea how insulting and degrading your offer is?" the beast spat and roared again.

Will waited patiently until the sounds subsided. "Do you have any better idea? Any idea at all? You don't want to get into the water. You don't want to wander away and get lost. You don't want me to hold your tail, but you don't have any other body part long enough to keep you out of the water and stay in touch."

"You can't imagine how degrading your offer is," the beast snarled. "Nobody holds a sphinx by his tail!"

"Any better ideas?"

Qu Sith sighed but didn't respond. The silence stretched into several minutes, but Will couldn't see what the beast was doing in the dark. It grew even more uncomfortable when he heard the beast's stomach playing loud marches.

"You can hold my tail," the sphinx sighed at last. "Nobody will see us in the dark. But you'll release it as soon as we see the light!"

"Of course," Will tried to pat the shaggy back but failed to find it. "Damn!"

"What? We haven't even started!"

"I can't find you! It's too dark..."

"Let's face it – it won't get any lighter even if we wait. Why don't you just come towards my voice?"

"I'll try," Will sighed but halted, met by another wave of growling guts from the darkness. He wasn't sure if it was safe to approach the beast. He wasn't sure of anything. Suddenly, he felt *afraid*.

"Are you coming?" asked Qu Sith.

"No," Will decided. "It will be difficult to find the creek together without risking splashing you with *water*."

"I see your point, human," Qu Sith squeezed through his teeth. "Go, find your creek but don't get in too deep. I don't want to get my feet wet."

Will backed a few paces away, still feeling uneasy. Then he turned left and stepped forward, keeping his hands outstretched to help with his balance. It was damned tricky, and he probed his way with his feet, afraid to stumble on some rocks. A few times, he stopped and listened. Once, he heard the growling of the sphinx's gut in the distance, but the beast didn't come any closer.

"Now!" he said when his feet hit the rippling surface. He took one more step just to be on the safe side.

"What do you want me to do?" Qu Sith asked.

"Come closer," Will shrugged in the dark. "We can begin moving once I've got your tail in my hand. I hope we'll be able to get out quite soon and you can hunt for some rabbits. I feel a bit hungry."

"Don't mention food, human," Qu Sith growled. "But I agree

with you – let's get out as quick as we can."

He heard the beast shuffling in the darkness, getting closer.

"Where are you, human?"

"A few more steps, I think," Will tried to direct him, his heart still trembling. *Damn!* He felt like a mouse! "And a little to the right."

A few more steps, a little more shuffling in the dark.

"Now – what?" The beast asked.

"Wait," Will extended his hand towards the voice. Something shaggy was under his fingers. "Which part of your body am I touching?"

"It's my head, stupid," barked the sphinx.

"I can't see a thing," Will complained but kept his hand touching the fur. "Now, turn your butt to the left so that I can reach your tail. You'll be facing in the right direction."

The beast moved. Will passed his hand along the spine of the sphinx, touching lightly.

"Be gentle and respectful," Qu Sith muttered. "Please."

"I will. Don't worry," Will sighed. "Are you sure there's no sting of a scorpion down there?"

"No, don't worry." Qu Sith chuckled. "I would know that."

"Let's move then," Will told the beast, carefully getting hold of the tail next to the tuft.

And they went like two moles in the dark tunnel, bound only

by the tail. Progress was slow, and the sphinx continually moaned about his hurt pride and his empty stomach. Will only listened as the steady stream of sighs and complaints didn't require any input from him. He kept his feet wet and tugged on the tail if the beast wandered too far away from the creek. His stomach was also growling, but he kept that to himself, not risking mentioning food to the sphinx. He was sure the shallow creek would offer little protection if the beast chose to fill his guts with Will's meat. He only hoped they wouldn't slip over the edge of madness.

A few hours later, they emerged out of the tunnel, but that didn't make their lives brighter or their struggles lighter. It was just another dark cavern where the guiding creek swelled into an underground lake, and they had to find their way around it, having no idea how big the grotto was.

"I'm very tired," Qu Sith complained.

"We can rest for a few minutes," Will agreed but didn't leave the safety of the water.

They rested three more times until they had crossed the cavern and found another stream escaping the lake. Then, abruptly, Qu Sith stopped there, at the mouth of the new tunnel. He didn't respond to the tug of the tail, and Will had to stop too.

"What is it?" he asked the beast.

"I smell a rat," the sphinx answered after a short pause.

Will didn't smell anything. *Was this a trick?*

"I must check this," the sphinx whispered. "Please, let go of my tail."

Will heard a few rocks falling as the beast stumbled upon them in the dark and quietly backed into deeper water. He took several steps forward as well without making a sound.

"Found them!" Qu Sith exclaimed; his voice sounded a few dozen paces to the right. "There's a whole nest of them but not exactly as I anticipated – all are dead and dried up. Do you want some?"

"No, you can have them all," Will sighed in silent relief. A stodgy sphinx was a safe sphinx. But the discovery worried him. *Who or what had killed those rats?* What dangers lurked in the dark? He kept his ears sharp, but all he could hear was the sphinx crunching tiny bones and munching on dried meat.

"Oh, one more nest!" Qu Sith exclaimed. "Are you sure you don't want some? It tastes like shit, but it's filling my belly quite well."

"No, thank you," Will declined politely.

The sphinx shuffled in the darkness for the better part of an hour, exclaiming joyously from time to time upon stumbling on a new nest of rats. It seemed as if an entire large colony of rats had been killed, mummified and left here to crumble to dust. The feeling was unsettling, but Will realised that it was almost impossible to part Qu Sith from the food, and he patiently waited until the beast could gobble up no more.

"I need a drink," the sphinx announced at last.

"We have plenty of water here," Will shrugged, still soaking his feet a few steps away from the shore.

Qu Sith crawled closer and then cursed when his paws slipped into the creek. The slurping sounds seemed to last forever.

"Are you full?" Will asked when the beast had stopped slurping.

"Yes," Qu Sith sighed. "We can proceed now. Just be warned, I'll kill you the instant you ever mention that I had feasted on dead rats!"

"It was a matter of survival, I understand. But don't worry, your secret is safe with me."

"You've been warned. Don't do anything foolish," Qu Sith said as he approached. "Now you can get hold of my tail again."

They carried on, led by the creek.

"I think we're close to the surface," Will broke the silence half an hour later.

"I like your conclusion," Qu Sith chuckled happily. "But what makes you think so? I can't see any lights."

"The rats. I doubt they would go too deep under the mountain to nest."

Qu Sith stopped. "I've told you not to mention that!" he growled.

"Relax. No one can hear us. I'm just stating the fact."

"I like your conclusion, but better forget that rat business now."

"Of course, I won't mention that again. But there's one more thing that's bothering me."

"What's that?"

"Why did those rats die?"

"Who cares? They're just rats."

"They might have been poisoned..."

"Poisoned? Poisoned?" Qu Sith gasped. "And you're only saying that just now! Am I dying?"

"I don't think so," Will tugged the sphinx into motion. "Whatever happened here was sudden and long ago."

"What makes you think so?"

"The bodies of the rats were dry when you found them in their nests. Their death was sudden and a while ago."

"I'd never have expected to encounter a seed of logic in that strange head of yours, human," Qu Sith said. "But yes, that sounds quite likely. Still, am I going to die?"

"I don't know. How do you feel?"

"I feel... strange... Goodbye, cruel world!" Qu Sith uttered. The next moment he slumped on the shore of the dark creek, motionless.

Will sat down next to the sphinx. *Damn! Was the beast dying?*

Dead? He placed his hand on the shaggy chest – it was still moving quietly! The signs were encouraging, and he pressed his ear against it, holding his own breath and listening. Will had never tried this before, but the situation was desperate. What he heard was shocking. His ear was hit by moaning and squeaking, sometimes rattling and splashing – it seemed like armies of dead rats were fighting for survival and battling hurricane winds at the same time. Then someone roared and sighed, but Will didn't back off until he heard the distinct sounds of the rhythmic drumming. The heart was beating! Qu Sith had just fainted, he realised. He must wait.

Will sighed in the dark – they needed some rest anyway. He quietly reclined on the rocky ground. He listened to the soft rippling of the creek somewhere next to his feet and wondered how to get back to the daylight more quickly. Nothing helpful came to mind. Those tunnels were dangerous, and several times he had to push away the rising wave of panic. He *must* get out or risk ending up like those rats.

Then a distant wailing reached him through the tunnel ending abruptly with an agonising scream.

He sprang to his feet, ears sharp, but neither the scream nor wailing came again. There was a dull silence and complete darkness around him, disturbed only by the soft rippling of water.

Will crouched next to the sphinx, feeling the chest of the beast.

It moved slowly in deep inspirations, and he patted the fur. The living body next to him felt like a lifeboat in a sea of terror. He was afraid.

Another half an hour passed waiting.

"Is it time to get up?" Qu Sith mumbled lazily.

"No," Will decided. "We'll spend the night here."

"How do you know it's night?"

"It feels like the darkest hour when demons wake up to the world."

"Demons? Have you seen any?"

"No. Relax. It's just a saying. How do you feel?"

"Strange," Qu Sith yawned. "I'd advise you not to sit next to my butt. I feel a strange storm building up in my gut, and anything might happen."

"I'd better move away," Will muttered. "Thanks for the warning."

He crawled away from the creek and stretched his tired body on the pebbles. It wasn't a comfortable position, but it was the best he could manage.

"Damned rats!" Qu Sith uttered before releasing a loud foul-smelling fart. "Have you figured out what killed them?"

"No," Will sighed. "Let's sleep." He decided not to mention the scream. The sphinx didn't have the bravest of hearts, and he didn't want any further fuss.

Will listened to the quiet sounds of the stream rippling down the corridor somewhere in the dark. He wasn't in a rush but didn't notice when his mind was carried away.

Ben was awake when Will opened his eyes. He was sitting naked on the edge of the bed staring at the rain pouring down outside the window. His gaze was empty, and Will thought that the young doctor might be having one of those fits, but then he noticed the tears rolling down his cheeks and splashing onto his naked chest.

Ben was silent, and Will didn't dare to disturb the silence. He simply watched as the young man's shoulders jerked in a soundless lament. He had no idea how to comfort the guy, what he should say or do to help Ben feel better. He just watched.

Fifteen minutes passed before Ben thought of casting a glance at Will.

"I didn't realise you were awake," he said quietly.

"I didn't know what to say," admitted Will.

"They drank Eric's blood," Ben's voice trembled. "They *ate* him!"

Will shrugged. "I don't believe they did," he said. "That *borwil* told us a lot of things that don't make sense. I think she just invented things to scare us away. She is a vile and heartless woman! Don't listen to her nonsense."

"She's not vile. She's more trapped than any of us," Ben said quietly. "And she has no reason to lie. She told us what she knows and whoever is connected to her knows."

"Wait and see," Will shrugged. "Perhaps, one day, your Eric will return to you. Don't be surprised."

"He won't. He's dead. And he died most horribly," tears rolled down the guy's cheeks, and Will felt an urge to comfort him but did nothing. "You can't undo that."

"I'm not going to undo anything," Will was persistent. "I just don't believe that creepy woman."

Ben sighed and shook his head.

"I need to wash my face," the guy said and stood up. "I look terrible."

He did indeed look like a wreck, Will thought but didn't say anything. For several minutes he just listened to Ben messing about in the bathroom. Then he got up and dressed.

Gusts of wind splashed rain against the window as Will stood next to it, watching silently. Going anywhere outside in such weather was out of the question.

Will watched the clouds when Ben sneaked out of the

bathroom. He didn't turn to look and patiently waited while the young doctor got dressed.

"I'll make us some coffee," Ben emerged behind his back, his voice was still grim and crackling, but he had managed to suppress the trembling.

"Do you want any help with that?" Will asked.

"It's fine. Don't worry."

Will didn't dare to say anything more. He watched the guy busy next to the stove from a distance. Ben wasn't fine. That was obvious – his hands were shaking, and he dropped the spoon a couple of times.

Will sneaked into the kitchen. "Let me help you," he embraced the guy and gently pushed him towards the table, but Ben didn't release him. His suppressed lament exploded, and the guy clutched Will as if his life depended on it. Hot tears rolled down Ben's face as he buried it into Will's chest; his shoulders jerked and trembled uncontrollably.

Will just stood awkwardly, embracing the young doctor and letting him cry his heart out. It seemed like an eternity, but he didn't dare say anything.

It took almost an hour for Ben to calm down. "Sorry," he whispered, wiping away his tears. "Thank you for understanding."

Will only shrugged. He didn't know what to say.

"Our coffee's gone cold," Ben noted and turned back to the stove. "I'll need to make some fresh."

He began to fill the kettle, but his hands still trembled.

"I'll do that," Will said softly. "You better sit down."

Ben seemed to shrink at his words but stepped back and lowered his still shaky body on the chair.

Will burnt his finger as he juggled with the kettle but stifled a curse. "Sugar? Milk?" he asked, frowning.

"Yes, one teaspoon, please," Ben's voice was barely audible.

Will placed the mugs down and sat on the other side of the table. The coffee tasted strange, but he was no barista. Ben said nothing, quietly sipping the brew, his eyes still red, his hands still trembling. "I can't face up to the fact that they killed Eric," he placed the mug on the table and buried his face in his hands. "How could they do that to him?"

Will said nothing, just sipped his coffee. His heart was breaking, and he felt helpless, watching the guy so deep in his sorrow, but he couldn't do anything about it, nor did he have any answers to that question. Heavy showers battered against the window outside, and they drank their coffee, watching the dark clouds scurrying through the sky and leaving the question unanswered.

"What are you going to do, knowing all the *borwil* said?" Ben asked when they had finished their drinks. "Where are you going to begin your search for the Sanctuary?"

"I must get home," Will said, inspecting the empty mug. "It was the most stupid idea to run away and come to London. I'd have been training in the gym at this time at home."

"But you don't have that home anymore," Ben reminded him. "Mrs Patel said you need to find that damned Sanctuary."

"She lied," Will cut him short. "I don't believe a word she said."

"I must disagree with you, I'm afraid," Ben sighed uneasily.

"It's as shitty a situation as itchy piles," Will shrugged. "You know they're there. You know it's wrong. But you can't prove it, and there's no one I would trust with my piles. I don't need some mystic Sanctuary. I must go back home."

"It's not safe back there..."

"I won't run away from home because of some stupid imaginary threat! I made a horrible mistake. Now, I must correct it. And I don't believe your Eric is dead. Maybe he just went to have fun somewhere and will come back anytime. Maybe he's home already but doesn't know you're in London. Shit! That might be the tragic truth. Don't trust that vile woman! She knows nothing."

Ben didn't even glance at Will. Instead, he sat, staring at his mug. "Don't play with my feelings, please. You don't know Eric," he uttered quietly. "And you need that Sanctuary to help you out of those caves."

"I don't need anybody. I've found the tunnel!"

"I'm glad you have."

"I don't believe that the Sanctuary even exists! Nobody seems to know anything about it!"

"There is a Sanctuary! It *must* be well hidden, or it wouldn't be a sanctuary. We should try harder..."

"We?" Will asked with too much irony in his voice, then his face suddenly blushed. *Had he barked too much?* He jumped to his feet and glanced at the elements raging outside the window. *Must he leave now?* Will regretted that slip of the tongue. "Sorry," he uttered and dashed into the corridor, unable to wait for Ben's response.

He didn't go far.

Will felt a nudge at his left side, and the corridor walls blurred and faded as he collapsed without uttering another word.

There was another nudge, and a familiar voice whispered, "Wake up! We must move. Now!"

Will sat up. It was dark with no hint of light anywhere. "What happened?" he asked. It was as silent as before except for the creek quietly rippling a few feet away.

"We must move now," Qu Sith repeated.

"Why? It's still deep night out there, and we just barely got any sleep."

"We must go without stopping until we get out!"

"You're the one who dropped off early yesterday," Will reminded him. "What happened?"

"We have ghosts here," said the sphinx seriously. "I heard someone wailing and screaming in the tunnels."

"I heard that yesterday..."

"Why didn't you tell me?"

"You were – how to say this delicately – very tired after your internal battle with those mummified rats," Will let himself sound sarcastic. "It was a great clash, and I wonder why nothing of it erupted outside."

"We must go!" Qu Sith sounded desperate. "Please..."

"Stop shouting," Will whispered. "I'm getting up. You can relax!"

"Get a grip of my tail, please," Qu Sith brushed against Will's thigh like an overgrown cat. "Let's move! Now!"

"I need to locate the creek," Will traced his hand along the spine of the beast. "I still don't understand what all this fuss is about – have you seen something?"

The question hung mid-air for a few long seconds. "I see it now..." Qu Sith whispered at last.

"I don't see anything," Will said, taking a grip of the beast's tail.

"Now it's gone... It just flashed past me," Qu Sith sighed. "I must be going insane."

"No, you're not."

"Have you seen it too?"

"No."

"Then I'm insane," Qu Sith was almost crying. "Nothing is more pitiful than a feeble-minded sphinx! I'm too young for this!"

"Shut up," Will cut short, his moaning. "Let's go."

His feet hit the lukewarm flow, and he was almost sure that

they were on the right track. It took a few more tugs on the tail to set the sphinx into motion. They hadn't gone more than a hundred paces when muffled distant wailing broke the silence.

Qu Sith stopped. "Do you hear that?" he sounded desperate.

"Yes," Will tugged the tail again. "Let's go. You woke me with a great desire to get out. Now it's my turn to urge you on!"

"But that voice – it's ahead of us!"

"The exit to the outside world is ahead of us too!" Will said firmly, although his heart trembled and his steps weren't so sure.

The wailing trailed off and died into silence. Will intently listened as he stepped along the slippery, rocky bed of the creek, but no more wailings were heard, and he sighed with relief a couple of steps later.

"Do you think it's a ghost?" Qu Sith asked.

"No," Will kept on going. "It sounds more like someone who has been badly hurt."

"You think that voice is human?"

"I don't know," Will shrugged in the darkness. "I'm not an expert. What does your predator instinct say?"

"It's silent," the beast sighed. "I need to hunt to make sure I've still got it."

"You'll be able to do that as soon as we get out."

"Unless some bloodthirsty ghost gets us first!"

Will was about to voice an objection, but Qu Sith cut him with a sudden cry, "Watch out!"

Will bent down instinctively and looked around. It was as dark as before.

"What was that?"

"A ball of fire attacked us! It's gone now..." Qu Sith sighed.

"I didn't see anything," Will chuckled a bit nervously. "It's your imagination!"

"Did you just call me a liar?" the sphinx snarled.

"No, of course, not," Will said firmly. "But when there's nothing around but darkness, you see things that aren't really there."

"Do you see them?"

"Maybe... Sometimes..."

"How do you know if those things aren't real?"

"You don't scream at them."

Qu Sith considered that notion for some time as they resumed their slow walk. "That's a brilliant idea," the sphinx admitted at last. "If you see something and I see the same thing – then it's real. If you don't see what I see – then it's my imagination! You're surprisingly wise, human!"

Will shrugged and blushed, but that wasn't visible in the dark. "Just tell me if you see something," he suggested. "We can safely move on if I don't see it."

"And you tell me when you see something, please," the sphinx said. "We won't miss any real danger then!"

"Great! Let's go..."

And they went. Will listened carefully, but that mournful wailing never came again. The way was difficult and slippery, and a few times, they had to go around the large crags since Qu Sith refused to step into the water, and Will was suddenly afraid to let the beast's tail go.

"Do you see the glowing green ring ahead?" the sphinx asked when Will's feet touched the water again.

"No."

"Good! Then it's my imagination. We may go on!"

They carried on, exchanging remarks every few hundred paces.

"Did you see that yellow orb on the right?"

"No!"

"Good!"

At first, it was frightening, but later it seemed funny. They even laughed at the things their imaginations created for them in the gloom.

"That orange flash on the left?"

"No. Ha, ha!"

"Ha, ha, ha!"

The passage was still arduous, but now they had cheered up a little by poking fun at their visions. They carried on for almost an hour, giggling. The predator's instinct of Qu Sith surfaced several times, and he began moaning about making too much noise but, just a few steps later, the chuckling and giggling took the upper hand again – it was dark, completely dark – *who on earth would want to live here?*

"That purple circle on the left?"

"No! Ha!"

"That faint silver cloud on the right?"

"No! Wait... Still, no! Ha, ha!"

"That red spark ahead?"

Qu Sith stopped. "I see that red spark too," he whispered. "It looks like a flame, not a spark."

Will frowned. Indeed, it looked like a small flame a few hundred paces ahead. They waited. The flame didn't move nor fade away.

"What shall we do now?" Qu Sith asked in a low voice.

"Let's get closer," Will suggested. "Carefully."

And they sneaked forward, stepping carefully and barely breathing. The flame could mean anything, but if it was one of those flaming caterpillars, they only had the shallow creek for their protection.

Will stepped forward slowly, his eyes fixed on the now clearly distinct flame dancing among the sleek rocks. He was ready to dash into the water at the sign of the slightest danger, but the flame didn't change its position, nor did more flames appear. His right hand still was clutching the tail of the sphinx, and he had to tug it as the beast kept stopping every few steps and carefully sniffing the air.

There were no sounds, or at least they couldn't hear anything.

"I can smell burning tar," Qu Sith whispered, "and something else I can't recognise."

"Let's get closer," Will answered. "Carefully."

And they crept on, quietly like two shadows. A few crags were in their path, but now the flickering flame shone in front of them like a distant lighthouse, and it wasn't the stormy sea they were crossing – the floor of the tunnel was dusty but even and they no longer needed the creek as their guide.

The rocky walls of the corridor emerged from the gloom as they got closer to the light.

"It's a torch," Will said and stopped. "A flaming torch!"

"You can let go of my tail," Qu Sith replied quietly. "Whoever brought that torch here might see us. I don't want to face any public humiliation."

"I don't see anyone around," Will observed. The torch had been dropped on the rocks, and its flame crackled softly, spitting out occasional sparks.

"I don't see anyone either," Qu Sith remarked. "But I can smell a human."

"I'm a human," Will reminded him.

"I know," the sphinx sighed. "It's a different smell. Your smell is musky, and that smell is acrid. I can tell the difference!"

They crept forward a few more paces. Will peered into the darkness beyond the light but couldn't see anything – not a shadow moved there. He couldn't hear anything either but the soft ripple of water in the creek.

"We were too noisy," the sphinx said. "They dropped the torch and ran away. We scared them."

"That's good news," Will mumbled. "Now we're sure the exit is near."

"But they might be preparing an ambush!"

"Anyway, whoever they are – they already know we're here," Will sighed.

"I only hope we don't fall into the hands of some more religious fanatics. I've had enough of sitting in a cage," Qu Sith said, stepping into the circle of light.

"Who knows?" Will sighed, following the beast. "It seems this world has an endless supply of idiots."

"They are not idiots."

"But they are dangerous."

Will picked the torch up.

"Why did you do that?" Qu Sith frowned.

"I'm tired of stumbling around in the dark," Will said firmly. "Rybbaths or no Rybbaths, I'm going to light my way as long as this torch is burning."

"As you wish," the sphinx stepped along the corridor. "Be prepared to think really fast if there *is* an ambush."

They went for another hour, watching their steps and peering into the darkness ahead. Everything seemed quiet, but the burning torch in Will's hand was a grim reminder that somebody knew that they were approaching. The thought was unsettling, and the tension in Will's head grew with each step he took, forcing his heart to race faster.

Qu Sith seemed increasingly agitated as well. The beast went a few steps in front of Will, now and then cautiously sniffing the air.

"That human wasn't alone. I can smell a few distinct odours," the sphinx whispered, and Will noticed the fur on the beast's back rising. "Are you sure we're doing the right thing?"

"Once, I was told that it's better to regret what I've done than regret what I didn't," Will shrugged. "I don't think we have too many options here. We're following the only way out. Let's hope those humans are more scared than us."

"Hope is a bad adviser, human," Qu Sith spat but didn't stop.

"Please, enlighten me if you have better ideas," Will said. "I hope you've got no plans to live in the darkness and wait until whoever or whatever mummified those rats comes after you. May I remind you that we have only water here..."

Will's voice trailed off as the tunnel ended unexpectedly in a large cavern. Qu Sith stopped.

Will quickly eyed the view – never in his life had he seen anything more grandiose. The cavern was no less than five hundred paces across, dimly lit by grey daylight that slipped in through a narrow slit in the ceiling.

It was no ordinary cavern – that was clear even with the scarce light they had. A grand colonnade held the pressure of the mountain on the left – the rose marble with white streaks, once magnificent, was now cracked and dusty but still stood proudly against the waves of black basalt. The marble floor, once laid in mosaic patterns, was now littered with chunks of crumbled stone. White marble statues were lined up on the right – a few still intact and magnificent, but most were broken. The window slits behind them, once opening onto sunlit gardens or distant mountains, were now blocked by black waves of solid rock. High ceilings, once painted with vibrant murals, were now cracked and faded.

The place looked like an abandoned place of worship. A wide dais was at the far end of the grotto with a giant sphinx statue carved out of black stone. Its back had been brutally destroyed by the partially collapsed ceiling. The statue's eyes glistened red even in the gloomy dusk, reflecting the flickering light of the torch with thousands of sparks. A tall pillar of black basalt rose high next to the statute, just below the crack where the flow of lava had spilt in and had frozen into a bizarre, elongated shape.

"Doesn't that statue look exactly like you?" Will whispered – it seemed inappropriate to be noisy in this place, holding his torch high and looking around with wide eyes.

"Nonsense!" Qu Sith cut him. "All sphinxes seem similar only to human eyes. It's not even close!"

Will shrugged but didn't dare to argue. "What is this place?" he asked.

It looked like a cathedral caught in the tight grip of stiffening lava. Fires had raged here long ago where the heat touched the flammable furniture; now, just a layer of soot marked the spot.

"I think we've arrived in Per Hathor," Qu Sith sighed, the tension growing in his voice. "This is a bit unexpected and greatly premature."

"Why?"

"You haven't found your damned blue flower!" the sphinx hissed.

"I don't think that you should rush into mating straight out of the caves," Will shrugged. "You need to have some rest and get to know your bride better. Then you need to have a wedding. The mating only happens on the first night after the wedding."

"Why?"

"To make your relationship official and your offspring legitimate."

"You never mentioned that the mating traditions were so

complicated. Why do you need to do all that?"

"I don't know. It's like some kind of guarantee of quality, I guess," Will blushed. "Everybody does it."

"Stupid traditions of stupid humans," Qu Sith moaned.

"Maybe sphinxes have different traditions?"

"Stupid sphinxes follow the stupid traditions of stupid humans to satisfy the human bits of our nature!"

"It's madness."

"I know..."

"But it can give you a credible reason to postpone your mating for a while until I find that blue orchid."

"That sounds like a plan," Qu Sith nodded thoughtfully. "If you don't run off with your flower."

"Have I ever left you behind?"

"No. That's why I still trust you."

"Then let's go," Will offered. "We have a perfect plan that needs to be implemented."

"We have a small problem here..."

The creek that had guided them entered the hall on the left and, a few paces later, disappeared into a crack in the floor, leaving them on their own. Will looked around. Four dark openings, gaping open in the distant stone wall, led out of the cavern. It was time for them to choose.

"Can you still follow that smell?" Will asked.

"Of course, I can!" the sphinx felt offended. "I just don't understand why you want to run into the hands of those people when you have three other options?"

"That trail surely leads to the way out," Will said. "Other options may end in a worse situation than the one that's waiting for us outside. We could die in those tunnels without even the slightest glimpse of the sun. And we would be wasting time in trying – somebody else could pick up my orchid, and then your mating difficulties would be your problem, dear sphinx."

"I don't want to get captured," Qu Sith mumbled, sniffing the air cautiously. "Not again."

"This time, we know they're stalking us," Will patted the back of the beast. "We'll move slowly and very carefully. They won't catch us off guard. And then we'll need to think something up rather quickly. We'll be prepared."

"Are you sure we're doing the right thing?"

"No. But we must get out. Let's follow those people. Carefully. We could come back at any time and try another way if we spot any danger."

"Very well," Qu Sith sighed. "Let's do as you say. Just remember my objections when we're sitting in a cage."

The sphinx raised his head and sniffed the air again. "Dirty humans," he squeezed through his teeth disdainfully. "What are they eating? They smell like pigs!"

"Remember your oath?" Will reminded him.

"I'm not feeble-minded," Qu Sith reminded Will as he slowly stepped forward, still sniffing. "But we might get to kill a few if we have to fight."

"Let's hope we won't need to fight if we run fast enough. All we need to do is to get out."

They quietly crossed the entire grotto. Will kept glancing around. He couldn't get rid of the feeling that the sparkling red eyes of the statue followed them.

Qu Sith stopped in front of one of the openings. "They went out that way," he said.

"Let's follow them quietly," Will urged, raising the torch. "It must be close. I don't think they had wandered half a day underground."

"Wishful thinking, human," Qu Sith stepped forward into the corridor. "You don't know Per Hathor. They might have been wandering here a few days. They might be as lost as we are. We can only hope to get closer to the surface by following them."

And they went. It was easier with the torch as they could now see their way, and Will was glad to be able to keep his feet dry. Now and then, they stopped and listened carefully, but even the sharp ears of the sphinx couldn't pick up the sound of any retreating footsteps or other noise.

"Are you sure we picked the right passage?" Will asked an

hour later.

"Yes, the stench here is even stronger than before," the beast answered without slowing down. "We're getting close."

The corridor – with multiple bends and turns that weaved a pattern Will couldn't understand – was full of obstacles. Piles of rubble and broken statues barred the way with the barely discernible path winding between them. Some walls were swollen, hanging at impossible angles. Some had collapsed, yielding to the pressure of the wave of black basalt. They even passed a few basins of the previously glorious fountains, now empty and filled with dust.

It was much easier to go with the light they had, but their happy strolling ended an hour later. The torch flickered and went out, leaving them in the darkness again.

"Shit!" Qu Sith cursed loudly. "I'd almost got used to that little bit of luxury..."

"We must keep going," Will dropped the useless torch on the ground. "Outside must be near if you chose the right corridor."

"This corridor is the right one. Have no doubts," the sphinx mumbled. "But now you must lead. I can't lean on the wall, and it is the only guide we now have."

"Well..." Will sighed, stretching out his right arm and touching the wall with his fingertips. "Let's go then..."

"Do you mind grabbing my tail?" asked the beast. "I don't

want to wander off in the darkness."

They sneaked forward as quietly as they could. This time there were no giggles or jokes. The way was arduous. With complete darkness and so many obstacles in their way, they stumbled and struggled with each step. A few times, Will almost fell, but his grip on the sphinx's tail helped him regain the balance.

At first, Qu Sith just sighed and snorted, but the beast exploded after one more painful tug: "That hurts!" he roared. "Don't do it again!"

"Sorry," Will apologised. "It's easier for you to keep your balance – you've got four legs!"

"Just be careful with my tail," Qu Sith snarled, but Will ignored him entirely. A faint, barely visible grey face glared at them from the dark just several paces away.

Will froze. "Do you see that?" he asked quietly. He had no idea if the beast was gazing in the same direction, but Qu Sith gasped.

They stood motionless for several long minutes. The face didn't move either.

"Stupid human!" spat out the sphinx at last. "It's a damned statue!"

"But why can we *see* it?" Will demanded.

"Must be some damned crack in the wall," Qu Sith said disdainfully. "Can't you see that, stupid?"

"We're getting closer to the surface!" Will grinned in the dark, ignoring the insult. "We might get out before dusk!"

The sphinx was silent for a few seconds, considering the thought. "Let's go," he mumbled at last. "We need to be more careful as now we're so close. Whoever is waiting outside mustn't get their hands on us."

They passed the ghostly face of the statue, and Will had to brush away a bunch of cobwebs, hoping that the spiders were away. They carried on slowly and silently. Will probed the way with his feet, trying to avoid stumbling on anything. Qu Sith sighed each time Will's grip on his tail tightened.

A few hundred paces and several bends in the path later, they found another crack in the wall. It was slightly larger, and Will caught a glimpse of the purple sky. The evening was nearing, and he realised that they must speed up to get out of the caves before dusk.

The cracks became more frequent as they went, and the darkness was no longer absolute. Will got a glimpse of a slit, no larger than a foot, high above his head in the ceiling, teasing them with the purple sky and part of a pink coloured cloud.

"I can see the way," Qu Sith announced.

"Still too dark for me," Will complained.

"Then hold on to my tail, and let's move faster!"

Qu Sith hurried forward. Will almost ran after him. It was still ghostly dusk to his eyes, and Will cursed silently as the haste left him with no time to even think about how to place his feet safely. The sphinx bent around all the bigger obstacles without slowing down, and Will just gasped, stumbling on small pebbles but somehow maintaining his balance.

Slowly it was getting brighter even to Will's eyes. Black bulging walls emerged on both sides of the corridor, seemingly engulfing the white marble colonnade on the left. The wall on the right had many cracks, and he was about to release the sphinx's tail when Qu Sith stopped abruptly.

"What is it?" Will asked.

"Shut up!" the sphinx spat angrily. "Listen!"

Will kept his ears sharp but couldn't hear anything at first. Obviously, the hearing of the sphinx was much better. He waited.

The sound came like a distant sigh at first. Then it rose to the harmonious heights of a melody as if a large crowd somewhere far away were singing their hearts out. Will couldn't make out the words. He only stood and listened to the magnificent melody rising and falling, luring them closer.

"What is it?" Will whispered.

"I don't know," Qu Sith said. "A hymn or a chant. I'm not familiar with all the nuances of human religion."

"Do you think it's religious?"

"Why else do humans sing?"

Qu Sith sniffed the air and took a few steps forward.

"Do you think it's safe to go there?" Will asked hesitantly. "Probably, there is a crowd!"

"Probably not," the beast whispered. "But let's have a careful look. Maybe we can make a plan how to break through them."

"Let's have a look, at least," Will shrugged and followed the sphinx. "I don't think it will be difficult to spot the singing ambush in plenty of time."

They went down the corridor, slowly emerging from the darkest dark into the flecks of purple and red of the evening dusk. Every twelve paces on the left, white marble statues lined the wall, depicting nude men and women in heroic poses. Most of them were broken, but a few were still intact and seemed to follow Will with their hollow pupils.

The chant grew louder as they sneaked forward, and the words became clearer. It was a magnificent hymn about the lost king who had wandered the dangerous lands searching for a way home. It was a sad story since the road was long, the obstacles the king encountered were great, and the dangers were deadly.

They sneaked closer and closer to the bright spot where the corridor ended between the broken statues. Will carefully peered over the rubble to the large amphitheatre that lay beneath. It was full of strangely dressed people in dark red cloaks, holding flaming torches high and chanting. All were facing the dais in front of the corridor mouth where the big empty throne, its seat too large for any human, faced the crowd. It seemed impossible to sneak away without attracting attention.

"I don't know how to get out of here unnoticed," Will whispered, his eyes still on the singers, searching. "Maybe, if we could just go back and wait until they've finished whatever they're doing?"

"That could take weeks if not months," Qu Sith whispered back. "Humans are quite stubborn when it comes to religion."

"We need another plan," Will sighed.

More singers joined the crowd as they spoke, passing freshly lit torches to replace those whose flames had faded. The chant now sounded stronger and more heroic as they sang about the great battles of the king.

Qu Sith took a careful peek at the crowd too. His face wore a deeply disappointed expression when he looked back at Will. "This could last ages unless we cause a bit of action," he said.

Will shrugged. He had no idea how any action could disperse the crowd and produce the turmoil necessary for their escape. He carefully peered out again, but his gaze now wandered to the left where the enormously large throne sat on a dais, flanked by two columns of white marble at its back.

A low altar of black basalt was in front of the throne, with two iron firepits blazing at each side. An old man with a strangely shaped brown hat stood in front of the altar, dressed in a long crimson tunic and holding a knife in his right hand. His left hand was high above his head as he directed the crowd.

"Stupid humans with their stupid religion again," Qu Sith mumbled, peering over Will's shoulder. "I guess he won't eat that girl? It must be only a performance?"

Will tore his eyes from the crowd and took a better look at the altar. A naked girl was lying on top with her arms and legs tied with red ribbons to the snake figurines carved out of the black rock of the altar. Her body looked lean and fragile, and her pale skin seemed almost blue against the deep blackness of the stone.

"Shit!" he gasped. "They're going to sacrifice her!"

"It's their stupid religion and none of our business," Qu Sith observed. "Stay low, or they'll pin your butt on that altar too."

The girl didn't scream or cry. She barely moved, probably drugged, and the chanting continued. Will's glances darted between her and the crowd, desperately searching for a way out of this madness, but nothing useful caught his eye. No realistic plans brewed in his head either.

"Qu'mun Almighty, God of temptation!" the priest shrieked, and the chanting stopped. "Have mercy for your children! Lead them out of the darkness!"

"Shit!" Will said in a low voice. "Let's go back! I don't like this."

"There's an arch on the left that's unguarded and unoccupied," whispered the sphinx, peering again. "That priest who is leading the ceremony looks rather frail. If we make our appearance sudden and unexpected and succeed in knocking the priest over, maybe we could slip through that arch fast enough without getting caught. I see woods behind it where we could lose anyone in pursuit."

"It's too risky."

"I know," the beast agreed. "Do you see any better options?"

Will was silent for too long. He was about to propose returning to the darkness and seeking a way out through another corridor but didn't have the chance to open his mouth.

"Run!" Qu Sith jumped forward onto the dais and roared with all his might.

Will had no time to check on the priest as he sprinted towards the arch as fast as he could without any preparation. He didn't reach it. Three bulky men in red cloaks pinned him down to the floor halfway to the arch.

Will couldn't see much of what was happening on the dais from where he was pinned or whether Qu Sith had succeeded in escaping. He couldn't understand what was happening as the whole red crowd dropped to their knees, including the men holding him, although their grip didn't relax one bit.

A few tense minutes passed in silence, disturbed only by the soft crackle of the flaming torches. Then the priest began to sing in his trembling old man's voice. Seconds later, everybody around was chanting. The melody was magnificent, rising high above the crowd and then falling. Will couldn't see any proceedings, but the ceremony didn't seem to have been much disturbed by their appearance.

The hymn faded with short echoes escaping through the underground corridors.

"Arise, my people," he heard the low voice speaking. There was a muffled shuffle of cloaks as the crowd rose to their feet. Then he heard the priest speaking again, but the crowd's murmur drowned out his voice – all Will could make out was the word *slave* repeated a few times.

"He's not a slave! On the contrary, he's my essential companion," he heard the sphinx shouting angrily. "Bring him to me at once!"

The priest gestured, and the red-dressed men lifted Will to his feet. To his surprise, Qu Sith was sitting on the throne, and an enormous golden chain, decorated with blue and red gems, hung around his neck. His fur was raised, and his eyes darted around, but the throne was surrounded by people dressed in red paying their respects. The beast had no way of escaping.

The girl on the altar was dead, her body had been cut wide open, and the priest's hands were elbow-deep in her chest. The old man paid no attention to Will, mumbling his prayers and tugging at something inside the body as the crowd watched in grim silence.

Will's captors pushed him to his knees in front of the throne Qu Sith growled impatiently and rolled his eyes.

"Arise, human, and come closer," the sphinx said loudly. "I want you by my side."

Someone wrapped a red cloak around Will as he rose to his feet. They made way for him to pass through.

"I guess we're deeper in this shit than we can imagine," the sphinx whispered in a frightened voice as Will came close enough to hear. "I've no idea what they want."

"They're treating you like a king," Will observed.

"I don't know what will happen when they find out I'm not their king!"

Will frowned, hoping that their quick exchange hadn't been overheard. He moved to the left side of the throne, trying to keep his eyes away from the gory body.

The priest turned around, his hands bloody red, holding a golden plate upon which lay the girl's heart, still trembling.

"Your majesty must be hungry after the long journey," a smile curled his lips as he bowed and extended the plate to Qu Sith. "Please, have a small offering from your humble servants."

The eyes of the sphinx darted towards Will before focusing on the heart. The crowd watched silently.

"Was she a virgin?" Qu Sith asked, at last, uncertainly.

"Yes, of course, your majesty," the priest nodded. "How could we dare to offer you something of inferior quality. I checked that myself!"

Qu Sith carefully sniffed the air and then darted another glance at Will. "And you think I'd be foolish enough to take part in your blasphemy?" the sphinx roared unexpectedly. "You sacrificed a virgin to Qu'mun! Then you must burn her properly! This heart is meant for Qu'mun! I won't steal from the Gods!"

The crooked smile slowly faded from the priest's face. He bowed before turning around and carefully placing the plate on the girl's body. Then he slowly lifted his bloodied arms to the sky. "Qu'mun almighty, God of Temptation, please, accept this simple offering from your children!" the priest screeched above the noise of the crowd. "We thank you for sending us the King!"

He passed his blood-dripping hands over his head, and only then did Will realise that it wasn't a hat he was wearing. The elaborate snake on his head was made from his own hair, shaped with hardened blood. He carefully rubbed his palms into the coiled tangle and then bowed his head in front of the offering. The crowd fell silent.

"You heard his majesty!" the priest barked at his aides around the altar. "Take her to the pits!"

For a few moments, he watched the men wrapping the body in

a piece of red cloth and carrying it away. Then he turned around to face the sphinx again, red droplets still rolling down his cheeks.

"You must be tired, your majesty," said the priest, and the wry smile returned to his face. "We've prepared your chambers for your arrival."

"Thank you, good man," Qu Sith said. "But I'm not sure if I heard your name correctly. Was it Cry?"

"Kroy, your majesty," the man bowed.

"Are you the priest of this temple, Kroy?" asked the sphinx.

"This is not a temple, your majesty," the old man replied. "It is what was left of your palace. We prayed hard and sacrificed many to direct the flows of Patna away from Per Hathor, and Qu'mun almighty answered our prayers."

"Indeed. I'm pleased, very pleased..." Qu Sith mumbled, although his voice had an ironic edge. "How did you know I was coming, by the way?"

"The Oracle of the Weeping Rock told us," the priest said. "And we hastened to make preparations."

"What exactly did the Oracle tell you?"

"*He is coming, and he will avenge*, your majesty," Kroy bowed. "Those were the exact words! It was the first prophecy of hope since the death of the Queen."

"Is the Queen dead?" Qu Sith nearly jumped off the throne.

"Sadly, yes, your majesty," Kroy nodded. "The Queen fell like a hero in a fight with the sky monster a few days ago."

"Fallen…" the eyes of the sphinx grew moist.

"We're preparing for the funeral, your majesty," Kroy said. "Your arrival is most timely."

Kroy's talk was interrupted by another hymn as the crowd stepped back a little, leaving some empty space in front of the dais.

"We have prepared your feast, your Majesty," said Kroy as the chanting stopped. "Proper food, fit for the King!"

"What is it?"

Kroy waved, and the crowd stepped back a little further, letting a young girl in her late teens dressed in crimson red pass through them. Two men followed her. They held nothing in their hands.

Qu Sith squirmed on the throne as the men removed the robes from the girl and stepped away. Will paled, slowly realising what was happening.

The girl held her back straight, slightly shivering, with her gaze fixed on something high above. Tears pooled in her blue eyes and rolled down her cheeks. The crowd fell silent again – all eyes fixed upon the sphinx.

Qu Sith stepped down from the throne and slowly approached the girl. Her white body looked incredibly pale in front of the crowd, all dressed in red. The sphinx carried on walking around, carefully sniffing the air. Will looked away.

"Very nice specimen, indeed," crooned the beast at last. "Sadly, I ate my fill of meat only recently, and I wouldn't like to spoil such beauty with any inadequate nibbling. That doesn't diminish your sacrifice, dear, but please, get dressed and go away before I change my mind. Do you have some mashed parsnips?"

A murmur passed through the crowd as Qu Sith returned to the throne. He stopped in front of Kroy just briefly. "Thanks for your trouble, but I don't want to waste a loyal servant when I'm already full," he said to the priest. "But a few parsnips would be nice."

"You heard what the King said!" Kroy gestured impatiently.

The girl got dressed and hurried away. A few minutes later, she brought a large tray of parsnips as Qu Sith had requested.

"Feed him first. He's my taster," the sphinx gestured at Will. "I don't want to be poisoned."

The girl didn't say a word and dutifully stepped to the left. Suddenly Will felt weak at the knees and sat down on the floor, leaning against the throne. *Could it indeed be poisoned?* The girl seemed frightened. She quickly placed the tray in front of Will and stepped away.

Will glanced at Qu Sith unsurely.

"Eat it!" the sphinx hissed quietly. "My guts are full, and that battle is still going. But you haven't eaten anything."

"But…" Will began to protest.

"Eat it! You're my official food taster," the sphinx cut him short and added, in a whisper, "Leave me a few bits, please."

Will hesitantly probed the mash. It tasted bland with just a mild hint of sour cream, but nothing seemed suspicious. The whole crowd waited as he ate. Then they waited a little more.

Will stood up and placed the tray in front of the sphinx. "Your turn," he winked and whispered. "I think we're together in this."

Qu Sith frowned but tried the parsnips. He didn't eat much, though.

"It's getting late, and we're tired after our long journey," he addressed Kroy. "Could you show us to my chambers?"

"Is your… food taster sleeping with you, your Majesty?" the priest asked.

"I'm tired, and he might be handy," the sphinx shrugged. "Is there a problem with that?"

"No problem, your Majesty," the priest tried to hide his embarrassment behind a smile. "But we have many concubines to attend to all your needs. And you may eat one at any point if you feel hungry."

"That won't be necessary," Qu Sith growled. "I'm tired and would like some rest. Just sleep."

"Of course, your majesty! Please, follow me," Kroy turned around and headed into the depths of the half-destroyed palace.

Qu Sith went after him, closely followed by Will, leaving the silent crowd behind. The corridors were dark, with most of the windows blocked with black rock and the only dim light coming from occasional torches. They followed the old priest who limped on with enviable strength. They climbed the stairs a few times, headed up, then turned right and stopped at a large wooden door. It was the King's chambers – Will could tell that by the concubines lined against the wall on the right. Qu Sith barely glanced at them.

"Your Majesty," Kroy opened the door and let them in. "If you need anything, just tell the concubines."

"When is the funeral of the Queen?" asked the sphinx, glancing around the spacious room with a window facing the remnants of the forest.

"Tomorrow, your Majesty, if you please," said the priest and bowed away. "The rollers have already been sent. We didn't know when you would come but if you need more time to mourn, just say."

Will watched as the priest went out and closed the door behind him. A few indistinct words were spoken in the corridor, and then the footsteps limped to the right, trailing away.

"Looks like we're sitting in a golden cage now. What shall we do?" Will asked, glancing through the window. The ground was far down below – they were in a tower. "We're trapped here."

"It's not an entirely bad situation," Qu Sith mumbled, circling the massive bed. "And they have an Oracle here. That might help you to find the flower. Sadly, that flower won't help me anymore."

"Why?"

"I think the Queen was a sphinx – that's why they promoted me to royalty so quickly," Qu Sith sighed sadly. "If she's dead, there's no way for me to have any offspring."

"We'll find out tomorrow."

"Yes," the sphinx crawled onto the bed. "We'll find out tomorrow."

There were no other beds in the room, and Will glanced around uncertainly. The sphinx didn't seem to notice.

"I'll sleep on the floor," Will decided.

"If that suits you," Qu Sith mumbled. "You can take one of those concubines if you need somebody to lull you into sleep."

Will ignored the remark. "Honestly, I thought you would tear that girl apart," he said, trying to make himself comfortable in the far corner.

"I remembered my oath," Qu Sith sighed. "Don't worry."

The night fell upon the world, and not much was visible through the window – the silver giant in the sky was covered with clouds, and the ground was almost completely dark. Will had trouble falling to sleep. He listened to the quiet breathing of the sphinx and tried hard to find any excuse to leave Ben's flat without upsetting the guy. Found none. Then he drifted away to the land of nod without even noticing.

❧ ❦ ✿ ❦ ☙

Will was lying flat in the hallway – a pillow carefully slipped under his head and his muscular body wrapped in a blanket. It was still in the early hours, and Ben was probably sleeping in his bed. Will yawned and stretched his body. *Damn!* Ben had taken care of him even when he had been so rude.

He got up quietly and rolled the blanket around the pillow. It was strange to sleep in a hallway but no worse than sleeping in a bin. Will went into the kitchen and sat down at the empty table facing the window. Not much was visible here either – a large tree obscured the view. Its branches were dark against the pale grey sky of the breaking day, and Will stared at the barely shivering leaves, wondering what to do next.

He was out of the caves and not in any imminent danger in Rehen, but his quest to find the blue orchid was still far from complete. Nevertheless, he felt stuck in London, and the situation was becoming more grotesque with each passing day. He kept bumping into weird people with their weird delusions, each telling him what to do. Those weird people were strangely obsessed with that Sanctuary – a place, Will was sure, might not even exist. *Where could it be safer than home?* The thought squeezed Will's heart as he remembered his mother preparing a Sunday roast or chasing him around the house with a plate of food. A shy tear rolled down his right cheek, and Will quickly brushed it away, but the pain didn't go away that easily. His heart remained squeezed with icy pliers, and he had to shed a few more tears to ease this. *He must see them. He must see his mother and his sister!* He must embrace them, no matter what! How could some crazy woman erase him from his family? Will didn't believe that. He couldn't believe that. It was just that crazy woman's delusion – a lie!

He wasn't alone for long. A shuffling behind his back told him that Ben was up. Will quickly wiped away the remnants of moisture from his face and turned around. Ben was an even bigger mess than Will. His eyes were red, and his face was swollen – he had probably cried almost all night. His hair was ruffled like a magpie's nest, and the stubble on his face needed shaving. Ben had a blanket wrapped around him and sneaked into the kitchen like a ghost.

"We both need a big mug of coffee," he sighed after a short greeting.

Will said nothing. He silently watched Ben at the stove, getting something out of the fridge, mixing something, preparing. He didn't really notice what the guy was doing, in fact, nor did he care. Again, it seemed as though his life was slipping away and didn't belong to him anymore. Somebody else was deciding for him, telling him what to do and where to go, while his mother was probably crying her eyes out, worrying for him. He felt guilty.

Only then he realised that Ben was talking.

"It's a pity Eric didn't leave any notes," the doctor said, mixing something in a pan. "But I've got a few thoughts on where to begin the search. We need to make a few enquiries but, I guess we won't succeed until we find another Sleeper who knows where it is. This quest is dangerous, I must warn you. We must be very careful... Here!"

Ben placed two mugs of black coffee and two plates of scrambled eggs on the table. "Eat this," he gestured. "It might be a long day."

Will picked up a fork and began to eat, not giving it too much thought.

"Thank you for taking care of me," Will quickly said before the young doctor could open his mouth again.

"I decided not to risk moving you – you're too heavy," Ben sighed and apologised. "I'm sorry you had to spend the night on the floor. I hope I didn't disturb your sleep."

"I've got used to harsh conditions recently," Will observed bitterly.

Ben shrugged. "I know," he sighed. "You need to find the Sanctuary, and your life will become much easier."

"Do you still believe that shit?" he asked. "That woman blatantly lied just because she was afraid. We were too brave for her!"

"Your belief doesn't change the fact that Eric is gone and you're away from your home, forgotten," Ben said, frowning.

"If you believe that those freaks drilled into my mother's brain and cut me out of there somehow," Will didn't notice that his voice had gained more decibels. "Then maybe they drilled into your brain and messed around in there too – implanted that crazy thought about a non-existent Sanctuary. Maybe Eric would be sitting here now, sipping coffee with you if not for those crazy thoughts? Now he's wandering around somewhere, looking for something that doesn't even exist! I admit I made a big mistake discharging myself from the hospital and getting on a train to London. Huge mistake! My mother is angry, and I'm stuck here. I need to go home, not further away from home. I'm not going to search for some non-existent place. No need for that. And it would be better if you woke up too. Maybe it's not too late to get Eric back."

Ben placed his mug on the table. His eyes were big, and his lips twitched – it seemed he was about to burst into tears again.

"Sorry…" Will placed his mug on the table too.

"I understand your doubts," Ben said quietly, staring at his coffee. "You know so little that ignorance becomes natural to you. But you can't ignore the real danger."

"What danger?" Will lowered his voice too. "I've got a vivid imagination, but I see no danger beyond that."

"Death is real – in this world or another. You need other Sleepers to help you."

"It's a stupid game, and I won't play it."

"It's not a game. You might die in those caves!"

"I'm out of those caves if you have my dreams in your mind," Will shrugged. "And I don't need any help with *my dreams*."

Ben gazed at his coffee a little too long, and Will began to wonder if he was having one of those fits. "I'm glad," he said at last. "That buys us some time."

"Time for what?"

"Time to find the Sanctuary."

Will sighed and shook his head. "I won't do this," he said, quietly but firmly. "You can choose to believe that crazy woman. I won't try to talk you out of it. Please, stop telling me that my family don't remember me. My mother is just angry. That will pass. She just needs time. I must get back. There's no safer place than home."

"How did they get Eric then?"

"Was he at home?" Will parried. "Of course, he wasn't. You wouldn't be asking some crazy lady what happened to him – you'd know."

Ben blushed bright red and swallowed.

"Did Eric ever even exist?" Will couldn't hold back his tongue. "If that woman is as powerful as you say, maybe she invented Eric and inserted him into your brain to torment you?"

Ben blushed even more but, before he could open his mouth and say anything, his body grew stiff and his face expressionless. A tear rolled down his right cheek, but he didn't lift his hand to wipe it off.

A fit! The thought flashed through Will's mind as he stared at the guy. Then he ate his scrambled eggs, drank his coffee, licked his lips and stuck out his tongue when he had finished eating.

Ben's face remained expressionless. They sat for several long minutes staring at each other. Then the young doctor slumped on the table, spilling his coffee.

Will jumped to his feet. The guy moaned, struggling to lift his torso from the spillage of the hot brew, and Will rushed to help. He lifted Ben easily like a doll in his muscular arms, wrapped him in the blanket and carried him to the bedroom. The eyes of the guy still aimlessly wandered around. The fit was over, but Ben was still struggling to get back to his normal self and needed some rest. He put him down on the bed and sat down on the floor next to it, waiting.

Nearly twenty minutes passed before Ben moaned again. "What happened?" he asked, still wrapped in the blanket.

"You had a fit. A bad one," Will said from where he sat. "Honestly, I think you need to go and see a doctor."

"I am a doctor," the guy mumbled, still a bit drowsy.

"You can't treat yourself, though, can you?" Will shrugged. "See a proper doctor. They'll give you some pill or an injection, and you'll be fine."

"If only it were that easy…"

"Have you tried?"

Ben just sighed. "I need to take a shower. I look terrible," he said after a short pause. "We must go to South London to get a few leads to find the Sanctuary."

"I'm not going, sorry," Will said firmly, getting up. "It's a waste of time, and I need to find a way to get home."

Ben looked at him, undisguised horror in his eyes. "You might die there…"

"So be it. You need to fight your demons, and I need to fight mine," Will said, avoiding Ben's gaze. "I must go."

"Did I offend you?"

"No," Will shook his head. "But I've no time for your

delusions. I must solve my own problems."

"I'm just trying to help you with this."

"No offence, but imaginary problems can only have imaginary solutions," Will shrugged. "I must get my real life back. You can't help me with that, but I thank you for what you have done."

Ben was about to object but thought better of it and just watched silently as Will packed his rucksack. "You're welcome back at any time if you change your mind," he uttered. "You know my address."

Will left without saying another word. He felt ungrateful but could stay no longer. Not with Ben trying to direct him away from home. Never had he felt more homesick than at that moment in Ben's kitchen when he thought about his weeping mother. He *must* get back home. Even if he had to walk all the way across the country. Even if he had to sleep rough again.

The street met him with the chill of the morning. Thin strands of fog still wandered here and there, and the grass was damp with drops of dew. Large droplets splashed down from the tree canopy above him, and Will couldn't decide if it was raining or just morning dew that had condensed on the leaves and was now falling. He pulled his hood up and went down the street, hunching over. He felt like the Titanic leaving the port of Southampton on its maiden voyage – big, strong but afraid of the yet unknown menace that was waiting ahead. He was homeless again.

Will turned left onto the main road and began his slow journey. He had no idea where he was but decided that going with the flow was the most appropriate approach. He decided to check his savings first. He still had a faint hope that his mother had read the letter and made the bank transfer.

He found a cash machine several hundred yards down the road, next to the underground station. But, unfortunately, it didn't deliver any good news. Will retrieved his card and sighed. He had no one he could rely on.

Will put a brave smile on his face and carried on down the street. It was crowded with the usual morning traffic of a big metropolis, and he went on trying at first to adapt to the hectic pace. An hour later, his enthusiasm had faded. He had nowhere to hurry, and his legs had begun to ache, but the street still looked no different – the houses, cafes, offices, shops all looked the same, and he had no idea of his location. A few red buses passed his way heading for the unfamiliar destinations burning in amber letters on their front screens.

Will went on, afraid to turn down any side streets, afraid to get lost completely. So far, he could retrace his way back to Ben's flat, he was almost sure. With every step, Will was less certain about his hasty decision to leave. He had a place to sleep and some food in his stomach. Now he was stepping towards the unknown, and although he wasn't sure if that was a good idea, he carried on anyway. His stubborn determination was still there. He was going to get on the train – no matter what, even if he had to sneak around the barriers or walk on the tracks, even if he had to beg on his knees for a place on the train home. The only problem was that he had no idea where that damned train station was or how to get there. It seemed pretty close to the centre of the city as far as he could remember.

Will went on, his steps now less sure. The street seemed endless, but the buildings gradually grew taller on both sides, and Will thought that was a reassuring sign. He even noticed a few skyscrapers on the left in the distance. The traffic grew more intense as he went, and Will glanced around in the hope of spotting the train station. Still, the place seemed unfamiliar.

His mother must be testing him. The thought struck like lightning, and Will stopped, still unsure how to react. She had always accused him of being too dependent on her, incapable of doing anything right on his own. That could explain her silence! *It was a test!* Will grinned – he must pass it! He must find his way back home and prove how wrong she was! He was a grown man now, able to take care of his own life. *Everything would go back to normal!* He just needed to find that damned train station!

Will crossed over to the other side of the street, hoping to get a better view of the buildings on the right. Cafes, offices, hotels appeared – still nothing that looked like a train station. His legs hurt a little, but Will wasn't prepared to slow down. Still, he was afraid to go too far off the main road and check the side streets. Half an hour later, he realised that he might cross the whole of London without finding what he had sought. *It must be the wrong street,* Will frowned, catching a glimpse of those skyscrapers at the end of a side street – the tall buildings were already behind him. He decided to find the river first and then retrace his way back to the train station. That seemed like a good plan, and he grinned, strolling at a faster pace but, a few paces later, his fear of getting lost crept back like a stray dog.

His doubts were forced to end half an hour later by the street he was following. For a few minutes, Will stood hesitantly gazing at the T-junction and then turned left, where another set of skyscrapers scratched the sky in the distance. He was sure this must represent the grandeur of the city centre.

Will spent the next few hours aimlessly wandering along the tangled, busy streets of London. He passed a few skyscrapers, but none of the places seemed to represent the centre – it was just another street, and he felt utterly lost. The day grew gloomy, with thick clouds nearly touching rooftops. Will's mood was dark too. It seemed as though he kept running round in circles, getting nowhere. Why had he left Ben's flat so hastily? He could probably have borrowed a hundred quid from the young doctor to buy his ticket home, but now he must spend days searching for the way out and suppress the spasms of hunger in his stomach and nights looking for shelter under some random shrub. It had been hours since he'd gulped down those scrambled eggs and drank his morning coffee, and Will felt his hunger rising. He cursed his stupid decisions, but that didn't bring any relief. Instead, his mood grew darker, crumbling his confidence into dust.

Still, he carried on, risking getting lost in this concrete jungle. He must find a way to return home. A night of sleeping rough on the streets beckoned ahead of him again, but he wasn't ready to go back to Ben's flat. He felt that he might drown in those irrational fantasies if he did.

He went on without selecting his way, without seeing anybody or anything. Twice he earned angry shouts from cyclists and once almost caused an accident by stepping in front of a moving car. Will barely noticed these incidents. He went on as dark as the darkest cloud, feeling lonely and abandoned. His mother had *pretended* to be angry for too long. This had never happened before, and it seemed suspicious. That damned tornado named Jill had wrecked his life, turning everyone away from him, and he was left alone to face all that dismay. Even that stupid ghost of Sheila had abandoned him entirely. Where was her advice when he needed it? Where were those best places to spend a night in London for a vagrant? He had left the safety of Ben's apartment, and now he had to find them on his own.

Small wonder was waiting for Will at the next crossroad. He had to stop and blink twice but still refused to believe his eyes. A witch, looking as wrinkled and horrible as you would expect of a witch, hovered almost three feet above the ground with her broomstick barely touching the pavement. Will was used to seeing flaming vipers and other horrible monsters in his dreams, but the sight of a witch in London was too unexpected, and he stopped, with his eyes popping and mouth gaping. The witch was frozen like a statue, with only her rags slightly moving in the light breeze. Will risked taking a few steps closer.

"Two quid for a photo," said the witch unexpectedly, and her voice sounded like a man's. "No freebies."

Will flinched but kept eyeing the witch, who seemed to be defying the laws of gravity.

"How do you do that?" he asked without risking another step. The broomstick barely touched the ground, and Will couldn't see any ropes that could suspend the witch in mid-air.

The witch glanced around before cursing and barked, "Go away! You're scaring away the clients. The real clients!"

Will backed off a few paces but kept his eyes firmly fixed on the weird sight.

"Go! Go!" the witch flashed a few fiery glances at him and froze as a happy family of five appeared from around the corner.

The children screamed with delight, and the head of the family was forced to drop a few coins into the witch's magical purse. Then they took a few pictures and went on without looking back.

"Go away!" the witch hissed when the family had disappeared into the distance. "You're bad for business!"

Will shrugged, sighed and went on, casting a few more glances at the witch over his shoulder. No more than a few paces away, a blonde lady in a delicate crinoline dress stood at the side of the road with a bouquet of plastic red roses in one hand and a white feather fan in the other. She pretended to smell the roses, but her eyes darted across the street in search of potential clients. Her glance focused on Will for just a brief fraction of a second. Clearly, he didn't look like a tourist. He was bad for business.

We should get you some superhero outfit, and you could pose for pictures in Covent Garden, Will almost heard Sheila's ghostly voice behind him. *People pay money for taking pictures...* He glanced back – of course, the princess wasn't there. Her murmur faded in Will's ears but not his mind.

Further down the road, Will noticed more living statues doing their business in a tight competition. *It's Covent Garden,* Will glanced at the red brick building of the underground station in the distance with the sign, "Covent Garden Station", on its wall. Crowds of tourists wandered around, and he noticed a small but almost steady flow of coins falling into the purses of the living statues. All they had to do was to pose.

That seemed like a good idea. Only his creased tracksuit didn't look like any of the fancy clothing those living statues had. Sheila was right. He needed a superhero outfit.

His empty stomach began to protest loudly at the thought. Those few quid left on his card could feed him for a couple of days, and Will couldn't afford to spend them. That money was the only thin and ephemeral protection that separated his still muscular body from real starvation. Those fancy outfits must cost a fortune. He passed the lady and the tin man and again saw a couple of quid disappearing into their purses. *Money for nothing!* Will cursed. He turned left at the first crossroad, trying to stay away from the crowds. A few more living statues were doing business here as well, and he sped past them as fast as he could.

He turned right into the next street and sighed with relief. All those strange people remained behind, and he could slow down and begin to create a plan for how to survive another day. He must stop running around the streets like a madman. That was a strenuous activity, and his situation demanded a slower pace. Aimless wandering was a waste of energy with the only purpose to kill time. But his time might be killed in other ways too. If only his mother would read his letter... With his worsening luck, Will wasn't sure if he could rely on this anymore. The timing might had been wrong. She might still be angry...

He stopped in front of a brightly lit shop window featuring masks, wigs, feathers and carnival costumes. His wallet almost screamed in his pants, and he stopped, torn by hesitation. The choice was simple – *to eat or to buy an outfit*. Will nervously hurried away and then, twenty or thirty paces later, stopped, turned around and sneaked back, not so sure in his steps. He looked inside through the brightly lit window. It was a kingdom of shapes and colours with fancy costumes hanging around the walls. A few stands with wigs stood on the right, and at the far end of the kingdom was a counter where a grey-haired lady was busy sewing something. She had no customers and was absorbed in her work.

Will peered through the window but couldn't make out if the old lady had anything suitable for him. He would have to inquire inside but was less and less sure if he needed anything at all. *Better to buy a baguette...* His stomach howled at the thought, and Will flinched, afraid that the old lady might hear.

He glanced around helplessly, trying to kick the view of coins disappearing into those purses out of his mind. A few hours of work like that could buy him a generous dinner. In a few days, he might have enough cash to buy a ticket home! *But those outfits must be expensive,* he sighed. He didn't feel rich enough to spend more than ten pounds. What could he buy for ten quid? Just a paper mask, perhaps...

The grey-haired lady lifted her eyes from her sewing and glanced at him over top of her specs. She had spotted him! It was too late to run away.

She smiled at him and put her work aside. Will felt pinned by her gaze like a dried butterfly, his eyes darting between the old lady and those fancy outfits hanging on the walls. *She won't have anything for ten quid*. The thought was comforting, but he had to ask the question. Will sighed and opened the door.

"Hello," the lady greeted him without leaving her spot behind the counter. "How can I help you, young man?"

Will stopped at the door. "I'm looking for a superhero outfit," he mumbled unsurely.

"You've come to the right place," she gestured at the walls. "Do you have any specific superhero in mind?"

"No," Will shrugged. "I need something inexpensive."

"Oh," the lady nodded knowingly. "Tight budget... I understand."

Will's cheeks burned bright red, and he almost turned around to run away. The situation was embarrassing.

"I don't have any expensive stuff here, don't worry, but I can order them from a catalogue if you want to do that," she left the counter at last and came closer. "Let's have a look."

Will backed away a few paces as she approached.

"Let's have a look," she repeated, adjusting her specs. "The top row has stuffed muscles. Those are the most expensive – fifty quid each, but you probably don't need one of those, young man. You have some muscles of your own. The bottom row is the cheapest – no fancy muscles, just plain cloth, thirty pounds each. Which one do you want?"

"I've only got ten pounds," Will mumbled.

"Then you're in trouble, young man," the lady adjusted her specs and frowned, measuring his frame with her eyes. "But don't worry, there's always a way to help you."

"What way?" Will gasped, not sure if he was willing to know.

She smiled, touching his elbow. "I've got a few returns that have been worn in the back room. Some are torn, but I'm sure we will be able to stitch something together. For ten pounds, of course."

Will was reluctant to accept the offer as a faint image of Jill flashed in the back of his mind. The lady hobbled back to the counter, then stopped and glanced over her shoulder. "Do you still need that outfit?" she demanded with some impatience in her voice. "Or have you already changed your mind?"

Will shut his eyes. Ten pounds, and he could earn those coins by simply posing for pictures. He decided to spend the first day's income on food. He must regain his strength. "Coming," he added and followed the old lady into the depths of her store.

The backroom was small, with piles of stuff on all the shelves that lined the walls. The old lady stopped in the middle of her poorly organised chaos, planted her fists on her hips and looked around with a faint smile. Will stopped at the door, unsure if he was doing the right thing.

"Do you have any idea about your costume?" demanded the old lady still standing in the middle of the room.

"No," Will shrugged. "I guess I don't have many options to choose from."

The old woman giggled. "You have plenty of choices, in fact. Only I'm not sure where to begin. Superhero, you said?"

"Yes, probably," Will admitted hesitantly. "I haven't decided yet."

"Oh," she grunted, picking a few random rags from the shelf. "How convenient it is for you to leave all decisions to somebody else. Maybe, you should go and make your mind up first?"

Will silently stared at her.

"Those big eyes won't make any impression on this old lady," she said and put the rags back. "I won't offer any bigger discount."

"I'll give you a tenner," Will squeezed the wallet in his pocket. "Please, help me. I need to impersonate someone, but I'm not very good at it. I need something really simple."

The old lady sighed and shrugged, adjusting her specs. "Would you mind taking off that tracksuit?" she asked at last. "I need to estimate your size, and I need some inspiration."

Will dropped his rucksack on the floor. He wasn't ready for the show, but she'd promised to help. Hesitantly, he stripped, dropping his sweatpants as well. The old lady clearly enjoyed the view.

"Oh boy, what a nice tattoo," the grey-haired gasped. "Is she your girlfriend?"

"No," Will blushed. "Not yet, at least."

"Still, there's hope!" she winked. "Do you love her?"

The question hung in the air for some time as Will carefully touched Hel's features on his chest. "Of course, I do," he squirmed under the intense gaze of the old woman. It was a silly question.

"Does she know that?" demanded the lady.

The question struck Will unprepared. He blushed, falling again into that awful pink colour, and failing to answer.

"Just as I thought," sighed the old lady when his silence stretched for too long. She made a wry smile and adjusted her specs. "You had enough courage to ink her face on your chest but not enough to open your mouth."

"It isn't that simple," Will murmured, suddenly feeling completely naked under the intense gaze of her faded blue eyes. "She is very proud and independent. It's not easy to get her attention."

"But you managed to get that attention, didn't you?" she

demanded as she stood in the middle of the room with her fists placed firmly on her hips. "Or are you still wandering around in the land of fantasy?"

"I had a few cups of tea with her," admitted Will, still blushing. "But then I did a few stupid things, and now she won't speak to me."

"I see," she relaxed her stance a little. "Did those stupid things involve infidelity?"

"Of course not!" It was a strange interrogation, but Will felt an urge to explain. "She gave me a present, but I've lost it."

"Oh boy, you are in trouble," her gaze left Will's torso at last. "How could you be so careless?"

"It just... happened," he felt it was a sufficient explanation.

"And what was the thing you lost?"

"A flower," Will said.

"A flower?" the old lady raised her eyebrows. "Can't you buy her another?"

"It was a very special flower," Will muttered. "There's no other like it. And I'm doomed if I can't find it."

"That girl must be insane to give something precious to a clumsy chap like you, I think. Or she was crazy in love with you to do it," the lady told him, going closer to the shelves. "You've hurt her feelings. It will be damned difficult to get her back but not hopeless."

"You think so?" there was a note of hope in Will's voice.

"I do," she shrugged. "I hope this masquerade is not an attempt to get her back? I wouldn't like to point you in the wrong direction."

"No," Will said firmly. "It's a matter of survival."

"Are you hiding from someone?"

"No," he shrugged. "No one is looking for me."

"Okay," sighed the lady. "Let's have a look at what we have here. You're huge. It will be difficult to find something suitable. Let me think a little..."

She mumbled something indistinctly and went around the room, picking things up from shelves, then glancing at Will and putting everything back. Will felt awkward. This situation was silly, and he regretted getting into it. It couldn't end well but, on the other hand, he had nothing to lose except his tenner.

Unexpectedly, the old lady planted something on his head. Will flinched.

"Here we go," she carefully adjusted the curly ginger wig and patted his shoulder. "Looks good. Almost real William. William Wallace."

"I'm not Wallace," Will began to protest, but the old lady was already back at the shelves.

"Of course, you're not," she resumed her search. "But we must begin with something."

She picked a few colourful T-shirts from the shelf, then glanced at the ginger wig on Will's head and put them back. She went along the shelf, picking things up, unfolding them and discarding them with a look of disappointment. Hunger played marches in Will's guts, and again he felt almost sorry for having started this whole affair. Better he had bought a baguette!

"Okay, put these on!" The old woman handed him a brown, dirty-looking shirt and a leather waistcoat. "I need to have a look to see if we're heading in the right direction."

The shirt had a faint odour of damp and mould, and Will frowned, trying to imagine how many men had tried it on before him. He didn't have much choice – he couldn't afford anything new. He had to take the ginger wig off to put the shirt on. The fabric felt sticky on his skin.

"Who is this guy Wallace?" Will asked, putting the waistcoat on.

"A hero," the old woman muttered.

"Never heard of him," Will shrugged.

"Never heard of Braveheart?" the lady kept on searching for something. "Not seen the movie?"

"No," Will admitted doing his best to fit the wig back on his head.

"What kind of a hole did you grow up in?" the lady asked disdainfully. "He was the true hero of Scotland, one of the most famous. But you know nothing about him? How can you play Braveheart, William Wallace, when you know nothing about him, Mr Ignorant?"

"I don't know..."

"Oh!" the old lady cut him short with an angry glare. "No good deed goes unpunished! I know that! Now it's my problem to tell you what you're supposed to do in these robes. You probably won't need to do much if we paint your face in white and blue, though..."

"I don't want any face painting!" Will began to protest.

The old lady only shrugged. "Then you need to begin practising a brave face. And stop looking at me with those eyes of a pregnant pussycat! I'll do what I can, but the rest depends entirely on you!"

"A brave face?"

"Scottish national hero Braveheart is supposed to have a brave face, don't you think?" she reached deep into the pile of rags on a top shelf.

Will frowned, practising that brave expression, but all he could feel was anger and hunger. His eyes popped out when he noticed the garment the old lady was dusting off.

"A skirt?" he gasped.

"It's not a skirt," she announced, inspecting the fabric closely. "It's a kilt!"

"I'm not wearing a skirt, and it doesn't matter what you call it," Will said fiercely. "I'm not a girl!"

"Yes! Yes!" the old lady smiled approvingly. "That's exactly the expression you need to impersonate William Wallace! Keep that expression, study it and remember how to recall it. Now, put that on!"

She handed him the kilt and turned back to face the shelves. "I need to find some socks to go with it!"

"Is this suitable for a man?" he asked hesitantly, less fiercely.

"Have you never seen the men of the Royal Family wearing kilts on TV? I'm sure you have unless you grew up in a cave without electricity," she didn't even bother to glance at him.

Will shrugged but was afraid to admit that he hadn't. She would certainly have a joke or two and laugh at his ignorance. The royals probably did walk around in skirts. If that man in Covent Garden could dress like a witch, then he could pretend to be Braveheart in a skirt. *It's just for money. Maybe that face painting wasn't such a bad idea...* Nobody knew him in this city. *I don't care if they laugh,* he decided. *I'll just take the money and go home!*

He put that strange skirt on, feeling like a shy schoolgirl. He probably looked funny, but the old lady kept a straight face. She barely glanced at him as she searched for those damned socks.

Will grimaced again, practising that "brave" expression.

"I think these will be fine," the woman handed him a pair of long brown tartan socks. "It's not the real thing, but I've nothing closer than that. Your shoes are not fit for the purpose anyway, but I'm not giving you proper shoes for a tenner."

"I understand," Will sighed, trying the socks on.

"By the way," the lady winked. "A true Scotsman has no underwear under his kilt, but that's for you to decide if you dare to."

"No way!" Will shook his head vigorously. "There's no way I'd ever go commando!"

"It's up to you to decide," the old lady shrugged. "Let me have a look at you."

Will stood up and walked a few steps around the room. It was a silly situation, and only some decent income could justify this drag act. *Just for a few days*, he squeezed his teeth, *just to earn enough for some food and a ticket home.*

The old lady seemed satisfied with his look, but Will still wasn't ready for the show. He hastily collected his sweatpants and hooded jumper and stuffed everything into his trusty rucksack.

"May I have my tenner, please?" the old lady asked when he was done.

"Yes, of course," he followed her back into the shop and paid with his card.

"Good luck," the lady said, adjusting his wig. "And don't

forget to tell her about your love, or all your efforts will have been in vain."

"I will," Will promised.

He carefully sneaked outside. The wind gusted up his kilt, chilling his treasures. It felt strange and uncomfortable, and Will wondered how girls could dress like that and still feel fine. He turned left and blushed, feeling a few gazes sticking to him. He felt like a starfish left ashore by the tide where strangers poked at him and made fun of his appearance. *Damn! I need to get that tenner back!* The thought flashed through his mind as he went down the street, trying to retrace his steps back to Covent Garden Station. *Just today, just to get my tenner back!* His stomach growled.

He turned at the crossroad. It was more crowded here, but the stream of people parted in front of him like a mountain creek parts in front of a towering crag. He stepped on, clutching the rucksack in his left hand, half expecting laughs and bullying and ready to run away any moment. *I must find a quiet place and change back. Maybe that old lady will take the outfit back for a tenner?* It had been a bad idea, a very bad idea.

He went down the street, looking for a cul-de-sac where he could slip back into his trusty sweatpants, put his jumper on and pull up the hood as far as it would go. In the distance, he saw the first living statue – a pirate – performing his pantomime.

"Braveheart!" a woman screamed behind him.

Will flinched and stopped. He was afraid to turn around and have a look. Someone patted him on his shoulder.

"Could we take a picture with you?"

Will eyed the smiling Chinese woman in front of him. She waved her tablet and nodded a few times.

"Two pounds," Will announced, lifting his gaze and added. "Each!" A busload of Chinese tourists gathered behind her with their smartphones ready.

"Yes! Yes! Of course," the woman happily nodded, opening her purse. "Here," she extended two shiny coins out to him.

The coins burned his palm, and Will clutched them with a trembling heart. The smiling woman grabbed his elbow and passed the tablet to her pal. The other tourists patiently waited, forming a queue.

"Smile, please!" announced the woman with the tablet.

Will suddenly remembered that he was supposed to impersonate Braveheart and did his best "brave" expression.

"Very good," nodded the woman as she took a few snaps.

For the following fifteen minutes, Will serviced the entire busload. A steady flow of strange people wanted to take a picture with a man in a skirt. They put on some silly expressions and made strange hand gestures in the process. Will didn't mind and displayed his "brave" grimace every time someone got him in the focus of a smartphone. But, most importantly, there was a steady flow of coins heading into his pocket. *First, I'll eat*, he decided firmly. Everything else seemed less important.

Will brushed his sweaty brow when the last tourist had pressed two quid into his palm and taken a few final snaps. It wasn't an easy way to earn money, but he had made it – his mother would be proud of him! He looked after the group of tourists with a broad victorious smile as they hurried down the street to torment the next living statue. The coins jingled in his pocket, and it was a small but solid victory. That old lady was a genius! *Braveheart!*

"May I take a picture too?" asked a male voice behind him.

Will turned around. "Two pounds," he said firmly to the balding man in his early sixties. Will noted the massive ring glistening on his finger – a strange brassy striated cube held by a thick gold band.

The man grinned and passed the money to him. "I'm not that quick with my phone," he said, getting closer.

"Take your time," Will said as he put on his "brave" expression.

The man's right hand slightly shook as he leaned against Will for a selfie. He squirmed, and Will wondered why it was taking so long to get a few snaps. Suddenly he felt the man's left hand getting under his kilt, squeezing his butt.

Will jumped away. "What are you doing!" This was ridiculous.

"I was only checking if you're a real Scotsman," the man grinned. "I was left a bit disappointed!"

"I'm not here to be groped!" Will snapped.

"Oh, yes you are," the man hissed back. "You're just not hungry and desperate enough! Not yet! But I'm patient. I'll wait. It would be a pity to waste such a decent specimen."

"I'm not gay!" Will told him firmly.

"That doesn't matter," the man winked. "You never know what may come your way... Now, may I take my picture, if you don't mind? I've paid you for it."

Will blushed. "Here! Take your money!" He extended out the two-pound coin as if it was a venomous snake.

"You owe me twenty pounds if you refuse to let me take a snap," the man said in an icy voice. "I paid you for the service – you'll owe me money if I don't get the service!"

"You groped me enough for that two quid!" Will paled.

"I was just checking the quality of the material," the man observed calmly. "It wasn't the service I paid for!"

Twenty! Will gulped as his stomach wailed loudly. He couldn't afford that.

"Well?" the balding man squeezed a foxy smile, waving his phone.

It was disgusting, but Will had to swallow his pride. "Take your damned picture," he said at last. "But keep your distance!"

"That's better," the man sneaked closer.

"I'll hit you if you dare to grope me again," Will said through gritted teeth, this time making horrible grimaces to spoil the man's pictures.

"Go ahead," the man grunted. "There's plenty of police around here."

Will quickly glanced around and lowered his muscular right hand, firmly gripping the edge of the kilt. He was almost ready to feed the bastard that damned twenty quid and wait for another bus carrying Chinese tourists. He only needed a spark.

The man took his time to get the perfect angle for his photograph and every second seemed like an eternity. He didn't pay any attention to the fact that Will was fuming but didn't risk getting any closer either.

"Are you finished?" Will asked minutes later, losing his patience.

"Here," the man handed him a small piece of paper. "Call me when you get hungry and desperate. You might earn more than two pounds if you behave. I could take good care of you. I've enough patience to wait. And yes – I'm finished. Have a nice day."

Will waited just long enough for the man to turn around and tossed the slip of paper away as if it was a black widow spider. He mouthed a few obscenities to the retreating back of the bald head and turned the other way. That would never happen! He only needed to act as Braveheart for a few more busloads of tourists and earn enough money to get his ticket home. It was a nice option, and Will was confident of it too.

Will hurried up the street with the coins almost burning in his pocket. His stomach rumbled in anticipation. He just needed to find a quiet place to change his outfit – going shopping in a skirt was out of the question.

He went back to Covent Garden Underground Station and then turned right. The street was crowded, and Will silently cursed as surreptitious glances slipped over his skirted frame. Some just smiled. Some laughed openly. He was leaving the other living statues behind, and his outfit seemed less and less appropriate with every step.

He found what he was looking for a little later – a narrow backstreet on the right wasn't a proper cul-de-sac but seemed to be dark and empty. Will rushed past a cafe's windows down a poorly lit path where several garbage bins were lined up on the left. He stopped in front of a residential entrance, squeezed between the two black bins and lowered his rucksack to the ground. Then he counted his coins – there were thirty-six pounds. *Thirty-six pounds!* It felt like a fortune, and Will's hands trembled as he stuffed the coins into his wallet. He grinned broadly and imagined a big juicy piece of meat in his mouth already. He just had to find some cheap eatery like Ali's back home where he could feast.

Will took his wig and waistcoat off first and folded them up. He must be careful with this outfit if it could bring treasure like this. It was tricky with the brown T-shirt that was a little too tight for his muscles and stuck to his skin. He froze as someone coughed behind his back.

"Nice muscles," a voice observed. A harsh male voice, chilly yet not threatening.

Will instantly decided he would not part with his money whatever threat may arise. He needed that money more than anybody else. His physique was usually sufficient to scare away any potential threat. Maybe it could help this time as well? He didn't rush to hide his diminishing self-confidence – he slowly pulled the T-shirt off over his head, folded it up and carefully placed it in his rucksack along with the waistcoat and wig. Only then did he turn around to face the intruder.

The Asian man was leaning against the wall a few paces away and smoking. He wore a black shirt, unbuttoned at the top, black jeans and a snow-white apron. He was much smaller than Will and incredibly thin. He probably worked as a dishwasher in a nearby eatery. Will couldn't imagine a chef being that thin.

"What do you want?" Will asked calmly.

"Just having a smoke," the man said without a smile. He

slowly exhaled, puffing out a grey-blue cloud of smoke.

Will shrugged, searching for the zipper in his kilt. The man seemed somehow sinister but was too skinny to pose any real threat.

"A very nice tattoo," the man observed and puffed out another cloud of smoke. "Who is she?" He pointed with his cigarette, keeping his distance.

"My girlfriend," Will wasn't in the mood for any explanations. He had found the zipper.

"Could you wait a moment?" the man suddenly tossed his unfinished cigarette away. "My friend really likes all kinds of tattoos. He must see that one. I think we could persuade him to pay you a few quid for the privilege of taking a snap. I'll be right back!"

The man hurried off, leaving his smoking cigarette butt behind. Will glanced at his retreating back and instantly decided not to wait. The backstreet was dark, and the haste with which the man had run away was suspicious. Will had no intention of meeting a pack of bad guys who could beat the money out of him. He quickly put on his old tracksuit and rushed the other way. He turned left at the corner when he heard a door slamming in the backstreet and many feet running. He ran as well, hoping that whoever was after him hadn't had time to spot him.

The street was almost empty, and Will realised that he couldn't run for long – they would spot him at once. He hastily glanced around and ran as fast as he could past the posh Indian restaurant with large windows. The signboard of the next shop promised food to takeaway, and Will rushed through the door without thinking twice. He glanced back before closing the door behind him – his pursuers were nowhere in sight.

"Hello," the girl at the counter greeted him. "What would you like?"

"Could I have a look at what's on offer first, please?" Will asked.

"Of course," the girl shrugged and handed him a menu with colourful illustrations.

It was a small establishment, and Will went to the corner on the right and sat down on a chair, facing the glass door. The position was as far from the entrance as he could get without raising suspicion.

The menu was a real torture for his empty stomach, but he slowly went through it, keeping his eye on the street outside the window. The prices were a bit too high for his budget, but he kept looking at the appetising pictures and reading the descriptions. A few minutes later, a gang of four men led by that Asian dishwasher sneaked past the shop window with knives and knuckle-dusters in their hands. Will lifted the menu, covered his face and pretended to read. He heard a quiet gasp from the other side of the counter but didn't risk having a look.

"God," the girl whispered. "They're hunting for someone."

Will braved to peek over the menu. The street was empty in front of the window. "Does that often happen around here?" he asked. "They seem to have already gone."

The girl was pale but forced a smile, pretending to adjust her hair. Will traced her frightened gaze – a balding man slowly went down the street shamelessly peeking through the windows of every shop and café. Will hastily lifted the menu, shielding his face. The girl said nothing.

The quiet sound of a ring scratching the glass made Will squirm. The girl stood as white as a pillar of salt. Her hand was still hesitantly touching her hair, but the smile was gone. Will saw a shadow on the floor – standing still at first, then slowly moving to the left. He held his breath – never in his life had he been more afraid. He traced the movement with unblinking eyes, waiting for the worst. A ring scratched the glass again. The next moment, the shadow was gone.

No one entered the shop. The girl slowly exhaled, regaining her colour.

"Are they after you?" she asked, her voice trembling slightly.

"Never seen them before," Will lied. "And don't want to see them again. I'm a visitor and have no idea about any gangs in London. Who are they?"

"Those thugs quite frequently hang around," the girl shrugged. "They hang out somewhere nearby. You saw them – country lines bandits at large, like in a movie. Probably, hunting someone if they're running around like that."

"Why would they want to hunt someone?" Will asked, lowering the menu.

"Don't ask me. I'm no expert in gangster affairs," the girl shrugged. "They're gangsters, bad people. Probably after some money or jewels. Who knows? And that last one was their chief. You know – like a godfather. He's the creepiest."

"I wasn't brave enough even to take a look at him," Will chuckled.

"Lucky you," she sighed. "He ripped my head off with his gaze and sucked my blood. That man is pure evil. I've heard rumours that he makes his men drink human blood. I don't know if you can believe that."

"A gang of vampires? That is weird, indeed," Will wasn't smiling anymore. "But they're running around in the bright sunshine. Aren't they supposed to burn?"

The girl rolled her eyes. "I hope you're just pretending to be stupid. You're too good looking to be a moron."

It was Will's turn to roll his eyes, but the move didn't reflect his true feelings or calm his fluttering heart. *A gang of vampires! Was that crazy Indian woman telling the truth?* After a few weeks in a cage next to the sphinx, flaming snakes and god-like knights, he was ready to believe almost anything.

"I'm not a Londoner," he reminded her. "I don't know which tales are true or not. But that gang did look creepy."

"I hope they don't come back any time soon," she sighed.

"Why don't you call the police?" Will asked, keeping an eye on the window.

"That's a stupid suggestion," the girl grunted. "I'd be dead before I had a chance to say hello."

"You know best..." Will shrugged. Indeed, that sounded stupid, but in a different way than the girl implied. So, there was some gang killing people, and no one had dared to report? *Timid rats!*

"Have you chosen something?" the girl decided to change the subject.

Will sighed and got up. "It's too expensive for me," he handed the menu back. "Looks fancy, I admit, but you won't stuff your stomach full with these. I can't spend more than just a few quid and then leave still feeling hungry."

"That's your decision," the girl shrugged and took the menu. "It's central London. I doubt you can find anything cheaper here."

"I'll try. Thanks," he said.

"For what?"

Will only shrugged. He sneaked out and carefully glanced in

both directions before closing the door behind him. Those men were nowhere in sight, and he turned right and mixed in among a group of Spanish speaking tourists. He ignored the loud growls of his stomach. He kept his hood low over his brow and his eyes wide open. *A gang of vampires!* That girl didn't seem crazy, and her words kept circling in his head. Those men were strange indeed. Why had they suddenly become so interested in a humble homeless person who had only thirty-six pounds in cash? That was strange and made no sense. *Did they want to eat him?*

He went with the crowd until they reached a crossroad. The guide led the tourists to the right. Will stopped just briefly. He glanced back over his shoulder and gasped. Those strange men had emerged from around the far corner of the street, glancing around and crawling forward like a pack of hunting wolves. He didn't wait for them to spot him. Quickly, Will turned left and mixed in with the crowd again. How fast could he run away? How far should he run? *Where should he run?* There must be a misunderstanding, Will was sure. He had nothing anybody would want. But how to explain that to those men?

The crowd dispersed in the square, and Will found himself in front of the colonnade again. He must hide somewhere, at least for a while. The entrance was in the middle of the colonnade; The Apple Market said the sign above it. Will entered without thinking too much – a market might be a good place to dissolve into the crowd. There were no apples inside, just a gallery of posh boutiques and souvenir shops. The gallery was almost empty, with just a few women wandering by the brightly lit windows, pointing at something and chatting.

Will hurried forward, going deeper into the market. He needed a quiet place to wait until those crazy men had given up running after him. Nothing suitable caught his eye. He slipped into a narrow corridor and quickly emerged in an even larger gallery. This one was different. He found himself on the mezzanine floor that lined all the walls of the gallery. A small crowd was on the left, cheering at someone playing a fierce melody on a violin. Will glanced around. It was dangerous to stay in one place for too long, and he dashed right, going down the stairs. Below there were several cafès, filling the area with glorious scents of food, and Will's stomach growled loudly, demanding its share. He stopped, feeling trapped. It had been a bad decision to come here. Now he had to hide in one of those ridiculously expensive eateries or risk bumping into his pursuers on his way back out.

The place on the right was selling crêpes, and that seemed like a safe option. They had a few rows of tables away from the window, and Will decided to wait there. He just had to buy something.

"Good afternoon," the girl behind the counter greeted him. "What would you like?"

"A cup of tea," Will said humbly, hoping that the order wouldn't deplete his wallet too much.

The girl quickly nodded and turned to prepare his drink.

"Any sugar? Milk?" she asked, working.

"With everything, please," Will sighed and got out his wallet.

He carefully counted out the coins before giving them to the girl. She tossed them into her drawer without even giving them a second glance.

"Take a seat wherever you like," she told him. "I'll bring the tea to you when it's ready."

Will scanned the place, which wasn't as spacious as he had hoped – five tables, separated with walls of artificial flowers that provided just an illusion of privacy. He sighed and selected the table opposite the door, ducking down as deep behind the plastic flowers as he could. The tea arrived a few minutes later.

"Hiding from someone?" the girl asked, placing the cup and a plate with a few biscuits in front of him.

Will shrugged, hiding behind a frightened smile, but didn't say anything. He had already paid his money and felt no obligation to explain. She might be working for those people, and it had been a foolish idea to go there. The girl smiled back, then turned around and returned to her desk. Will stirred his tea nervously.

His tranquillity didn't last long. The door opened, and the balding man stepped inside, strolling unhurriedly and glancing behind each flower wall.

"How can I help you?" the girl stopped him before he could reach the table where Will was hiding.

The man halted his search and turned to face her. He came closer and placed his hands on the desk. For a few moments, he just watched the girl. "I'm looking for a muscular young man," he crooned at last.

In an instant, Will fished the curly wig out of his rucksack and placed it on his head, trying to camouflage himself as much as he could without making too much noise. He froze, peering carefully through the gaps between the flowers.

"We're not that type of establishment," the girl said calmly.

"I know," the man tapped his right hand impatiently on the table, and it sounded like a metal band striking the wood. It was a band – Will saw the familiar golden ring on the man's finger with the brassy faceted stone. "Have you seen him?"

"I work here. I don't spy on boys," the girl answered without a trace of hesitation.

"Clever girl..." the man cast a few glances around but didn't step any further. "Here's my phone number," he placed a card on the table. "Call me if you see him. I'll pay, and usually, I pay a lot."

"I don't even know what to look for," the girl shrugged.

"Tall, muscular, ginger."

The girl shrugged again and shook her head.

"Call me," the man said firmly and turned to leave. "You won't regret it."

The girl didn't answer, nor had she time to do that as two chatty old ladies stepped through the door.

"Greetings, dear," one of the ladies smiled at her and placed a couple of banknotes on the counter. "We'd like two cups of tea – Earl Grey with milk, no sugar and two scones with jam and cream, please."

"Take a seat, ladies," the girl took the money. "I'll bring everything over as soon as it's ready."

The man left, but Will still couldn't calm his insanely beating heart. He sipped his tea and tried a biscuit, but his hands still trembled slightly.

The old ladies took a table nearby without stopping their chatting. It seemed they hadn't met for a long while, and now they were eager to fill each other in with all their news. Will chewed his biscuits and quietly sipped his tea, unsure how to leave the café without getting caught. He was certain that the strange man wouldn't give up easily.

"I told you many times, Eleonor," said one of the old ladies. "You should give up your posh London life and come up North. It would be fun to have you closer. I was spending a fortune every time I come to visit you."

"Those train tickets are so incredibly expensive," sighed Eleonor. "But I'd hate to move and leave all this culture behind – the performances, the theatres…"

"Are you still going to the theatre, my dear?" the other lady asked, probing her scone. "You're as blind as a bat, and they don't have any seats in the orchestral pit!"

"With your hearing, that would be the right place for you too, Winifred," Eleonor chuckled. "You said the ticket *was* a waste of a fortune, dear. Have you found a cheaper way?"

"What?"

"Have you found a cheaper way to travel, Winifred?"

Will absentmindedly nodded but then stopped chewing, his ears suddenly alert. Winifred took a bite of a scone and waved her finger teasingly. Eleonor shook her head impatiently, but she wasn't as impatient as Will was – he could barely sit still, but both were forced to wait while Winifred adjusted her prosthetic smile after vigorously chewing and washing the scone down with a few gulps of tea.

"I did," she smiled. "I took a bus! Maybe less comfortable and takes longer to get to Victoria Coach Station – but here I am! And just for a fraction of that terrible price. So now that I saved some money – let's feast!"

Will couldn't stop grinning. *Victoria!* That sounded like a victory! He just had to slip away without falling into the hands of that terrible gang. The thought cooled down his enthusiasm a little, but still, his butt was almost jumping off the chair.

The ladies chatted on, but he didn't listen. *Victoria! Victoria Coach Station!* Maybe his scarce savings bolstered by the coins he had earned as Braveheart could take him home? The thought felt dizzying.

The ladies ordered more tea, but Will sat grimly staring at the cold brown brew in his half-empty cup. He tried to glance through the window a few times, but it was difficult to see anything from his hiding place.

"Do you want more tea?" Will nearly jumped at the question. The girl met his eyes with a serious face, but her lips barely twitched with suppressed laughter. "You can take off that wig. Is it you that man's looking for? Don't worry – he's gone."

"But you have his phone number."

"I won't call those weirdos," the girl placed the slip of paper next to Will's cup. "You can have that number."

"Thanks for saving me." Will took the slip of paper and put it into his pocket before the girl had a chance to change her mind.

"You're welcome," the girl smiled at last. "What about another tea?"

"I still have some."

"It's gone cold," she shrugged. "Give me the cup. I'll bring you a warmer one."

"I don't have much money for that."

"It will be the same cup," the girl shrugged. "Just warmer."

She didn't wait for Will's approval. A few minutes later, the cup reappeared in front of him, full of a hot brew and with four biscuits at its side.

"Thank you," Will blushed. The girl only shrugged and turned to go away.

"Wait!" Will stopped her. "Is Victoria Coach Station far from here?"

"Four stops on the underground," she said without thinking too much.

"I won't be using the underground," Will sighed. "Is it far to walk?"

"Not far, a couple of miles, probably," the girl said with a trace of disappointment in her voice. "You need to go left after you leave the market, take any street and carry on until you reach the Strand. Then turn right and walk all the way down to Buckingham Palace. Then take the left-hand street and carry on until you see Victoria Station. It's easy."

"Sounds easy," Will gave her an awkward smile. "Thank you."

The girl nodded and went back behind the counter, leaving Will to meditate in front of his teacup. He was embarrassed to accept free food from a girl. Still, he felt hungry and afraid. Very afraid. He was cornered. *Would she allow him to sleep here on the floor?* He could safely sneak outside in the early morning while those hunting hyenas were still asleep. *Probably, not...* He regretted leaving Ben so hastily. He could be eating lasagne, sleeping in a normal bed and not worrying about some crazy bloodthirsty weirdos, but then he wouldn't be on his way to find out what had happened to his family either. And he hated to sit in a swamp of tears.

"You're very difficult to find, my friend," someone whispered in front of him. A hand appeared next to his cup. A transparent hand.

Will lifted his eyes. The man's face in front of him was barely visible and unfamiliar, and he could see some plastic flowers through it. "Do I know you?" he asked a little impatiently – all he needed was a ghost to add to his growing pile of problems. "I don't remember you."

"Of course!" the transparent man nodded happily and sat down in front of him. "No one remembers a beggar! I was sitting in front of Euston Station, and you gave me a tenner!"

"Yes, now I remember," Will mumbled. "I guess you're not here to return that tenner?"

"I came to thank you," the man said. "I felt so rich! I bought myself a bowl of soup and a mango! Can you believe it? I bought a mango! A divine, delicious, sweet ripe mango! I hadn't had a mango for years!"

"I'm glad for you," Will said and sipped his tea. "But, as I can see, that tenner didn't help much."

"Why do you say that, my friend?"

"You're dead."

The man giggled and dismissed Will's statement with a gesture. "It was an accident. My fault – I ran across the street without looking both ways properly, and a double-decker ran me over. I'm sorry for the driver – he probably had a heart attack, but I died happily. It was quick and painless. And I decided to find you first and thank you before going to meet my goddess."

"You already thanked me," Will shrugged.

"You look distressed, my friend," the transparent man observed. "Is it for because of the 10 pounds? I can't give that back to you, sorry."

"No," Will quickly assured him. "I've got my own problems. They're not related to you in any way."

"Good," the transparent shape nodded. "Kali doesn't like folks with problems."

Will glanced over the right shoulder of the ghost and froze – the balding man had emerged from the souvenir shop on the opposite side, glanced around and went right towards the staircase. *The hunt was still continuing!*

"Your problem is related to that one?" the ghost asked, tracing Will's gaze.

"Yes. The most pressing one, at least."

"Then you're in big trouble, young man," the ghost sighed. "These are ruthless people. I would rather avoid even glance from that man."

"So it seems."

"You must stay away from them."

"Unfortunately, that advice is too late."

"I'm sorry I can't hide you. I'm just a mere souling," the ghost sounded distressed. "I don't know how I can help you."

"Perhaps, you can."

"How?"

"They're looking for a tall, muscular redhead," Will said quietly. "But it seems they are unaware that I'm here since they keep looking in other shops. I must get to Victoria Coach Station and get out of London, but I can't move while they're still hunting around, and I can't stay here for too long. They can't see you – can they? Maybe, you could help me to sneak out when they're not looking?"

"Even if they can see me, they won't pay much attention. I marched in here right in front of their noses! I can do that!"

"Thank you."

"Wait for me here."

The ghost vanished, leaving Will to contemplate over his cup of tea. Now he had doubts if he had done the right thing by entrusting his fate to a spectre he barely knew. *Maybe he was already assembling and positioning the hyenas somewhere outside?* It was a chilling thought, and Will unhappily sipped his tea, unsure what to do next.

He barely noticed that the two old ladies had finished their tea and had left. His thoughts were far away, where his mother was roasting a chicken for dinner. Will closed his eyes, imagining the delicious smells, her smile as she watched his sister eat, his empty place at the table.

He nearly jumped when the door of the café opened. Will carefully peeked from behind his plastic flowers – it was a young couple who had decided to spoil themselves with some crêpes and two mugs of coffee. He felt like a sitting duck, but there wasn't much he could do – that gang might still be waiting outside.

It took an hour for him to drain his cup of tea and eat his biscuits. He cringed every time the door opened, but nothing serious happened. Customers came in, placed their orders, ate their treats and left. The girl at the counter worked like a bumblebee, barely coping with the flow. She never glanced at Will again.

Will watched the café fill with people and decided that it was about time to move – with or without the help of that ghost. It was easier to hide in a crowd if those men were still sticking around.

"It's time," Will heard a sudden whisper. The ghost of the scraggy man appeared next to him. "Those terrible men riddled the place, but now they're holding a meeting on the Eastern side. We could safely sneak out to the West!"

Will's heart sank. *Could he trust the ghost?* It seemed he had no other options. He collected his things and placed the empty cup on the counter.

"Thank you," Will said quietly, but the girl was busy preparing some snacks and didn't seem to notice. He wasn't sure if she heard his acknowledgement. That didn't matter anyway.

Will opened the door and looked around. Nothing seemed suspicious – music played on the other side of the market, and crowds loudly cheered at the familiar melodies.

"Let's go upstairs," said the ghost. "There's no other way out of this hole."

Will didn't answer but took the stairs and then turned left, heading to the exit. He had no time to look if the ghost had followed.

It was even more crowded outside the market. Will pulled up his hood and turned left, joining a large group of youths on a stag do. The groom was a big muscular guy, nearly as big as Will, wearing a pink tutu. He went down the street with a big red umbrella in his hand like Mary Poppins, clutching a can of beer in his right fist. The noisy company laughed and shouted obscenities, and Will strolled amongst them, feeling a little safer. He left them at the first crossroad.

The street was narrow but crowded, and Will rushed forward, hiding under his hood. Nobody stopped him. Nobody looked at him. All were preoccupied with themselves, looking in the windows of posh boutiques and dining in stylish cafés. The street ended a few hundred yards later, giving way to a busy dual carriageway. The red-topped sign on the corner building said "Strand WC2", and Will realised that he was going in the right direction. *As long as the girl had told the truth.*

"I can't go any further," there was a quiet whisper in Will's left ear. He looked around – saw nothing.

"Thank you for helping me out," Will responded quietly.

"Well… good luck with the rest of your problems then."

"Good luck with your afterlife."

The ghost didn't answer. Will turned right and blended into the crowd.

He went on, his heart beating faster in anticipation. He barely noticed the banks, grandiose hotels, magnificent cafés and restaurants and posh boutiques on either side of the street he was passing. If those old ladies were telling the truth, he might even catch a bus tonight!

His daydreaming ended several hundred yards later in a large square with chaotic traffic. Will stopped, unsure where to go next.

None of the buildings surrounding the square looked grand enough to be a Buckingham Palace – he had seen it on television. He crossed the street along with a crowd of cheerful wanderers and stopped again in front of a large column guarded by four iron lions. He felt lost again. The girl hadn't told him everything.

Will wasn't accustomed to asking someone for directions – he knew almost every corner in his hometown, but the situation was critical. He hesitantly approached a policeman who was directing crowds crossing the street.

"Excuse me," he asked, blushing like a schoolgirl. "Do you know how to get to Buckingham Palace, please?"

The policeman glanced at him just for a second. "Follow the Mall," he pointed at the three arches in the curved building just across the street.

"Thank you," Will mumbled and went away. He was sure the policeman had misunderstood his question – the road he pointed at looked like just another service road from a distance. But then Will recognised the place – indeed, it was the same gate he had walked through with the ghost of Princess Sheila, and there was a broad street behind that gate.

He sent a mental "thanks" to the policeman and hurried across the street, grinning widely. The journey home seemed close, very close. If only he had known about the coach station before when he had wandered around that street with Sheila – he could be munching on a chicken by now, deliciously roasted by his mother.

Will almost ran, doing his best not to bump into other people. He was stopped by a furious glance from marble Queen Victoria sitting on her marble throne in the middle of a roundabout. *This must be Buckingham Palace*, Will looked at the building, frowning – it seemed much grander on the television. But he had no time for a better look. Evening dusk was falling on London, and he must get on the bus quickly or risk another night sleeping rough in some forsaken cul-de-sac.

He turned left and crossed the street, trying to keep away from the crowds of tourists wandering in front of the gates of the Palace.

Take the left-hand street and go until you see Victoria, the girl said. *Don't turn off anywhere. Keep straight*, Will hummed to himself. And he hurried on. He never looked back. Those dreadful gangs, living statues, Ben, that strange Indian woman – all seemed distant and irrelevant, especially when his destination was so near – he could almost feel it.

The street was as busy as any other street in central London – squeezed between the walls of tall buildings. A few buses passed up and down the road, but these weren't the usual red double or single-deckers that Will had seen in abundance over the past few days. Some were dark blue, some green, some white. Will wondered which one of them could take him home. He was so absorbed in wondering that he almost missed the bright blue sign on the tall white building in front of him, with "Victoria Coach Station" written on it in bold white letters.

He rushed in and stopped abruptly, finding himself in a small, round hall and unsure where to go next, feeling like Alice, who had reached the bottom of the rabbit hole at last. Then a bunch of wandering tourists carried him down the corridor on the left. Will looked around – eyes wide and ears alert – still he had no idea where the buses were.

Then the whole retinue came to a halt at the end of the queue for the ticket office. *He needed a ticket!* The joy subsided, replaced by a sudden wave of fear – he wasn't sure if his meagre savings would be enough to buy a ticket, and he waited, ready to find out if that old lady had been telling the truth.

The line progressed slowly, and some tourists left to search for another ticket office. Will patiently waited to find out his fate.

"Where are you going?" asked the sleepy woman behind the counter. She sipped coffee from a paper cup, but that didn't seem to be helping her much. Will had to repeat his destination several times until she heard it correctly.

"One way or return?" she asked.

"One way, please," Will told her. "I won't be returning, for sure. Not in this life!"

The woman fiddled with the computer for several painfully

long seconds. "Twenty-seven pounds and fifty-two pence," she announced at last. "Cash or card?"

Will's heart almost jumped out of his chest, and he felt the urge to kiss the woman. "Card," he decided, opening his wallet. His hands shook as he keyed in his PIN number and took his ticket.

"The bus will be at bay twelve at 23:20," the woman told him and took another sip of coffee. "Be at the bay thirty minutes before that!"

"I will. Thank you!"

He left the ticket office, a broad smile splitting his face – *he was going home!* That was the most important thing, and Will couldn't be happier.

Suddenly he felt immensely rich and popped into a nearby café to buy the biggest baguette he could find. He ate it slowly, savouring each bite, taking large gulps of apple juice between them. When he had finished eating, Will went to look for bay twelve. It didn't take him long to find it.

The waiting area was big and almost empty – there was still more than an hour until departure, but Will was determined to keep a firm grip on his chance. He took a seat next to the bay door, waiting.

It probably wasn't a very popular destination. No more than a dozen passengers gathered around the bay door when the sleepy girl finally opened them. She checked their tickets and rushed them on to board the coach that stood a few yards away.

Will found his way to the back of the bus and sat down next to the window. Clouds were gathering in the darkness above London, and a few bolts of lightning pierced the sky. Will smiled, looking at the first heavy raindrops splashing on the pavement – it would have been difficult to find a place to sleep with those elements raging. It didn't seem important anymore – he was on his way home!

"Goodbye, London," he whispered when the doors of the bus closed. "I won't miss you."

The bus rolled onto the tangled streets of the metropolis, and Will closed his eyes, feeling deadly tired. His mind wandered away a few minutes later.

The morning was merry, but the view was blocked by backsides – twelve almost naked female backsides, barely veiled by transparent silks. The concubines stood between Will and sphinx's bed – water, towels, precious oils, perfumes and jewellery in their hands – waiting for the King to wake up. He could hear Qu Sith still snoring.

"Good morning," Will uttered quietly. None of the girls stirred or glanced at him. They were here not for his entertainment.

He sat, leaning against the wall, and waited, enjoying the view, which wasn't bad at all. Half an hour later, Qu Sith yawned in his bed, and the concubines stirred into motion.

"What's all this about?" the sphinx snarled.

"This is your morning refreshment, your Majesty," one of the girls blushed, suddenly afraid of her own courage. "What would you like for your breakfast?"

"Get your hands off me!"

"We must prepare your divine fur for the funeral of the Queen, your Majesty," the other girl dared to say. "And we need to dress you for the occasion."

"Who ordered that?"

"Priest Kroy, your Majesty," the girl paled. "He is in charge of the funeral."

"When is the funeral?"

"At noon, your Majesty," the girl quickly nodded. "What would you like for breakfast?" she repeated the question.

"Three or four rabbits will be fine," Qu Sith growled impatiently. "And be careful with those refreshments of yours – don't pour that water on me!"

The concubines were only briefly baffled by his request.

"As you wish, your Majesty," one of them said as they all curtsied. They soaked three or four towels and wiped the sides of the beast with a firm determination to get all the dust of the underground out of the sphinx's fur.

Qu Sith grimaced fiercely, and Will couldn't help but stiff involuntary giggles, watching the girls rub the beast. The procedures seemed endless. The girls poured scented oils on Qu Sith as soon as they had cast the wet towels aside. Qu Sith looked pitiful like a damp cat as the concubines massaged his sides and combed his hair.

"Could you get on a bit faster?" the sphinx growled. "I've one really urgent matter to solve!"

"It won't take long, your Majesty," said one of the girls, combing his fur.

They braided his mane in intricate patterns and hung tiny golden bells at the end of each braid. They tinkled softly with each move of his head, making the sphinx grimace even more.

Then they put a thick golden chain around his neck, richly decorated with rubies and aquamarines.

"Are you done?" Qu Sith growled with a pained expression on his face.

"Yes, your Majesty," the concubines curtsied.

He sighed with relief. "Then I need the smallest room in the palace for some privacy," the sphinx requested.

"You can choose any room you want, your Majesty," one of the girls said, a comb in her hand.

"I need it right now!" Qu Sith exploded in a roar. "Where is the latrine!"

"The whole world is a latrine for the King, your Majesty," another girl said, curtsying.

The sphinx roared in frustration. "Fine!" He backed a few feet. "Then deal with it! All turn around!"

The prolonged sound that followed was the final blow from the battle of the rats inside the sphinx's gut, accompanied by the acrid odour of wet gunpowder. Qu Sith sighed with relief. "Now I can have my breakfast and pay my final respects to the Queen," he said, addressing no one in particular. "But we may need another room for that."

The door opened without knocking, and the head of Kroy peered in. "Oh! Your Majesty is ready, as I see," his face broke into a smile. He smelled the air, and the smile became even broader. "I've come at a perfect time!" he exclaimed.

Qu Sith glanced at him suspiciously. "What is it you want?"

"I'm the High Priest of the Oracle, your Majesty," Kroy mumbled, coming closer. "I can't waste the opportunity to get a glimpse of what your reign in Per Hathor will look like. I hope it will be long and prosperous, your Majesty."

Qu Sith just shook his mane, the bells tinkled.

The concubines moved away from the pile of shit as Kroy approached. He produced a slim silver stiletto from his robes and stopped in front of the pile, mumbling a few incomprehensive words.

Will stood up, trying to get a better look. The future written in the pile of shit sounded like utter nonsense, even if that shit was royal – or was it a shitty future? He wasn't particularly interested, just curious.

Kroy waved to the nearest concubine to come closer. The girl paled but obeyed. Her slender, almost naked shape looked fragile next to the priest, richly garbed in silks and gold. Kroy raised his hands, murmuring something under his breath and grabbed the girl's left hand. She just gasped when the priest sliced her palm with the stiletto. Bright red drops poured over the foul-smelling pile, and Kroy began to sing in a low voice, the words still indistinct. A few minutes later, he dropped the girl's hand and pushed her away as if discarding an infested apple core, frowning.

"All out!" Kroy roared unexpectedly. "I need to speak to the King!"

The girls curtsied and left without even turning back.

"You too!" the priest pointed at Will.

"He can stay," Qu Sith shrugged.

"But the matter is private, your Majesty," Kroy whispered. "Not suitable for the ears of an outsider. You won't need a food taster for this conversation."

"No worries, I can wait outside," Will said and turned to follow the girls. The sphinx didn't stop him.

The concubines lined the far wall of the corridor, all facing the door of the royal boudoir.

Will quietly closed the door and sneaked aside. He didn't want to give the impression of spying on whatever nonsenses Kroy was whispering into the sphinx's ears. *Nobody can see the future* – he was certain. Not in a pile of shit, at least.

He went several paces down the corridor and stopped, leaning against the wall. He half expected the eyes of the concubines to follow him but was left utterly disappointed. His physique in the dream wasn't as impressive as in the real world, and the girls preferred Qu Sith.

An hour passed in dispersing the mists of the future behind the closed door. Then Kroy stuck his head out and barked a short command to the concubines. Qu Sith giggled behind his back, and the priest closed the door again without even glancing at Will.

The girls rushed down the corridor, then turned right towards the magnificent staircase and disappeared, leaving Will alone to meditate next to the closed door.

He felt growing frustration. He was wasting time! He must hurry back to the lava fields and search for the flower! Instead, he was leaning against a wall waiting as the priest groomed the sphinx and told tales by looking at that pile of shit! *Damn! Could he somehow sneak away from the palace?* Will glanced down the empty corridor. He was alone, but he didn't know the way. Those corridors might get tricky – some of them were probably blocked, some ruined. *Do they have guards here?* Will kept his ears sharp, but all he could hear was the muffled indistinct talk behind the closed door. Then the door opened.

Qu Sith emerged, grinning widely. Kroy strolled next to the sphinx with a mysterious expression on his face. He patted the sphinx's back a few times, but Qu Sith didn't seem to object.

"Follow us," the beast said to Will as they passed. Kroy ignored him entirely.

They went on down the corridor, talking quietly. Neither of them glanced back or waited for Will. He went after them, feeling forgotten utterly. He saw the priest whisper something to the sphinx from a distance, and Qu Sith nodded his head vigorously, making the bells tinkle.

They didn't stop until Kroy opened a heavy wooden door and let the sphinx in. The room wasn't big, with just two windows showing the vast frozen lava field beyond. There was a dais on the right, richly scattered with embroidered cushions and probably meant for a sphinx – Kroy took Qu Sith there and helped him settle down comfortably between them. A low table was placed in front of him with a feast for a king. Two girls stood at either side of the table, ready to help the sphinx with whatever he chose. The rest of the concubines lined along the far wall, waiting.

"Come closer, human," Qu Sith addressed Will. "Please, help yourself. There's enough food for both of us." The beast didn't invite Kroy nor the concubines.

Will approached the dais hesitantly. Something just didn't seem right, especially the foxy smile on the face of the priest.

"Have a seat," Qu Sith crooned. "Would someone bring the best wine for my friend?"

One of the girls dashed out. The others stayed at the wall,

expectantly. Will sat down at the foot of the dais, his stomach growling, but only one thought spun around his head. *Ben said, avoid any danger! Avoid any danger!* Nobody and nothing threatened him here. Why then were his hands shaking?

Qu Sith didn't wait for him and began to devour one of the rabbits. Will scanned the table – no cutlery. *Of course, sphinxes don't need any!* He quietly ripped the leg off the nearest rabbit and began to chew. The meat tasted funny, but he had never tried rabbit before anyway.

Qu Sith nodded approvingly. "I didn't realise how hungry I was," he said as he chewed. "Dear priest, could you order a few more rabbits to be brought since you're taking care of everything. I'd like them raw, with blood!"

"Of course, your Majesty!" Kroy impatiently waved to the concubines. "You heard our King!"

Another girl rushed out without saying a word. They feasted silently for some time under the close observation of the priest. Then the wine arrived in a dark red pitcher.

"You try it first," Qu Sith ordered the priest. Kroy paled but filled the goblet with the noble dark ruby liquid.

"To my King," he said and gulped the wine down in one go. The priest's hands were steady as he refilled the goblet and passed it to Will. He wasn't very keen to mess with alcohol, especially in such a slippery situation as this, but didn't dare to object.

"To my dear friend," Will raised the goblet and drank. The wine was bittersweet with a quite distinctive aftertaste of citrus. It warmed his throat, and he could trace the sultry wave as it reached down to his stomach.

"Now it's my turn to have some delight," Qu Sith observed. "Would you mind holding the goblet for me?" he asked Will.

Will didn't understand the game but refilled the goblet. Nobody moved a muscle as he approached the sphinx.

"Go ahead," the beast nodded. "I'm feeling thirsty."

Will raised the goblet, and Qu Sith drank. Then the door burst open, and the raw rabbits arrived on a large silver tray. The girl was breathless but smiling as she approached the table and placed the tray in front of the sphinx.

"All out!" Qu Sith said cheerfully. "I want to enjoy my meal undisturbed by your glances!"

"I need to supervise the preparations for the funeral, your Majesty," Kroy said, bowing. "Would you excuse me?"

"Yes, you may go too," Qu Sith nodded.

Will watched the priest leaving the room, then placed his half-eaten rabbit leg back on the table and rose to his feet too.

"Sit down, human," the beast hissed. "We must talk!"

They watched the concubines depart and close the door. Only then did Will sit down at the foot of the dais again.

"Let's eat first," Qu Sith got closer to the tray and sank his teeth into the first rabbit.

Will was reluctant at first, but the pleasant warmth of wine in his stomach and the mild light-headedness it brought eased the tension a little, and he grabbed his half-finished piece of meat and began to chew again. Then he ate a few salad leaves, which served as the garnish and helped himself to another bit of roasted rabbit.

"I need you to clarify for me one delicate matter about a certain promise I gave you before we escaped captivity," Qu Sith whispered between two gulps.

"What is it?" Will instantly grew sober and stopped chewing; his heart skipped a few beats.

"If I remember things correctly, we were talking about tasting human flesh, and I agreed to your request," the black eyes of the beast drilled into Will's face. "The situation has changed."

"I won't release you from your oath," Will quickly shook his head. "It's for your own benefit."

"I'm not asking for that," Qu Sith said. "I need you to clarify if I would be breaking any part of my commitment if I killed an enemy but refrained from eating the body. I'm the ruler of Per Hathor now, and I think such a necessity may arise."

Will paled. "You're right," he sighed. "We only spoke about tasting."

"Good!" Qu Sith painted a happy smile across his face. "Then I can kill a few enemies without condemning myself to that degrading eternal service in the Tower, which is the essential part of my oath."

Will had no chance to respond. The door opened without warning, spitting in Kroy, garbed in the dark crimson cloak.

"It is time, your majesty," he announced. "All is ready."

"Stay close to me at all times!" Qu Sith ordered Will quietly.

"Yes, your Majesty," Will mumbled sarcastically and got up to his suddenly shaky feet. He didn't understand what was happening, and all that small talk with the sphinx had raised more questions. *Avoid any danger!*

Kroy led the way again, slowly this time. The sphinx went after him, a few paces to his left, and Will ambled along at the left side of the beast, as ordered. The whole entourage of concubines followed them, trailing behind at a respectful dozen paces.

The way was long and dark. A few times, Kroy was about to begin another session of whispers with the King but cast a few fiery glances from under his hood at Will and thought better of it. The girls followed silently with only their robes softly rustling in the dim light.

The corridors and terraces were strange – some of them were immaculate and brightly lit by the sun as it approached midday. Others were dark and gloomy, littered with pieces of broken marble, framed with cracked statues and colonnades, half-swallowed by black waves of frozen basalt. It was a strange palace in the ruined city that once was sacred. Will tried hard to keep up with the sphinx and barely had time to look around. His steps weren't sure, and his heart still trembled, troubled by the strange enquiries of the beast. This wasn't fun anymore. He wasn't sure what was going on inside the sphinx's head, and he realised that he might die here.

A few times, he contemplated taking a different turn at one of the forks of the route they were following but was afraid of getting lost. He had no doubts that these strange people would be able to locate him in no time at all, although he wasn't prepared to serve as a sacrificial lamb for their weird beliefs.

The gloomy corridor led into a burnt garden with charred dead trees on both sides of the paved path. They didn't stop or slow down.

"I thought the funeral was to be in the palace," Qu Sith mumbled.

"The Queen needs a big pyre, your Majesty," Kroy explained, leading them out of the garden and onto the narrow, cobblestoned street. "We built it in the pits."

"Oh," Qu Sith sighed.

The street wound between grim, half-destroyed houses that looked at them with empty eye sockets of absent windows. This part of the city seemed dead as they moved like restless ghosts among the gravestones.

Several intersections later, they turned right into a broader but just as lifeless avenue, heading south. Will looked at the empty windowless eye sockets of the buildings, and a creepy feeling took a firm grip of his heart. Countless figures in dark robes stood in the empty frames. Countless eyes stared at them silently as they passed down the street. The only sounds were the soft tinkling of the golden bells in the sphinx's hair and the never-ceasing mumbling of Kroy. The girls shuffled along in their long gowns a dozen paces behind them. Then the sound of shuffling grew stronger. Will glanced over his shoulder and gasped – dark-robed silhouettes were emerging from the houses they had passed and joining the procession.

The broad avenue was filling with people who moved after them silently like an army of ghosts. Will frantically looked around, searching for a way out of this nightmare, but it seemed that all possible routes were blocked, and he walked on unhappily next to the sphinx, heading to meet his fate.

"Who are these people?" Qu Sith asked.

"They are your people, your Majesty," Kroy said without slowing down.

"Why are they dressed in rags?"

"Your people are poor, Sire," Kroy shrugged. "And not many are left after the last devastation."

"What devastation?"

"When the lava wiped out half the city, Sire," Kroy said. "Sadly, I must point out, Sire, that your treasury was on that other side and perished in the fiery flow."

Qu Sith gave him a long stare.

"Yes, your Majesty," Kroy nodded absentmindedly, stroking the five rows of massive golden chains around his neck. His eyes were fixed somewhere ahead as he added. "There was no way to save your gold. All is lost. Most of your people there lost everything, too, except their rags. But, your Majesty, you are, of course, the King of a proud ancient nation!"

"Shit!" Qu Sith whispered and shook his mane, jingling the bells.

The avenue ended a mile later at the shore of a pit that had once been a deep lake, teeming with life. Its rugged bottom now lay dark and dry. The avenue climbed onto an arched bridge that rose high above the pit propped up by evenly spaced columns. It didn't go far. The southern bank was empty, buried deep under a thick layer of basalt, and the south part of the bridge lay crumbled to pieces on the bottom of the pit. They climbed onto the bridge and stopped a few paces away from its collapsed end, waiting. The crowds gathered along the shore of the lake behind them.

"Here is the Queen, your Majesty," Kroy uttered, gesturing beyond the edge of the crumbled bridge.

Will looked. A tall pyre had been built at a distance of no more than thirty paces away, and the huge body – at least twice as big as an adult man – of a Queen who was full of incongruities lay on top of it. Her three crowned heads peacefully rested on crimson cushions, staring at the sky with sightless eyes. Only the middle head was human – with the features of an attractive brunette with red eyes. Her left head stared at Will with the muzzle of a lioness. Her right head, barely visible on the other side, had the scaled features of a viper. Her body seemed randomly covered in patches of fur, scales and feathers, with just her breasts bare and seemingly human. Her hands, resembling the talons of a bird of prey, rested on her chest, clutching the golden sceptre of Per Hathor. Her lower body had been lost in the fight, the remnants covered with a crimson gown that ran in great folds down to the base of the pyre.

"Shall we begin, your Majesty?" Kroy cast a fiery glance at Will. "All is ready."

The bells in the sphinx's mane tinkled in the wind, and the priest raised his hand to give the signal without waiting for the word.

Only then Will noticed twelve men, dressed in black, at the base of the pyre. They held flaming torches and moved on as soon as Kroy waved.

Qu Sith rolled his eyes and growled impatiently as the men placed their torches at the base of the pyre and backed away a few steps. The wood was dry, and the flames rapidly flared up, devouring what was on offer. Nobody said a word or moved, but all eyes turned to Qu Sith when the flames rose.

"Why are they staring at me?" Qu Sith whispered.

"They're waiting for your sign, your Majesty," Kroy said quietly.

The sphinx frowned and nodded impatiently, and those twelve men did the unthinkable – they began to climb the flaming pyre.

"What are they doing?"

"They are companions to the Queen, your majesty," Kroy explained. "They are accompanying her to the Road of Gods."

Will watched the twelve figures in flaming robes climbing higher, slowing down, halting. None of them reached the top. None of them uttered a sound, drowning in flames, dying.

Clouds of dark fumes and smoke rose to the gloomy sky. When the flames, at last, touched the royal body, the priest lifted his hands in the air and began to sing. The crowd picked up the elaborate chant moments later and set it into motion.

The long line of mourners in dark robes slowly moved along the broken bridge and past the right side of concubines who had gathered in the centre. Each one of them approached the edge, bowed and threw something into the raging flames, uttering a few words, then bowed again, backed a few steps away, turned left and returned down the bridge back to the sacred city.

"What are they doing?" Qu Sith demanded.

"They are sacrificing their most valuable possessions to the Queen," Kroy explained between his chants. "Something they cherish most. I was about to suggest your Majesty do the same if you think it's appropriate for you to honour the Queen." He nodded slightly towards Will.

"Well..." the sphinx said uncertainly. "That might be a nice gesture, indeed."

Kroy waved his hand, and several men from among the mourners grabbed hold of the protesting Will. His brief life flashed in front of his eyes as he beheld the raging flames of the pyre.

"Stop!" Qu Sith roared. "Release him! I'm supposed to do that myself. Am I not?"

The hands holding Will froze then backed off after a slight nod from the priest.

"Did you say one must sacrifice something of the highest value? Something most desirable and unique?" the sphinx asked.

"Yes, your Majesty, of course," Kroy nodded with a foxy smile. Then he screamed as Qu Sith suddenly grabbed his thigh and hurled him high in the air, landing him on top of the pyre next to the Queen. Then he shrieked a few more times until the flames silenced him forever. The chant continued as if nothing had happened.

"I told you to stay close to me!" Qu Sith hissed at Will angrily.

"Yes, your Majesty," Will mumbled, barely coping with his trembling knees.

Will looked at the perishing skeletons in the flames of the pyre, feeling weak and barely able to move. The heat was immense, and everyone backed a few steps away, watching the flames rising high above the crumbling bridge. The stream of mourners seemed endless, and the chanting didn't cease for a second.

"How beautiful the ceremony is," the sphinx said with his eyes moist. "They must have loved their incredible Queen!"

"Or maybe they're just afraid of you?" Will mumbled. "As they were afraid of her." The beast didn't seem to hear.

For a few more hours, they stood on the bridge and waited as the mourners chanted their psalms and tossed their valuables into the flames of the pyre. The body of the Queen had perished before the pyre collapsed. The flow of mourners drained away soon after that.

"Let's get back to my chambers," Qu Sith said when the last mourner had tossed his gift to the flames. "I'm hungry and deadly tired."

And off they went, surrounded by the concubines, retracing their way back to the palace. The streets were empty as the mourners dispersed among the ruins, returning to their still habitable homes. The girls gently directed them each time the sphinx was about to take a wrong turn.

Will went grimly, watching his steps. Deadly fear still fluttered in his temples like the dark wings of a giant moth. *Would he have died in those flames?* Probably... *If the sphinx hadn't interfered, he would be roasted by now!* He felt ashamed for underestimating Qu Sith. Still, this business wasn't over yet, and he wasn't sure if he could trust the beast. The sphinx was a King now and could do whatever he pleased, and Will felt an urge to run – as far and as fast as he could. He didn't feel safe in this crazy city, but it wasn't the first crazy city that had tampered with his life.

They turned left and crossed the burnt garden again, disappearing into the long maze of corridors and passages of the palace.

"Two roasted rabbits for my human and four raw rabbits for me," Qu Sith ordered at the door of his chambers. "And someone gets these damned bells off me!"

The girls obeyed without wasting a second.

Qu Sith stretched out on his bed, frowning and mumbling without a moment's break as the concubines swarmed around him, disentangling the braids in the sphinx's mane. They had finished well before the rabbits arrived.

Will grimly watched the scene from the corner, sitting on the floor and leaning against the wall. He thought he knew the beast, but he hadn't been a King as they waited for their deaths in the cages. Qu Sith held absolute power over these people, and a single gesture from him could cause lives to be lost. Several men had ruthlessly died in front of his eyes today. *Would he be next?* Will sighed and firmly decided to sneak away at the first opportunity.

"Your rabbits," one of the girls woke him up from his daydreams and placed a silver tray in front of him with roasted meat, bread and a pitcher of wine.

A table with a much larger arrangement was placed in front of the sphinx's lair.

"All out!" Qu Sith growled. "I don't want you to count how many I eat!"

The concubines rushed out, casting back a few frightened glances. Will rose to his feet as well, leaving his food on the floor.

"You stay!" Qu Sith barked at Will – he flinched but obeyed.

"Do you want me to face the wall while you eat?" Will asked when the concubines had closed the door.

"Don't be silly," the beast rolled his eyes. "You've seen me eating, you've seen me shitting – sit down and eat your rabbits in peace!"

The peace didn't last long. Will had taken no more than a dozen decent bites of meat and a few gulps of wine while the sphinx had munched all of his rabbits and was licking the blood from his lips.

"The Queen was a beauty," Qu Sith sighed with sadness in his voice. "Don't you think?"

"A beauty?" Will said without thinking too much. "You call *that* monster a beauty?"

"You know nothing, human," the sphinx said, his eyes growing moist. "You must be a bull to understand the sexual appeal of a cow!"

"If you say so..." Will decided not to argue. "But was she a sphinx? She had no resemblance to a sphinx in my eyes."

"You're right," Qu Sith sighed. "She was a chimaera, an even more rare and ancient breed than sphinxes. Rhey, God of Creation, made her with her own hands!"

"That's good," Will took a large bite of the roasted meat, began to chew and added. "Then you're lucky!"

"I see no luck in this whole situation," the beast cut him short grimly.

Will shrugged. "If the Queen was a chimaera," he winked. "Then the female sphinx is still waiting for you somewhere."

"You are genius, human! I must find her," Qu Sith beamed a smile but wiped it away in the next instant. "But I can't leave my people."

"They weren't your people just two days ago," Will reminded him.

"But I'm their King now! They need me!"

"If you say so, your Majesty," Will put another piece of meat in his mouth and began to chew.

Qu Sith shook his head and growled. "Fine! You have a point, human. Still, we could benefit from the situation."

"How?"

"Kroy mentioned the Oracle," Qu Sith whispered as if afraid that somebody might overhear. "If it had predicted where and when we were about to emerge from the underground, maybe it can tell you where your flower is and tell me where to find the female sphinx."

"Is it that simple?"

"The Oracle is supposed to know everything," the sphinx shrugged. "We could try, at least."

"Time is ticking," Will reminded him. "We may lose the flower."

"I know," Qu Sith sighed. "Have you finished your rabbits?"

Will gulped down the last mouthful and drank his wine before nodding.

"Get me those girls then," the sphinx took a regal pose on his bed. "With Kroy roasted, I think they can arrange a meeting with the Oracle for their King."

Will obediently opened the door and nearly jumped out the way as the girls rushed in without any invitation, their transparent gowns and evening toiletries in their hands. Qu Sith rolled his eyes and roared at the top of his lungs before the concubines had a chance to get their hands on him.

The girls stopped, stunned.

"New rules!" the sphinx announced. "No grooming without me asking! And dress decently – I hate naked humans!"

"Yes, your Majesty," said one of the girls. "As you wish."

"Tomorrow, I will visit the Oracle," the beast added in a calmer voice. "Please, arrange everything that is necessary."

"Yes, Sire."

"Now - out! It's getting late, and I feel tired."

The girls curtsied before leaving the chambers. Qu Sith sighed and shook his head but didn't say anything until they had closed the door.

"Good training but in the wrong direction," the sphinx observed.

"Kroy's efforts, no doubt," Will agreed, going back into his corner.

"Are you comfortable there?" the beast asked.

"Yes," Will nodded. "I don't want to disturb your royal highness."

"Shit!" Qu Sith said, grimacing.

Will stretched out on the floor, still feeling the warmth of the wine in his stomach. It had been a stressful day, and he still felt some twitching in his muscles, remembering the funeral, but at least he had managed not to fall into the flames.

He hoped that his life was slowly getting back to normal. He didn't have that feeling yet, but he was going home. His heart raced faster at the thought, and a shy smile secretly sneaked upon his lips.

Will closed his eyes and let his mind slip away.

It was early morning. The sky had barely brightened over the dark, sleepy rooftops, but the streets were familiar. Will blinked, gazed through the window and smiled. *He was almost home!*

"Damn you all," he said softly, addressing no one in particular. "I'll prove you're wrong."

The traffic was non-existent, and the bus quietly made its way up and down hilly streets with sleepy houses with black windows gazing indifferently at Will. He closed his eyes, anticipating the morning quiet of his home. It would be bliss to stretch out in his bed like he had done before and think about nothing, listening to the muffled sounds of eggs being scrambled for breakfast or the making of an omelette – he always guessed incorrectly.

They passed his old gym – the windows dark and lifeless. Will sighed, suppressing the rising wave of emotions. *Boys don't cry!* But he would gladly shed a tear, being so close to home after sleeping rough in that indifferent metropolis. Will sighed again, squeezed his fists, turned away from the window and closed his eyes. He opened them only a few minutes later when the bus stopped at the station.

Will grabbed his rucksack and sprinted off, gasping. He hadn't got far from the bus when suddenly he felt weak at his knees as he watched the bus depart and he crawled to the nearest bench.

His life was getting back on track – he had escaped from London. But instead of feeling happy, he was sad, his eyes watered, and shy tears rolled down his burning cheeks. *Why?* Will sighed one more time and wiped the moisture from his eyes with slightly trembling hands. He quickly glanced around – it was early morning, and no one was around to witness his shame.

His hometown was slowly waking up around him. Will took a few deep breaths as if preparing to lift the heaviest barbell, and a cold fear crept into his heart. What if he had indeed somehow been erased from his family? Even if it did sound crazy, and he had no trust in those tales told by creepy Londoners. Still, his heart trembled like a frightened robin in the deadly grasp of a stray cat. *What if they had done that?* He didn't dare even to think about what might happen.

Will spent almost an hour on the bench, trying to fight off the irrational fear. He was almost home. *Almost!* But he had no plan B and couldn't permit himself the luxury of failure. *Everything will be fine!* He kept repeating this until he almost began to believe it.

Finally, that cold grip of fear eased a little but didn't go away completely, and Will spent some more time on the bench organising his thoughts and watching the early passengers hurrying into the train station across the street.

Everything will be fine...

Coming home didn't seem to be as easy as he had anticipated.

Above him, the sky grew milky blue with a hint of rose pink as the street filled with early cars and the pavements with pedestrians. It was time to move. He took a deep breath, stood up and pulled his hood up. His feet still felt limp as he left the bus station and turned right, heading uphill.

The crowds grew larger as the day broke and traffic filled the street. Will kept his steps steady, his mighty frame towering amongst the scurrying people when the sudden memory of the menace in the red car made his heart skip a beat. *Damned Jill!* He frowned, peering at the steadily moving traffic. A few cars in the traffic line were red, but they didn't move erratically, and the drivers were all male.

Will hastily turned right at the first crossroad, slipping into a side street. Some time had passed since the last encounter with the fatty blob before he had run away from the hospital, and Jill might already be roaming around freely. He might be forced to deal with her somehow and claim his life back, but later, not now. He must stay away from red cars. He had more pressing problems to worry about. Will forced Jill's protesting image out of his mind and went down the street under the shade of chestnut trees.

He went slowly. Occasional dry leaves gently crunched under his feet. His steps were hesitant, and it seemed that he had left all the joy of coming home on that bus which was now miles away, speeding north on unknown roads. Fear followed his steps closely like a dark shadow. *What if his mother rejected him again? What if she was still mad?* He wouldn't be going back to London in any case – he decided firmly. These streets were as good for sleeping rough on as the streets of the capital. Maybe even better. If she needed more time, he would wait here.

The road went uphill, winding between the neat houses and sleek gardens. Will carried on, ignoring the beauty and seeing nothing, his worries piling up with every step. The street was quiet – just a few cars and even fewer joggers had passed him. His feelings were mixed and confused. The anticipation of a home was thrilling by itself, but Will was terrified by the difficult conversation that awaited between him and his mother.

He emerged onto the main road just a few hundred yards away from his home. The windows were still dark, and Will stopped, hesitating – he hated to begin that awkward conversation on the wrong foot by waking his mother up too early. She was probably still asleep and might get angry if she was disturbed. He owed her a massive apology already and didn't dare complicate things even further. He needed to adopt a slow approach and appropriate timing. And he needed a good and believable story that could save his skin from further humiliation. He had no idea how far his troubles had advanced in his absence, but he decided against mentioning Jill.

Will turned left and went a few paces downhill. He sat down on a low bench at the bus stop, waiting. Several cars passed down the road, but the real morning traffic was still almost an hour away.

The morning chill calmed down his muscles, but his heart remained uneasy. The breaking day had woken up anxiety that made him shudder, drowning in a flow of desperate thoughts. He didn't recognise himself anymore. *What if she was still angry?* Will glanced at the distant rooftops down the road. *Where should he go then? Wait here? She might call the police again!*

The traffic grew steadily, and he was no longer alone at the bus stop. A few women from the neighbouring houses came to wait for a bus, and he moved to the far edge of the bench, making space for them to sit down. They just glanced at him once but didn't take the offered seat. A bus arrived a few minutes later, and they left without saying a single word.

Will waited.

A light wind brought him the pleasant aromas of freshly made coffee, scrambled eggs and toast from the nearby houses where people were getting up and preparing for the new day. His home was still dark, and Will began to worry if something terrible had happened to his family. It seemed like his sister would be late for school. Still, he waited on the bench, battling the growing anxiety.

More people gathered at the bus stop. There was a small crowd in a matter of minutes, impatiently glancing at their watches. An elderly couple sat down on the bench next to Will. He peered at them covertly, but their faces weren't familiar.

A few minutes later, a bus stopped in front of them, and all the crowd began to squeeze on, paying for their tickets, getting into their seats and obscuring Will's view of what was happening on the other side of the street behind the moving traffic.

When the bus left, at last, his heart skipped a few beats as his mother emerged from the house with his sister and locked the door. Will jumped to his feet and waved happily, but his efforts went unnoticed. *Almost unnoticed!* His mother's gaze slipped over him without stopping as if he was an empty space.

Anxiety gripped Will's throat, stifling a cry as he watched helplessly while the two dearest women in his life got into the car, his mother started the engine, and the car joined the flow of traffic. They were gone in an instant, leaving Will's mouth gaping.

My sister must be late for school, the thought flashed through Will's mind, trying to soothe his heart. But his mother still was angry, he was sure about that. Some hard times lay ahead for him

– he was certain about that too.

Will slumped back on the bench, sighing helplessly. He must get closer. *She'll probably be back in about fifteen minutes – the school isn't far away.* Her heart couldn't be made of stone. He was her only son! She must give him a chance.

Another bus stopped in front of him, halting some of the traffic, and Will dashed forward, ignoring a few curses and loud shouts. Trembling, he sat down on the doorstep and closed his eyes, afraid of the tears spilling out. His home was so close yet on the other side of the locked door. He must wait.

An hour passed, waiting. The morning rush was over now, with just occasional cars passing along the street in both directions. Will leant against the door but jumped to his feet when his mother's car finally pulled into the driveway. A terrible wave of fear washed over him, his knees shook, and he had to lean against the door again to steady himself.

His mother got out, collected her grocery bags, locked the car and then turned to face him. Will attempted a shy smile, but his greeting wasn't returned.

"Please, forgive me, mum," he whispered, getting closer. "I'll be different. I promise..."

She didn't answer, standing still with the bags of groceries in her hands, and Will dared to embrace her. Tears rolled down his cheeks, and his muscular body trembled like a leaf in a high wind.

Then, for a few minutes, he just held her, grateful for not being told to go away. He could feel her heart galloping terribly in her chest, but not a muscle moved in her body, and not a single sigh escaped from her mouth.

Something wasn't right.

"Mum?" he kissed her cheek and looked at her uncertainly. Her body felt frozen like a marble statue, with just her grey eyes following him. Was she having a fit? He embraced her tightly. A few seconds later, it was over.

"Get off me, you pervert!" she suddenly exploded and hit him with a grocery bag. "Go away!"

Will backed away a few steps.

"Mum? I'm your son, Willy..."

Her face was furious.

"I don't have a son!" she retorted through gritted teeth. "Stay away from this house! Stay away from my daughter! I know your kind, you pervert! Go away, or I'll call the police!"

"Mum?"

"Go away!" she placed the bag on the ground and got her phone out. "I'm calling the police!"

Will knew she would do it and backed away a few more steps. "Could we talk, mum?" he asked her meekly.

"I'm not your mum! Go away, you pervert! Now!"

Will picked up his rucksack and dashed down the street before she could dial the number. He knew from her stance that she meant business. He knew her well. She was still angry! Still very angry!

He stopped a few hundred steps later and looked back. Hot tears rolled down his cheeks, but he didn't care if anybody could see them. He had failed to convince her. *He had failed!* Maybe she needed more time?

His mother picked up her groceries and went inside without even casting a second glance at him. *Damned Jill!* Will sighed, his body still trembling with sorrow. He must calm down. And he needed a plan.

Almost ten minutes passed before his tears dried as he gazed at his home – so close yet out of his reach. Then he brushed the moisture away, pulled his hood up as far as it would go, turned around and went downhill.

Will had no doubt – this was Jill's doing. She had probably let her tongue loose. *Shit!* Maybe she had even let her fantasy loose too. It might involve much effort to undo the damage.

Will sighed. His heart was breaking and bleeding as he stepped away from his home. To retreat was the only option left to him. He had returned too soon while his mother still fumed and called him a pervert.

It was a glorious day, but Will crawled down the street like a zombie, seeing nothing around on his way. Fear squeezed his mind into a tiny spiky ball, sufficient only to process putting one foot in front of the other. He had been a lone wolf his entire life and had been quite happy about that, but now Will felt lonelier than ever. He circled the town centre a couple of times until the deadly grip of frustration eased and the ability to think returned. His mother might still be angry and remain stubborn for a while, so he needed a mole, a secret ally in his home.

He must find his sister! At least she could help to pinpoint the best moment to approach their mother.

Will sighed as the day became a little brighter. He still had no idea where to spend the night, but at least he had a plan for immediate action. It was already early afternoon, and classes at school could finish any time soon – he must hurry to catch her.

Will hastily crossed the road and slipped down a side street on the right. He knew the place and almost ran uphill in the shade of giant chestnuts. He was breathless, and his heart insanely raced when he reached the top, but he didn't slow down – he had no time to rest.

Will turned right at the next crossroad and dashed across the street, dodging between two moving cars. He didn't stop to listen to the curses aimed at him.

The street was long and narrow, winding between the neatly trimmed gardens and attractive houses on the right and a tall brick wall on the left that hid the park and the school grounds.

Will cursed as a bunch of children in school uniform burst through the gate, and the cars of concerned parents began to line the street. He thought he saw his mother's car parked at the end of the road, although he wasn't certain. Will cursed and slipped through the gate. He forced his shaking hands and trembling heart to calm down, carefully making his way amongst the chatting pupils like an elephant in a shop of delicate porcelain.

Will spotted his sister in the field on the left, talking with two other girls. They looked happy, joking and giggling, and his hands trembled slightly as he hesitantly approached them.

"Hello, Rose," he said.

The jokes and giggling ceased, and all three girls turned to face him.

"Do I know you?" his sister blushed, but her voice was cold, and Will's heart sank.

"Can we talk for a minute?" his voice almost begged.

The other girls giggled and ran away, leaving Rose to face Will. He knew he hadn't much time – his mother was waiting in the car and would come to look if his sister didn't show up after too long.

"My mother doesn't allow me to talk to strangers," she said. "Especially, men."

"Don't you recognise me?" he asked, his voice breaking.

She squinted at him but shook her head firmly. "No."

"I'm your brother, Willy," he uttered. "Don't you remember

having a brother?"

Rose shook her head again. "I have to go," she said.

"Wait!" Will was almost ready to kneel in front of her. "Think harder, please! My room is opposite yours, just across the landing. Don't you remember?"

"The storage?" she chuckled. "Do you live in the storage room?"

"It's not storage – look inside! My bed, my table and my laptop are there! And you can find my photos on the laptop! I'm your brother, Rose!"

"I don't have any brothers. I have to go."

"I know you have to go," Will said. "Our mother is waiting. I don't know what they've done to you to make you not remember, Rose. There is proof. Just promise to have a look inside my room. Please, look at the photos on the computer. You'll remember. Please!"

"I have to go," Rose repeated firmly.

Will nodded. "I'll meet you tomorrow. Please, have a look. Just have a look. You can keep the computer if you find the photos!"

"I'll go into the storage room. I promise," Rose said and went away, leaving Will trembling.

He slumped to the ground helplessly. *Maybe that crazy Indian bitch had been right?* Indeed, it all seemed very strange. Maybe they had done something horrible to his family while he was away?

Will watched Rose go, and a dark bird of guilt began to spread its shadowy wings over him. Would everything be different if he hadn't run away from the hospital?

Will looked helplessly around. His world was crumbling before his very eyes. Still, he had a slim hope – Rose had promised to have a look at his photos. Maybe then she would be able to remember him?

Clearly, another night on the streets awaited him. Will sighed and stood up, picking up his rucksack. He had no idea where to go, just pulled up his hood and sneaked back onto the street, hunching over.

He saw Rose in the distance, getting into his mother's car. The car left a few minutes later, and he went after them, pulled by some invisible force. He knew he was unwelcome but couldn't suppress the desire to see his dearest, at least from afar.

The car speeded up and out of sight, but the streets were familiar, and he knew the way. There was no need to rush.

Will crept on, hunching over like a thief, his hood pulled up over his eyes, his gaze fixed on the cracks in the pavement. *Damn!* How could his life have got this low? *Damned Jill and her fantasies!* She was the driving force behind his mother's anger – Will was sure about that. But he had no idea how to explain his sister's behaviour. They had never been close, but now her distance was really over the top. She hadn't smiled once and seemed embarrassed to speak with him.

Will went on drowning in grim thoughts and lifting his eyes only to cross the occasional side street. Of course, he had expected some misery, arguments and accusations, shouting, swearing and crying, maybe even the breaking of a few plates. But he hadn't expected total and complete rejection.

A few crossroads later, the road ended at the High Street, and he turned right, heading uphill. The grim thoughts followed him like a dark cloud.

Will went slowly, barely paying attention to the growing traffic as people finished their nine-to-five jobs and headed home. He was heading home too but was unwanted, neglected and ignored. Hope was fading.

His mother's car was parked in front of the house. Will stopped, suddenly unsure how to proceed. He crawled along a few more paces and then stopped again, gasping. His mother was in the kitchen. She peered at him through the window – her face expressionless, the phone in her right hand, standing still like a statue. Will hunched over and ran forward. It still wasn't the right time to approach her again. *Not yet!*

He stopped a few hundred paces later, breathing heavily. His heart raced liked mad, and he had to spend a few minutes calming down and regaining the ability to think.

He must wait! If he kept angering her, he might end living on the streets forever. He must wait for a more appropriate moment to soften her heart.

Will turned left at another crossroad. The sign clearly labelled it as a cul-de-sac, but it was only a dead-end for cars – he knew this place! There was a narrow footpath between the two houses on the left, and Will sneaked there, walking down the narrow track with rampant weeds on either side.

He went on in no-man's-land beneath the shade of shrubs and trees, squeezed between the sleek backyard gardens of the nearby houses. It was a damp place in perpetual shadow, and Will slowly carried on forward, pushing away occasional cobwebs and trying to get a better view of his home.

The backyard looked exactly as he remembered. He stopped, peering at the windows from the dark shrubs, and immense sadness squeezed his heart. *Home.* It was there, on the other side of the fence. It was still unreachable.

Life in the living room went on as if nobody was missing. The TV was on, and his sister was reading a book. His mother went into the room several times to ask her something. Obviously, Will couldn't hear what his sister replied.

Will gripped the fence as he silently watched his family. Then the weeds shuffled to his right, and he tore his eyes away from the living room window to have a look. A pitiful white one-eyed stray cat emerged onto the path and stopped, peering at him. Her scraggy body trembled, and she held a tiny kitten in her mouth. She put her treasure on the ground and opened her mouth. Her miaow was barely audible.

Will cursed. "Go away!" he said to the cat.

The cat didn't move but answered something in her own language, her single eye still fixed at Will.

"Go away! I can't care for your kid!" he exploded, waving his hands. "I don't have a home! I don't have food! I can't even take care of myself! Go away! Go! Go!"

The poor animal jumped a few feet down the path, then sneaked back, grabbed her kitten and dashed into the thick shrubs.

Will cursed again. Now, as he said it aloud, the wave of loss and helplessness splashed over him with full force, submerging his soul in unbearable pain. He gasped for air as if he was drowning. Here was his home – the place where he had grown up and the place where he was safe. Here was his sister – reading a book in the living room. His mother was roasting a chicken in the kitchen – he could smell the familiar delicious aroma. Only he was standing on the other side of the fence, feeling like a starfish on the shore – observing the unreachable familiar life and slowly dying inside.

Uncontrollable tears rolled down his cheeks, but all he could do was watch and wait for his sister to glance at his laptop and end all this misery. He didn't care if anyone spotted him crying.

An hour passed before his cheeks dried. Dusk was already spreading over the town when Rose put the book aside, turned off the TV and left the room. She never glanced through the window across the backyard where Will was gripping the fence. She just put the lights off and left.

They're in the kitchen – a thought flashed through Will's clouded brain. He could see the narrow band of light across the living room. It was dark when that narrow band of light went off, and soft yellow light squeezed through the floral curtains of his sister's window. A few minutes later, the windows in his mother's bedroom lit up too. Will patiently waited. Then the light went on in his room. It was the light of hope, and his heart began to beat faster as he saw Rose enter the room. Will couldn't see what she was doing, but she didn't stay in there for long. The lights soon went off.

Will turned around and left his hiding place. *She had been to have a look!* The hope was tiny but alive, and he didn't want to scare it away. *One more night* – he sighed – *one more night...*

He sneaked back to the cul-de-sac and turned right. The street was quiet at this time, and he stopped in front of his home. The windows were already dark. Will looked up at the cloudless night sky but couldn't read any assurance in the stars. Hesitantly, he stepped closer, ready to run away at any moment.

The door was cold to the touch, but he leant against it, unable to resist. His heart trembled, and tears pooled in his eyes again. Will pressed his ear to the door, listening. Nothing... The house was quiet.

He sat down on the doorstep. The home was so close but still unreachable. He sighed and stretched out his body on the porch, placing the rucksack under his head. If he must sleep on the street, this place was as good as any. And it felt safe.

He closed his eyes, feeling deadly tired. The next instant, his mind had been carried away.

Ray Zdan

❧ ✿ ☙

The King was alone in his bed, still sleeping. Will sat up, leaned against the wall and quietly stretched his muscles. It was early morning. He glanced at the pale blue sky outside the window where a few fluffy clouds slowly travelled eastwards, painted pink in the warm rays of the morning sun.

It was time for him to leave this nonsense and get back to his mission. He had wasted too much time already. Anybody could pick that blue orchid up, and he could almost physically feel his luck diminishing with each passing minute. Could he sneak away while the King was asleep? He hated goodbyes but was sure he wouldn't be able to go far without the sphinx's blessing. He must remind Qu Sith of the importance of his mission. The beast might be less interested in obtaining the flower with the Queen dead, but he must return the blossom to Hel.

Will sat and looked at the sleeping beast and contemplated the most convincing words for his farewell. Nothing useful came to mind. Then a distant turmoil broke into his consciousness. At first, he dismissed it as an annoying fly without paying much attention, but then the noise grew louder. People were arguing somewhere down the corridor, their voices rising to higher notes and getting closer to the King's bedchamber.

"What is it?" Qu Sith asked impatiently, lifting his head from his bed.

Will shrugged, but the sphinx wasn't looking at him. His angry eyes were staring at the door, which suddenly burst open without a preceding knock. Three men, dressed in dark blue togas, walked in, bowed and closed the door.

"Excuse us for the intrusion at such an early hour, your Majesty," one of the men said. "But the matter is urgent and requires your immediate attention."

"Who are you?" Qu Sith growled with growing agitation.

"Senan, Cathal and Cillian," the man said, bowing.

"Who are you?" the sphinx repeated the question, frowning.

"We're the priests of the Oracle, your Majesty!"

"What do you want?"

"Our establishment is small but very important for the city, your Majesty," one of the men stepped forward uncertainly. "And now we no longer have a high priest. We were told about your Majesty's desire to visit the Oracle, but we don't have a high priest to supervise it!"

"And you came here to cry for Kroy?"

"No, your Majesty, of course not," the man shook his head. "Your notorious sacrifice was the most heartfelt gesture for the late Queen. She must be delighted to have her adviser accompanying her on the Road of Gods."

"Then why are you interrupting my sleep?"

"I beg you to excuse us, your Majesty," the priest took one more step forward. "But maybe you could appoint a new high priest?"

"Appoint you?"

"Or Cathal. Or Cillian, your Majesty." The other two men quickly nodded.

"You haven't a very broad priesthood, have you?"

"No, your Majesty. We have had no time to expand," Senan said, blushing. "There were four of us who found the Weeping Rock. Now, as Kroy is accompanying the Queen, we need a new leader."

"And do you think any of you are suitable for the job?"

"Yes, your Majesty."

Qu Sith took his time to inspect the faces of all three men. They squirmed under his gaze, waiting expectantly.

"I can't decide," Qu Sith said at last. "I need advice from the Oracle."

"Now?" Senan asked.

"Yes, now."

"The Oracle might not be ready…"

"You're not worthy of being a high priest if you can't make the Oracle ready when your King requests this."

Senan swallowed before nodding.

"The Oracle will be ready," he said and glanced at the other two for support. "We will do what we can."

"Let's go then," Qu Sith jumped off his bed and briefly stopped in front of Will. "I want you to accompany me at all times," the sphinx told him, leaving no room for argument. "Let's go. You'll be able to ask your question too."

The concubines were lined along the wall and facing the door, holding bowls of water, soaps, brushes, combs, towels and perfumed oils in their hands.

"None of those things will be necessary today," Qu Sith ordered them. "Leave everything here and follow us." He didn't wait to check if his order was being carried out correctly.

The three priests led the way, walking half a step ahead of the sphinx but constantly arguing and quarrelling. Qu Sith went after them looking bored and barely listening to their squabbling. Will walked to the right of the sphinx, and the entire entourage of concubines strolled after them, maintaining the respectful distance of a dozen steps. They went the same way as they had done yesterday, passing the shady corridors, dead gardens and semi-ruined streets. The crowds they had seen yesterday were gone.

They went past the broken bridge where the ashes of the Queen's pyre were still smouldering in the light breeze. The priests didn't stop here; they barely noticed the site, immersed in some weird theological discussion.

They carried on along the beach of the dry lake. Then, half a mile later, they went underground again through the entrance of a grand palace, half-swallowed by a giant frozen wave of black basalt.

Unlike the King's chambers, the place was guarded by five men armed with short swords and crossbows. They sat in a big hall around a fire pit quietly talking but jumped to their feet as soon as the whole entourage entered.

"Torches for the King!" ordered Cathal, and the men stirred into action.

Will looked at the commotion with indifference and a certain distant sadness. He was wasting time. Maybe some other guy was picking up that lost orchid at this very moment! Why had Qu Sith dragged him here? He must find the flower! *No time for this nonsense!* He must go as soon as they got back into daylight. He needed that blossom! He just hoped it wasn't too late. No more delays from the sphinx – King or no King, he must attend to his own business.

The guards brought several torches and began to light them

one by one from the flames of the fire pit. Cillian was the first to grab a lighted torch. "Follow me, Sire," he turned to the right where the black mouth of a corridor gaped in the gloom.

Qu Sith ignored him, waiting for the other torches to be lit. "I've had enough of wandering in the dark," the sphinx squeezed quietly through his teeth for Will's ears only. "I won't go after one fool with a torch. I'll wait for more light!"

"I must go and search for that flower!" Will told the beast, keeping his voice low as well.

"You can ask the Oracle about its whereabouts," Qu Sith shrugged. "We'll eat first after we return, and then you can go if you wish."

That sounded good enough, and Will nodded.

"We're ready, your Majesty," Senan announced. All three priests held a flaming torch as well as three concubines from the sphinx's entourage.

"Let's go," said the King. And on they went, surrounded by the flickering light.

A sickening stench met them in the corridor. The priests bravely carried on, but Will heard some unrest among the concubines.

"What's that smell?" Qu Sith asked. The answer revealed itself a dozen steps later – decomposing corpses pinned to the walls. "What's this?" the beast demanded on a higher note.

"Kroy ordered the sacrifice of the first pilgrims," Senan offered an explanation. "He thought that the Oracle was a great gift from the Gods, and we should pay something back."

"How many?"

"All of them, Sire," it was Cillian's voice from the gloom. "Twelve."

"And now they are decorating these walls?"

"Don't you find this appropriate, Lord?"

"No," Qu Sith told them firmly. "Have them removed and placed on a pyre!"

"It will be done as you wish, your Majesty," Cathal nodded in the flickering light. "That is a noble decision of the King."

They went on, passing more corpses. Will tried to look away, but his nose failed him each time they got nearer, sending his stomach into painful spasms. This time he was glad they had skipped breakfast as the air was thick with the unbearable stench.

Senan seemed slightly nervous as they left the corridor several hundred yards later and stepped into a colossal cavern. Steep black walls ran almost three hundred feet up to meet a high dome with a hole in the centre – Will could see the clouds passing lazily overhead. It used to be a large square of the sacred city with a small fountain in the centre before the volcano had claimed the entire place. Some houses at the perimeter had been flattened to rumble by lava, some were still standing, but all were engulfed by countless layers of black basalt that framed the rugged walls and dome of the cavern.

A long stalactite, formed by the once fiery flow, hung from the northern edge of the hole in the dome, thin, resembling a bloodied sword in the light of the flickering torches, its tip hanging almost halfway to the ground. As shapeless and ugly as a crushed mushroom, its stalagmite counterpart rose nearly thirty feet above the cobblestoned square and hung over the dry fountain like a frozen wave.

The priests went closer to the fountain, raising their torches as high as they could.

"This is the Weeping Rock, your Majesty," Senan said with notes of piety in his voice.

"Impressive..." Qu Sith said flatly, clearly disappointed. "Why is it called Weeping? I see no tears..."

"We had no time to prepare the Oracle for your visit, Sire," Cillian said.

"What is needed for the preparation?"

"A few bundles of firewood and a little time, your Majesty," Cathal explained, gesturing to the empty fountain. "We need to warm the Rock. It speaks only then."

"It speaks?"

"Yes, your Majesty."

"Then do it!" Qu Sith ordered rather impatiently and added

with disdain. "Amateurs! And those damned retards want to serve the Oracle?"

The firewood wasn't far away – a few piles had been dumped near the left wall of the cavern. Qu Sith didn't have to repeat his order. The priests obediently fixed their torches on the wall of the dry fountain and hurried to pick up the firewood. They made that journey twice.

Then Cathal slipped into the dry fountain and began to build some elaborate structure resembling a hexagonal pyramid. He checked the position with the overhanging basalt a few times, and once he moved the structure half a foot to the left. Cillian and Senan made a few more trips to bring more firewood.

Qu Sith watched the progress with growing impatience. "Is this Oracle known for correct prophesies?" he asked.

"It predicted that you were coming, your Majesty," Senan answered, passing firewood to Cathal. "That has been its only prophecy so far, and it was true."

"I see..." Qu Sith said. "What questions were asked by those cadavers?"

"We don't know, your Majesty. Kroy ordered their sacrifice before they had a chance to open their mouths."

"I see..."

"Would you like to sacrifice somebody to the Oracle too, your majesty?"

"Yes," Qu Sith nodded grimly. "I'll sacrifice any one of you who talks too much!"

For some time, they silently watched the priests working.

"I don't like this situation," Will whispered to the sphinx.

"Me neither," the beast sighed. "They sacrifice humans too easily and in too great a number. I'll run out of peasants if that doesn't change!"

"May I go now? I must find the flower!"

"I want you to test the Oracle, human," Qu Sith told him quietly. "Ask where your flower is, and then you can send me a message if you find it there. This might save you time searching, and I'll get to know how truthful that rock is."

Will sighed. "I'll do that for you."

"Thank you."

They were interrupted by Cathal. "We're ready, your Majesty."

"Go on!" Qu Sith nodded. "Do it!"

Cathal raised his torch and carefully inserted it into the base of the firewood pyramid. Then he backed away, nodding, bending his head and mumbling something incoherent. He jumped out of the fountain pit as soon as he reached the edge.

"Well?" Qu Sith demanded.

"Now, we must wait until it begins to weep," Cathal said, keeping his eyes on the rock.

The wood was dry, so the flames climbed quickly to the top of the pyramid, licking the overhanging cliff. Then it happened. At first, it was a sigh, quiet and barely audible as if a late autumn wind was making its way through dead leaves.

"Why?" a voice asked quietly somewhere from the top of the overhanging cliff and broke into a sob.

"We seek your knowledge," Cathal said, addressing the rock.

The rock didn't answer but kept sobbing for some time. Nobody dared to interrupt, only watching the flames go higher.

"You are cruel people," the Oracle said at last. "You will be harshly punished for your deeds. All your cruelty will return to you tenfold! I know he will come and punish you! He will punish you for all those sufferings! Be afraid, cruel people! Be very afraid! He is coming! He is coming!"

"He is here already," Cathal dared to interrupt the prophecy. "The King is here..."

The Oracle of the Weeping Rock stopped sobbing. "Bryn?"

Will flinched as if struck with a stick. Qu Sith glanced at him just briefly, then turned his angry gaze at the priests.

"Bryn? Is that you?" the rock demanded.

Will hesitantly went closer to the rock. The voice seemed familiar. "Gudula?" he asked.

"Bryn!"

"What's going on?" Qu Sith asked.

"I'll explain later," Will dropped hastily and began to climb the rock. "Please, have the flames extinguished!"

"You heard him!" the sphinx roared at the priests.

Will had no time to look at the turmoil behind him. He cursed, climbing. It was hot, unbearably hot, but he didn't stop. Thick acrid clouds of smoke engulfed him as he got higher, his eyes began to water, and he had to stop twice, struck by a vicious bout of coughing. The cliff wasn't high, but the way up seemed as if it took an eternity. The stench of burning flesh hit him as he reached the top. The priests did something to the pyre as the clouds of smoke began to clear a little by that time.

Still covered with smoke, the clifftop seemed empty, Will's eyes watered, and he couldn't see anything but the rock. Then he saw something move – something at first resembling a broken dry branch of a tree.

"Gudula?" he asked, taking a few steps forward uncertainly.

"Bryn!" the dry branch waved a little, and then Will saw her. He had to look away and fight a terrible bout of sickness before he could glance at her again.

The girl – what was left of her – was half-buried in the black rock. What had looked like a dry tree branch among the receding smoke was her left arm – the skin burned down, a few fingers missing, barely moved by parched dark brown muscles. Her head rested on a rock, turned slightly to the right, her hair, nose and left ear were gone, her skull almost bare, looking at Will with empty eye sockets. Her blackened right breast was scarred and deformed. Her left breast had melted away, and her beating heart was visible through the charred ribs of the chest wall in front of the collapsed left lung. Her waist and the lower trunk were buried in the rock.

"Bryn? Is that you?" her mouth barely moved, white teeth shining like pearls behind the parched lips.

"Yes, Gudula," Will sighed. He didn't dare to object to her using that wrong name. She had been dead when he gave her body to the flames. It was the blue orchid that had revived her and kept her alive through this entire ordeal. It was he who had placed the orchid on her chest before pushing the body into the flowing lava. The guilt now was unbearable. "I'm sorry," he said, keeping his eyes away from her.

"It's not your fault, Bryn," she whispered. "I always knew you would come to save me. It is not your fault that there's not much of me left to rescue. I'm tired, Bryn. Very tired. I'm long overdue for my journey to the Road of Gods. I must go, but that thing keeps me."

"What thing?"

"I don't know, Bryn," she sighed. "I can't see. There's something in my chest. I feel some immense cold there, which is holding my soul. It won't let it go. I don't know what it is."

He kneeled next to her. The smoke had cleared completely, but the rock was still uncomfortably hot. He frowned, trying to bend closer and to get a better look at her chest.

"Do you see it?" she demanded.

Will watched the beating heart for a few seconds. The left lung was collapsed – he saw the black spurs of basalt seeping between the ribs. There was nothing inside the left walls of the chest. Then he saw something move behind the beating heart, and Will realised that it was the right lung still doing its job and pumping air. There was a faint flash of blue between the heart and the moving lung, and Will sighed.

"Yes, I see it," he said.

"What is it?"

"A blue flower."

"A flower?"

"Yes, there's nothing else inside but the blue flower. It's right behind your heart."

"Can you see my heart?"

"Yes, it's there, beating."

"Oh, Bryn! I can just imagine how ugly that looks. Forgive me, love, please."

"There's nothing to forgive."

She felt silent for a few long minutes. Will patiently waited.

"I know it's very much to ask, love," she said at last in a low but firm voice. "Could you take that flower out of me, please?"

"But that will kill you!"

"I've died thousands of times already," she said, her voice still firm. "I can handle one more time. It's not a life to be half-buried in rock and wait until some feeble-minded folks build a fire beneath. You must free me – free me from this burden. It is much better to be dead than this!"

"I'm sorry..." Will whispered again.

"Don't be sorry, love," she whispered back. "This is the only way you can help me."

"I'll try," with a heavy heart Will moved closer.

The smell of burnt flesh was sickening, and his hands shook as he touched the charred rib cage. Gudula stirred and sighed.

"Is it painful?" he gasped. "My fingers are too thick to get in."

"Could you break a few ribs?" she asked. "I won't need them anyway."

"That could be painful."

"Don't worry, love. Just do it, please."

"Sorry," he said, then clenched his right fist and punched her chest. She screamed. The ribs shattered and crumbled easily, and he didn't need to hit twice. "Sorry," he apologised again when she had finished screaming.

"Thank you, Bryn," she said, gasping. "Now take that flower, love..."

"Goodbye, Gudula," Will sighed and reached behind her heart.

She didn't answer, just jerked a few times and grew still. "Rest in peace," he added, standing up, the blue orchid in his hand.

He had no strength to touch the dead girl again. He had found the lost blossom, but there was no joy in his heart. There was a heavy feeling there, and he almost cried, holding it in his palm. The girl had been annoying, but she hadn't deserved everything that had happened to her. *Damn!* It was his fault! He looked again at the charred remains in the gloom of the cavern, unsure now if it was appropriate just to leave her here. She didn't even have any eyes that he could close.

"Goodbye, Gudula," he whispered again and began the descent.

The way down took much longer than it had up.

"You found your flower," Qu Sith observed as Will came nearer.

"But you lost your Oracle, your Majesty, I'm afraid," Will shrugged. "Could you order a proper pyre to be built one last time? There's a body on top of that cliff."

"Did you have to fight to get your flower back?" the sphinx demanded.

"No," Will responded sourly. "It was given back to me with love."

"Then why did you kill the Oracle? This might be a problem."

"She was dead already," Will sighed. "That flower was the

only thing that was holding her. She gave it back to me voluntarily. She wasn't an Oracle after all. She was just a stupid innocent girl in love."

"I've heard that love makes humans crazy," Qu Sith sighed and then turned to the priests. "So, you retards, never bothered to have a look at the Oracle? Never seen who was talking? Now she's dead! No more Oracle and no more priests of the Oracle! Bring the firewood – all of it! You're building a pyre on top of that cliff. We must help your Oracle to reach the Road of Gods!"

The sphinx didn't have to repeat his orders to Senan, Cathal and Cillian. The men disappeared into the gloom of the cavern, shuffling firewood around. They didn't dare to disobey.

Will grimly watched them as they gathered the firewood, brought it to the cliff, climbed clumsily on top, gasping at the sight of dead Gudula and then begin to build an elaborate structure around her. They made multiple journeys to different parts of the cavern, bringing all the firewood they could find. It took the better part of the day for them to build a proper pyre. Qu Sith watched, constantly mumbling barely audible obscenities.

"Hey, put your togas on the pyre! You won't need them!" the sphinx ordered the priests. "You're cremating your Oracle!"

Will grimly watched as the priests stripped, their fat naked bodies glistening with perspiration. They silently placed their blue togas over the pyre. Even from a distance, Will could see their hands visibly shaking.

"We're ready, your Majesty," Cathal announced in a trembling voice. "We're ready to accompany our Oracle to the Road of Gods."

"That's not necessary," Qu Sith barked at them and then sighed. "Human stupidity has no limits. Start the fire and get down! I may find a better use for your feeble heads."

There was no response from the three naked men. They lit the pyre and got down the cliff as fast as they could, joining the entourage of royal concubines behind the sphinx.

Will watched the flames slowly climbing the dry firewood, tasting the blue togas before they reached the top and spat a cloud of fumes up through the hole in the ceiling of the cavern. Nobody said a word. Waves of mixed feelings beat through his chest with overtones of dark guilt mostly taking the upper hand. He couldn't explain why he felt that way. Gudula had been an obstacle, an irksome feature of his dream at first, and he hadn't even noticed how she had died. He hadn't killed her – he had found her dead. *So why did he place the orchid on her chest?* He could have just burned the body as he had with the other two, and the entire story would have been completely different. She had died because of him. Was it a sense of guilt that had guided his hand then on top of that cliff next to the lava flow? It had all happened so quickly at the time, and he couldn't remember clearly. But it was certainly a sense of guilt that overwhelmed him now as he watched the pyre. Gudula's sufferings had been his doing. Hel's orchid had kept her alive through all that terrible ordeal but hadn't made her invincible. And then those weird priests had kept torturing her! *Damn!* Will clenched his fist as those horrible thoughts flashed through his brain. With the heat rising, the whole entourage took a few steps back, leaving Will to face the flames. Again, he felt nothing but guilt.

The guards had come in a few times to bring new torches. Will had barely noticed that. He watched the pyre. The flames rose higher, almost touching the ceiling, scattering fistfuls of sparks in all directions. He awoke from the trance only when the blazing structure began to collapse, filling the dry fountain with embers.

"Let's go," Qu Sith said quietly.

Will nodded, and they went. He barely remembered how they got back to the King's bedchamber. It was late afternoon when they arrived, and there was some disturbance around him – the sphinx declared that he was starving, so the concubines hurried to feed him rabbits. They offered Will food as well. He politely declined and just sat on the floor in the corner, leaning against the wall and holding the blue orchid in his hands.

He didn't notice how Qu Sith selected two concubines for his late night entertainment, nor did he see what they were doing on that vast bed.

It was dark when his mind went blank too, and he slumped against the wall, still holding the orchid.

It was a damp and foggy morning. And as chilly as a dead man's grip. Will stiffed a yawn and sat up, leaning against the door of his home. A few early cars passed down the road, but it wasn't the cars that made him curse. A massive female frame barred his way. The frame was familiar but transparent.

"Hey, handsome!"

"Hi, Jill," he responded with a sigh.

"I've been looking for you, haven't seen you anywhere around lately."

"I was away."

"Working, I guess," she nodded knowingly. "Are you not glad to see me?"

"You're damned right. I'm not glad. Go away."

"You know I won't. I begged you to meet me, but you kept your silence. But here we are – you still tall and handsome and me still old and ugly. Yet I thought there were some sparks between us on *that* night. I did all I could and even did what I couldn't, but I never expected my love to become a one-way street. My life became meaningless when you vanished so unexpectedly," she paused, but Will remained silent. "But now that you are back, I'm not ready to abandon it, and I don't care what you think about that."

"You're dead," Will reminded her with a cruel smile.

"Glad you noticed," Jill chuckled. "That makes things a lot easier. Now I know where you live, and I can see you as much as I like."

"I don't live here," Will mumbled. "Leave me alone."

"You're lying," Jill was persistent. "Yesterday, I saw you peering through the windows and sobbing like a schoolgirl."

Will blushed. "That's none of your business!"

"I can't look calmly at a sobbing beauty; that sight was breaking my heart," Jill said. "What was that terrible thing in your life that they dumped you out? And don't pretend you've just lost your key!"

"You were that terrible thing," Will spat out. "And don't pretend you don't know what I'm talking about! You've ruined my life!"

"I'm so sorry to hear that your life has been ruined," Jill shrugged. "But could you be more specific about my part in that?"

"You told my mother everything!" Will exploded fiercely. "Everything that happened that night!"

"Nonsense," the ghost of Jill was calm. "I didn't. I knew nothing about your family."

"You're lying!"

"Why should I lie? I'm dead anyway."

Will shrugged. "I don't know. Maybe to get a better afterlife if your real life was shit."

"Nonsense!" Jill cut him. "No one has ever called my life shit! You know nothing..."

"It doesn't matter now," Will shrugged. "You're dead and won't be here for long. You'll be caught in no time; I've seen that in London."

"Nonsense!" Jill cut him again. "Our town is not London. I know our *nesyns* – all three of them. Old buffers see nothing past their noses until you start jumping on them. Why do you think there are so many ghosts in the North?"

"Shut up!" Will hissed. He heard footsteps behind the door –

his mother had probably got up and went to prepare breakfast for his sister. "I must go!" he said, getting up and grabbing his rucksack.

"Where? This is your home, isn't it?" the ghost frowned. "Why must you run away?"

"I don't need to explain anything, do I?" he mumbled, stepping directly through the transparent shape of Jill.

"That was rude," she observed calmly.

"Bye!" he said, going downhill.

Jill didn't follow, but Will had a bad feeling that this wouldn't be his last encounter with that crazy woman. The day had begun on a nasty note. Will cursed but walked firmly forward.

He must speak with his sister again. He had seen Rose go into his room last night, and maybe she had found his photos. She must remember him, and perhaps she'd be able to persuade his mother? The plan had holes with plenty of "ifs", "buts" and "maybes" but he had no other. He must just stay away from his mother until she's ready to forgive him.

Will strolled down the street, barely paying attention to the surroundings. The hour was early, and the traffic was light, but he felt rising tension. What if Rose had failed to find the proof? How could he persuade her to look again? What if she wouldn't talk? How could he convince her to stop acting like a demented old bag? He *was* her brother – why did she have to pretend she didn't know him?

He stopped and waited until the line of several cars had passed then crossed the road. A few hundred yards later, he turned left into the tangle of side streets, getting closer to the school. He must talk to Rose and stay out of his mother's sight. It was a difficult task but not impossible, and he still had plenty of time to prepare.

The side streets were quiet, but the day was breaking, and windows lit up as he went. People were getting up, brushing their teeth, showering, having their coffee and toast and rushing around during their morning routes. Will barely noticed any of that, torn with fear of failure and hesitation. He stopped in front of the tall brick wall that separated the school premises from the street.

He looked around. The street was still empty, but it wouldn't be for long, Will was sure, the buses and cars were already on their way with their cargo of children, and it wouldn't take long for them to unload them here, unleashing a cacophony of shouting and laughing through the gate.

He glanced a few more times at the still-empty street and took a good grip of the top of the wall. He was tall and strong, so it wasn't hard for him to lift his body and climb get over.

Will landed among the weeds behind the thorny shrubs of wild blackberries. The place was shady under large maple trees and smelled of damp rotting leaves.

"Are you hiding from me?" Jill asked, emerging from the wall. "Did you think I wouldn't find you here?"

"I'm not hiding," Will looked across the field where a man was coming to open the school gate and moved behind the trunk of the maple tree. "I need to settle some family business here."

"Oh!" Jill planted fists on her hips and asked with suspicion. "I thought I was your family."

"No, you're not," Will said, watching the man open the gate and return to the school building.

"I knew it! I knew it!" Jill blasted. "All this time, you've had another woman! That's why you didn't answer me! I'll kill her! I'll make her life so miserable that she'll kill herself!"

"Calm down, crazy woman," Will squeezed through his teeth, keeping his gaze fixed on the gate. "She's my sister!"

"Oh, you mischievous beauty," the ghost crooned. "Then all this time you've been thinking about me? I kept reminding you every single day!"

"Yes, I noticed that," Will sighed. "My thoughts were daily."

"Oh, how lovely this is! Did you have any disgusting fantasies about me?"

"You don't want to know that."

"Naughty boy!" the curvy ghost floated closer. "I knew butterflies were flying between us! Shit! How sad that I'm now dead. We could have had a bright future!"

"I don't think there were any butterflies involved," Will said, keeping his gaze fixed on the gate where the first children began to emerge chatting. "And I'm not sure about any future."

The ghost frowned. "Do you want me to spook her? She'd accept everything you ask."

"No," Will shook his head, his eyes still fixed on the children. "Stay away, please. I must talk to her without interruption."

"Oh, nasty boy! You said the magic word!" Jill crooned. "Yes, you can talk to her, but not for long. You're mine!"

The statement sent a wave of chill down Will's spine, but he didn't say anything. His eyes searched for Rose. Then he saw her. His sister was walking alone. Children ran around her, shouting and laughing, but Rose went silently as if an invisible force field had created a bubble of void around her.

"Rose! Rosie!" Will slipped from behind the tree. "Wait! We must talk!"

Rose stopped and turned to face him. Her lips were pressed tight without even the hint of a smile.

"Have you found the photos? I saw you in my room yesterday," Will asked her, breathless. "Have you found proof that I'm your brother?"

"No," the word was as cold as ice. "We have no computers in our storage, and I have no brother."

"But, Rosie, here I'm..."

"You could ask my mother. She knows better."

"*Our* mother is still very angry for what I did. She won't speak with me."

"Why should I speak with you then?" she asked.

"Because we're family!" Will sounded desperate.

"No, we're not..." Rose let her voice trail off, her face suddenly expressionless, her head drooped down.

Will's heart sank. "Rosie?" he asked cautiously, his voice slightly trembling.

She lifted her face in a few jerky motions. Her eyes fixed on him.

"Rosie?" Will repeated. "Are you okay?"

"We have told you many times to find the Sanctuary," she said, her voice sounding distant. "Why won't you listen? We won't let you back to your dismal life! Don't have any empty illusions."

"Rosie?"

"Go and find the Sanctuary," his sister said harshly. "You have no home here."

"Rosie..." Will whispered, slowly realising. "My sister is a damned bloody *borwil*!"

His extended hand froze in mid-air, trembling. Then, even bigger tremors shook his heart as his hopes for normal life died and crumbled to dust. He looked at his sister's face, which had become a mask for some alien monster, and tears began to pool in his eyes and roll down his cheeks uncontrollably.

Then Rosie's face lost the tension. "I must go," she whispered. "I'll be late for my maths class." She turned and ran away, leaving Will gasping.

Will felt the ground slipping under his feet, and he slowly sank, his knees unable to support him anymore. He sat down on the ground and looked helplessly at Rose running off, unable to utter a word. The realisation came a few moments later and crushed him with its weight like a mountain – *they've taken away my home! They've taken away my family!*

Will had no idea how much time had passed before he regained the ability to think. The yard was empty, and he looked helplessly around, trying to figure out in which direction he should move. There happened to be only one direction available – through the open gate. He got up onto his feet and crawled out, turning right outside the gate.

Each step he took carried him away from his home, and away from his family, he had no more. He went, barely looking around, letting his feet choose the way. The town was familiar but suddenly felt alien, and Will just pulled up his hood, afraid to meet anyone he might know. He crossed the High Street, barely waiting for the traffic to stop at the red lights.

The mighty crowns of trees in the shady park were ahead, and Will needed a quiet corner to organise his thoughts. He hadn't expected that turn of events and had been utterly taken aback.

Will sighed as the rusty gate swallowed him up like a hungry mouth. He went down the shady alley, dead leaves rustling under his feet, but his thoughts were far away, and his worries dragged behind him like a pack of hyenas following an injured wildebeest.

He couldn't believe fate. It was entirely his fault that his mother's life had become as miserable as Ben's. Or even worse. Ben seemed to have pieces of his own personality left simmering between those horrible fits. His mother seemed worse, far worse. And his little sister Rosie had become the bloody *borwil*! It was all his fault, entirely his fault.

Was there any way to help them? Any way to get his family back? Probably not. Ben was a doctor, and he wouldn't want that miserable life; he would have taken even the most risky and narrow path out of that swamp. The young doctor seemed to be firmly stuck with no hope left. And his family was now in that murky swamp too!

Will sighed. It was entirely his fault!

He carried on without picking the way, barely noticing anybody around. He didn't stop until the river barred his path. For a few minutes, he stared dumbly at the geese and seagulls in the slow-moving water. Then he sank onto the nearest bench and buried his face in his palms. His mind was as empty and lifeless as the lunar surface. Will had no idea what to do or where to go next.

A few hours later, his meditation was over.

"Here you are, beautiful!"

Will raised his head, glanced at the transparent shape and buried his face again. "Go away, Jill."

The ghost wasn't one to be scared easily away. "I presume the conversation didn't go well," she said.

"No, it didn't," Will sighed. "They won't let me back."

"How dare they!" Jill exploded. "Stupid sluts! If you want, I can organise the worst poltergeist in the world for them! They'll howl like two bitches after a few nights and crawl on their knees to beg for your return! Oh... I'll show them their place! They'll grovel at your feet!"

"No!" Will cut short the tirade. "And don't ever think of doing that!"

"Why? Wouldn't it be funny?"

"Don't ever go even close to my family!" Will told her harshly. "Or I swear I'll find someone to put you on the express to the Tower to see Mantus!"

Jill gulped. "Okay," she hastily agreed a few seconds later. "I'll do as you say. I'll stay away from them."

"Now, leave me alone, please," Will sighed. "I must think about where to spend the night."

"You don't need to think about that, beautiful," she said flirtatiously. "I'm an attractive curvaceous woman, and I live alone in my house. I'd gladly invite you to spend as many nights as you want."

"You're dead," Will reminded her.

"You can't have everything," Jill shrugged and chuckled. "There's always some stinky tiny piece of shit in any package. But I still own a house. And if I can trust my damned old arthritis, it might be raining tonight."

"You're a ghost," Will said. "Ghosts don't have arthritis."

"You don't believe me – look at the clouds!"

Will raised his eyes. *Shit!* The clouds were gathering. They were dark, and it might indeed rain. It might be risky without a roof over his head.

"Well?" Jill planted fists on her hips and moved her tummy in round motions, teasing. "To soak or not to soak?"

Will cursed loudly. "You win," he said sadly. "But on one condition?"

"What condition, beautiful?"

"You'll keep your hands off me."

A smile crooked the face of the ghost. "Deal!" Jill said. "Let's go catch a bus before that downpour. I guess you have a few coins for the ride?"

"Don't worry," Will got up and picked his rucksack. "Let's go."

They went back up the shady alley to the rusty gate. Jill chattered on without a break, and Will had to hush her before stepping into the street.

"Why?" She asked. "Why can't I talk?"

"Others might think that I'm insane talking to an empty space."

"I'm not an empty space!"

"Other people don't see you."

"True," Jill carried on, making faces instead of chattering on, but Will remained grim-faced, his thoughts with his family.

They boarded the bus, and Will paid the fare with his card. He didn't look where the ghost parked her wide bottom. He went to the rear and dropped onto a seat by the window.

Will looked at the familiar streets, and an immense sadness gripped his heart as the bus began to move, taking him away from the home he no longer had. He pulled the hood over his head as hot tears rolled uncontrollably down his cheeks. This time he didn't care much if anybody saw them.

The sky darkened and responded to his mood by pouring down streams of water. It rained all the way to the remote suburb where Jill's lair was. He had stopped crying a little earlier.

"It's time," she crooned in his ear.

Will nodded silently. A cold drizzle dripped from the dark sky when they got off the bus.

"This way..." Jill went ahead, stepping directly through the large puddles. Will followed, feeling increasingly unhappy with each step.

He stopped in front of the dark red brick house at the far end of the street. High shrubs guarded the house on both flanks, partially obscuring the dark windows. The place stirred unpleasant memories, and he sighed, taking a few more steps closer.

"Go in quick!" Jill urged him. "You'll get wet!"

"I'm not a ghost," he reminded her. "I can't walk through the walls."

"Just a temporary problem, soon sorted," she said with a vicious smile and pointed. "See that pot with the white petunia? Lift it – there's a key underneath."

"Are you sure we're doing the right thing?" Will suddenly felt hesitant.

"It's my house, isn't it?" Jill asked fiercely.

"You're dead," Will shrugged. "It's not your house anymore."

"Then this damned house belongs to no one, and you just found a key," she told him. "Lucky you! Lift that damned plant!"

Will swept the cobwebs aside and lifted the petunia pot. A small brass key was stuck in the ground like a tooth of a dragon. He picked it, replaced the pot and carefully brushed away the lumps of dirt.

"Open the door!" Jill urged him. "I don't want those damned neighbours to see you!"

"Why have you suddenly become worried?" Will mumbled,

fitting the key in the lock. "You weren't that sensitive the last time."

"Just get in!"

The door squeaked open, and Will stepped in. Jill whizzed past him and disappeared into the room. He heard her humming something indistinctly. He closed the door, locked it, leaned against it and took a deep breath. He was in the place he dreaded most with the woman he hated most – a dead woman. He only hoped that she had died in hospital and he wouldn't be forced to share a bed with her corpse.

"Come here, beautiful. You must be hungry," Jill called from the kitchen. "I left the fridge full when I went to the hospital, so something might still be edible in there. But you need to take a look yourself."

He exhaled and hesitantly stepped further in.

The transparent shape of Jill stood in the middle of the kitchen, her fists firmly planted on her hips. At first, it wasn't apparent if she was facing him or the fridge, but then she pointed at the fridge door and ordered, "Open it!"

Will got hold of the handle, carefully pulled and peeked inside from a distance. The whole situation seemed surreal, and he half expected at least a horde of rats to leap on him from in there. The light didn't come on, but a wave of stench slapped his face, and he slammed the door shut.

"Shit!" he barely had time to whisper as the ghost rushed past him and disappeared into the fridge.

He heard some muffled curses inside, then Jill's head appeared through the closed door.

"Damned fuse blew while I was in the hospital!" she exclaimed. "But maybe not everything has spoiled. Do you want to have a look?"

"No," Will told her firmly. "I don't want food poisoning."

"Oh..." Jill emerged from the fridge. "It's not a bad idea. But we need something stronger than ruined food, I'm afraid. You're a genius, beautiful!" She emitted a burst of eerie laughter.

Will paled, taking a few steps back. "I'd better go," he whispered.

"Where?" Jill exploded. "You don't have a home anymore! Rainy night in the yard!"

"It's better that than your ruined food," he shrugged, backing away one more step.

"Wait, love!" Jill whispered, desperation in her voice. "You've got me wrong! I won't rush you. I'll wait until you're ready. But wouldn't it be fine to unite again for eternity? That thought only sends shivers down my spine!"

"You don't have a spine," Will reminded her. "You left it in hospital."

"I don't need it anymore!" Jill chuckled. "We could haunt this house forever! Wouldn't that be great, love?"

"I'm not your love," Will told her coldly. "You're not my type at all."

"Appearance isn't what makes a person, dear," Jill cut him. "Would you prefer this shape?" The chunky transparent blob transformed into a slender feminine silhouette. "Does look better, doesn't it? Think about the endless possibilities!"

"No," Will said firmly. "I'd rather have my life back."

"I doubt that's possible in your situation."

"What do you know about my situation?"

"Not much. But it doesn't look good. You're freaking out even from your sister."

"Don't ever talk badly of my family!"

"I won't, I promise," the ghost said, blurring back into the fatty blob. "But you completely misunderstand my intentions, Willy. I want just to help."

"Why?"

She went to the window and looked at the rain before answering. "Because I'm an old and stupid woman who fell in love with you!"

"Yes, you're stupid, indeed," Will shrugged. "And you can't help me. No one can."

"Maybe I can, just a little," she crossed the kitchen. "Come with me. I'll show you."

She led him to the bedroom. Will frowned but followed. Jill crossed the room and stopped in front of the old dark oak wardrobe. "Open the bottom drawer," she ordered.

"It's your old knickers," Will frowned even more. "The old knickers of an old lady. How can that help me?"

"Move them aside," Jill waved her hand impatiently. "Don't worry. They're clean."

Will touched the underwear hesitantly. It felt repulsive as if stirring a spider's nest, but he pushed the knickers aside and withdrew his hand immediately. A few packs of banknotes were at the bottom.

"There's five grand. Take it – now. This money is yours," Jill said. "I was preparing for the meeting with you, but death came first."

"I'll be clear – I'm not having any more sex with you," Will told her firmly. "Not even for that money. I'm out of that business. No more selling of my meat."

"That's technically impossible, beautiful," Jill chuckled. "Sorry to point this out, but I'm dead. You're alive. We're on different planes, so it's simply not possible. Not yet. Take that money without thinking about it too much."

"But it's your money!" Will began to protest.

"Don't be silly," Jill shrugged. "I don't need it anymore. It's my money, and I can give it to anyone I like. You seem as though you're in great need. Take it!"

"But I promise you nothing!"

"I'm not asking for any promises," Jill shrugged. "Take it before I change my mind."

Will reached into the drawer and took the money out. Never in his life had he held that much money in his hands, but strangely this treasure didn't bring any happiness. He quickly stuffed it into his rucksack. *At least, I won't go hungry* – a thought flashed through his mind, but that didn't feel comforting either.

"It's getting late," Jill observed. "You can take a shower if you want and get some sleep. I'll go do some ghost things."

"Just don't shake your chains too loud," Will told her. The idea of taking a shower didn't seem bad at first, and he felt deadly tired. He felt hungry too but decided not to go near the kitchen. He didn't trust that ghost anyway.

"There's the bathroom," Jill pointed with a too wide smile. "Careful with the light – it flickers sometimes."

Will stopped like jolted. He had a sudden nasty feeling that somehow flickering electricity and showers didn't go together. "No," he told the ghost firmly. "I'm too tired for a shower. I can sleep on the floor if you're afraid that I might spoil your bedsheets."

"Fine!" Jill frowned, half fading. "Do as you wish; I won't interfere with your stupid decisions. As you said – it's not my house anymore, but it is a place I haunt!"

Will didn't answer. The bedroom stirred unpleasant memories, and he picked his rucksack up before heading back to the hallway. It was narrow, but all he needed was a plain wall without anything hanging overhead.

The wind and rain raged outside but only muffled sounds leaked through the tightly shut door. The floor squeaked as he settled his muscular body down and placed the rucksack under his head. He was sure Jill was watching, but he couldn't see anything in the dark and just closed his eyes. He felt a cold ghostly hand moving over his manhood but was too tired to protest. Then he drifted away.

Will's mind floated in the darkness, listening to some distant moans and groans. These were the few remaining moments of oblivion when he could hush his worries away and simply exist somewhere in the darkness without paying too much attention to anything. But, of course, those moments couldn't last long.

"Get out! And bring breakfast; I'm ravenous!" he heard a hushed shout, then some barely audible commotion moving from the left to right and then the door closing quietly.

When he opened his eyes, the sphinx was alone in his vast bed, lazily stretching his paws and yawning.

"Good morning, lazy bum!" the beast greeted him with a smile. "Have you slept well?"

"Not so well as you, as I see," Will mumbled. "I'm having a lot of troubling dreams lately."

"I had an excellent relaxation. My balls have never felt so shiny clean!" Qu Sith yawned again. "Humans are so perverted, but I found it kind of enjoyable."

"As you say..." Will was in no mood to argue. Instead, he watched the sphinx yawn again. The morning had begun strangely.

"Now that you have your flower back," Qu Sith crooned, watching Will through narrowed eyes. "What are you going do next?"

"It's not my flower. I must return it to Hel," Will said simply. "That orchid belongs to her. I must go back to her castle and wait."

"And then? What will you do then?"

"I don't know," Will shrugged. "I've done a few terrible things, and I'm not sure if Hel will be able to forgive me. Some people couldn't and have turned me away. Maybe she'll do the same. I'm no longer certain of anything. But I must try."

"I had the untimely loss of my most senior adviser recently," Qu Sith said. "Would you be interested in that position?"

"I saw that untimely loss," Will reminded him. "Would be quite reluctant even to consider your offer if that's your usual way of creating vacancies."

"You're completely safe from that," the sphinx growled. "I gave my oath to you, and I wouldn't ever do that to my friend."

"You didn't consider me as a friend when we were sitting in those cages."

"Still, many things have happened since then, and we've been through a lot of dangerous obstacles together," Qu Sith told him fiercely. "I think I can now consider you as a friend, human."

Will shrugged but didn't answer.

"Would you consider that position, at least?"

"First, I must talk to Hel."

"Would you consider that position if she turns you away?"

Will didn't get the chance to answer. The door opened, and the concubines brought in the King's breakfast – roasted rabbits, cheese, freshly baked bread, fruits and wine. They ignored Will, as usual.

"Come closer," Qu Sith invited him as soon as the concubines had left. "Eat something."

"I'm not hungry," Will said dourly from his corner.

The feast of the sphinx didn't last long. First, there was a growing commotion outside, then cries in the corridor before the door burst open.

The young man was breathless and barely able to speak. He seemed vaguely familiar to Will, but he couldn't pin a name to the features. "The Dark Priestess," the young man squeaked from his dry throat. "She demands your presence, Sire."

"Where is she?" Qu Sith sprang to his feet, the fur on his back rising.

"At the pits of sacrifice," the guy had to lean against the opened door, gasping for air. "She's waiting, and she seems quite impatient."

"Damn! I knew this couldn't end well," Qu Sith hissed and glanced at Will, panic flooding his eyes. "It seems your conversation will happen much sooner than you expected. I hope you'll be able to put a word in for me too if she's in a mood!"

Will raised to his feet, carefully holding the orchid in his right palm. His heart raced with excitement in anticipation of seeing his love again and deadly fear too. *Would she accept his apologies? Would she give him another chance?* He had hoped to prepare his speech on the way back to the black castle but, unexpectedly, everything was happening sooner. *Too soon!* He didn't feel ready, and he hated to improvise in such a delicate matter. "Let's go," he said sternly.

"You'll show us the way," Qu Sith ordered the messenger as they went into the corridor, leaving their unfinished breakfast behind.

"Of course, your Majesty," the young man bowed, still breathless. "Please, follow me. I'll show you the quickest way."

The concubines stirred into motion as they went by. "You all stay here!" Qu Sith dismissed the girls without slowing down. Will went with a trembling heart after the sphinx. What was supposed to be a bright and joyous reunion now descended into the dark abyss of fear with every step. Never in his life had he ridden the train of failure this fast. Would it be another failure? Yet another foul-up in a long line of self-inflicted disasters?

Will quietly cursed a few times, but this didn't help to reduce his anxiety. The sphinx was mumbling something too, and only the young guide was silent, leading the way. They descended the stairs but then, instead of going down the long gallery they had passed through a few times before, the guide opened the first door on the left and crossed a trashed room.

"What is this?" Qu Sith asked, cautiously sniffing the air. "Are you sure this is the right way?"

"This way is the quickest, your Majesty," the young guide explained, climbing through the burnt frame of a broken window.

"The Dark Priestess seemed very impatient."

"Shit!" the sphinx approached the window and glanced outside. The garden was even more of a mess, framed by black waves of basalt on two sides and ruined buildings on the other two. A few blackened rib cages gathered dust under the charred remnants of a tree as Will peered over the sphinx's shoulder.

"Do we go that way?" the beast asked, peering at the bones.

"No, your Majesty," the guide pointed to a barely visible path on the right. "We'll go down there. First, we must get around this lava field and then we'll come out at the pits."

"Let's go," Qu Sith hesitantly went through the window and stopped, waiting for Will to catch up.

The air was stale with the sour stench of decay. They turned right where the path slipped between the piles of rubble and later disappeared behind the broken down door of a derelict building. The hall behind that door was large, dark and dusty, with only narrow rays of light falling like daggers through the slits in the broken roof.

The gallery on the right was even darker since most of the windows on the left had been blocked by frozen lava, and they had to step carefully, curving around the crumbling statues and crushed pillars.

"Where are we going?" Qu Sith demanded, stepping in the gloom.

"To the pits, your Majesty," the guide answered without stopping. "The Dark Priestess requested that you were brought at once."

"Why must we go through all this wreckage?"

"Two-thirds of Per Hathor is wrecked like this, your Majesty. There is no more glory," the young guide shrugged. "And this is the shortest route."

"This shortest route is not suitable for the King," Will pointed out wryly.

"Ruins are always suitable for the King of ruins who is ruling over alive in the kingdom of Death!" a harsh male voice told them from behind.

Qu Sith froze as Will turned around to face their doom. A tall, large and muscular man emerged from behind the pillar they had just passed. Light armour covered his body on top of a soft fur vest and black leather pants. His long curly hair seemed a little messy, but his black beard was neatly braided. Will couldn't see his eyes behind the furrowed bushy brows, but the naked sword in his right arm meant business.

"This doesn't look like a friendly welcome," Qu Sith observed. "And you don't look like the Dark Priestess."

"True," the man said calmly. He raised his left hand, and a dozen more armed men appeared from behind the rubble. "I'm not the Dark Priestess, and you're not the King. You were just a decoy for the true King. You didn't ask how many sons he had before throwing him into flames. You did a foolish thing. Now, those sons will make you pay, and your pet monkey will die with you."

Will's throat went dry.

"Oh. Kroy was quite prolific, as I see," Qu Sith grunted. "And all this small army is to fight an old, tired unarmed sphinx and his pet monkey? Doesn't this seem a bit over the top?"

"I don't think so," the man said. "You had no trouble throwing a grown man up onto the pyre from more than a hundred paces away. I don't think this small army is over the top. We anticipate it might be quite difficult to persuade you."

"On the contrary!" the sphinx blasted a smile. "I'm very easy to persuade. We'll gladly leave Per Hathor right now if this is what you wish."

"That won't be enough, I'm afraid," the man frowned. "I want to put you both on a pyre."

"That's ridiculous!"

"I told you this would be difficult," the man sighed and motioned with his sword. The other blades sang as one as they left their scabbards. "You'll die today – this way or the other."

"Are you going to kill us here?"

"If that's necessary," the man shrugged. "But I'd prefer to put you on the pyre alive. I want you to suffer and die the same way our father did."

Will hastily glanced around, but there wasn't much he could see in the gloom. The gallery was narrow with the windows blocked on both sides and almost empty except for a few broken statues – most pieces too large for him to lift and a few pebbles that could scarcely offer any defence against men with swords.

"You better follow me, Sire," the young guide said, now holding a foot-long knife in his hand. "There's no other way out of this."

"And don't even think of outrunning us," the man with the sword warned. "I must warn you that another small army is waiting at the other end of the passage. Indeed, there is no other way out of this for you."

The sphinx roared and shook his head helplessly, the fur on his back raised. The man just laughed. He waited until the beast had calmed down. "That won't help," he said with a smile. "No one can hear you here. No one will come to rescue you."

Qu Sith darted a fiery glance at him, but this didn't make any impression either. "Well," the beast sighed. "Let's go and have a look at this pyre of yours."

The man nodded and gestured with his sword.

"This way, Sire," the young guide said as he began to move down the gallery.

Qu Sith slowly went after him. Will strolled at the right side of the beast. The small army followed them, brandishing weapons but keeping a distance.

"They're still afraid of me," Qu Sith whispered a few paces later. "If that army ahead isn't big enough, we might have a chance if you can find a stick to use to fight against those swords."

"I don't know if I could fight a sword – never done that before," Will whispered back. "I'm not a fighter!"

"Don't worry. You're immortal with that flower!"

"But not invincible," Will reminded him.

Qu Sith shrugged as they crept along in the gloom. "We must kill them somehow, or they'll most certainly kill us!"

Will swallowed the thought, but it didn't feel very terrifying, and that numbness frightened him. Those idiots were about to roast him, and all he could do was sheepishly stroll forward. His calm seemed almost religious. Qu Sith was still agitated, mumbling something indistinctly, but Will didn't say a word. He went after the young guide, barely looking around and paying no attention to the small army crawling after them.

It took a while for him to realise that the sphinx was asking a question.

"What?" he spat quietly.

"I said, if you could hold me tightly on that pyre, maybe the protection from that orchid will extend to both of us?" the beast repeated the question.

"I don't think that's a good idea," Will shrugged. "That flower makes you immortal, but your body still burns. You didn't see the Oracle. That flower makes life not worth living."

The gallery took a turn to the left as they carried on, and a spot of faint grey light appeared at the end of it.

"We're close," Qu Sith whispered. "Oh, gods! I'm too young to die!"

Will said nothing. He went on, stumbling over occasional pebbles, still unable to trigger at least a shadow of self-preserve. His life didn't seem worth saving. Where was he? Sleeping on the floor in the house of the woman he hated most, her ghost spawning around his genitals! Could he ever be more miserable? He had found Hel's orchid, but would she ever spare a glance for such a miserable guy? She must have found her handsome and strong man already, that's why she left him behind. A woman like Hel would never want to become close to a loser. *A loser!* Will frowned. The word tasted alien but was true. He had lost everything except for the blue flower. He had no more hope.

"Faster! Faster!" the man growled behind them angrily. "Move!"

Qu Sith attempted to roar a few more times, but nobody paid much attention to his efforts. The men with the swords kept going, and the beast was forced to crawl forward too.

Will carried on without saying a word. The blurred grey spot shaped into an opening as they got closer, with a large pile of rubble blocking the view. The guide held his knife high, brushing off a few cobwebs on the way. He stopped only briefly in front of the wreckage, glanced at the sphinx and turned right. The beast roared one more time before shaking his head and sadly following the guide.

They emerged into what once would have been a pleasant promenade by the lake. With the water gone, only stinky dry pits remained, now probably used as the burial grounds for Per Hathor. The crumbled bridge was further to the left, where the large grey pile of ashes marked the burial place of the Queen.

A new pyre had been built in the pit a few hundred paces ahead, waiting for them. Will glanced around – no crowds this time to mourn for the King. They were alone.

"Where is Odam?" the man with the sword growled behind them. "Bloody fool! Late as always!"

The young guide shrugged, glancing around, knife still in his hand. "I don't know. He..."

He didn't finish the sentence. The air shivered in front of him, and a dark, slightly fuming spear pierced his chest. He was dead before he hit the ground. Swords rattled against gravel as their captors silently slumped to the ground too, found by dark spears.

"It's our turn!" Qu Sith reared to his hind feet and roared with his all might.

Will glanced around. A line of dark knights had emerged in the distance on the right, and his heart skipped a few beats. "There's no defence against them," he told the beast. "We'll die if that is their will."

Qu Sith whimpered like a small kitten. "I'm too young to die!"

Will didn't answer. He stood still, carefully holding the blue orchid in his palm. *Utter loser! It's better to die from the hands of her knights than to face her like this!* He sighed and closed his eyes.

Nothing happened for the next few minutes. Then there was a quiet clopping sound on the gravel, nearing. Finally, it stopped in front of Will.

"I see you have found the flower," Hel said in a soft voice. "I'm glad. I was worried that it might end up in the wrong hands."

Will slowly opened his eyes. She was sitting on her black stallion and smiling faintly. Will blushed and lowered his eyes. Qu Sith was lying in the dust at his feet and pretending to be dead – he could clearly see the beast's chest moving.

Will's throat was dry. He had rehearsed this conversation in his mind thousands of times. He had been ready to grovel in front of her but now, with Hel before him, his mind went blank. "Here," he extended the orchid. "I've brought it back to you."

"I don't take my gifts back," Hel frowned and made an impatient gesture with her left hand.

"I didn't realise its power until I found it," Will shrugged. "It's a little frightening."

"So, it was in the wrong hands then..." the smile slowly vanished from Hel's face. "Now you know it's power. I gave it to you, and the flower is yours. I won't take it back."

Qu Sith grunted, rising from the dust. "May the sun shine brightly on your path and your enemies walk like shadows in the darkness, great Priestess," he said, bowing his head. "I did not have the pleasure of welcoming you to Per Hathor."

"And are you the new King of Per Hathor?" Hel turned her eyes to Qu Sith. "I'm sorry if my knights killed your entourage, Sire. They have been told to make sure that no one carries a weapon in my presence. Another group of fools with swords is right there, up the street. These are difficult times, you must understand. My apologies."

"No need to apologise, great Priestess," Qu Sith crooned. "Those are the exact fools who deserved to die. I'm immensely grateful that your knights did such a righteous job."

"I'll make sure they learn their lesson well in the Tower," Hel shrugged. "If you so wish."

"Please, include their father as well," the shadow of a vicious smile crossed the sphinx's face. "I think it all started with him."

"I will, if you ask, Sire," Hel nodded.

"Thank you, great Priestess," Qu Sith bowed his head.

"Sadly, I can't stay with you much longer," Hel said and patted the neck of her horse. "I must attend to few pressing matters at my castle."

Will felt as though the ground was slipping away from his feet. "Wait!" his voice sounded almost to be begging. He knew that he must invent something really quickly, or she would go away.

"Yes?" she looked at him askance.

"The ghosts in your Tower..."

"Soulings?" Hel asked. "What about them?"

"They badly wanted to see your flower," Will shrugged. "Do you know why? That wasn't just innocent curiosity, was it?"

"Selfish bastards!" she smiled. "Did they ask you to select them?"

"They did."

"They're desperate to get back to the world of the living. They would promise you anything for that flower, but I'm not sure if they would ever keep their promises," Hel said, her face suddenly serious. "Yes, you can save one souling from the Tower with that blossom if you wish. Or you may keep the flower for yourself. The choice is yours. Choose wisely."

"Still, I think I owe them a chance," Will sighed. "Would you permit me to do that? Please?"

Hel frowned as she considered that. "Indeed, you are a strange man, Will, but I admire your courage and selflessness," she said at last. "Yes, you can do that."

"Thank you," he bowed his head, afraid to ask more.

"So, as I happen to be travelling home now," she said. "You can join me if you want. My Shaitan is strong enough to carry two of us."

"I never dared to dream of such a privilege," Will said.

"Let's waste no more time," she extended her hand. "Get up behind me!"

Will's heart loudly pounded as he took her grip. Her hand seemed small and fragile, but her strength was enormous – she lifted him like a tiny poodle, not a grown man, and placed him on the horse behind her.

"Goodbye, my favourite human," Qu Sith said sadly.

"Goodbye, sphinx," Will sighed. Mixed feelings bubbled in his heart. He had become used to the mischievous beast and was sad to part from him too. The numbness he had felt before had fallen away like a broken cobweb, carried by the wind. Hel was here, next to him, and everything else seemed less and less important.

"Hold on tightly," she told him. "It will be a fast ride, so don't fall off."

Will's hands slightly trembled as he got hold of her slender waist. Shaitan reared, and he had to cling to her even harder as the horse flashed forward like a bolt of black lightning. Yes, it was fast, much faster than he had anticipated. The ruins of Per Hathor blurred as they galloped amongst them at incredible speed. It was a dizzying sight, and Will closed his eyes, wondering how Hel could endure this. She didn't seem disturbed, firmly holding the reins in her right hand, her long blonde hair flowing in the wind.

They left the ancient city, heading steadily up the slope of the volcano, but the forest they entered was even worse, with lights flashing insanely between the intertwined branches. Will glanced back. The dark knights looked like living statues amongst the streaming landscape, moving at the same incredible speed and maintaining their distance. He felt dizzy and shut his eyes firmly, afraid of slipping off the horse. He pressed his body against Hel's, but she didn't seem to object.

Will dared to open his eyes just an hour later when they began to slow down. All around them were lifeless basalt fields with the flaming river of molten rock speeding down the slope on their left. The sky was a dirty grey with just a few flashes of red from the large lava lake swirling and spitting fountains on the left. The landscape had changed beyond all recognition since he had last seen it. Still, the black castle on top of the high cliff in front of them remained the same.

Shaitan stopped at the foot of that cliff. The dark knights passed them like shadows and took their usual post halfway up the ridge.

"I'll wait here," Hel told him, helping him off the horse. "Just remember that only the souling you name can touch the blossom.

You must make your choice alone. Be careful. Don't let them trick you."

Suddenly Will felt lost, standing next to her glistening black stallion. He wasn't sure about his decisions anymore. He looked at the flower in his palm and sighed.

"You could still keep the flower for yourself," Hel reminded him, tracing his gaze.

"I must try," Will told her. "But I'll be back shortly."

"We'll see, Will," Hel sighed. She dismounted Shaitan as well. "Go if you must."

He nodded quickly and turned away, hiding his slightly shaking hands and facing the winding way uphill to Hel's black castle. He knew the way, but this time he went openly, not sneaking about and not hiding his tracks.

He eyed the dark knights standing halfway to the top. They didn't move as he approached, their faces indifferent, eyes fixed on Hel. Their features seemed blurred a little as he neared them, the spears in their hands lightly smoking. He felt uneasy this close. They had threatened him before; he had seen them killing. But now they stood motionless as if Will was just a wisp of fog drifting uphill, not worth a glance.

He crossed the line of knights with a trembling heart. The Black Castle stood in front of him, dark and silent. He noticed the gate was slightly ajar as he got closer.

He turned back when he reached the gate. Hel still stood next to her stallion, reins in her hand, looking after him. It was too far to see clearly, but it seemed that she was smiling. Will sighed and lifted his eyes to the grey sky above the black lava fields. The high clouds didn't bear any rain, but they did obscure the sun and nor were there any birds on the high winds. He waited a few more moments for the sign that never appeared, then nodded his head and entered the Black Castle of Death.

The inner yard looked the same as he remembered and as empty as before. Will crossed it quickly as if any hesitation he had was left on the other side of the gate.

The heavy door quietly opened as he pulled it and then just as gently closed when he had entered. Will went forward, each footstep echoing from the walls of the giant hall. He didn't go far. A dozen steps later, the air in front of him began to blur and swirl as if boiling.

"He has the flower!" the words were repeated thousands of times in different voices as if passing down a heavily distorted grapevine. Shadows crawled from every corner, dancing in a crazy tornado around him. Will could see pale, distorted and transparent faces – some smiling, some scorching bitter grimaces but most of them begging. He saw transparent hands reaching out to him; he heard voices promising riches and pleasures. "Please! Pick me!"

He waited for a few more heartbeats, observing the turmoil.

"Gudula!" he then called softly.

The tornado of soulings lifted, showering curses on Will, and dissipated in an instant. He waited a little longer. "Gudula!" he called again, a little louder this time. Murmurs stirred somewhere around the high ceiling.

The shape of a girl appeared from the shadows, floating a few feet above the ground. Will couldn't see her face, but the form looked like Gudula. She stopped hesitantly a few paces away.

"Please, forgive me for all the suffering I forced you through," Will uttered. "It was horrible and entirely my fault, though I had no such intention."

"All forgiven, my love," the girl said. "But don't ask me to forget it."

"I was told that the flower that brought so much suffering could give you a new life and a new body if you accept it," Will glanced at the orchid that was sitting peacefully on his palm and lifted his eyes back to the transparent shape. "Do you want it?"

"A new life with you, Bryn?" she asked hesitantly.

"No," Will shook his head. "I'm not included in the offer."

The transparent body shook as if jolted with electricity. "Then keep your gift for yourself, Bryn! That means I suffered in vain," she said fiercely. "I would rather dwell here!"

She dashed to the right and disappeared into the shadows.

"Did you see that gawk?" A voice screamed from the height. "She rejected the flower!"

"His name is Bryn!" A voice whispered, and the whole swarm of soulings descended again.

The faces, begging, smiling, angry, vicious, hands put together as if in prayer and clenched into fists, inviting and threatening – all swirled together in a dizzying whirlpool.

"Remember, Bryn – we went fishing when we were kids!"

"We used to be lovers, Bryn! Don't you want your girl back?"

"I'm your aunt, Bryn! I always brought you sweets!"

"We stole apples from our neighbour! Don't you remember, Bryn?"

"I'm your brother, Bryn! Help me out of here! Please!"

"I'll crush you like a fly if you don't give me that flower at once!"

"Don't you remember your father, Bryn?"

"Stop!" Will felt dizzy amongst all the shouting and the swirling ghosts. "I don't know you! I don't remember you!"

"Think harder!"

"I'm not Bryn!"

He shut his eyes just for a second, and thousands of cold ghostly hands began slipping under his robes. "Stop!" frightened he glanced at down. The orchid was still peacefully resting in his palm. *They can't touch the blossom until I name them!* He remembered what Hel had told him. Still, that didn't make things easier – the soulings were touching everywhere else.

Will took a deep breath. "Eric!" he called out loudly.

The crazy whirlpool ceased immediately, cursing.

"Eric!" he called again. "Are you here?"

The lonely figure of a young man approached him uncertainly from the gloom.

"Do I know you?" the man stopped a few paces away. "I never thought that I would hear someone call my name. Not in this world, at least. And you don't look familiar."

"Dullard!" an angry hiss dropped from above. "You've been *named*!"

"No, you don't know me," Will said. "But I know Ben."

"Ben?" the young man gasped. "Then you're a Sleeper too! Is he all right?"

"He was drowning in tears when last I saw him a couple of days ago in London," Will shrugged. "One bitch told him what had happened to you with all the nasty details. He needs you badly."

The ghost sagged his transparent shoulders.

"That simply won't happen," Eric said sadly. "I'm stuck in this world. Even if your flower gets me a new body, I'll lack the spark to cross back to him. I'll be stuck here forever. And your flower will simply have been wasted."

"If you need the thing that you put in the tattoo ink, you can take it back if you know how to," Will sighed. "Technically, it's yours, I guess."

"You've got a tattoo?"

"Yes."

"Where?"

"My left pec."

Eric came closer.

"Well... yes... It can be done in these circumstances, but it involves a bit of juggling and depends on luck, and it could be deadly dangerous for you since I'm dead anyway," he told Will seriously. "If we succeed, you'll be stuck in this world forever without any chance to cross back. You won't return home. Is this what you want?"

Will thought just for a second before answering. "Yes, that's what I want. I've nowhere to return to anymore. I don't have a home. And you, at least, have somebody who loves you."

"I understand," the transparent shape of Eric sighed. "Let's do it then. But you might be killed in the process, and you don't have another flower."

"What do you want me to do?" Will asked, ignoring Eric's warnings.

"Just stand still and don't move," he said. "I need to grab the spark after I touch the flower and get it out before my hand solidifies. You'll be dead if I fail, and I'll probably be dead too. So, keep still."

Eric stepped closer. Will had no fear as the transparent shape extended his hand out and touched his chest. The touch was cold, but Eric wasn't the first ghost that had touched him, so Will just frowned slightly but didn't move a muscle. The transparent hand sank deeper, and Will felt an unpleasant wave of chill spreading through his chest.

"Here it is, I feel it," Eric whispered. "Where's the blossom?"

Will extended out his hand, the blue orchid sitting gently on his palm. "Let's do it," he whispered back and closed his eyes.

"We have just one go," Eric growled. "God help us!"

Then it happened. At first, it felt like he had been shot – an intense pain as if a white-hot metal rod had pierced his chest. Will cried out but didn't move a muscle, trying hard to ignore the pain and move it out of his mind. He wasn't sure if he succeeded, but the pain eased a little and then drifted out of his chest. Then it was gone.

"Here we go," Eric said.

Will opened his eyes. The guy was no longer transparent, and he smiled as the bright red spark slowly melted into his palm. "We did it! It's so good to breathe again!" he said cheerfully, then grew serious again. "Was it bad?" he asked.

"Bad enough," Will admitted sourly. "Won't do that again."

Suddenly Eric embraced him. "Thank you!" he whispered. "Thank you so much, brother! I'm in debt forever. Whenever you need anything – just ask." He released his embrace and looked into Will's eyes. "Do you already regret it?"

"No," Will said firmly.

"No way back anyway," Eric shrugged. "What are you going to do now?"

"No idea yet," Will sighed. "You?'

"All this has happened so suddenly, and I've had no chance to think about that," Eric smiled. "Do you know where I can find Ben?"

Will told him the address. "Just avoid Covent Garden. Those creepy guys are hunting me."

"I know. They got me too. They're hunting sparks. Had to get me killed in this world to spoil their plans."

"Did they really eat you?"

"They did. But they gained nothing. The link was already broken."

"Fools!" Will grinned.

"Fools, indeed," Eric grinned too. "Do I need to know anything before I get into your body tonight?"

"Take the rucksack and get out of that house. I doubt she'll follow you to London."

"She?"

"One crazy ghost. Just get away, and you'll be fine. You'll find some money in the rucksack, so don't forget to take it."

"Sorry to ask, but I must know – is your body crippled somehow? Some disease, perhaps? Must I be careful about anything?"

Will smiled sadly. "No. It's just a nice body. Please, take good care of it."

"I will," Eric promised. "And thank you again, I'm immensely grateful."

Will sighed and just nodded.

Eric passed his eyes around the hall as if saying goodbyes. "We better go before Hel returns," he said at last.

"She's waiting outside," Will told him.

"Shit! How will we escape?"

"We'll walk out through the front door," Will shrugged.

"She'll kill us!"

"No, she won't," Will sounded certain. "She knows what I'm doing here."

"You're crazy!"

"I am," Will grinned. "Let's go. I doubt if there's any other way to sneak out of the Tower anyway."

"There isn't, I know."

"Let's go then."

Eric paled and visibly shrank, his shoulders sagging, but

quickly nodded. Angry murmurs and curses followed them from every corner of the Tower until they reached the door.

"I just hope you didn't sell me to Hel for experiments," Eric whispered.

"No, I didn't. Relax," Will opened the door.

The yard was empty, as before, and they quickly passed to the gate. Eric stopped unsurely at the sight of the black knights, and Will had to urge him on again. The knights stood like black statues, unmoving, smoking spears in their hands, looking down the slope where Hel was standing next to her stallion in the distance. The knights were aware of their presence, Will was sure.

They followed the winding path between the splatters of basalt. The knights didn't move as they passed them. It was an uneasy feeling to turn their back on the smoking spears, but Will kept his eyes on Hel too, and Hel was faintly smiling.

"This is quite a strange decision of yours. I was expecting a girl," she raised an eyebrow, glancing at Eric. "But who am I to judge?"

"The girl of my desires is not in the Tower. That would be a long and boring story if you do want an explanation," Will shrugged.

"No," Hel cut him. "You don't need to explain your decisions. Do you have any regrets about what you did?"

"I'd better go," Eric said quietly, but Will just waved to him absentmindedly.

"No," Will watched Eric walking away down the vast lava field. "I've no regrets."

"Aren't you going with him?" Hel asked.

"I don't want to go with him. I've no place in his life," Will said after a short pause. "Could you let me stay with you?"

Hel was silent, studying Will's face.

"Are you sure you want that?" she asked at last.

"Yes. More than anything else!"

Hel came closer, embraced him and put her head on his chest. Will's heart pounded insanely. He was much taller and bigger than her, but he trembled like a poplar leaf on a high wind. He had wanted this moment so badly.

She raised her head and looked at him with that strange, sad expression in her blue eyes. Then, without thinking, Will took her face in his palms, bent down and kissed her lips.

His garments then changed into black armour, and his body acquired a ghostly semi-solid look. This wasn't painful, the world around him grew dim, and his mind numbed to a certain strange indifference.

Hel stepped back, lowering her head.

Will followed her up the slope of the mountain. She pointed him to the first place on the right in the line of her black knights.

The following days, he stood there motionless. He watched her walking in the lava fields among the black rocks. She never looked back.

Afterword

You have just read a story from the Sleeper Chronicles series and may wonder which book will take you deeper into the world of the Sleepers. It's a difficult question and the advice is not as straightforward as it may seem. The Sleeper Chronicles are a non-linear series where the story in book B doesn't necessarily follow the story in book A and book C doesn't precede the story in book D. Each main character tells his own story as a piece of a jigsaw puzzle. That piece may be as short as a short story or may grow into several books. Still, not one single piece can reveal the picture of the whole universe, but more details emerge when those pieces are added together.

The stories are listed on the webpage www.sleeperchronicles.com – in no particular order. It's up to you to decide which piece of the puzzle to pick up next.

Ray Zdan